PAULA SMEDLEY lives in London  writing at a very young age, winnin poetry and short stories. *The Inconve* debut novel. An extensive traveller, Pa in Nigeria, escaped post-tsunami rad......... ... japan, parued in a favela in Rio de Janeiro and left her debit card in a cashpoint in Sri Lanka.

CU00920868

The Inconvenient Need to Belong

PAULA SMEDLEY

SilverWood

Published in 2020 by SilverWood Books
This edition independently published in 2020

SilverWood Books Ltd
14 Small Street, Bristol, BS1 1DE, United Kingdom
www.silverwoodbooks.co.uk

ISBN 9798635065822 (KDP paperback)

British Library Cataloguing in Publication Data
A CIP catalogue record for this book is available from
the British Library

Page design and typesetting by SilverWood Books

For Joan and Trevor, who always led lives much larger than the ones they were given.

And for Baker, without whom this book would never have happened.

Chapter 1

Alfie Cooper opened his canvas bag and carefully placed inside the bread he had stolen from breakfast, wrapped in the cheap napkins the care home used. He checked his old and battered watch and realised it was time to go to the park.

Technically, he thought the staff couldn't stop him from going, but he liked to sneak out nonetheless. It avoided any questions and made him feel a bit daring, despite his eighty-six years. He thought one of the nurses – Julia her name was – knew he snuck out, but she'd never asked and he'd never told.

He picked up his hat, almost as old and battered as his watch, and stole out of his room, down the hall and through the TV lounge, turning right before he got to the day room. Once out the side door, Alfie sprung the gate and began the walk to the park. It wasn't far, only the end of the street really, but at his age it took him a while to get there. He shook his head, remembering the days when as a cabinetmaker he'd spend hours lugging wood around and still have the strength and energy to do his daily fifty push ups.

He negotiated the crossing at the end of the road and entered the East Slatterley Community Park, relishing the fresh air and the smell of lavender that always reminded him of his mother. He closed his eyes briefly and inhaled, picturing her reaching up to adjust his tie before the regular family Sunday outing to church, the smell of her hand lotion wafting up.

It wasn't a big park by any means, more of a green really. But it was his. He slowly shuffled in to the middle of the park to assume his customary position on the bench by the lake under the park's solitary oak tree, carefully stepping around the pine cones and dog poo.

He came every Saturday morning to sit on the bench and feed the ducks with the bread he stole from breakfast. Great care was taken to ensure that each piece of bread was the same size and that no duck received a second piece before each had received their first. It was a fair and equitable duck feeding.

With all of this done in a slow and methodical way, it was a necessarily time-consuming practice. Alfie didn't mind. It kept his mind and his hands occupied for a few blessed hours every Saturday. Enough time for visitors to Pinewood Care Home for Aged Residents to have moved on to the more interesting parts of their days. Of their lives. By the time Alfie got back around eleven-thirty, the day room would be empty of visiting relatives and he could get on with the business of lunch.

It didn't have to be this way. Not if he actually had visitors. And it was his own fault he had none of course. But without the ingredient of visitors, visiting hours, he felt, became somewhat redundant.

He still hated the name of the place too. You would have thought that a home whose residents only left by dying would name themselves after something other than a coffin.

He wondered if the boy would be at the park today. Alfie had been coming to the park since he moved in to Pinewood and, excluding the odd irritating morning when someone else plonked themselves on the other end, for most of those six years he'd had the bench to himself. But lately Fred had been joining him. Sometimes staying for hours, sometimes only a few minutes. Not every Saturday, but most of them, and Alfie wondered again what drew the boy to the unremarkable suburban park. To him.

He'd tried to get rid of the boy at first, naturally, but he'd just kept coming back. He had tried to ask Fred about himself, but he was always evasive, and Alfie suspected that his situation at home wasn't ideal. Why else would a teenage boy spend his Saturday mornings sitting in a park with an old man?

Alfie got the impression that Fred didn't come from an affluent family; his clothes were clearly hand-me-downs from some time ago, given the style, and he didn't have a mobile phone even though kids were practically born with one in their hand these days. Alfie didn't know how they managed to walk and fiddle around on them without getting run over all the time. Evolution of the species perhaps.

Alfie was trying to impart some of his life's learnings on the boy to make sure the lad didn't make the same mistakes he had. He was having varying degrees of success, with Fred smug in the superiority of his youth. But with no family to bestow his memories on, secretly Alfie was grateful for the largely receptive ear and the promise of regular contact with the world outside Pinewood.

Alfie reached his bench and read the brass plaque screwed to the seat back, as he did every week. *For Rosalind, who loved this park. Mother and beloved wife.* And as he did every week he wondered who Rosalind had been, who the unimaginative sod was who had written the plaque, and then tried to come up with something better. *For Rosalind, who would have been an astronaut if she hadn't been so lazy.* Or *For Rosalind, who played a mean pinball.* He chuckled to himself, especially pleased with his astronaut creation. Probably a result of *Apollo 13* being on the telly this week.

He couldn't see Fred anywhere so he settled on his bench, placing the bag on his lap. He looked over the lake and savoured the view for a few minutes. He knew it wasn't the prettiest of lakes, or indeed actually a lake. More of a pond really. But it held a special place for him, being his sanctuary outside of Pinewood.

A pine cone rudely dropped to the ground in front of him, startling him out of his tranquil little moment. He glared at it and wished his flexibility and reach was what it had once been so he could kick it. Or his height. He had been over six foot once upon a time. Before old age gradually stole his stature from him, like he'd been shrunk in the wash.

"Hi Pop," said a voice loudly into his right ear, giving him another start.

"I'm not bloody deaf, Fred," Alfie said. "And besides, you shouldn't do that to an old man. You'll give me a heart attack."

Fred chuckled, dropping his lanky frame onto the bench next to Alfie and immediately slouching down, his legs spread wide. He reminded Alfie of a rag doll when he sat like that. No bones, just a puddle of clothes with a head sticking out the top.

"Do you really have to sit like that? I'm sure it can't be doing your back any good."

Fred shrugged – a feat in itself in that position, thought Alfie. "You sound like my mum."

Alfie waved a hand, "Fair enough. It's your spine. You just look a little untidy, that's all." Alfie gave him a sidelong glance. "So how are you, Fred? Keeping well?"

Fred shrugged again, a favourite mode of communication. "I guess."

Alfie sighed inwardly. He could never get a lot out of Fred about his private life. But maybe that was just because as he'd never had kids he had no idea how you were meant to talk to them.

"Can I have some bread for the ducks?" Fred asked suddenly.

Alfie glanced at the bread on his lap, unconsciously pulling his hands around to build a wall. He realised what he was doing and forced himself to relax. It was a breakthrough with the boy, he told himself. And it's also just bread. If Fred didn't break it up quite as precisely as he did, what did it matter? Still, he hesitated, unable to quite let go of total control.

"Forget it," Fred kicked the ground. "I don't care."

"No, no it's fine," said Alfie. "Here, take this bit of wholemeal. Now, the trick is to break the bread into equal size chunks – you want all the birds to get the same."

"Why do you care so much? About if each bird gets the same? They're just dumb birds."

"Not to me they're not," he said quietly, looking at his hands in his lap. He picked up a slice of white bread and started to methodically tear it into pieces. "But besides, it's just fair, isn't it? You don't want one of them getting fat and one going hungry."

Fred shrugged again, sitting up a little straighter to throw his bread further away.

"So what were we talking about last week, my boy?" asked Alfie.

Fred threw some bread clear into the lake, putting his back into it. "You were telling me that you worked in a funfair – again. But you never tell me anything about what it was like or what you did. How did you end up in a travelling funfair anyway?"

Yes, it was time to tell the story, thought Alfie. His story. He couldn't die with it untold and he couldn't put it off any longer. "All right, let's get started," he said, settling in to a more comfortable position. He just hoped he had the courage to tell it.

Chapter 2

He took one last look around his childhood bedroom before shouldering his holdall and his tool bag, turning off the light and quietly closing the door. He knew his mum would be upset – and his dad would be furious – but he had to leave. He couldn't handle another day of being teased on the building site. And he definitely couldn't handle another day of his parents' smothering and overbearing morality. Of his father's rages.

He felt like one of those seedlings his mum had planted outside the front room. Desperately struggling to grow, but his parents kept piling soil on top of him. And besides, he thought, he was twenty – a man. He should be able to go off and start his own life. He knew men his age who were already married and yet he'd never even kissed a girl, let alone had a real girlfriend.

He felt a twinge of guilt at not saying goodbye to his sister, Betty, but knew she would understand. She was also being slowly strangled by their parents, but at sixteen there was little she could do about it just yet. Once she turned eighteen he thought he could invite her to visit wherever he was living. That would be nice. He could buy a gammon and get a tin of pineapple for dinner. He'd never understood Betty's love of gammon with cheese and pineapple rather than a delicious fried egg on top, but then she was a girl. Doris, his older sister, would be altogether less forgiving or envious of his flight. He wouldn't invite her to come and stay and eat gammon.

He would write once he was settled somewhere, put his parents' minds at rest. He'd left a note obviously; he wasn't just going to disappear into the night. But he would write to let them know where he was staying and that he was doing well.

He didn't have a firm idea where he was going, apart from a direction. He had thought about going north, but he'd heard northerners didn't like Londoners and he just wanted to fit in. But then, sticking to the Home Counties didn't seem far enough away. So he thought he'd try his luck south-west, down Devon or Cornwall way. People said it was tranquil and pretty down there, and he was already on the right side of London. Maybe it was a sign.

He double-checked his note was still propped up against the fruit bowl on the kitchen table and quietly left the house and his old life behind, the echo of his parents' disapproval ringing in his ears.

By the time the first signs of daylight were appearing on the horizon, he thought he was getting to the outskirts of London. The houses were further apart with proper front gardens, and the signs of war weren't as bad.

He'd only been six when the war broke out, and he remembered terrifying nights being woken by the sound of the warning sirens. The whistles as the bombs dropped. The inevitable explosions, rattling the windows like an earthquake. His mother had been too scared to leave the house to go to the air-raid shelter so they'd all huddled in the cellar. He and his sisters should have been evacuated to the country, but his mother hadn't been able to let them go, not with their father away fighting.

So far tonight, his grand adventure had been less adventure and more just an ambitious attempt to get some exercise. The hours and the unexpectedly cold June night had dragged on interminably, the biggest excitement coming from stumbling across a fox going through some rubbish on the side of the road. They had both eyed each other up, trying to decide what the other meant to do. Once the fox was comfortable he wasn't a threat, he'd gone back to inspecting the rubbish, ignoring him with almost wilful disdain.

The only other event of note had been when he'd caught his foot in a tree root and gone face first into the dirt. He wasn't sure exactly what he'd had in mind when he set out, but he was certain it involved more exciting things than being ignored by a fox and narrowly escaping a sprained ankle.

He heard a lorry rumbling behind him and stuck his thumb out, praying it would pull over. He was exhausted from a night without sleep and the miles he'd walked carrying his heavy tool bag, and wanted nothing more than to just rest his tired legs and feet. He heard the swoosh of the brakes and thanked his lucky stars. He didn't even care if the lorry was going in the right direction at this point, he just wanted to sit down and get warm. He'd thought upon setting out that he was rather fit from years as a cabinetmaker lugging wood and toolboxes around, but it appeared while he had strength, he somewhat lacked stamina.

He stood right back to give the lorry room to pull up. He saw a bloke in his thirties with close-cut hair looking at him through the passenger window. "Where you going to, kid?"

Not overly impressed about being called kid, he replied rather more confidently than he felt, "Anywhere other than London."

"Amen to that," said the driver. "Bleeding shithole. Hop in."

He climbed into the cab, thanking the driver for pulling over. "Don't mention it, mate." Wiping his hand on his worn and grubby trousers, he held it out saying, "The name's Michael. What do I call you?"

He took a breath to reply and then stopped himself. Why not a new name for a new phase, a new adventure? A new him. "Alfie," he said, shaking Michael's hand. "The name's Alfie."

"Well, Alfie, welcome aboard! Do you have a destination in mind or just out of that heaving pile of shit? Or was the coronation of our good Queen this week an inspiration to get out and see more of our fair country?" Michael laughed, clearly in some way finding what he'd just said amusing. "I'm bound for Plymouth and you're more than welcome to ride with me the whole way if you'd like – I could use the company."

Alfie sized Michael up, wondering if he was trying to lure him in so that he could rob him at a later stage. He was a big man, broad-shouldered and muscular, but he seemed nice enough, with an open face and a friendly smile.

"Sure," he said, smiling at Michael. "That sounds great."

Michael reached into the console and fished out a packet of Player's. "You want?"

"No thanks, I don't— Actually, why the hell not?" said Alfie, deciding that if he was going to start again as a new person, then perhaps this new person smoked. He took a cigarette and the lighter, coughing on the initial inhale.

Michael laughed, reaching over to give him a friendly thump on the back as he doubled over coughing. "Don't worry lad, they grow on you." He took a long draw and closed his eyes briefly before exhaling and filling the cab with smoke.

Alfie tried a tentative second time and managed not to cough, although the sting down his throat did start to make his eyes water. He rolled the window down a little to get some air, on the pretence of flicking off the ash.

"So Alfie, are you off to seek your fortune in the country then? Settle down on a farm with a pretty country girl and milk cows?"

"I don't know," he said honestly. "I just know I had to get out of London."

Michael chuckled. "I know what you mean about London. Time was I worked at a dive of a pub in Soho. The Bell if you know it. Then again," he said, looking Alfie over, "maybe you don't, clean-cut boy like you. Anyway, I worked there behind the bar for a few years after the war but I just couldn't take it anymore. The same sad drunks telling the same stories and drinking themselves further and further into the ground. Mainly ex-servicemen like me, although these poor sods had been on the front lines. Dave had been in the Battle of the Bulge, poor bastard." He shook his head sadly. "Bloody sad."

Alfie nodded and finished his cigarette – it had not grown on him – and threw it out of the window before replying. "My dad was on the front lines too. I don't remember too much of what he was like before the war, but my mum tells me he wasn't the same when he came back." He tried not to picture his dad towering over him, his eyes crazed and far away. His face contorted with whatever he was seeing that wasn't his terrified son.

Alfie, grown weary of talking and tired from all the walking, settled back into his seat, closing his eyes briefly as he relished the warmth and comfort enveloping him like a cosy blanket.

"Wake up sleeping beauty," Michael said not unkindly, giving him a shove.

Alfie blinked, disoriented, struggling through the mental fog to recollect where he was. The lorry was parked and the sun was well above the horizon. "Sorry Michael, I didn't mean to fall asleep. Where are we?"

"No worries mate. You looked like you needed it. And we're in Exeter. I'm stopping for a late breakfast. I would have stopped sooner but wanted to give you a chance to get some shut-eye. Fancy some eggs?"

Alfie realised he was ravenous, and readily agreed. "I guess I haven't made a great passenger, have I?"

"Don't worry about it, lad. You're still not the worst passenger I've picked up – remind me to tell you about the drunk Scotsman."

"Well, let me buy you breakfast as a thank you," he said. "I can at least do that much."

"All right then, Alfie, if you're so inclined that would be mighty generous of you." He clapped an arm around Alfie's shoulders and steered him across the street towards Esme's Café. It had a worn, somewhat faded interior and a welcome smell of grease.

The place was half full, and they took a table towards the back, immediately poring over a laminated menu. After a few minutes, which seemed like an eternity given how hungry they were, the waitress came over, pad in hand, pen poised. "What can I get you?"

"Scrambled eggs and tomato with toast please," said Michael. "And a tea."

"How would you like the tea?"

"With milk, thanks darling. Nice and strong," said Michael.

Alfie sat quietly stunned while Michael ordered. The waitress was beautiful. Lips painted a shade of red that made him think of roses and big brown eyes that matched her glossy brown hair. She was perfect in every way.

"And what can I get you?" she asked Alfie.

He struggled to regain his thoughts and bring them back to the present. He'd already started to picture what their wedding would be like.

"I…I…uh…what he's having please," Alfie eventually said rather desperately, blushing.

"Right you are." She nodded and jotted his order down on her little pad. "Scrambled eggs and tomato, toast, and strong tea with milk."

"Oh, no, not the tea," Alfie fumbled. "Coffee, please. Black."

She scribbled on her pad some more. "Anything else?"

Blessedly, Michael took over. "That's it, thanks love." She put the pad away in her cute little apron and walked towards the kitchen.

Michael chuckled. "Not that clean-cut then, I guess, are you lad?" Alfie blushed even further, causing Michael's chuckle to turn into a roar of laughter as he pulled out his cigarettes. He offered one to Alfie who politely declined. It turned out the new him didn't smoke after all.

"So then, Alfie, will you stay in Exeter or keep with me until Plymouth? Don't worry, you get used to the accent."

Alfie nodded. The waitress' accent had been very strange, but he'd been too dumbfounded by her beauty to take proper notice. "I don't know – I don't know anything about either of them. What would you do?"

Michael rubbed his chin. "Exeter is probably better for work, depending on what you're after?"

"I'm a cabinetmaker by trade, but I've trained as a carpenter as well."

"Well, there's a lot that needs rebuilding here after the war. Although there is in Plymouth too, and it's by the sea. But don't rely on my advice, lad." He dug back into his shirt pocket and pulled out a shilling. "This," he said, waggling the coin in front of Alfie with a cheeky grin, "this is what you should let decide for you. It's my lucky shilling – hasn't let me down since I found it on Whitstable beach. What do you say? Heads for Exeter, tails for Plymouth?"

Chapter 3

Alfie glanced at Fred. "Didn't I tell you it was a story?"

"Story? You've still not told me how you actually ended up working in a funfair. All you've done is tell me about some ride in a lorry."

"Ah, but that's just the beginning. And all stories need a good beginning. If you're here next week, I'll tell you all about how I got from that café with Michael into Crompton's Travelling Funfair." He glanced at his watch. "Now though, it's time for me to get back before someone misses me." He hesitated. "See you next week?"

Fred shrugged. "Maybe."

Alfie sighed. The boy was always the same. He heaved himself off the bench, groaning a little at the effort. Even though it wasn't a cold day, the cold still always seemed to seep into his bones.

"Well then, until next time…maybe," he said, tipping his hat and starting to shuffle back in the direction of Pinewood.

As always, Alfie snuck back in half expecting a cry of outrage after his absence had been discovered. And as always he was left a little disappointed when there was none. He ambled down the corridor towards his room to tuck away his canvas bag, passing Julia who raised an eyebrow at him. Yes, he thought, she does know, or at least she suspects. He liked it this way though, the not quite knowing. It was like a game of spies between the two of them.

Trevor, with whom he shared a room at Pinewood, blessedly wasn't there, and he walked past Trevor's side of the room, pulling the curtain closed behind him. He put away his jacket, bag and his hat, enjoying the temporary silence.

He went to the window to check on his bird bath and feeder. Grand terms for what were a plastic ice cream container filled with water and an ashtray he had nicked from Trevor filled with seeds. But the house sparrows that regularly came for a feed and a bath seemed to think the facilities were decent enough.

He'd had to look at a book to be able to identify what type they were, but he liked to know. He liked the way they would cheerfully hop around, vocally expressing their delight as they played around in the water. Or maybe they were telling him he needed to renovate the bath, he chuckled.

Trevor, messy as he was, had never noticed that his ashtray was outside the window. Alfie thought of it less as stealing and more of a civic duty he was fulfilling to try and get the man – who had emphysema – to stop smoking. Not that it had helped one whit. Not while the man's pushover daughter-in-law smuggled in cigarettes for him.

Suddenly there was a wheezing cackle. "Alfie! I've got a great one for you," called Trevor as he came in the room. "If James comes next week I'll tell it to him too."

Alfie's smile vanished. Trevor grated on his nerves and had done ever since he'd moved in after Arthur, his previous roommate, had died. Arthur had been a wonderful roommate; quiet, clean and with absolutely no interest in dirty jokes that he couldn't remember the punchline to.

The curtain was whisked back and Trevor beamed at him, his straggly grey beard and wild, unkempt hair irritating the clean-shaven Alfie just by looking at it. Although not as much as the ridiculous fake diamond stud Trevor wore in his right ear like some sort of geriatric pirate. "Do you want to hear it, Alfie? It's a cracker

– James is going to love it if he comes next week. He couldn't come again today, but I'm sure he'll come next week."

Alfie couldn't help himself. "James won't come next week, Trevor. James never comes, only Beth. Remember?"

Trevor wasn't listening to him, repeating the joke softly to himself to try and commit it to memory. "So listen. A guy is walking on the beach one day when he finds a genie bottle. He rubs it and a genie pops out and— No wait, it's two genies that pop out – and the guys says 'Two genies, that must mean six wishes' and the genie – I can't remember which genie but I don't think it matters – says, 'Sorry buddy, you only get three wishes'. Seems a bit of a rip-off if you ask me but anyway, the guy wishes for the most beautiful girlfriend and to be super rich— Oh wait, no he whispers that to the genie, you're not meant to know that yet." Trevor waved his hand. "Forget I said that. Let me go back. So the genie – I can't remember which genie – says 'Sorry buddy—"

"Trevor! Please shut up."

Trevor looked hurt and shrugged his shoulders. "Your loss," he said, moving back to his side of the room and turning his back to rifle through his overflowing and utterly chaotic cupboard.

Alfie closed eyes that once had been a startling blue, but were now watery with age, and took several deep breaths, trying to calm himself. He was sure that once upon a time Trevor wouldn't have irritated him so much. But almost thirty years of living on his own before coming to Pinewood had made him decidedly less tolerant.

He saw Trevor leave and brought his attention back to look at the bird facilities, which were in need of some attention. He retrieved the small bag of birdseed from his bedside cabinet and started the loop through Pinewood to get to the outside of his window. It was a circuitous route he had to take, going down the corridor, through the TV lounge and the dining room and then out the back door. Once outside, he then had to loop back around the outside of the building to his window. But he could get a cup of water in the dining room on his way through for the bath.

He had slightly misjudged the timing today though and most people were already sat down for lunch, the staff filling the plastic cups with water or juice. The birds would have to wait. He'd never make it all the way around and back in time, not at his speed, and he didn't want to miss lunch.

He looked at where the available chairs were, groaning at the choices he had available. Normally he timed it better than this so he didn't end up having to eat lunch with someone he despised.

It reminded him of being back in school and being the last person to the dining room and the only kids left to sit next to were the fat kid with the terrible body odour or the unattractive girl who wouldn't stop prattling on. In fact, he thought, that wasn't dissimilar to his choices today. He could either sit next to Mavis, who talked interminably about everything with false authority, or next to Ben, who farted uncontrollably and almost incessantly. At least he could tune Mavis out, he thought. There was no chance he was suddenly going to lose his sense of smell.

He took the chair next to Mavis, placing the bag of seed on his lap. Mavis was already in full flow with Joan. "...definitely faked, I tell you. You can see the flag moving! It was all filmed in a studio somewhere. The cousin of a friend of my son's brother-in-law works at NASA and he's confirmed it."

"Oh shut up, Mavis," Joan snapped. "No one with any sense believes that." She looked at Alfie and her eyes sparkled mischievously. "You may as well say that Santa Claus doesn't exist."

"Well now, that's an interesting topic because you know there's debate about the historical origins of the made-up Santa Claus. Some say—"

"Mavis!" Joan cut her off. "It was a joke. I do not want to hear about the origins of Santa Claus. It's only April. If I'm still alive in December, tell me then."

Alfie chuckled, pleasantly surprised by Joan's humour. He'd not spoken to her a great deal, although he'd not spoken to anyone a great deal, even after six years at Pinewood. But as she normally sat with Trevor, the two of them having some sort of romantic affiliation, and him getting more than enough of Trevor having to share a room with him, he supposed he'd spoken to Joan less than most. She had lipstick on and small blue earrings in the shape of a clam. He liked that she put a bit of effort in to make herself look nice. And she did look nice. She must have been a real looker when she was younger.

One of the nurses appeared with a cart carrying the day's lunch. They were meant to get a choice of two meals at lunchtime, but frequently it was a choice of one.

"What's on the menu today? Any prawns?" asked Joan hopefully. Alfie stopped himself from laughing. Prawns? They were lucky if they got boiled fish.

The nurse, Claire her name tag said, shook her head. "Sorry, Joan. It's corned beef and mash today." She placed a plate in front of each of them and both Alfie and Joan looked in disappointment at the grey meat and grey potatoes. "But I do have ice cream for dessert," Claire said, with a wink and a smile to Joan before moving on.

"Will you be coming to bingo later, Alfie?" Joan asked him. "It's a lot of fun. I'm sure if you tried it just once…" She tentatively took a small mouthful of greyness.

Alfie shook his head. "Nice try, Joan, but no. Besides, I wouldn't want to win and deprive you of your chocolate winnings." Joan had an enviable record at bingo within Pinewood, winning more chocolate frogs than any other resident. And given Joan's sweet tooth it couldn't go to a more receptive winner, he thought.

With Mavis determined to ignore them and speak only to the almost deaf Clyde, lunch passed pleasantly enough, chatting with Joan. He learned she had four children, but only two lived locally. The other two lived abroad, one in New Zealand and one in the US. "It's hard sometimes, but you know with Skype and FaceTime these days it's a whole lot better than it used to be. I can see my grandkids and great-grandkids. Of course, I need someone to set it up for me – I'm not that much of a techno granny," she laughed. "What about your family, Alfie? Do they live away too? I've never seen you have visitors."

Alfie shook his head. "I never had children, no."

"What about siblings?" pressed Joan.

He looked away. "A sister in Bath." He pushed himself back from the table. "Anyway, must get on and fill up my bird bath. They'll be thinking the star rating has dropped even further at Alfie's Bird Motel."

He was dozing peacefully in his chair by the window a few hours later, Gold radio station playing softly on the radio, when Trevor burst into the room, much as a tortoise would burst through a paper bag. "I won!" he announced gleefully. "I bloody won the bingo!" He did as much of a jig as his eighty-four-year-old body would allow him, cackling to himself before the cackle turned into a hacking cough, sending him almost doubled over. "I gave the frog to Joan, of course," he wheezed, once he'd caught his breath a little. "Got a kiss for it too." He smiled broadly, his eyes twinkling. It was probably just the tears in his eyes from all the coughing, Alfie thought meanly.

Trevor started rooting around in the disaster he called a cupboard. Alfie had no idea how he found anything in there, it was such a jumble of chaos. Eventually, after pulling out a sweater, a slipper, a floral shower cap and a balled-up parka with a fur-lined hood, he came upon what he was after. "Ah ha!" he exclaimed, pulling out a half empty bottle of Scotch and shaking it at Alfie. "Fancy a Saturday night snifter?"

Alfie looked at his watch. "It's hardly Saturday night, Trevor. It's only four o'clock."

Trevor shrugged. "Suit yourself," he said, taking a swig from the bottle. "And besides, you know we'll all be in bed by eight-thirty, so it kind of is Saturday night. It's all rock and roll at Pinewood, Alfie me boy." He took another swig and then put it back in the cupboard, shoving the excavated items back in and closing the door quickly before they could fall back out.

"Right, I'm for a spot of telly, I think," he said, rubbing his hands. "See you at six for *Pointless*?"

Alfie nodded, vaguely waving him off. The game show *Pointless* was the one show he watched regularly. He wasn't sure what it was about the game, but he enjoyed it. And god knew he enjoyed precious few things these days. He sighed. Two hours to kill until then. He picked up his book and decided to read in the garden.

The sun was out so the garden was busy, and he picked as secluded a seat as he could find. He was halfway through *Strangers* by Dean Koontz and it was getting rather good. He knew some people thought of him as a sub-standard Stephen King, but Alfie infinitely preferred him. Koontz's novels were darker. Plus, Alfie liked the fact that Koontz wasn't as well known. He didn't like to be seen doing what other people were doing. Which is why it irritated him that he enjoyed *Pointless* so much.

He still had a hundred or so pages left of *Strangers* and he wasn't sure he'd get through them all before the weekly trip to the local library on Wednesday. If he could get enough peace and quiet from Trevor, he might.

Apart from his escapade to the park every Saturday, the weekly trip to the local library was the other highlight of his week. Pinewood had a minibus, which ran them to the library and back. It was his only other regular contact with the outside world. It was also free, which was very welcome, given he had virtually nothing left once Pinewood had taken its cut of his meagre pension.

Lately, he had also discovered that seniors could use the internet on the public computer in the library for free for an hour. He wasn't as technically savvy as Joan with her tablet and Skyping, but he'd been given a quick lesson on the computer and how to log on as well as how the mouse worked. It was enough to be able to read the news on the BBC and look at the weather for the coming week. Sometimes he'd even watch a video on YouTube.

He picked up his book and started reading, glad to lose himself in the pages for a while.

Julia watched Alfie through the window. He was an odd fish. Compulsively private and by turns irascible and kindly. The turns between mood weren't odd in themselves, not in elderly care where most of the residents swung between peevish and saintly. But there was something about him. He wasn't even the most cantankerous of the bunch – Mavis won that crown. She couldn't quite put her finger on it and she sighed, annoyed with herself that she couldn't work it – or him – out.

She knew that he disappeared somewhere every Saturday morning for a few hours. At first when she'd noticed it, she had been about to raise the alarm, but then he had wandered back in looking happy as Larry. She should have raised the alarm. She should have told him he wasn't allowed to just leave or she'd need to report it.

But he looked so dammed happy whenever he came back and god knew he rarely looked happy any other time. And he had all his marbles still and wasn't a danger to anyone. So she kept letting him sneak out, always keeping an eye out to make sure he was back by eleven-thirty for lunch. She thought the old devil quite liked the excitement of having one over on them too. Besides, she felt sorry for him, never having any visitors. She'd looked at his paperwork and there was no next of kin listed. She sighed. She should make an effort to try and break through to him, although she suspected even her Australian charm might fail her this time. Still, it was her job to try even so.

"Shit!" She turned to see Joan and Trevor sitting together in a corner of the day room, a large puddle of water and an overturned plastic cup on the floor between them.

"All okay?" she asked, walking over. "I mean, spillage aside?"

They both nodded. "My fault," said Trevor. "I was getting a little overexcited. At least I didn't spill it on my trousers – it would have looked like I'd pissed myself!" He laughed that wheezy laugh of his and Julia couldn't help laughing with him.

"Let me get a cloth and I'll clean this right up."

"Sorry love," Trevor apologised. "It's just that this one here gets me so excited." He patted Joan's arm affectionately.

Joan playfully swatted his arm away. "Get on with you. You're just clumsy."

Julia went to the kitchen to get a cloth, smiling. Joan and

Trevor were her favourites at Pinewood, making a very cute almost-couple. They reminded her of her own grandparents, although both had sadly passed away years earlier. Thinking about them got her starting to think about her parents, who were also now getting on a bit. She really should make an effort to get back home more to see them, she thought.

In the sixteen years she'd been in the UK she'd only gone back three times, and even those had been flying visits. She realised if she kept up her one visit every five years or so she'd likely only see her parents five times before they died. Tops. It was a sobering thought and she set an alarm on her phone to Skype with them tomorrow and float the idea of a trip home.

She'd always meant to get home more often. But there was such a big world out there to explore, and if she had to choose between two weeks exploring Morocco or Japan and two weeks in Jimboomba, then anywhere other than Jimboomba would win every time.

She mopped up the spillage as best she could, thankful she was mopping up water rather than urine. Not that she could complain about the latter too much. Pinewood was a care home rather than a nursing home. Once the residents got too frail and in need of constant tending they were moved to other facilities. It was one of the things that had attracted her to Pinewood, as she got to see the residents as people rather than patients. The fact that she rarely had to clean up urine was an added bonus.

The next Saturday saw Alfie back at the park at the usual time. Part of him was irked at being so predictable. He hated routine and it was a source of constant irritation at Pinewood that every part of his day was dictated to him – wake up and lie there until someone came at seven-thirty to help him out of bed and give him a shower or a sponge bath. Get dressed. Eight am breakfast. Activity or free time until lunch at twelve. Activity or free time until dinner at five. Then TV in the lounge until bed at eight-thirty. And of course, all the talk of activity time sounded grand, until you realised that really there weren't that many. The trips to the library, bingo and singing were about it. Although he had heard talk of chair yoga recently and shuddered at the thought.

But the pleasure he got from coming to the park and the simple company of the birds, and somewhat less simple company of the boy, made it all somewhat bearable. It was an escape, both physically and mentally, for a time.

As usual he made up infinitely more interesting plaque inscriptions for Rosalind. *For Rosalind, who really owned that moustache in later life* or *For Rosalind, who had a phobia of unripe bananas.* He could understand her on that last one if he was honest. Bananas should definitely not make your teeth squeaky.

"Morning, old timer," Fred shouted behind him, making him start.

"I'm not bloody deaf, Fred, I keep telling you. What's wrong with just coming up and saying hello like a normal person?"

"Where's the fun in that? Besides, you'd miss having it to complain about."

He was right, thought Alfie, and that also irritated him. Bloody kids.

He passed a slice of bread over to Fred, eyebrows raised. Fred accepted it with an almost imperceptible dip of the head and started to break it up into equal pieces, Alfie noticed with pride and delight.

"So, fancy hearing some more of the life of Alfie Cooper then? Where were we up to?"

"You were in some cafe with a lorry driver."

"Oh yes, Michael. But the coin, lad, the coin really did seal it all."

Chapter 4

Michael flipped the coin up in the air. They watched it with bated breath but it was up and down so fast Alfie barely saw it. Neither did Michael apparently, as it bounced off his hand on to the floor and rolled beneath the table next to them. The man at the table retrieved it for them, leaning over to hand it back.

"Thanks," said Michael. "I don't suppose you saw what it was?"

"Sorry me boy, I didn't. But I couldn't help overhearing, and if you need a decider on where to settle down I could do with a pair of hands on a job I've just picked up this morning. Especially those of a skilled cabinetmaker-cum-carpenter. It's not glamorous work, mind, but I'll pay you a decent enough wage."

Like the waitress, the man's accent was incredibly strange to Alfie and he wasn't sure he'd actually understood half of what the man had just said. But he thought he'd understood enough. Alfie leaned forward, hardly believing his luck that it could all be this easy. "I'm not worried about glamorous, believe me! What's the job?"

"The army has some land not too far from here that they use for training. There's a house on it that they use as part of that training, for when they go into civilian areas and to help them practise explosives work." He chuckled. "Basically the army will go in and either blow the house up or shoot it to shreds and we then need to go in and reconstruct it so they can come back in and blow it up again. Now, we're obviously not talking fully functioning house with plumbing and electricity and the like, but it does have the façade of a normal house and it's a bit more than just a shell inside, with a fitted kitchen and the like. What do you think, lad? Your skills would be perfect if you can do the cabinet-making interior bits and also the structural carpentry. I take it you can?"

Alfie nodded vigorously. He'd been evaluating the man as he spoke and he seemed honest. Around forty, with close-cut brown hair and a cleft in his chin that his mother always told him denoted a nice man. His father didn't have one, Alfie couldn't help but think whenever she'd said that.

"Good. In between that I've also got a ton of work rebuilding bits of the town – there's still a lot of work that needs to be done after the war. I can pay you eight pounds, four shillings a week. I know it's not a lot, especially once the taxman has his share, but it's enough to live modestly off."

Alfie shook his head, certain he'd never heard anything as stupid as building a house just to blow it up, but it sounded like good honest work, and it had practically fallen in his lap.

"The name's Derek. I'm off to the site now, but come and see me in the office at four-thirty and we'll get you sorted." He scribbled an address down on some paper and handed it over before standing, ready to go.

Alfie jumped up and introduced himself, noticing as he stood how tall Derek was – a good inch taller than himself. "Thanks very much, Derek. I'll be round this afternoon. You can count on it."

"Well, didn't I tell you, lad? You can always count on the coin!" said Michael, after Derek had left.

Alfie wasn't quite sure that was how Michael had intended the coin's intervention to play out, but he couldn't doubt that the shilling had neatly solved his dilemma of what he was going to do for work.

Breakfast was delivered and they both tucked into the plate with an appetite and appreciation bordering on lustful.

"So tell me, lad," said Michael, in between mouthfuls of egg, "which part of the rat-infested shithole that is London do you hail from?"

"I grew up in Fulham," Alfie said, trying not to inhale his tinned tomato. "It actually wasn't so bad around there. The house we had was a bit rundown – there's a crack in the load-bearing wall downstairs that's been growing every year since I can remember. I think it was there when Dad bought the place and he just never quite got around to fixing it properly." Alfie remembered growing up thinking that the crack was growing to keep pace with the darkness in the house, absorbing his father's rages and displeasures. His mother's disapproval. If so, he could only marvel that the house was still standing. "There's damp in the cellar too," he continued. "But Bishop's Park was nice to play in growing up." He smiled as he remembered chasing Betty in and out of the shrubbery, trying to avoid the park keeper. Her squeals as he would dunk her in the paddling pool.

Michael finished chewing his toast and smacked his lips, grabbing a napkin to wipe the grease from his mouth. "Well, certainly sounds a lot nicer than the East End where I lived, lad. And now that you're out in the proper country you don't need parks – just walk five minutes out of town and you're in the countryside, with cows and everything."

After breakfast they stood a little awkwardly by the lorry. "Well, best of luck, lad. I'm sure the shilling will have steered you truly." A hearty handshake, a wave and Michael was off, leaving Alfie standing in the lay-by with his holdall and his tool bag.

"Well Alfie," he said, looking around, "looks like we're living in Exeter." He shouldered his bag and set off according to the directions Derek had given him.

He found the place easily enough. A small office squeezed between a bakery and a corner store, Derek's Building Services painted a little clumsily onto a makeshift sign. He checked his watch; he was three hours early. Looking at the watch, a present from his parents and his two sisters for his last birthday, got him thinking about how they were all doing, and he hoped they weren't all too angry or upset.

He'd been intending to write to them, but maybe he should call his dad at work at the butcher shop. He'd passed a telephone box half a mile or so back and he had some coins.

He was in luck and there was no queue. Of all the people he could have spoken to, his father would have been his last choice. But he had no way of calling his mum or his sisters; a butcher's wages were a good deal short of the Cooper family having its own telephone.

As he dialled zero for the operator he wondered how long he should say he wanted. Not too long. Not long enough for this father to start yelling. He gave the operator the number and asked for one minute, duly feeding the amount she told him in to the top of the box. He liked the sound the coins made as they fell through, although he couldn't have said why. He held his breath while it rang. Half hoping no one would answer.

Then he heard his father's voice rattling off the number. His hand was over the button to open the call but he hesitated, unsure if he was ready for what would inevitably be a very difficult conversation. Then he thought he should just do it rather than risk his father getting angry and pushed the button.

"Hi Dad, it's me."

"Son? Where the devil are you?"

His dad sounded like he was down the bottom of a well. "I'm fine, Dad, I just…I just needed to get away and make my own mark."

"Yes, so your note said. Your mother was in floods of tears when I left her this morning. You couldn't have just sat us down and told us? You had to sneak off in the middle of the night like some criminal?"

"I'm sorry, Dad, I really am. I just didn't know how to tell you. But I'm okay. I'm in Exeter and I've picked up some work already. I'll write and let you know where I'm lodging." The pips went, letting him know his time was up. "Look Dad, I've got to go, the phone is about to run out. Tell Mum I'm sorry. I—" The line went dead.

Probably for the best, he thought. It avoided any awkward goodbyes. Or further recriminations.

To pass the rest of the time before he was due to meet Derek, he ambled about exploring Exeter. It was a pretty town, despite the highly visible scars of the war. The High Street was busy, and he thought Friday afternoons must be the time most of Exeter did its shopping. He was pleasantly surprised to see a Marks & Spencer and a Co-Op, and realised he'd had no real idea of what to expect outside of London. Everyone was speaking in the same thick accent that Derek had, and he realised it must be the way people spoke in the West Country. He'd have to get used to it.

At four-thirty he returned to Derek's office. He opened the door to find Derek in a cramped room sitting at a desk too small for both his height and the amount of paperwork on it. Derek waved him to the only other chair in the room. "Glad you found me, boy. Sit down." The chair was awkwardly low.

"Apologies for the smell of bread. You get used to it if you're in here long enough. So, boy, you're a qualified cabinetmaker then who is also trained in carpentry?" Alfie nodded. "And I can see you've got your own tools." Derek motioned to the tool bag at Alfie's feet. "We've agreed your wages, so the next thing is when you can start. The army job starts on Monday if you can be available then?" Alfie nodded again. "Good." He paused, looking Alfie over. "Do you have somewhere to stay, boy?"

Alfie, originally bristling at being called boy, realised it must be part of the West Country dialect as Derek was using it so often and without malice. So he simply shook his head. "No, I hadn't got that far yet."

Derek searched for a scrap of paper. "Go and see Hilda," he said, scribbling down an address. "Tell her I sent you and that you need a room. They're not fancy, but she doesn't charge the earth and her cooking won't kill you."

"Thanks, Derek. I really owe you one."

"Don't mention it. Be waiting at the bottom of South Street past the cathedral at six on Monday morning and you can jump in the van. It's about a mile from Hilda's, give or take." He stood, shaking Alfie's hand. "Welcome aboard and I'll see you bright and early on Monday."

He found the boarding house easily enough. Aside from the bright blue front door it was a nondescript terraced house with a slightly overgrown front garden and a front gate that appeared to be hanging from just one hinge. He took a deep breath and knocked on the door. A short redhead, hair bound in a scarf, answered the door, drying her hands. Alfie estimated her to be in her late forties.

"Alright me 'andsome. What can I do you for you? If you're after Matthew, he's at work." She noticed his bags on the ground, "Although I think maybe you're after a room?"

He nodded, shifting his bags awkwardly. "Derek sent me. He said to ask for Hilda."

"Well, you've found me!" She beamed at him, revealing crooked teeth, and opened the door wider to show a narrow hallway. "Well, come on in, me boy. Don't just stand there like a goose. What's your name?" she called over her shoulder, turning to walk down the hall.

"Alfie Cooper," he called, following her into the front room. It was painted a shade of purple that made him think of a turnip.

"You can put your bags down in the corner over there. Would you like a cup of tea?"

"Yes please, Mrs...? Strong and with milk please." Alfie floundered for how to address her. Using her first name didn't seem right somehow.

"Of course it is. And no Mrs this or that, call me Hilda. Right-o, I'll be back in a flash." Hilda left the room in a swirl of cheap perfume and the swoosh of her skirt.

Alfie took the opportunity to have a better look around the room, now that he'd adjusted to the paint. It was cosy, with a fireplace and three armchairs arranged around it. A shelf above the fireplace was home to a small assortment of books, a framed photo of Winston Churchill, a small radio and a clock. Underneath the window was a sideboard so filled with ceramic animals that it was a veritable menagerie.

He walked over to have a further look, finding tigers, owls, dogs, frogs, horses, fish, penguins, squirrels, elephants, zebras and even a unicorn. Forget a menagerie, he thought, this was a collection to fill the ark. He picked up the unicorn, an unexpected whimsy in a sea of ordinary.

"I'm particularly proud of that one," said Hilda, coming back into the room and startling him, so that he thought he might drop the bloody thing. He put it back carefully in its place between a cat lying curled in a basket of flowers and a giraffe. She handed him his mug of tea. "Una comes from a little village in North Devon. I hadn't seen a unicorn before."

"You've named them?"

"Oh yes. That's Gary the giraffe, Pam the poodle, Oscar the otter, Reg the rhino – you get the idea," she chuckled. "Of course, I can't remember them all, so tomorrow it might be Rebecca the rhino and Oswald the otter. But that just makes it more fun. Una is always Una though."

"How come?"

"Well, apart from the fact that names starting with U are a bit harder to come by, she was the last one that my husband bought me, god rest his soul."

"Oh I'm sorry," said Alfie, flustered. "I didn't mean to…"

"I know you didn't, me dear. How could you know? And it's not like you killed him, is it? You weren't out there directing the drunk sod into the big hole he fell down. I always told him the drink would kill him. Of course, I'd meant with his health, but there you go." Alfie didn't quite know how to respond to that and was searching for something even vaguely appropriate to say when she rescued him.

"So, you're here for a room anyway, aren't you, me dear? The price is three pounds, two shillings a week and that includes your room, two meals a day and your laundry. Breakfast is served in the dining room, but I know Derek likes to start early so I expect you'll be needing something before I'm up and about. I can do some boiled eggs for you the night before and you can help yourself to some porridge – how's that for you?" Alfie nodded.

"That would be very nice, thank you Mrs— Sorry, Hilda."

"Right, good then. Dinner is served at six, also in the dining room, and is whatever I've felt like cooking up. Like it or lump it, I'm afraid." She finished her tea and placed the mug emphatically on the sideboard, upsetting Gary the giraffe. "He's so clumsy," she said affectionately, putting the animal back upright. "Anyway, assuming that's all acceptable to you, Alfie Cooper, then I'll show you your room.

"It's not much," she continued, walking ahead of him up the stairs, "But then I'm not charging you much, am I?" She stopped on the landing at the top of the stairs. "Right, that's Matthew's room, that one there is Joe's and this is your room here. My bedroom is downstairs at the back with the bathroom."

She was right, thought Alfie. It wasn't much. But it would do. It had a single bed, a small desk under a window that looked out to the road, a cupboard and a small basin and jug. He did a quick mental calculation of how much money he'd have left every week. Not a lot by any stretch, but it should be enough for his needs.

"Bath day is Sunday and I go first so I can get a start on dinner. You can work out the rest of the order between yourselves. In between you've got your own basin there for freshening up."

Alfie nodded, wondering what Matthew and Joe would be like; how old they'd be, if they'd be friendly. And, most importantly, would they like him?

Chapter 5

Julia walked down the hall and noticed Trevor sitting on the edge of his bed, crumpled in on himself like a ball of screwed-up paper. "Trevor? Is everything okay?" she asked, going to sit next to him.

"James didn't come again. I really thought he would this week. It's been months. Beth said he had to work, but I wonder if he just doesn't want to see his old man."

"Oh Trevor, I'm sure it's not that," Julia said, patting his leg, secretly thinking it was probably exactly that.

"I don't think he's ever forgiven me for the divorce, you know," Trevor continued. "But that wasn't all my fault, was it? Sylvia and me, we just didn't work. We drove each other to drink and argued – bloody hell, could we argue!" He shook his head. "Jeez, just talking about her has made me want a drink!" He opened his cupboard, fishing out a stapler, a box of tissues, an old newspaper and a bowl, before he put his hands on his bottle of Scotch and took a long swig.

"I'll pretend I didn't see that," said Julia, "although I don't think I'd be able to find it again in that mess anyway," she joked, trying to lighten the mood.

"Now you sound like Sylvia! That woman would hoover twice a day, I swear to god. Twice a day! How can the floor possibly need to be hoovered twice a goddamn day?" He took another drink and waved the bottle wildly to demonstrate his indignation at the concept of hoovering twice a day. "How is a man supposed to live with that, Julia? 'Trevor get your feet off the table'. 'Trevor use an ashtray.'" He shook his head, taking another mouthful. "I was a bloody saint to put up with it for so long. A goddamn saint."

"What does Joan think of it all?" Julia asked, hoping to shift the focus of conversation and get Trevor to put the Scotch away.

"Now there's a good woman! Kind and funny, my god she's funny. And even better, she thinks I'm funny!" He laughed his wheezing chuckle. "Oh I must go and tell her that joke. She'll love it!" He quickly stashed the bottle and left the room. "Joan love," he called out. "Where are you? I've got a great joke for you."

Julia followed him to the TV lounge to continue her original errand to start helping some of the frailer residents through to the dining room for lunch.

"Joan sweetheart," Trevor called exuberantly. "I've got a cracking joke for you!"

In a chair by the window, she waved a hand at him distractedly. "Hang on Trevor," she said. "I think I've almost got the nine-letter word." She looked at the screen for a few more moments before tapping away with her stylus. "Yes, that was it. Abduction." She looked at him, beaming. "I hardly ever get those!"

"Well done, darling," he said, giving her a big kiss on the cheek.

"Oh away with you," she said with a smile. "So what's this joke then? You've really sold it now."

"Okay, here it is. Are you ready for it? A pirate walks into a bar with a ship's steering wheel hanging from his knackers. The bartender says, 'What the hell is that?' The pirate says, 'I don't know, but it's driving me nuts!'" Trevor roared with laughter, clearly pleased he'd remembered the punchline. Joan laughed with him, pausing after a few moments.

"I don't get it."

"What? Well, he's got a steering wheel attached to his bits right?"

Joan nodded slowly. "Ye-es…"

"And so the steering wheel is hanging from them, and it's driving him nuts."

"Oh!" Joan laughed heartily, before saying, "No, I still don't get it."

Trevor rolled his eyes, starting to get exasperated. "It's a steering wheel, Joan. Attached to his nuts. So it's driving him nuts…"

"Oh, now I get it!" she exclaimed, laughing again.

"Thank god for that! I'm not sure I could remember it again!"

Julia smiled. They made a funny pair. The man who could rarely remember a joke and the woman who could never understand them without explanation. But she could sense they were kindred spirits. Two larger-than-life people reduced to shrivelled, bent bodies, trapped in small green rooms. But together they defied their surroundings, their age. Refusing to let Pinewood and old age put out their fire and zest for life. She loved them for that and could only hope that she retained even a semblance of their spirit when she got that old.

She spotted Alfie come out of the corridor and skirt the edge of the room before leaving by the opposite door. She wondered once again what his story was. She was sure it would be an interesting one if anyone ever got to hear it. But then she supposed everyone had an interesting story to tell. Her own story was probably interesting to other people, although she was so bored of it she could barely even bring herself to think about it. Thankfully there were enough stories in Pinewood that no one bothered too much about hers.

Joan, for instance. Julia had only heard snippets, but what she'd heard so far was fascinating and frankly just inspirational. A single mother in the 1950s with four kids, working two jobs to keep a roof over their heads and put food on the table. And the two of Joan's children that she'd met were absolutely lovely and doted on her. Knowing Joan's story you could understand why, although Joan was so sweet she suspected that they'd dote on her anyway.

Childless herself, Julia wondered – not for the first time – who would dote on her in her old age. She'd probably end up like Alfie, reliant on kind staff at the care home to buy her what she needed. But instead of being daring enough to sneak out, she'd just end up sitting forlornly in the corner while other residents received visits from family.

At thirty-eight she was running out of time for kids too. She and Siobhan had talked about having kids and they'd always planned on it. They'd even discussed whether they'd go for a sperm donor or adoption. And while they'd liked the idea of having their friend Nick be the sperm donor, the fact that one of them then wouldn't be a physical part of the child didn't sit right with either of them. And which one of them would get to carry the baby? Adoption seemed to navigate those dark and perilous waters, while also giving a home to a child who needed one. They'd even gone so far as to have an initial meeting with an adoption agency and take home the forms. But then of course that had all gone out the window. Now she was thirty-eight, childless and single.

She shook herself out of what was increasingly becoming self-pity and went to help serve lunch.

Wednesday. Alfie's second favourite day of the week. He was ready and waiting in the day room a full half an hour before the minibus was due to take them all to the East Slatterley Public Library. He'd finished *Strangers* on Sunday, and so he'd had nothing to read since then but the paltry selection of newspapers the nurses provided. He was sure they just supplied the cheapest ones, the *Sun*, the *Express*, the *Daily Mail*. All the tabloids. Nothing with serious journalism. He had to content himself with the *Daily Mail* as the least bad of the bunch. At least it had a half-decent cryptic crossword.

Of course, he was allowed to borrow more than one book from the library, but he only liked to have two at any one time and his second book choice was always taken up with *Persuasion* by Jane Austen. He had the book on effective permanent loan from the library, re-borrowing the book once each loan period was up. He kept it in his bedside drawer so Trevor or one of the nosy nurses wouldn't notice and start asking questions. He didn't want to talk about it.

The current loan on *Persuasion* didn't expire for another week though, so this week he was just taking back *Strangers*. He thought he might have a break from Dean Koontz and try something else. Maybe he'd try a Lee Child. He always saw one of the nurses reading Lee Child and despite the adage, he couldn't help being attracted by the covers he'd spotted. There seemed to be quite a few of them too, based on how many he'd seen the nurse reading over the years so he'd probably be dead before he got through them all.

He looked down at the copy of *Strangers* in his lap. Being a larger sized paperback, his big hands hadn't dwarfed the book, which had been a nice feeling. He didn't like the hardbacks, too many sharp edges and corners. But the small paperbacks felt like a child's book in his hands. He wondered if he could get any of the Lee Child novels in the larger size, but he didn't like his chances. They were less common than either the smaller paperback or the hardback and he wished the publishers would do them more often. He didn't understand why they insisted on publishing such small paperbacks, like they thought women with dainty hands were the only ones who read.

He'd always had big hands, but somehow they felt even bigger now, as the rest of his body had shrunk with age. Well, except for his ears and nose. They also hadn't shrunk, and some days he felt like a deformed clown.

"Right, you lot," said Julia as she walked in. "Are you ready for your outing to the library? Brian is out the front in the minibus so let's go!" Those who were able slowly levered themselves out of the chairs while Julia helped those up who couldn't do it themselves, getting them settled on their walkers. They moved out to the minibus at a pace that would have made a tortoise blush, thought Alfie.

He remembered watching a David Attenborough documentary about the Galapagos Islands and there had been an ancient tortoise that was all alone with no mate, the last of his kind. He'd fittingly been named Lonesome George and Alfie had identified with the poor tortoise, wondering if he should start calling himself Lonesome Alfie, but it didn't have quite the same ring to it. He'd also promptly started hating himself for being so self-pitying. He'd made his choices in life and he had to live with them. Nevertheless, he'd been quite upset to learn about Lonesome George's death a few years back.

Eventually everyone was on board and they were on their way. They passed the park and Alfie peered out the window, instinctively looking for his bench. He was startled to see Fred there, sitting on his own and staring out across the lake. Alfie hadn't known or realised that Fred went there on days other than Saturday. If he was honest he was a little hurt. It made their hours together on a Saturday feel less special somehow, although he'd never tell Fred that. It also occurred to him that Fred should be in school. Perhaps he should have a word; school was important and he didn't want Fred ending up uneducated and ignorant.

Alfie continued to stare out the window as the minibus negotiated its way through what passed for the town centre. A young couple were having an argument outside a WHSmith, gesticulating wildly and angrily at each other while a toddler cried in its pram between them. And despite being a good yardarm before noon, there was already a collection of drunks outside the Wetherspoons, pints clutched in one hand while they desperately sucked on cigarettes with the other.

In a short time they arrived at the library, where it took them almost as much time to get everyone off the minibus as it did to drive there. Impatient, Alfie went on ahead. He wanted to be able to use the computer today and there were only two of them. He didn't want to get stuck behind someone and have to wait.

He entered the library and waved at Emma the librarian, making a beeline for the computer. Emma was one of the few people who could elicit a smile from him. He wasn't sure what it was; there was just something about her. Perhaps it was the big open smile. But he also thought he saw a kindness in her eyes that for a change wasn't tinged with pity.

Thankfully, one of the computers was free and he eased himself slowly into the uncomfortable plastic chair. He logged on and went straight to the BBC weather site to see what the forecast was for Saturday. The weather had been unsettled lately and he hoped that rain wouldn't prevent him from going to the park. He entered in the postcode for Pinewood and was disappointed to see the little grey cloud with rain for Saturday. Although when he scrolled down, he could see that the rain wasn't forecast until the afternoon so maybe he'd be lucky.

He then went to the *Guardian* website to get some proper news. As he was reading an article on Brexit, an ad caught his eye: *Lonely? Want to meet people around the world without leaving your house? Try our email pen pal service! It's free and you can choose the pen pal that's right for you!* He went to leave the page but stayed his mouse. He was lonely. And the idea of being able to talk to someone without having to actually see them and talk in person appealed to him.

The reason he spurned conversation with people in Pinewood so much was because he didn't want them asking questions that he didn't want to answer. He was all right with Fred, as the boy never asked questions; he just listened. A pen pal would be different. Even if they did ask questions he would have the time to write a response that he was happy with. He hesitated for another moment, his pointer hovered over the ad before deciding to go for it and clicking through.

A new page appeared, telling him a bit more about all the different countries the pen pals were in and asking him to create an account. The form was easy enough to fill in until he got to the part where they asked him what sort of pen pal he wanted so they could show some possible matches for him to choose from. Country? Age? Gender? He didn't really know. Maybe someone in another country would be best. Someone in the UK he'd be worried he'd bump into them or something. Which he knew was totally irrational as he never just bumped into anyone, given his entire world was Pinewood, his park bench and the library. But even so. Someone from America might be nice. He clicked on the US button next to country. Now, what gender? He caught sight of Emma chatting with Julia and thought having a female pen pal would be nice. Ladies always seemed to be kinder than men. He clicked on female and moved on to age. He looked at the brackets and discounted 60+. He was already surrounded by old people – why would he want to be pen pals with another one? He thought someone younger might be a breath of fresh air, but not too young. He considered for a few moments and then clicked 30-40. He clicked the complete button at the bottom of the page and up came a list of possible pen pals. It was a much longer list than he had anticipated and he was a touch overwhelmed.

Each result had a name and a brief description of the person and he scanned through the top few, his eyes coming to rest on Anne. *I'm a primary school teacher and mother to my son Ethan, living in New Jersey. I'm looking for a pen pal from somewhere international to bring a bit of the world outside to my little corner of the US.* She seems nice, he thought. And she can clearly write in proper English rather than that ghastly text-speak he understood kids used these days.

He clicked on the connect button and a window popped up for him to write his message to Anne in. He stopped, stuck. He'd thought this was a good idea, but now that he was faced with a blank page, he didn't know what he'd say. What would a young woman in America want to hear about from him? Probably nothing. He was on the verge of closing the window when he thought, why not? What did he have to lose? If she never wrote back to him then he'd lost nothing. And if she did, then he'd gained another small piece of contact with the world outside Pinewood.

He settled in and thought for a good few minutes before slowly bashing out his message with his two index fingers.

Dear Anne. My name is Alfie and I'm eighty-six years old. I live in a care home in a small town in England called Slatterley and I have no children. I see you have a son Ethan. How old is he?

He stopped then, out of ideas for what to write. He'd not had to write letters to anyone for such a long time. And he'd never been very good at writing them anyway. He spotted the Dean Koontz novel next to the keyboard, waiting to be given back to Emma.

I like to read Dean Koontz novels and am about to try Lee Child. Do you read? I also like birds and go to feed the ducks once a week at the local park. I have an ashtray I took from Trevor filled with seed outside my window and house sparrows come and visit to eat it. Occasionally I even get a redwing coming to visit in early spring. I've never been to America although I did travel a lot of the UK back in my twenties, working with a travelling funfair. Have you ever been to England or the UK?

He stopped typing, out of things to say to someone he'd never spoken to. He wondered if it was still considered speaking if you were doing it over email, then decided he didn't care.

He read over his email and wondered how he should sign it off. *Hope to hear from you* felt a little desperate but if he didn't say something like that maybe she wouldn't write back. And now that he'd invested some time and written the email he discovered that he actually did want her to write back.

Hope to hear back from you.

Regards,
Alfie Cooper.

He hit the send button before he could lose his nerve and sat staring at the screen for a few moments. He wasn't sure what he was expecting, but the rather bland message telling him his message had been sent and that he could see any replies in his pen pal inbox felt like a bit of an anti-climax.

He looked at his watch and realised his free hour was almost up anyway and that he only had an hour left. He stood with the inevitable sounds that come with standing up when you're eighty-six and walked to the desk to give Emma the copy of *Strangers*.

She smiled at him as he approached and he found himself smiling back. "Another one finished, Alfie?"

"Yes, and that's almost all of your Dean Koontz books read, I'm afraid. I was thinking of trying someone new. The nurse at Pinewood is always reading Lee Child so I thought I'd give him a go. Is he any good?"

"Yes, I'm afraid we've got a rather slim Dean Koontz selection here. I could order one in for you from another library?" Alfie shook his head. "All right then, Lee Child it is. I've not read any Lee Child myself, but I can show you where they are." She came around from behind the desk and started leading him towards the shelves. "The Jack Reacher books of his are very popular. If not, you might like John Saul. He's meant to be quite like Dean Koontz and Stephen King." She stopped and pointed to the shelves where Alfie saw at least twenty Lee Child novels lined up. All of them small paperbacks.

He thanked Emma and took a book off the shelf at random. *Never Go Back*. A fitting title he thought to himself, turning it over. It was one of these Jack Reacher books Emma had mentioned, although it wasn't the first one. He opened the front of the book, hoping for a book list so he could identify the first one in the series. He found the page and looked at the top of the list for the first title. *The Killing Floor*. No, that wouldn't do. Hands shaking, he put the book back and looked at the rest of the titles – *Die Trying, A Wanted Man, The Affair, Worth Dying For*. No, these were not books for him.

He went back to the desk to ask Emma about the other author she'd mentioned. "Back so soon, Alfie? I take it Lee Child isn't for you?"

He shook his head. "No, I thought I'd try that other fellow you mentioned. Can you show me where he is, please?"

"Of course I can!" she said jumping up. "It is my job after all." She smiled kindly at him and took his arm. "Come on then, this way to John Saul."

Saturday. Once again, Saturday. His life seemed to be a never-ending metronome, swinging back and forth between the bright rings of Saturday and Wednesday, with arcs of silence in between. Alfie looked anxiously out of the window. The clouds were grey and ominous, carrying the threat of rain like an unwelcome messenger.

He decided to brave it. The worst that could happen was that it would rain and he'd catch pneumonia and die. Actually no, the worst that could happen was that it would rain and he'd catch pneumonia and be bedridden for weeks on end with no escape from Trevor. The thought of that did actually make him reconsider going out, but he decided to go anyway. If the worst did happen he could always go on hunger strike. He was thin anyway so he was confident it wouldn't take too long.

He got his hat and canvas bag and checked his watch. Yes, time to go. Trevor blessedly was already in the day room waiting for his visitors, convinced that this week would be the week that his son James paid him a visit. At least I don't have to worry about being disappointed by my children, Alfie thought, as he shuffled down the hall. Although he had to admit he'd done a good enough job of disappointing himself.

As he walked to the park he thought he might finally have to relent and start using a cane. He was beginning to feel a little unsteady on his feet and the cane would help. Besides, he could use it to whack Trevor with when he got annoying.

He entered the park and stopped to take a big lungful of the lavender and pine. A small white dog ran in circles on the grass nearby, excited about being out for a walk. He knew the feeling.

He got to his bench and paused before he sat down, musing on his words for Rosalind this week. *For Rosalind, who was a demon at noughts and crosses.* Or *For Rosalind, who was rubbish at skiing but great at falling over.* Not his best effort, he realised, but still a damned sight better than the original.

He sat and waited to see if Fred would appear this week. He wasn't sure if he should bring up that he'd seen him at the park on Wednesday. Probably not. It would surely spook him and scare him off. Besides, it didn't matter really. Well, not beyond Fred missing school. That did concern him. But so what if Fred came to the park without him? He wasn't sure why he'd got upset in the first place really.

A pine cone suddenly appeared in the air in front of him, arcing down into the lake and startling the few ducks that had been napping on the edge. He's literally ruffled their feathers he thought, half amused and half annoyed.

"Hello Fred," he said, without turning. "I guess I should be grateful that you're not shouting in my ear this week."

Fred dropped onto the other side of the bench with a thump, his hair flopping over his eyes. I remember having hair, thought Alfie. It had been the same sort of colour as Fred's, blonde tinged with a little red. Strawberry blonde his mum had used to call it, which Alfie had always thought sounded about as masculine as telling him that he had the feet of a ballerina. Now he had no hair, masculine or otherwise.

"Right," said Alfie, handing Fred a piece of wholemeal. "Let me tell you about Joe and Matthew."

Chapter 6

Alfie paced the front room waiting for Matthew and Joe to come home, unable to sit still. He'd already examined the contents of the ark, making up names for the ceramic animals all in Hilda's own style. Terry the tiger. Claire the camel. Paul the polar bear. He could see why she stuck with Una for the unicorn. He was struggling to think of another name starting with U himself.

He'd taken a book on horticulture from the small shelf above the fire, left behind by a former boarder, so Hilda had informed him. But try as he might, he just couldn't get enthused about the best way to grow tomatoes or plan irrigation channels.

He heard the front door open. "I'm telling you, Matthew, he's a fecking eejit. He's no sense at all," said a broad Irish voice. Before his companion could reply, they had both spilled into the front room, stopping short when they saw Alfie.

"Well, how's it going there?" asked the Irishman looking him over. "Who do we have here? A new boarder?"

Alfie nodded. "Alfie Cooper," he held out his hand.

"Joe O'Leary," said Joe, holding up his grease-stained hands apologetically.

"Matthew Rogers," said his companion, shaking Alfie's hand.

Alfie covertly gave them a sizing up. Both appeared to be

in their mid-twenties. Joe was short and stocky, with blonde hair and blue eyes that Alfie knew his sister Betty would go crazy over. Matthew was much more like Alfie, tall and wiry, with the West Country accent that he was beginning to get used to.

"So Alfie," said Joe, "what brings you to Hilda's Fine Establishment for Single Working Boys in Exeter?"

"I've just arrived from London."

"London! How grand! I'm trying to get to London," said Joe. "Just need to save up enough money."

"Which would happen a lot quicker if you didn't spend it all on beer and women!" Matthew laughed.

Joe shrugged and grinned. "What can I do? I'm Irish, it's in the blood." He held up his grease-stained hands. "Anyway, better go and clean up before Hilda has kittens. Grand to meet you, Alfie. I'll see you at dinner." He disappeared up the stairs, making a clumping noise that made Alfie think of a suitcase being dragged up the stairs, step by step.

Matthew clapped him on the shoulder. "Well, I don't have to wash and I've got a bottle of Old Fitz upstairs with two glasses that haven't forgotten what it was like to be clean. What do you say, Alfie? Join me for a pre-dinner snifter?"

"Sure, thanks. I've seen the ads for Old Fitzgerald but I've never tried it," he admitted rather shyly. Something else his parents had never let him do.

"An Old Fitz virgin, hey?" Matthew said with a chuckle. "Well, that definitely calls for a drink! I'll be back in a jiffy." He glanced at the horticulture book open on the side table. "You can finish your chapter on cucumbers in the meantime."

Alfie opened his mouth to explain, but Matthew was already gone, his tread up the stairs positively cat-like compared to Joe. Alfie put the book back on the shelf and tried to decide which chair to sit in. Suppose they had usual chairs that they sat in? There were only three armchairs, all colours that clashed quite spectacularly not only with each other, but also with the turnip walls.

He couldn't decide whether to go for the one with red flowers that reminded him of a chair his nan had, the green chair that had a rip in the arm or the huge armchair with a pattern in orange that Alfie thought might have been meant to represent flowers but wasn't quite sure. Maybe it was just meant to be swirls. He was still dithering when Matthew came back, armed with a half full bottle of Old Fitzgerald and two small glasses stacked inside each other.

"Sit, sit!" he said, waving Alfie into the red floral armchair and dropping himself into the orange ambiguity. He set the glasses down on the side table and pulled the cork from the bottle, breathing in deeply. "That's the proper job. I'll never get bored with that smell, I tell you." He poured two generous measures and passed a glass to Alfie. "Cheers," he said, clinking glasses and settling comfortably back into the armchair and lighting a cigarette. "So Alfie, how did you end up in Exeter?"

Alfie gave him a short summary of his ride with Michael, leaving out that he'd snuck away in the middle of the night and been ignored by a fox. "So are you actually a horticulturalist then?" asked Matthew. "Or were you just that bored that you thought you'd read up on potato growing?" He laughed. "Joe would heartily approve of that!"

"I'm a cabinetmaker." Alfie paused. "And yes, I was that bored."

Matthew nodded. "Already named all the animals, had you?" He caught Alfie's look of surprise and laughed. "We all do it, mate. Joe and I have a competition going to see who can come up with the best ones. So far I'm winning with Zachariah the zebra." He sipped his whiskey and waved the glass in Alfie's direction. "What do you think of the Old Fitz anyway?"

Alfie nodded enthusiastically, despite the fact it felt like it was burning a hole in his throat. It was pleasantly warming afterwards though, he noticed. And he suspected that unlike cigarettes this might be something that would grow on him.

"So what about you, Matthew? How have you ended up in Exeter?"

"Well, that's a short story and a not so interesting one, truth be told. I finished National Service and arrived back in my home town of Granton, which is about an hour north of here, and promptly fell head over heels for a cute little maid called Lucy. I'd known her before I left, of course – Granton isn't all that big – but she'd got all grown up while I'd been away, and I was smitten. You know what it's like when you get back from National Service – I think I was a little demob happy!" Matthew chuckled and took a drink of the Old Fitz.

Alfie sat guiltily. He didn't know. He'd been so excited about National Service too. Getting out. Getting away. The day he'd turned seventeen, bursting with excitement about the possibility of escaping his suffocating home life, he'd gone for his medical and been rejected. A heart defect. He'd secretly cried himself to sleep that night, his dreams of being called up by the RAF dashed.

He'd had it all planned out too. They would train him as a pilot and he'd finally get to not just go in a plane but fly it and leave the world behind. Leave his world behind. He would be deployed to Africa and make a name for himself, before returning home and immediately finding a bride from the swarms of women swooning over him as he proudly showed off his medals of honour.

"Anyway, I followed her to Exeter when she found a job at a dress shop. Turned out though that I was cuter on her than she was on me." He shrugged. "It all worked out in the end though, I guess. I found a job at the Co-Op on the High Street and a room here with Hilda and I've never looked back. They're training me up to be manager at the store and that's more than I could have hoped for in Granton. We didn't even have a Co-Op there."

He swallowed the rest of his whisky and stood. "Come on, we best go into the dining room. Hilda hates it when we're late."

The dining room was in keeping with the autumnal vegetables, Alfie thought, taking in the brussel sprout-green walls. Like the front room, the furniture was mismatched both in style and in colour, giving the room a chaotic look despite being tidy. The long table was set for three and Alfie and Matthew sat facing each other, leaving the head of the table for Joe.

"Hilda's actually a rather good cook," said Matthew. "I mean, it's a pretty limited menu, given that meat's still being rationed and you tend to get the same thing a lot, but her liver and onions is a right proper meal."

Having not eaten since his late breakfast of eggs and tomato, Alfie was ravenous and thought that he'd probably even find his father a good cook he was so hungry.

They heard an elephant on the stairs, shortly followed by the appearance of Joe. "Lads! You left me the head of the table, how kind." Joe elegantly slid into his chair, sitting tall with the hint of a smirk. "So, what have we been talking about? Was it me?" He turned around to look in the direction of the kitchen. "Was it Hilda?" he asked in a whisper, pulling Matthew's packet of Woodbines towards him and lighting a cigarette.

Alfie wasn't quite sure what to make of it, but Matthew laughed. "We're always talking about you, Joe. I don't know what we'd do for conversation without you."

Joe laughed with him. "As it should be! You know I'm the most interesting person you've ever met." Joe turned his eyes to Alfie. "You, however, Mr I've-Come-From-London. You probably have met more interesting people. Hmm?" Joe raised his eyebrows in question as he inhaled on his cigarette and Alfie sat there totally incapable of fathoming how he was meant to respond.

"Come on, Joe," said Matthew, "leave him alone for the first night at least. He doesn't know yet to not take you seriously. About anything."

Joe continued to eye up Alfie for a few moments before relenting. "Oh all right! I'll go easy on him. But just for tonight. I'm not promising any more than that." He stubbed out his cigarette in the nearby ashtray.

Hilda bustled in with plates piled high with salmon rissoles, mashed potato and green beans. "Here you go boys, tuck into that." She put the plates down with a flourish and Alfie noticed that the plates were as mismatched as the rest of the place. He thought of the matching dinnerware and furniture in his house and decided that he preferred Hilda's way. It felt more whimsical. More happy.

Hilda stopped by his shoulder. "How are you settling in, Alfie?

I hope Matthew and Joe have been kindly to you?" she asked with a raised eyebrow in their direction.

"Of course we have, Hilda," Joe replied in his lilting Irish accent, before raising a pile of mashed potato on his fork that Alfie was convinced was too big to be eaten until it disappeared.

"Well I'm glad to hear it." She gave Alfie's shoulder a squeeze. "If you need anything, me dear, let me know." She disappeared back into the kitchen leaving a temporary life-size hole in the room in the shape of a floral pinafore.

There was silence for a few minutes as the three of them gave full attention to the food. Joe was the first to remember there was a world outside of his plate.

"So Alfie, I know Matthew will have already asked this," he waved his fork at Matthew, tiny bits of mashed potato falling on to the tablecloth, "but what brought you to Exeter and caused you to leave a grand city like London? Was it a girl like our lanky friend here?"

Alfie was glad for the mouth of food as it gave him some thinking time. He got the feeling he needed a better answer than 'to get away from my parents'. Even if one of them swung between unpredictable, violent rages and sobbing uncontrollably.

"Not a girl, no." Well, not yet, he thought, remembering the waitress at the café. "I just wanted to get out and see the world really. Or, at least see more of England. What about you, Joe?" He asked quickly to prevent follow-up questions. "What caused you to leave Ireland?"

"Ahh…the lovely Emerald Isle. 'Tis a rather unfortunate story, my departure from Cork. I…accidentally set fire to the garage where I worked." Joe ducked behind a fork laden with salmon rissole, while Alfie stared at him, mouth open.

"You set fire to the garage?"

"Not deliberately, mind. I may have had a snifter or two down the pub at lunch and got a little careless with my cigarette and some oil. Amazing how quickly that stuff lights up. Anyway, to cut a long story short, my services were no longer required and so I decided to try my luck in London. As you can see, I've got as far as Exeter. And that, my dear Alfie, is the story of Joseph O'Leary." He finished with a flourish of his fork and a mini seated bow. "And you, Alfie, what is your work? And do you have any?"

Alfie nodded, his mouth full of salmon rissole. "I'm a cabinet-maker. And a carpenter as well," he finally managed. "I was fortunate enough to meet a chap called Derek this morning who has given me some work."

"Derek's Building Services?" asked Matthew. "Over by Tennyson's Bakery on Sidwell Street?"

Alfie nodded again, stabbing some beans. "That's the one. Do you know him?"

"Not personally, I just remember seeing the sign. Remember the maid Lucy? The dress shop she works in is across the road." Alfie tried to bring the shop to mind but could only recall the bakery and the pervading smell of bread.

After dinner, they retreated to the front room and Alfie noticed that Matthew took the orange chair again while Joe flopped into the green armchair, groaning under the weight of dinner. Alfie sat in the red floral number, assessing it with the new appreciation of it now being the only chair that he would sit in in this room.

They both lit up a cigarette, offering him one, which he declined with a shake of his head. Having had one of Michael's, he was inclined to agree with his parents that he couldn't understand how anyone could enjoy those things. Joe shrugged. "More for me."

Matthew brought out the Old Fitz again but Joe grunted and waved it away. "It's Friday night, let's go out for a drink. The Crown and Goat would accommodate us all for a drink and it's good craic. Besides, we need to show the new boy the town! Don't we, Alfie?"

Feeling a little put on the spot, all Alfie could think to do was nod, while his brain frantically tried to calculate how much money he had left after paying Hilda upfront for his first week of bed and board.

"Well, that sounds good by me," said Matthew, heaving himself up off what Alfie was beginning to think were meant to be abstract fruits. "Let's get spruced up and meet back down here in ten minutes."

Ten minutes later, Alfie was back in the front room having changed his shirt and counted his money four times hoping to come up with a different number. He knew the small amount he could afford to spend and he would just have to stick to it, even if it did mean having to be firm with Joe and Matthew. An act of assertiveness he was in no way used to performing and was mildly dreading.

Joe and Matthew joined him shortly after and with a jaunty step from them and a vague sinking feeling from Alfie, they all set off for the Crown and Goat.

The pub was almost full and the noise, warmth and dense smoke hit Alfie like a wall when they pushed open the heavy wooden door. It was a cosy pub with lots of dark wood, in the shape of an inverted L, with the bar an even smaller inverted L inside it. The door was in the corner of the L where the two arms met, meaning everyone in the pub could see them as they walked in, making Alfie blush self-consciously, even if no one was looking at them.

Alfie's feet stuck a little to the red patterned carpet as they made their way to the bar, and several people called out greetings to Joe and Matthew.

Having been to so few pubs in his time that he could count the visits on one hand, Alfie was a little overwhelmed and unsure what to order. Should he stick with drinking the Old Fitz? But how much did it cost? He knew that other men his age in London drank bitter but he couldn't see anything marked bitter. If he just asked for that would they know what he meant or would they laugh him out of the pub? In the end he wasn't given a choice anyway.

"Three Young's please George," said Joe, slapping some coins down on the bar. George was a bald man with a pale complexion and a paunch that threatened to propel his shirt buttons across the pub at a frightening velocity.

George nodded and began pulling their pints. He glanced across at Joe as he pumped. "All right then, Joe? Business good down at the garage?"

"It's busier than a whorehouse on payday. Still, keeps me out of trouble!" He grabbed his pint of beer and downed half of it in one go, smacking his lips. "That's the stuff!" He waved his glass in the direction of Alfie. "Now George, this is our new fella, Alfie Cooper. He's staying with us at Hilda's. He's a carpenter! Or a cabinetmaker. I forget which." He waved his pint back in George's direction. "Alfie, this is George, the best landlord in all of Exeter. Be kind to him. If you're broke come the end of the month sometimes he'll let you put a pint or two on credit."

"All right, all right, keep it down. I don't want every bugger asking for credit."

Joe tipped an imaginary hat. "Right you are, guv. My lips are sealed." George shook his head and went to serve another customer while the three boys sat themselves at a small round table at the top of the small end of the L. Joe scanned the room, eyeing up his fellow punters. "Not so many in tonight, Matthew. And no Barry the Burglar, Beetroot Tony or Jack the Beaver which is most unusual."

Alfie laughed. "Another naming game?"

"I'm shocked and offended at such a suggestion! As will they be! They are three very real regulars in this grand establishment. Or maybe that should be grand regulars in this real establishment."

Alfie glanced at Matthew, unsure if Joe was playing with him. "It's actually true, believe it or not. We're not short of a nickname in this place."

"The sign of a proper local if you ask me," said Joe, draining the last of his pint and lighting a cigarette. He looked at Alfie's barely touched and Matthew's half-drunk pint and snorted derisively. "Blazes lads, it's Friday night! This is a piss poor show indeed. Speed it up. I'm thirsty and I'm bloody certain it's not my round."

"We're not all as eager to drown ourselves as you are, Joe. But right you are, we are going a little slow. Ready Alfie, one, two, three and down!"

Before Alfie had a chance to protest Matthew raised his jug and finished off the rest of the pint. Joe and Matthew then both turned eyes to him. "Come on, lad," said Joe, seeing his hesitation. "I promise it won't kill you."

*

Several hours, several pints and decidedly more money than he'd intended to spend later, Alfie spilled out on to the street with Joe and Matthew, the three of them attempting to sing a bawdy Irish folk song Joe had made a poor show of teaching them.

Alfie was drunker than he'd ever been in his life and he liked it. Although come to think of it he'd never actually been drunk before. He still liked it. He had an overwhelming sense of everything being warm and fuzzy. It was like his brain had gone into soft focus and for the first time he could remember he wasn't second guessing what people thought of him or what he was saying, what he was doing. He could get used to this.

Matthew stumbled and crashed into a telephone box, causing a riotous outburst of laughter from Joe, who then slipped off the kerb and fell on to his hands and knees, exclaiming, "I'm locked out of the tree like a monkey who forgot his keys!" The fall, and this preposterous sentence prompted more laughter from both Matthew and Alfie and the three of them stopped there, laughing like the drunkards they were until a window opened and a blurry head stuck itself out of a window yelling at them to be quiet.

"Shhh! Shhh!" they all shushed each other. Joe, still on his hands and knees, held a finger up to his mouth while doing so and promptly keeled head first into the road.

Trying to contain their laughter, and doing a bad job of it, Matthew and Alfie helped him up off the road and the three of them staggered and stumbled their way back to Hilda's.

Reaching the top of the street they began to compose themselves and quiet down. "Hilda's a good maid," said Matthew somewhat solemnly. "She doesn't deserve to be woken up by a bunch of drunks."

They crept up the stairs, stifling giggles and Alfie flopped down on his narrow bed, passing out as soon as his head hit the pillow.

When he woke he discovered a dead animal had taken up residence in his mouth overnight – probably fleeing from the jackhammer in his head. He stumbled blearily to the basin and gulped water directly from the jug before sinking to the floor and praying to god that he was dead like the animal in his mouth.

He looked as his watch and realised that it was late – very late. Not only had he missed breakfast but half the day had gone. He stumbled downstairs and Hilda came bustling out from the direction of the kitchen, tutting at the sight of him.

"Look at the state of you," she shook her head.

Alfie tried to make his thoughts focus. He was pretty sure it was Saturday and he hadn't slept through until Sunday. "Where are Joe and Matthew?"

"They're out playing football. They're in a local team. Although Lord only knows how they manage it every week after writing themselves off like they do. Still, they're good boys at heart."

Having struggled to get down the stairs without falling over, Alfie couldn't even imagine being out playing football today. He wasn't even going to manage his push ups.

Hilda looked at the clock on the mantelpiece and announced she had to be off. "Don't forget dinner is served at six," she said, as she put on some dainty white gloves. She gave him another once over. "I hope for your sake you're looking and feeling a lot better by then."

The door closed behind her and Alfie sank down into the nearest chair, not even noticing it was the orange one rather than his red floral armchair. After several long minutes feeling sorry for himself, Alfie heaved himself up to see if he could successfully scrub the stink off. He was starving and needed food but he couldn't let himself be seen in public like he was. Although with bathing night not until tomorrow night he would have to make do with what he could manage from the sink in his room.

He'd go back to Esme's for food, he decided. He didn't know anywhere else yet and his brain was incapable of useful thought. He thought of the attractive waitress and realised he'd need an even more vigorous scrub than planned.

Chapter 7

Fred laughed as Alfie tailed off and Alfie glared at him. "It's not funny, Fred. Drinking is no laughing matter."

"It certainly sounds like it was!"

Alfie shook his head, his eyes closed. "You'll see, lad, you'll see," he said sadly. "But that's enough for today." He checked his watch. "For now I need to get back to Pinewood before they miss me." He glanced at Fred. "What are you doing with the rest of your Saturday? Hopefully something a little more exciting than counting the hours until *Pointless* comes on the television like I will be."

Fred shrugged. "Not sure. Maybe spend some time with my sister."

This was the first Alfie had heard of a sister. He was curious, but stopped himself from asking any further questions, knowing it would just irritate the boy. He tipped his hat to Fred. "Until next time."

Alfie slowly made his way up the path, his mind still back in Exeter. It had been a turning point in his life and he wondered – not for the first time – how life could have turned out so very differently.

Slowly the week ground on to Wednesday. He still hadn't finished the John Saul novel as it was almost 400 pages, but he always went to the library even if he didn't have a book to return. He especially wanted to go this week to see if he'd had a reply from Anne.

Gradually the other library regulars trickled in to the day room, clutching various books. Mavis had her usual book with a pastel watercolour in soft focus on the cover. Romance, or something soft and drippy, he thought dismissively. It was an unusual choice for her though, given that Mavis was all about being sharp, both in personality and looks. He expected her to be reading about sharks or something.

Ben had a book on World War II. Ben was one of the younger residents in Pinewood, being born the year the war broke out. He regularly borrowed books on the war, and Alfie privately thought he was trying to make up for being too young to remember it.

"Good morning, Pinewood people!" Julia exclaimed as she walked in. "Are we ready for our trip to the library?" A few slow nods. "Right, well, let's get cracking!"

Thankfully the rain had stopped so they didn't need to complicate the already painful process of getting them into the van with umbrellas. Alfie made sure to take a seat on the left side so he could look and see if Fred was at the park again.

He kept his eyes peeled as they passed the park. The bench was empty. He wasn't sure if he was disappointed, relieved or something else. He tried not to dwell on it and instead looked for anything interesting out the window.

There were the usual smokers out the front of Wetherspoons, and outside an Indian restaurant he spotted an Indian lady replenishing the takeaway menus by the door. With her black hair and yellow sari she reminded him of a golden oriole that he'd spotted once in East Anglia.

They stopped at a red light and the minibus came up alongside a mother and her young daughter, probably about six years old, in tears. "No, Betty!" he heard the mother snap. "I've already said no and I won't hear any more about it."

"But Mum, it's my turn!" the little girl wailed, tears streaming down her face. "Everyone gets a turn to take Fluffy home and look after him and this weekend it's my turn! Please can't I take him home? If I don't I'll miss my turn and Susan will get two gos and that's just not fair."

Alfie never got to hear how it turned out as the lights changed and the minibus was off. Betty. He'd not heard from his sister in a long time. The last he'd heard she was living in Bath, but that must have been, oh, forty years ago now. He wondered if she was still alive and what she was up to. He knew that Betty had married and had two children, but he'd never met either of them. Even after all these years, it hurt that his little sister was essentially a stranger. His own fault, but it stung nonetheless.

He thought sadly about his family and everything he'd lost. He knew that Doris had died back in the early nineties from cancer, although he couldn't remember which one exactly. Bladder maybe. He hadn't gone to the funeral, knowing without asking that he wasn't welcome.

He also knew his father was dead, but only because he'd be too old to still be alive. His mother had died many years ago. He'd only found out about Doris because he'd happened to spot an obituary in the newspaper. He'd stopped reading them after that.

He was nudged out of his increasingly maudlin mood by the minibus' arrival at the library. He remembered his letter to Anne and for the hundredth time since last Wednesday wondered if she had replied to him. He was trying not to get his hopes up too much in case she hadn't. Even with himself he never liked to appear that he cared too much.

He waved at Emma on the way in and she called him over, coming out from behind the desk to meet him. "Hi Alfie," she greeted him with that big smile of hers. "I wanted to ask how you're getting on with John Saul? Is he living up to the hole left behind by Dean Koontz?"

He nodded. "He is indeed. He's got a good pace. I'll need to read a few more though before I can comment on whether or not he'll match Koontz. I'm only halfway through the first one so we'll see how it goes."

"Well, I'm glad I could be of some assistance for a change!" She smiled to take any sting out of the words. "I take it that means nothing to return this week then? Or is *Persuasion* up for renewal?"

"Nope, not until next week." Emma had never pushed him on why he had the book on perpetual loan, not since she met resistance on her first enquiry, and for that he was grateful.

"Right then, well, until next week I guess! But give me a shout if you need any help with anything today of course."

Alfie nodded and moved to the computers. He sat and logged on, attempting to get himself comfortable in the stubbornly uncomfortable chair while the machine woke up. He didn't know how old it was, but in computer years he figured it was probably as old as him.

He launched Internet Explorer and typed in the web address, his heart giving a little flutter. Oh stop it, you old fool, he told himself. She's probably not even written back. Why would a bright young woman in America want to talk to a crotchety old man like you?

He sighed and diligently put his details in to the little box, almost holding his breath while the thing reloaded. He exhaled heavily, his shoulders slumping. There was nothing. He should have known, should have expected it. Still, he continued to scan the screen hoping to see something. Nothing. Oh well, he tried to tell himself, it had been a good attempt, but he should have known better really.

He clicked on his name at the top to see if he could close it down and forget all this foolishness and lo and behold on his account page there was the word 'inbox' with a big red 'one' and 'new message' next to it. She had written to him after all!

With a slight tremble in his hand, whether from age or excitement he wasn't sure, he clicked on the new message.

Hi Alfie,

It's real nice to hear from you. I'm Anne, although I guess you already know that! I'm an elementary school teacher (although I guess you know that already too!) and I live in New Jersey. My son, Ethan, is six years old and he's a little terror but I love him. I teach fourth grade at Petersville Elementary and I just love it.

She sure did love a lot of things, he thought. But then, he remembered that was the American way.

> I'm a single mom, my husband and Ethan's dad being killed in Afghanistan three years ago. He was a soldier and he died in the line of duty. A car bomb.

Oh god, well that was just awful. He felt mean now for his previous thought, thinking that anyone who could lose their husband like that but still find things in life to love had to be someone to be admired.

> So here I am, thirty-two, a single mom with a six-year-old kid and I thought why not register with penpals4u.com? I don't get out much anymore and most of the conversation I have on a day-to-day basis involves people under the age of eleven so I thought it would be a good way to meet some new friends and have some adult conversation. I was especially looking for an international pen pal, having never travelled myself. So I've not been to England and you've not been to the US. I guess we're even!

> You'll have to tell me all about England. Does it really rain as much as they say it does? And do your police really not carry guns? I can't imagine a life without guns – I bet it's wonderful. They're everywhere here and it's awful.

> I've never read any Dean Koontz I'm sorry, although I googled him and it says he's a lot like Stephen King and I have read one or two of his books. Have you read any Jodi Picoult?

> So your funfair sounds real interesting and I'd love to hear more about it. I take it it's the same as what we'd call a carnival here in the States? What did you do there? Were you a carny? I'm not sure if that word translates to England or not...

Hope to hear back from you soon Alfie!

Take care.
Anne

Alfie sat back and absorbed it all. She doesn't like Dean Koontz – didn't even know who he was! He wondered if Jodi Picoult was one of those pastel watercolour books that Mavis read and wondered if she was if that would be a good enough reason to not write back.

He caught himself. Was he really prepared to throw away a new friendship over Dean Koontz? He realised he was looking for excuses to put an end to it and gave himself a mental shake. Come on Alfie, he chided himself. You wanted this, there's no excuses now. And that, he realised, was the problem. There were no excuses now. No reasons to be cranky to keep her at a distance as this conversation, this relationship, could be on his own terms. But it was the habit of such a very long time that it was going to take some breaking.

The big blue reply at the bottom of the message seemed to taunt him.

Just take it slow, he told himself. One sentence at a time. He stabbed the mouse key over the reply button, irrationally getting pleasure from bashing its smug face.

Dear Anne,

It was lovely to get your reply.

He stopped. What next? It was lovely to get your reply but you have awful taste in books? It was lovely to get your reply and I'm sorry your husband got blown up?

Dear Anne,

It was lovely to get your reply and hear more about Ethan.

Does he go to the school that you teach at?

Where to now? He wasn't sure if he should bring up the dead husband or if it would be worse to pretend that she hadn't mentioned him.

I was very sorry to learn about your husband and Ethan's dad. War takes a terrible toll on everyone. I was only a boy during World War II but I still remember the carnage and the enduring aftermath. I'd like to hear more about Ethan if you wouldn't mind. I don't have any grandchildren – or children – of my own. Regarding books, no I haven't read any Jodi Picoult. Does she have pastel watercolour covers? As regarding your questions about England, no it doesn't rain that much. It just drizzles a lot really. And you're right, our police don't carry guns. At least not the normal police. I think these new terrorist police do though. And isn't that a sad state of affairs that we need a separate police force for terrorists. If I'm not careful though I'll start to sound like Mavis and so I won't say anymore on that matter. Except for the fact that it must be awful over there with all those guns. Hardly a day goes by where I don't read in the *Daily Mail* about another shooting in the US somewhere.

He didn't add that being in the *Daily Mail* they were obviously buried back in the newspaper in the foreign affairs section, the meat of the paper being taken up by stories about Nazis in wheelie bins and secret cameras in Britain's bathrooms. Not for the first time he asked himself why he read such rubbish.

I hope it's not like that in New Jersey though. I don't really know that much about New Jersey except that it's somewhere near New York. But then I guess you don't know much about Slatterley either do you? It's not very near London at all, thankfully. It's out in the Midlands and it's fairly peaceful, although very

What was a nicer word than boring? He didn't want Anne to think that he was just rotting away in some forgotten corner of England or she'd stop writing to him. Best just to delete that last part.

> It's out in the Midlands and it's fairly peaceful.

He re-read Anne's letter, anxious to make sure he'd answered all her questions. He knew how irritating it was to ask people questions and for them to just pretend that you never asked them. If he didn't want to know the answer then why would he have bothered asking the question? He got to the bottom of Anne's letter and realised he'd not said anything about the funfair.

> Travelling with the funfair as a young man in my twenties was wonderful. And no, the word 'carny' doesn't really translate to the UK, but I am familiar with it. I think it's because we call them funfairs in the UK rather than carnivals. I wonder if that makes them 'funnys' over here?

He chuckled, pleased at being able to demonstrate some wit.

> I guess I wasn't really a true carny as I didn't run any of the rides or stalls, just set them up and pulled them back down again. Still, it was a good job for a young man who needed work. I better go now as my hour is almost up on the computer. Hopefully you can write back before next Wednesday as that's library day and the only time that I have access to a computer.
>
> Regards,
> Alfie Cooper

And then, as always, the week inexorably rolled back around to Saturday. He'd spent the past two days anxiously keeping a watch on the weather, worried it would thwart his weekly foray to the park. But, true to the British weather's ability to constantly surprise, Saturday morning dawned with blue skies and brilliant sunshine. True, by nine it was grey and overcast, but Alfie was confident the rain would hold off.

He grabbed his hat and his jacket and his small bag with the bread safely stowed and left, passing Joan in the TV room, comfortably ensconced in one of the armchairs with her tablet, murmuring to herself. She looked up as he walked past. "Are you any good at these puzzles, Alfie?" she called. "It's infuriating me today – I can't get the nine-letter word for the life of me."

Alfie paused, torn between wanting to get to the park and his love of a good anagram. He went over to her.

She held the tablet up for him as high as she was able, a slight tremor in her hands. As a fellow octogenarian she was aware of his age-inherited inability to lean forward. At least not without danger of toppling over. He gave her silent thanks and looked at the square of letters for a few moments.

"I think it's discomfit," he said, annoyed that he found himself having to squint a little. He prided himself on his eyesight, but he'd been noticing more and more that he had to squint to read things. Still, he had to admit that to get to eighty-six and only just be starting to squint wasn't too bad going.

"Oh yes, of course it is!" Joan exclaimed. "I can't believe I didn't see that. Especially as I got comfits." She tapped away with her little stick at the screen and then put it down, beaming at him. "Well that's yesterday's done then! Only a day late isn't so bad."

"Well then," he said a bit awkwardly, not knowing how to close the conversation and all too aware that he should have been on his way to the park already. "I'll be off now then. Right. Bye." He beat a hasty retreat, moving as fast as his aged body would allow.

Fred was already on the bench when he arrived at the park, lazily throwing pine cones into the lake and scattering the ducks.

"Hey now!" said Alfie peevishly. "Stop that. If you scare them all away we'll have no one to eat the bread. And besides, what have they ever done to you?"

Fred shrugged but did desist from throwing any more pine cones. Alfie settled himself onto the bench, realising that he'd have to think of Rosalind's plaque alternatives on the walk back to Pinewood instead now. He'd not shared the game with Fred, scared the boy would mock him for it.

He didn't like having to do it differently this week. He liked the way he normally did it, when he first arrived. That would teach him for being nice.

Chapter 8

Alfie woke bright and early on Monday morning, equal parts excited and anxious about his first day in his new job. Two early nights had helped to clear the last of the hangover cobwebs and as he did his push ups he was feeling good about the day ahead.

As promised, Hilda had left him out some boiled eggs she'd done the night before. He put them in his pockets to eat on the way and quickly gulped down some porridge before striking out for the cathedral and South Street.

The sun was out, but the sky had yet to take on any colour, making Alfie think it looked almost see-through. Or like a blank canvas he could write his dreams on. He pulled an egg out to eat while he walked, discarding the shell in the brambles on the side of the road. His mum had always told him eggshells were good for plants.

He found what he assumed was the 'bottom' of South Street in good time and was waiting on the corner at five to six, the last of the eggs gone. A few moments after he arrived, a man in his forties approached, with the obvious build of a labourer. He eyed Alfie up. "You waiting for Derek?"

He nodded and thrust his hand out. "Alfie Cooper."

"Bob," he said, shaking his hand with a grip that made Alfie wince. "Welcome aboard, Alfie. Got your own tools I see."

Alfie shrugged self-consciously. "Just some bits and pieces I managed to scrape together."

"Well, they'll be welcome." He glanced down the road. "Here comes Derek. You'll meet the other boys in the van. They're a good bunch. Just mind you don't talk about the war with Harold. He's still a bit twitchy."

The van pulled over and Alfie bundled in with Bob. "Boys, this is Alfie," called Derek from the driver's seat. "Make him feel welcome, won't you."

Alfie introduced himself to Harold, a heavy-set man in his thirties with thick curly black hair and to Adam, a boy even younger than himself with pimples still on his face. Space was limited in the van and he awkwardly balanced his tool bag on his lap, aware that the others were staring at it as Bob had done.

He knew it was unusual for a labourer to have his own tools, a labourer's wage not being enough to be able to afford them. The few tools he had he'd been gifted by Jimmy's widow. Jimmy was the reason he was unofficially a carpenter.

Alfie had dreamt of being a pilot. Flying above everything and leaving the world behind. Leaving his parents, that house, that life behind. Even before his National Service medical though, his mum had crushed those dreams, flatly refusing to let him even consider such a dangerous job. So he'd decided to apprentice as a carpenter as he liked working with his hands and there was plenty of work going rebuilding everything after the war. But his mum crushed that too, too scared about him being up on ladders or falling off roofs. So she made him apprentice as a cabinetmaker. Made him promise to stay on the ground.

He'd told this to Jimmy, the team's carpenter, while he was doing his apprenticeship. Jimmy had promptly offered to unofficially train him up. "Can't have you obeying your parents all the time can we?" he'd asked with a wink and a chuckle.

Jimmy was an open-hearted and generous chap with an infectious laugh, and Alfie had secretly idolised him. He was only ten years older than Alfie but had lived such a full life. Doing exactly what he wanted to do rather than what his parents forced him to do through guilt or violence. Then he'd gone off to Korea and never come back.

In some ways it was Jimmy's life that he was hoping to find by leaving London. Not to finish it for him or anything like that. But to live his life his way, on his terms. Meet a girl and get married and settle down.

This got him thinking about the waitress at the café. She'd not been working on Saturday when he'd gone in, which was probably a blessing given the state of him. But he'd not stopped thinking about her. The way her hair shone and those pretty brown eyes. He thought that she would make a fine wife and mother to their two children.

Alfie realised he was getting lost in his own head, as he was wont to do, and forced himself to look outwards. Thankfully everyone else in the van appeared to be lost in their own early morning musings too.

Derek turned off the road onto a narrow track and the van bumped along for a while. Then they turned a corner and the view opened, revealing a house standing on its own in a clearing.

It looked large from the outside, and Alfie put it at around twelve or even fifteen rooms. Certainly much larger than anything he'd ever worked on or been inside of. As they drew closer, Alfie could see the damage that the army had clearly wreaked during their last exercise. The front door was kicked in and some of the walls had partially collapsed where explosives had been detonated. He thought the damage inside must be even more extensive.

"Right boys," said Derek, swinging the van around at the front of the house. "Let's get to work."

The rest of that week passed uneventfully for Alfie. Wednesday they moved from the army house to the school, and Alfie found the work incredibly satisfying. It was the kind of structural work that he had wanted to do more of in London, instead of rebuilding kitchens for rich women.

Evenings were spent listening to the wireless or shooting the breeze with Matthew and Joe as they all sat on their appointed chairs in the front room. He'd grown fond of them both and was enjoying the friendship that was blossoming between the three of them. Joe had some pretty adamant political views that Matthew liked to wind him up about, just for the hell of it.

One night he suggested that the declaration of the Republic of Ireland was a mistake, and that all of Ireland should come back under the monarchy. A staunch republican and what Alfie was beginning to think was bordering on communist, Joe roared back an argument. Impassioned, his Irish accent became so thick he became almost indecipherable. Alfie was too insecure about his knowledge of politics to contribute, but he enjoyed it enormously nonetheless.

Every evening a bottle of something would be brought downstairs by Matthew or Joe for a post-supper snifter while they talked or listened to the wireless. Alfie was aware that once his first pay packet came in he would have to buy his own bottle of something to contribute. But Matthew and Joe were too good-natured to make him front up his share before he'd been paid.

Thursday evening found them in the front room, half listening to a play on the wireless in a haze of cigarette smoke.

As the play finished, Joe stood up. "Well lads, I'm for bed now." He raised his glass, "But here's to another night of good craic at the Crown and Goat tomorrow." Joe drained his glass, followed by Matthew and belatedly Alfie, who was a little alarmed that the previous Friday night was due to be repeated.

It had taken him the rest of the weekend to recover last time, and he wasn't sure he could deal with Hilda's disapproval again. Matthew and Joe had been out again on the Saturday night, leaving him in bed with a thumping headache and a great deal of self-pity. He did not want to do that again. Still, he would deal with that tomorrow. Tonight, he was too tired and more than a little tipsy. He'd come up with an excuse tomorrow.

*

The Crown and Goat was busy again when they arrived, the cigarette smoke curling around the pillars above the bar like some sort of ephemeral vine.

Alfie had been paid and was feeling flush, ordering the first round. He had to admit that he was secretly rather chuffed when George remembered his name.

Joe and Matthew began chatting with three men on stools along the top end of the bar. "Alfie," said Joe, as he brought the pints over. "Meet Barry the Burglar, Beetroot Terry and Jack the Beaver." Joe swept his hand across the three of them by way of introduction. "Gents, meet Alfie. He's lodging at Hilda's with us."

Alfie shook hands with the three of them, calculating all to be somewhere in their sixties. Barry was quite small in stature with a thick shock of black hair and a heavily lined face. Jack looked like the sort of bloke you wouldn't want to meet in a dark alley, tall and broad-shouldered, although Alfie noticed a distinct paunch. He was red-faced and mostly bald but still had what Alfie always thought of as a monk's ring of hair, which was tinged with red and matched his beard. Terry was in the middle in terms of stature as well as the amount of hair he had, with a modest amount of nondescript brown hair atop an averagely sized body. All three were smoking.

"Nice to meet you all. Joe and Matthew told me about the three of you last week."

"Oh really?" said Barry, his expression darkening. "And what exactly did they say?" He narrowed his eyes and looked the three of them over.

"Nothing, Barry, nothing," said Matthew. "We were just telling him that you three are the best locals at the Crown and Goat, that's all."

Alfie nodded furiously, blatantly aware he'd messed up somehow. "Yes, they just told me all of your names and that you were regulars here. Honestly."

Barry continued to regard them intently for a few moments before bursting into laughter, along with Terry and Jack. Alfie laughed too, relieved that the mood had lightened.

"I'm just messing with you, boys. Go on and enjoy your pints."

The three of them sat at the same table in the corner as last weekend, at the end of the bar where Jack, Terry and Barry were sat. Alfie sensed that he should probably get used to the view of the bar from this table.

He gulped down half of his pint to try and calm his nerves and looked at Joe and Matthew. "What just happened exactly?" he asked, making sure to keep his voice low.

"Don't worry about it," said Matthew with a reassuring smile. "They wouldn't hurt a fly, honestly. They just like to have a bit of fun."

Alfie glanced over at the three at the bar, careful to keep his eyes lowered. "Are you sure?" he asked doubtfully. "I mean, why is he called Barry the Burglar anyway?"

Matthew shifted in his seat. "He's not anymore, I'm told. I think that's all behind him."

"Right," said Alfie, trying to take it all in. "And Jack the Beaver and Beetroot Terry? Where do they come from?" The general hubbub in the pub died just enough at that moment that the subjects in question overheard him. Almost as one the three of them swivelled around on their stools.

Terry looked at Jack. "Shall I go first?"

"By all means," said Jack with a sweep of his arm.

"Well boy, since you asked, Beetroot Terry is because I used to own a greengrocers. And back during the war there weren't always a lot of veg around. But one thing we did always have a lot of in the shop was beetroot. Trouble was, the ladies never liked to buy it uncooked and so I'd spend Saturday nights cooking the dammed things and then Sunday mornings skinning them. Took all week for the pink to get off my hands, just in time for them to turn pink all over again." He gave Alfie a mock half bow from the stool. "Hence Beetroot Terry. At your service." He looked to Jack. "Over to you."

"Well now," said Jack, settling comfortably in to his stool. "Mine is not so interesting, I'm afraid, me boy." He bared his teeth and tapped the two front ones. "It's all to do with this gap between my two front teeth. Apparently it reminds some people of a beaver. And the name just sort of stuck." He looked slyly at Alfie. "Don't you want to know why Barry is called Barry the Burglar?"

"I'm sure I don't need to know," said Alfie hastily, not wanting to encourage further conversation with Barry, who still scared him a little despite his small size.

"Sure you do, me boy," said Jack. "Go on, Barry, tell him why you're called Barry the Burglar."

"Tell me where you live and find out!" Barry cackled, followed by Jack and Terry, all three of them thinking it a great laugh. Alfie laughed half-heartedly along with them, not sure if he should be laughing too or not.

"Relax, Alfie," said Barry. "I've been retired for a long time."

"That's right," said Terry. "He's just drinking his profits now! Speaking of which, it must be your round Barry." He turned back around to the bar. "George! Another three this way please." Jack and Barry also swung around, their attention now back on each other and a fresh drink.

"Well that was…interesting," said Alfie, downing the rest of his pint to resettle his nerves that once again felt like they were strung taut enough to play music on. Although it had been a pleasant enough conversation it had rattled him.

"Trust me," said Joe, collecting the empty glasses to get his own round in, "they're all really solid. They've got a heart of gold and would do anything for you."

For the rest of the evening the conversation bounced between the serious and the silly, from the Korean War crisis and Matthew's concern he'd be called up again, to football and the extraordinary fee paid in March for Tommy Taylor's transfer to Manchester United.

Matthew shook his head in disbelief. "Thirty thousand pounds. It's obscene to think that one footballer is worth that much."

"Not thirty thousand," said Joe. "Twenty-nine thousand nine hundred and ninety-nine. Big difference," he chortled into his beer.

Eventually the conversation turned to music, and Frankie Laine's song 'I Believe'. It had been sitting at number one in the charts for nine weeks.

"It's all right," said Joe, shaking his head. "But we could do with something a bit more upbeat couldn't we?" He stood up and attempted to sing it to a double beat, swinging his body in a vague parody of what one would call dancing.

A screwed-up piece of paper hit his head and he drunkenly spun around to attack the thrower only to be confronted by George. "Shut up, will you Joe? You sound like a drowning cat."

Matthew and Alfie roared with laughter and Joe sat down with a thump, grumbling to himself. "You've got no idea about the future of music!" he shouted to George.

"He's right, though," Matthew managed finally, once his laughter had subsided. "You did sound bloody awful."

Joe swatted his hand in Matthew's direction. "It's because my lovely Irish voice is more suited to good Irish ballads. Come on lads," he said, standing up and swaying, "let's go treat the good people of Exeter to some grand Irish songs."

Alfie woke the next morning and discovered that the dead animal from last week had decided to return. Although his head was thumping a little less than last week and he didn't feel quite as bad. He looked at his watch and was pleasantly surprised to discover that he was still in time for breakfast downstairs.

He splashed some water on his face, changed and lumbered rather heavily down the stairs. Joe and Matthew were in the dining room finishing the last of their breakfasts and dressed for football.

"Well, there's sleeping beauty!" said Joe with a smile. "Or should I say singing beauty?"

Alfie looked at him, confused, as he dropped heavily in to a chair. "What are you talking about?"

Joe looked at Matthew and burst out laughing. "He doesn't remember!" He looked back to Alfie. "You seriously don't remember?"

Alfie looked to Matthew, who was grinning broadly. "What? What is it?"

Joe stood and flung his hands in the air singing, "Look at that girl she's like a dreeeaam…"

Alfie's mouth hung open as vague recollections from last night began to surface, like an apple slowly bobbing to the surface in a murky pond. He looked to Matthew. "Not Esme's…?"

Matthew nodded, doing a bad job of containing his mirth. Joe didn't even try, laughing heartily as he sat back down to finish his cup of tea.

Alfie hung his head in his hands, feeling his face grow hot. "I wouldn't worry too much – your singing actually wasn't too bad," said Joe, grinning broadly.

Alfie groaned. "Well, thank god she wasn't there to hear it anyway," he said miserably, desperately trying to find anything salvageable in trying to court a waitress whom he'd only spoken to on one occasion, and whose name he didn't even know, by drunkenly serenading an empty café in the middle of the night.

"I wouldn't worry too much about it, Alfie," said Matthew sympathetically. "We've all done equally stupid things when we're in our cups. I raided the Brocklebanks' garden one night, picking flowers to try and woo Lucy. I was so drunk and made so much noise I woke up Mr Brocklebank and he chased me off their property in his pyjamas!"

Joe nodded. "I remember that. Bloody funny it was."

Matthew gave him a dark look. "Not as funny as you getting your head stuck in the fence down on Murray's farm."

Alfie looked at Joe. "How did you…?"

Joe shook his head. "I'm not even really sure myself, truth be told. I remember wanting to go and talk to the cows and deciding I'd climb the fence and the next thing I knew my head was stuck."

"How did you get out?"

"With a lot of pulling," said Joe ruefully, rubbing his ears.

Alfie smiled. "You're right, that does make me feel a bit better. Still, not something I'm looking to repeat!"

"Or at least learn her name before you do it again," laughed Joe. "You can't keep calling her Esme."

"I had sort of been planning on going in again some time to see if she's working. She wasn't there last Saturday when I went."

"Probably a good thing given the state of you when we saw you later that day!" said Matthew with a grin. "I must say you're doing remarkably better this week. You'll be playing football with us in no time!" He looked at the clock on the sideboard. "Speaking of which Joe, we must be off or old Peterson will make us do laps again for being late."

Joe pushed his chair back and saluted Alfie. "Alfie, a pleasure as always. Come Matthew, we mustn't dally." He literally marched out of the room in an exaggerated step, leaving Matthew behind shaking his head. "It's going to be one of those days," he said sighing and following him out. "See you later Alfie!" he called over his shoulder.

After a hearty breakfast and a good scrub he was feeling better and decided to go for a walk and get some air. He spotted the paper and pencil he'd bought earlier that week with a view to writing a letter home. Perhaps he could find a nice spot and finally force himself to do it.

Downstairs, he took the book on horticulture and carefully slipped the sheets of paper inside. Not only would it protect the paper, but it would give him something to lean on while he wrote. He stuck the pencil behind his ear and set off.

He wandered aimlessly through Exeter, letting his feet take him wherever they felt like going. Before long he'd crossed the river and found the western outskirts of the town and a lovely open field with a large oak that looked like it would serve nicely for something to rest against.

He got himself comfortable and took out his paper.

Dear Mum and Dad, he wrote and stopped. How to start? Sorry I took off in the middle of the night? He shrugged; he could do worse than starting off with that.

Sorry for taking off in the middle of the night. I know I should have told you in person rather than just leaving. But I'm doing well here. I've got a job and I've made some friends. And Hilda, the lady who runs the boarding house is looking after me really well.

He stopped again. He'd wasn't very good at writing letters. Then again, he wasn't very good at talking either. Maybe he just wasn't meant to get on with people, he thought.

I hope that everybody is well back home. Has David proposed to Doris yet? And I hope Betty is good and not too upset with me?

He stopped and thought some more. He looked over what he'd written already. Was that enough? He knew his mother in particular would want more details of his new life but he wasn't really sure what to tell her.

He certainly wasn't going to tell her that he was now frequenting a pub. And not just any pub but a pub whose locals were people like Barry the Burglar. And he most certainly was not going to tell her about his evenings spent at the boarding house drinking Old Fitz every night. She frowned upon drinking of any sort and thought pubs were dens of debauchery. How little she knew, he thought with a smile. The debauchery took place once one had left the pub, desecrating people's gardens and getting stuck in fences. He decided to see if he could grind out a few more lines.

The people I work with are really nice and we've been working on rebuilding part of a school that was bombed during the war.

Knowing his mother would worry as it was exactly the sort of work that she kept him from doing in London, he added, *But don't worry Mum, I'm being very safe. The boss, Derek, is paying me pretty well and the work is hard but satisfying. There are two other lads in the boarding house, Joe and Matthew, and we've become good friends and they're looking out for me.*

He knew his mum would like to hear that. Best say something to his dad. He'd have no room to sign the letter, but they would know who it was from.

Dad, I hope everything is going well at the butchers and thanks for not hanging up on me.
    I'll write again soon.

Chapter 9

Fred was smirking at him.

"What's so funny?" Alfie demanded, knowing the answer.

"Serenading an empty café? Really?"

He sighed. "I was young and stupid. Let that be a lesson to you – young, stupid and drunk do not mix."

"Did you really have to rebuild the house after the army shot it to pieces? It sounds like the stupidest thing I've ever heard."

Alfie nodded. "Yes, to me too. But you couldn't argue with work back then. Things were still a bit tough from the war and jobs didn't exactly grow on trees."

He checked his watch and almost swore. It was a lot later than it should have been. "Time for me to head back." He walked up the path, his mind already on how he might get back in without being spotted. So consumed was he on figuring that out that he forgot all about his delayed game with Rosalind.

He looked at his watch again as he crossed the car park at Pinewood. Eleven forty-nine. Too late. Way too late. He stopped and thought about what he'd do. By now his window to slip back in unnoticed would be well and truly over.

"Alfie?" He heard a voice behind him, making him start. He turned and saw Julia walking towards him. "What are you doing out here?" He opened his mouth to reply but didn't know what to say. He'd never been good when put on the spot. She gave him a knowing look.

She was about to say something further when the door to Pinewood opened and one of the other nurses appeared. Alfie recognised her as the one that read Lee Child books.

"Julia?" she called across to them. "And is that you, Alfie? What are you doing out here? You really shouldn't be out here, Alfie." She crossed the carpark to where they were stood.

Again, Alfie opened his mouth to reply but couldn't think of anything to say. Julia stepped in. "Alfie said he felt like some air and a change of scene and as I had to come out to my car to get some bits anyway, I told him he could tag along for the walk."

Alfie was flabbergasted and looked at Julia, but she wasn't looking at him, speaking to the other nurse instead. "I hope that's not a problem, Helen?"

Alfie looked to the other nurse, realising that he hadn't actually known her name up until now, despite the fact she'd worked at Pinewood for at least a year.

Helen shrugged. "I don't have a problem with it, just don't let Meredith catch you, she'll flip. Anyway, that's the end of my shift so I'm off. See you on Monday, Julia. Bye Alfie."

They both watched her get into her car and drive off. It was a pleasant blue, Alfie noticed, with leopard print seat covers, a nodding dog of some kind on the dashboard and a dangling thing hanging from the rear-view mirror that caught the sunlight as she passed them. Not at all like a gruesome-sounding Lee Child novel.

He turned to Julia, about to ask why she had lied for him, but she stopped him. "The less I know the better. Come on, it's well and truly time for lunch and you don't want to get stuck next to Mavis or Ben."

Later, while clearing up after lunch, Julia asked herself why she hadn't pushed Alfie about where he'd been. She'd been dying to know what he got up to every Saturday morning ever since she'd noticed him sneaking out. She'd surprised herself when she'd told Alfie not to tell her anything. She supposed she didn't want to rob him of one of the very small pleasurable and private things in his life. Perhaps the only thing.

While Pinewood wasn't a hospice, residents were still told when and what they would eat, when they would be bathed and dressed and even when their friends and relatives were allowed to visit.

Julia had learned that years ago Pinewood had operated a 'come when you like' policy for visits from family and friends between the hours of nine and five, seven days a week. But it had been felt that haphazard visits weren't in the best interests of the residents as it was disruptive to their routines. Privately, Julia suspected that doing it the new way just made the nurses' lives easier. A mean part of her also thought that the families probably preferred it this way too as it gave them an excuse to only come once a week. And while she knew that routine was important, she also knew that it wasn't everything. And she knew how much the residents looked forward to those visits all week. Well, all apart from Alfie. She sighed. It obviously wasn't her place to say anything but it smacked of jail and visitation rights to her.

She checked the clock. Almost time for bingo and it was her turn to run it and draw the numbers. She knew that some of the other nurses dreaded bingo duty, frustrated by the glacial speed at which some residents located their numbers. But she rather enjoyed it. She loved the excitement of whoever had won. It was almost childlike, the joy in winning a cheap chocolate frog. She supposed once almost everything else had been stripped away from you that a chocolate frog would seem exciting.

No, she was being unkind. It wasn't about the chocolate frog for them, it was just the excitement of winning. She especially liked it when Joan won. And not just because she had a soft spot for Joan, but because Joan was so indescribably gleeful when she won. Her girlish delight as she dabbed the winning number, the lipstick she insisted on wearing a defiant fuck you to old age and people's perceptions of it. Her eyes sparkled and a new life was breathed into her for a few moments.

Julia realised that she was in a peevish mood and blamed the phone call from her parents early that morning. They'd caught her as she was getting ready to come to work, innocently pretending they'd forgotten she worked on a Saturday. In reality, Julia knew they'd felt guilty about not speaking to her in so long but at the same time didn't really want to speak to her. So they rang at a time when they knew that she couldn't talk for long. Guilt assuaged and only twenty minutes of pain on the phone. Bam.

She didn't know if they'd ever accept her for who she was. And quite frankly if they were going to take this long about it then she didn't care if they did or not.

She shook her head, determined to stop dwelling on it and letting it ruin her day. She finished up and went into the day room to set up the bingo.

Alfie finished lunch and then went to tend his bird motel. He was still musing on why Julia hadn't given him up. Not that she knew what she was giving him up for. He was also at a loss as to why she hadn't asked him where he'd been. He could tell that she was curious about where he went and why. Still, he'd been lucky today and he would have to be more careful in future.

Once his avian facilities were back up to standard, he took his John Saul and went to the day room to read for a while. He stopped in his tracks when he entered the room. With his mind half on his run-in this morning he'd completely forgotten that it was bingo today.

"Alfie!" Joan beamed at him from her seat at the long table. "You've come to join us for bingo!" It was a statement more than a question, although Alfie shook his head all the same.

"No… I was…" He held his novel up helplessly.

"Oh come on, Alfie," said Julia mischievously, walking around the table dishing out the number cards and non-toxic, non-permanent markers. "You know you want to really."

"Oh yes, please do, Alfie," said Joan. "It would be lovely if you joined us."

He looked around the table with growing alarm as he saw not only Mavis, but also Ben and Trevor. He thought Julia might be extracting some sort of pound of flesh for covering for him earlier and, as he wanted to stay on her good side, he relented. "Very well," he said, looking as enthusiastic as Trevor did when Alfie told him to clean up his side of the room.

"Come sit up the top near me," said Julia, now back at the head of the table, unable to contain a grin. He glowered at her and stalked the length of the table. Julia handed him a laminated card with four squares of numbers and a large marker pen. He sighed and shot her a dark look, but she merely smiled brightly at him.

"Right then, Pinewooders! Let's get this bingo party started!" Dear god, he thought, it was worse than he'd feared. Julia shook the box – Pinewood didn't have the money for one of those fancy tombola-type things – and pulled out the first number. "Two fat ladies! Eighty-eight!"

Alfie dutifully marked off the two eighty-eights that he had on his card and then waited expectantly for the next number. When none came he lifted his head to look around and realised that half of them still hadn't found their matching numbers yet. This was going to take forever.

A gruelling hour later the game was finally finished, his patience with it. Although he had been pleased to see Joan win and take out the chocolate frog. He went to his room, clutching his book and praying that Trevor would stay with Joan and he could finally get some peace and quiet.

He sat in the window watching the birds outside and tried to think exactly when it was he'd become so intolerant of other people. And so disinterested. The nurses for instance. He barely knew any of their names apart from Julia. Prided himself on the fact if he was honest. In contrast, the other residents knew not only the nurses' names but also the names of their children and husbands. He, on the other hand, deliberately tried to remain as ignorant as possible. To not see them as real people.

He sighed and leaned over with difficulty to open his bedside drawer and pull out *Persuasion*. He gently stroked the cover and opened the book to a random page and started reading.

Wednesday. Back to Wednesday. The week turning like an inescapable grindstone. He had finished his John Saul book and was ready for another one. But more importantly he wanted to see if Anne had written him back. He hoped she had.

He was sitting patiently in the day room with the other library regulars when the Lee Child nurse – he'd already forgotten her name – walked in. "Right everyone, let's go to the library!"

"Where's Julia?" he asked, with something approaching alarm. "Julia takes us." He heard himself stating the obvious like a child and hated himself for it.

"She's off sick today," said the nurse. "Flu, I think, so she'll be off for a while I would have thought. You're stuck with me today. But that's okay, isn't it?" She asked the last question in a patronising tone and smiled at them like they were idiots.

"Fine," he harrumphed, pushing himself up off the seat with the help of the adjacent table. "Let's go then."

At the library, he settled himself at one of the computers and went straight to the pen pal site and logged in. Now in the know, he scanned the page for the red number next to the word inbox that would tell him he had a message. His eyes widened in slight disbelief. Two! He had two messages! Surely someone else hadn't written to him? He didn't really know how these things worked but he didn't think he'd signed up for other people to write to him.

He clicked on his inbox and saw it was two messages from Anne. Tempted though he was to read the second message first, he dutifully started with the first one to read them faithfully.

Dear Alfie,

It was wonderful to get your letter. It sounds like your time in the carnival must have been a real adventure. I know you said you're in a care home now, so you must have been traveling in the carnival back in the 1950s or 1960s? What was it like back then? Were the swinging sixties as great as everyone always makes out? I wasn't born until the 1980s and no one in my family ever speaks about what it was like back then.

How long have you been at the care home for? I hope it's a nice one? A lot of them here aren't very nice at all. My grandma was in a nice one but she sadly passed away. I miss her.

Thanks for your thoughts about my husband too. Mark was a good man and it was heart-breaking to lose him so soon and so young. We'd only been married three years when he was taken from me. Worst of all is that Ethan is growing up without a dad. And not only that but he's growing up not ever knowing his dad. I try to tell him stories about Mark so he can hopefully understand a little about what his father was like but it's really tough. He's a good boy though and does his best to understand. And these days it's not like he's the only kid in his class without a dad for whatever reason. Almost half his class are kids with single moms. There's even a single dad! A little bit different to how it was in your day I guess!?

Ethan is the centre of my world and is so so dear to me. Although sometimes he looks so much like his dad it hurts. The same blonde hair, so blonde it's almost white, the same sparkling blue eyes. You said you don't have any children or any grandchildren – do you have any other family? I hope you do.

I looked up Slatterley on Google Maps to see where it was. And also the Midlands as I didn't know where they were either! Made sense though that they're kind of in the middle of the country. Say it like you see it I guess! I ended up reading a bunch of stuff while I was online about England and I'm thinking about doing a lesson on England for the kids. It's not in the curriculum but I think it would be good for them to learn about other countries.

Speaking of the kids, I better sign off and get my lesson plan for tomorrow sorted. It was good to (sort of) speak to you Alfie. Hope to hear from you after your next library visit.

Anne.

Alfie sat back, absorbing the contents of her letter. She really did seem like a lovely lady, and he was sad she had lost her husband. And Ethan sounded like a wonderful boy. It was a shame he would never know his father. Alfie was of the opinion that in most cases it was better to know your father, even if he was an arsehole.

He thought of his own father, so taciturn and hard-edged. So unforgiving of mistakes or transgressions. Or anything that he perceived as weakness, which included showing, or even feeling, any emotion other than anger. When he'd been posted to France during the war, Alfie remembered how he'd wished that his father wouldn't come back. But he did, and he was a changed man. Even more silent and unforgiving, but now prone to unpredictable and violent rages.

Alfie could still remember the terror of his dad erupting over him, his eyes seeing something other than his young son. There were even a few times when his father had tried to kill him, roaring that he was a stinking Jerry. His mother had rushed in to calm his father down and bring him back to the present. Maybe it was better that he'd not had children after all, much as he had wanted them. At least it meant he couldn't perpetuate the cycle and damage his own son.

He suddenly remembered the second message and duly went back in to his inbox and clicked on the second message.

PS Who is Mavis?

He stared blankly at the screen. Mavis? Was she talking about the Mavis at Pinewood? The one that he could currently hear spouting off about fracking to some unfortunate soul behind him? But how did she know about Mavis? He went and opened his last letter and spotted his reference to her. An offhand comment he hadn't expected her to pick up and he barely remembered writing, even now he was looking at it. But then he thought if she had casually mentioned someone in the same way then he would have asked too. How best to answer that question?

Dear Anne,

Thank you so much for your return letter. It was lovely to hear about Ethan. I bet he's a good-looking boy. What does he like to do? It is sad that he'll never know his father but with a mother like you I'm sure he'll be just fine.

He stopped. Was that too familiar? Did it come across as flippant about Mark's death? He certainly hoped not. Maybe it would be better if he deleted it. He backspaced all the way back to 'do?' and tried again.

It's terrible that he'll grow up never knowing his father. I don't know you very well yet but I'm sure you're doing a great job of being a mum.

Yes, that was better. Now, how to address her question about his family?

You asked if I had any family and the answer to that is yes…and no. Yes I have, or had, family, but I don't, or haven't, spoken to them for a very long time.

I've been at Pinewood for six years. It's not the best place but they do what they can. All the residents are on state

> pensions as far as I know, so the place doesn't really get a lot of money. Our weekly trips to the library are about it, apart from some games that they organise in the day room. I have to share a room with Trevor who drives me up the wall. I liked Arthur. He was a great roommate, but he's dead. Sorry to hear about your grandma.
>
> In answer to your questions about what life was like in the fifties, I remember rationing, having to bathe weekly on bathing day, the BBC's Light Programme on the radio, tins of Pascall Fruit BonBons and huge white five pound notes on thin paper. Although not necessarily in that order.

He reread what he'd written and decided that was all he was going to say about those years. He did remember all those things. And he wasn't prepared to talk anymore about that time. Not yet. It was different with Fred somehow. He didn't mind talking about those times with Fred.

> In answer to your question on your second message, Mavis is a know-it-all who also lives in Pinewood and thinks she knows more about everything than everyone else.

He looked at his watch. Time to finish up his letter or he'd never have enough time to exchange his book before he had to leave.

> I must go now or I won't have time to get a new book. I hope your lesson on England went well if you gave it.
>
> Alfie Cooper

Julia was still off sick come Saturday and Alfie hoped she wasn't too ill. If he believed what his mother used to say he'd be convinced there was some divine significance to her getting struck down by illness just days after lying to cover for his unsolicited outings. It was a good thing he had never believed her then.

Trevor had been quiet all week, not bothering him with any half-forgotten jokes, and this morning there had also been no yabbering about James finally coming to visit. Was there something wrong with him? Alfie glanced at him on his side of the room and thought that he did look a little dejected. Alfie then also realised that he'd not touched his bottle of Scotch all week and knew something must really be wrong. Trevor was a good-time drinker, and for him to be off the Scotch it meant a serious absence of good, or even vaguely good, times. It was the opposite of himself, who when he had been a drinker all those years ago, had only ever drunk when times were bad. Apart from those brief days with Joe and Matthew.

He thought about asking if anything was wrong but decided it wasn't his problem. He'd done enough caring about other people recently. And he didn't want to be beaten to the park by Fred again. He'd been out of sorts all week after last Saturday.

So instead of doing what he fully realised any decent person would do and ask his roommate what was wrong, he grabbed his hat and jacket, picked up his canvas bag and slipped out of the room, not even looking at Trevor as he left.

The squirrels in the park were in a whirl of activity when he arrived. There weren't many that called the park home, but those that did currently seemed to be engaged in a fast-forward version of chasey. He stopped to watch them. They were chasing each other so quickly up, down, around and along trees that his eyes could barely keep up with them. He lost track of exactly how many he was looking at.

He continued to his bench, sighing with relief when he saw it was empty. He hated that such a small thing could put him so out of sorts, but then he had to acknowledge that he was eighty-six and there had to be some concessions for his age.

He stopped in front of the bench and read Rosalind's plaque. He'd spent the week wondering if he needed to come up with four to make up for last week or if two really really good ones would suffice. He then realised that it was his game and he could do as he dammed well pleased. *For Rosalind, who loved to sing, and didn't mind a bit that she couldn't.* Or, *For Rosalind, who always smelled mildly of cinnamon.* He had decided that two was enough. It was becoming increasingly difficult to think of amusing replacements every week and it wasn't like his life provided him with a lot of new material.

He sat quietly, enjoying the tranquillity of the park and relishing that smell of pine and lavender that brought back memories of his mother. He remembered sitting by her knee as she patiently taught him how to do the cryptic crossword in the newspaper. He'd hated it at first, not understanding all the rules and how to read the clues. But gradually the clues had untangled, and the secret cryptic parallel universe had been revealed and he'd been hooked. From then he'd got better and better, until those hours spent with her, just the two of them enveloped in their cryptic world with their own secret language, became his favourite times of the week.

One of the squirrels ran in front of him and stopped suddenly, looking at him quizzically. He stared back, realising that the squirrel was holding a large acorn and that that was probably what the other squirrels had been after.

"Don't let them take it from you, little man," he said softly. "You keep what's yours." The squirrel tilted his head as if considering Alfie's advice before zooming off and running vertically up the trunk of the oak tree at a rate of knots. Alfie tried to follow him with his eyes but lost him as soon as he hit the foliage.

Fred suddenly appeared and dropped onto the bench in his usual fashion with a big sigh. Alfie glanced at him. "Long week?"

"I guess." Alfie waited to see if he would add anything else but realised that was all he was getting. It was like conversing with a Neanderthal sometimes.

He'd just about given up when Fred suddenly spoke. "Are you ever going to get to the bit where you get to the carnival?"

"All in good time, Fred, all in good time. I haven't even told you about what happened with the waitress."

Chapter 10

The weeks passed in a pleasant repetition of the first, both at work and at Hilda's. He had surprised himself with how much he enjoyed the work at the school. The satisfaction he got from seeing what was once rubble and ruin being turned back into a working school. Sure, he'd done plenty of rebuilding in London after the war, but he was always part of a much bigger team, working on smaller parts of the job and usually inside using his cabinet-making skills. And certainly never up a ladder.

He'd also discovered that he enjoyed the company of the men he worked with. It was an easy and amiable atmosphere, with no unnecessary chatter to make him worry he was saying the wrong thing. And he'd been careful to not talk about the war so as not to upset Harold. Adam was a good lad too, bright and eager to learn.

He whistled as he ate his eggs and walked to the pick up point, the July morning already heating up. Although it had only been a month, he felt like he was settling in to Exeter. He had a job he enjoyed, Joe and Matthew had become friends, and he was earning a decent enough wage. And Hilda fed him so well he thought he might eventually put some bulk on his wiry frame.

Bob was already on the corner when he arrived. "Morning, Bob!"

Bob's eyes narrowed. "Why are you so bloody cheery?"

Alfie grinned at him. "Life is good, Bob! Today is going to be a good day, I can feel it." Bob grumbled something he didn't quite catch in retort. But before Alfie could ask him what he'd said, he spotted Derek's van approaching them.

"Morning all!" Alfie cried as he climbed in to the van.

Derek looked at Bob through the window. "What's up with him?"

Bob rolled his eyes. "He's in a good mood apparently." Alfie grinned and settled in to watch the world go by on the short ride to the school.

Derek motioned him aside as they all spilled out of the van in the car park. "Alfie, I'd like you to take Adam around with you for the next few months so he can learn from you. You've got good skills and I think you could teach him a lot. Think of him as your apprentice. Nothing formal though, of course."

Alfie was taken aback. He had never dreamed that Derek would do him such an honour, especially after only a little more than a month on the job. He nodded furiously, unable to contain his grin. "Yes, of course, Derek, I'd be more than happy to."

By the end of the week Alfie had to admit he was enjoying mentoring Adam. He'd not realised himself until now exactly how much he did know, and that he was really rather quite good at what he did. That, and the satisfaction of imparting that knowledge to a willing and captive audience had served to make it a very enjoyable week indeed.

The only thing that threatened to dampen his good mood was the ongoing lack of a return letter from anyone in his family. Of course, they may have been busy and hadn't found the time to get the letter in the post. Or indeed hadn't yet found the time to write a reply. But then, he knew his mum and knew that the first thing she would have done upon receiving his letter would have been to start writing the reply. Never put off until tomorrow what you can do today. He could hear her voice in his head.

He forced himself to forget about it so as not to ruin his good mood as he walked home at the end of the day. He had decided that he was going to go back to Esme's café this weekend to see if he could talk to the waitress again. Even though she hadn't been in the café when he had decided to drunkenly serenade her, he'd still been too embarrassed to go back in. He was also uncertain about what to say, how to approach her. He'd never gone out with a girl before and he had no idea how to go about it.

Instead, he'd taken to walking past the café every Saturday, stopping outside to look in and see if she was there. If she was he would stop for a time and watch her through the windows from the opposite side of the street. He'd picture himself going in and confidently talking to her, making her laugh. He'd ask her to go out with him, which she would blushingly accept. Often, he just stood on the footpath outside and told her about his week in his head, like they were already married. Sometimes he'd imagine going in and sweeping her off her feet – literally – before carrying her out and into a romantic future. Tomorrow he would go in.

He was whistling to himself as he opened the door to Hilda's and he heard her call out from the front room, "Well someone's in a good mood then." He stopped to stick his head in and saw that she was dusting her menagerie. He nodded at the penguin she had in her hand.

"Percy the penguin?"

"I'd actually been thinking he was a Perry today, but I think Percy is better." She smiled at him. "So how come you're in such a jolly mood then?"

He grinned. "What can I say? Life is good Hilda!"

"Well I'm glad. Just don't go spending all your wages down the pub tonight."

"I won't," he promised. "In fact, here's next week's bed and board." He counted out the money from his pay packet and pocketed the rest. He then watched agog as the money he'd given Hilda disappeared inside the bodice of her dress. She winked at him. "Guaranteed I won't lose it from there!"

He nodded and beat a hasty retreat up the stairs. As long as he lived he didn't think he'd know what would be appropriate to say in that situation.

The next day, freshly scrubbed and fed, and dead animal safely disposed of following another night at the Crown and Goat, Alfie summoned the courage to go back to Esme's. His goal was simple: order a coffee, ask the waitress her name and not make a fool of himself. Tasks that while they looked quite easy, actually got harder with each one, despite – or perhaps because of – the fact he'd already had so many conversations with her in his head that he felt he already knew her.

He'd agonised over what to wear. He didn't want to appear too formal, but likewise he didn't want to look too casual. In the end he didn't have a lot of choice given he'd only left home with a few clothes, and he was dressed in a blue shirt and grey trousers, his second best outfit from home. He hadn't brought his Sunday best away with him. It had felt wrong somehow. He hoped that the blue would bring out the blue in his eyes. His mum had always said it did but then you could never really believe everything your mum told you.

Thinking of his mum got him thinking about the fact he still hadn't had a return letter from home. It worried him. At first he'd worried that they were so angry with him they didn't want to reply. Then he worried that something had happened to them so they couldn't reply. Then he worried that they didn't have time to reply because he'd deprived them of the portion of his income he always gave over to his mum and they'd all been forced to find more work. Then he worried that he was worrying too much and fell into a pit of mental and emotional exhaustion.

He gave himself a mental shake and set off for Esme's. It was going to be hard enough as it was to get her name, order a coffee and not embarrass himself. He didn't need to be distracted by thinking about his mum. What if he did something truly awful and called her mum because he'd been thinking of his mum? His face grew hot just thinking about it.

He squared his shoulders and marched on, determined to get her name or die of embarrassment trying. And if that did happen well, Exeter had been fun while it lasted.

He took a square table roughly in the middle and pretended to read the menu while he looked to see if she was working. He couldn't see her at first but then like a ray of sunshine she appeared from the kitchen.

He hid behind the menu, overcome with shyness. He was doing such a good job of hiding that he was then startled when she asked for his order. He peered over the menu to see her looking as lovely and radiant as the first time he'd seen her. Her rich brown hair shone under the cheap lights and her bright red lips leapt from her face like a luscious invitation.

He hastily put the menu on the table, already flustered and still yet to utter a word. "Umm…err…just a coffee please."

"Anything else with that or just the coffee?"

He briefly considered ordering something else to go with it but remembered he still needed to buy a bottle of Old Fitz. "Umm, just coffee please." He then wondered if he could just order a coffee. "Is that allowed?" he asked, faintly panicked.

She gave him a small smile. "Of course it is. Black?" He nodded furiously.

"I'll be right back." She walked to the counter and Alfie took the reprieve to desperately suck in some air, unaware until now that he'd been holding his breath. He frantically tried to think of something funny to say when she got back. As he drew a continued blank, he realised that he'd happily settle for something vaguely interesting that didn't make him sound like a moron.

All too soon, with Alfie still blank as to witty, or even mildly interesting openers, she was back with his coffee. "One black coffee," she said putting it down in front of him.

"Have you worked here long?" he asked desperately – and rather too loudly – as she turned to go.

She stopped and looked at him a little quizzically. "About two years, I suppose." She looked like she was about to go but then asked

"Are you new into town? I've not seen you in here before have I? Or have I?"

"Yes, I was in the day I arrived a month or so ago. I'd hitched a ride in with a lorry driver – that was the chap I was with that morning." As soon as the words were out of his mouth he cursed himself. She'd think he was some sort of vagabond.

Her eyes widened. "How adventurous and daring! I can't imagine ever doing something like that. Where did you come from?"

He was mentally so far down the route of apologising for what he'd said and trying to figure out how to convince her he wasn't a vagrant that he floundered. "Uh…Um, from London. West London. Fulham actually to be precise."

"London! I've never been to London. Is it truly like everyone says?"

"Uh…that depends what everyone says," he said, somewhat at a loss.

"That it's so big and dirty and noisy and cramped and at the same time utterly wonderful."

"Oh. Umm…Err…I guess so?"

She sighed. "I've never left Exeter."

"I like Exeter!" he avowed, somewhat too passionately.

"Really?" She looked unconvinced.

"Really. Much more than London. In fact, I've decided that I'm staying for good."

"Well, in that case I guess I'll be seeing more of you then, Mr…?"

"Cooper. But please call me Alfie."

"Okay then, Alfie," she said, starting to walk off to serve another customer.

"What do I call you?" he called out after her.

"Grace," she said over her shoulder. Grace. Grace. He savoured the name and the word in his mind. And as he watched her walk around the café while he drank his coffee he thought what a very apt name it was indeed.

*

The next few weeks passed in a blissful haze. Not only had he not disgraced himself, but he'd got her name! And she knew his now too! If he'd been a girl he would have skipped down the road. As he wasn't, he had to settle for grinning like an idiot. Although he was still tempted to do a little bit of skipping. When no one was looking of course.

He'd taken to walking past Esme's on the way home after work every day now as well, not just Saturdays. Watching her. Dreaming of their life together. He'd started saving a small amount from each pay packet so that eventually he could ask her out. Unfortunately, it meant he'd not been able to afford to go back in for a coffee and talk to her, but the imaginary conversations in his head while he watched her through the café windows sufficed.

And on top of all that, his working life was good. Adam was continuing to be a diligent and conscientious apprentice, sucking up knowledge from Alfie like a newly emptied vacuum cleaner. Looking up to him. It was a completely new experience and he felt himself grow bigger with the attention. With pride.

He was humming to himself and mentally picturing his next meeting with Grace as he walked through the door to Hilda's after work one day.

"Alfie," he heard Hilda call out from the kitchen. "Is that you?"

"It's me, Hilda," he called back, taking his shoes off in the hallway. "Something I can do for you?"

She appeared in the hallway drying her hands on a tatty tea towel and reached into her apron pocket. "This came for you today," she said, handing over a water-stained and crumpled envelope. "I fear it's a little worse for wear. Lord only knows what's happened to it. Thankfully the postman could still make out the address. I only knew it was for you because of the 'ooper'. The rest has been washed away."

His heart leapt. A letter from his family! It had to be! As July had turned to August he'd lost all hope of hearing from them. But the letter looked like it had been around the houses, and possibly a few ponds, which probably explained it. "Thank you, Hilda!" he cried over his shoulder as he raced up the stairs to read it in the privacy of his room.

He flung himself on his bed and stopped to examine the envelope, taken aback when he recognised Betty's handwriting bleeding through where the letter had clearly got wet, and not that of his mother. It was strange that Betty should be writing to him on her own and he was immediately worried, a pit opening in his stomach. He hesitated, almost not wanting to have the letter now he finally had it. But it had to be done. He tore open the envelope and pulled out two folded sheets of paper. The first few lines were illegible from the water.

...take a little while to reach you as our father has forbidden any of us to write back to you, so I shall have to wait until I can find the right time to post this off.

Our mother was distraught when you left, and aside from telling her that you'd called to say that you were all right, our father hasn't said a single word about you until your letter arrived when he told us all that we were not to reply. If he wants to go off on his own, then let him go off on his own, he said.

Not that there was a lot of danger in Doris replying to you anyway! She's ever so cross with you. I'm not cross, but I am rather envious. Although I am a little cross that you left without me. I think Mum would have liked to write you back but she's too scared of our father.

What's it like out there? Is it as incredible as we always imagined? Being able to do what you want must be intoxicating. I'm giddy just thinking about it. I'm glad you're making friends. I couldn't bear to think of you being miserable out there all on your own.

Not a lot has changed here. Although you were right in your surmise and David has indeed proposed to Doris. She's as happy as Doris ever gets about anything. Father is Father. If anything, he's grown even more taciturn and unpredictable since you left. Although I don't want you to think badly of yourself! You know what he's like.

Mum was ever so upset when you first left but once she knew
that you were safe after you telephoned, and even more since we
had your letter, she's been a lot better. I overheard Mrs Cooke from
down the road talking to her too, telling her that it was perfectly
natural for a man of your age to want to strike out on his own and
leave the family nest. So although she's still rather upset, I think
she is beginning to understand. As for me, you know perfectly well
that I understand already.

You will write again soon won't you? I fear our father will
destroy any more of your letters, so best to send them to me at the
store. Mrs Barnes won't mind and I'll tell her to keep a look out.

Your sister,
Betty

Alfie read and reread the letter several times before collapsing back
on his bed. He had known his dad would be angry, but he'd never
dreamed he would stop the rest of the family from contacting him.
His heart ached that his dad was forbidding his mum from writing
back. They all did what he said, of course. Even before the war his
word had always been one to be obeyed without question. But after
the war he became someone to tiptoe around, and Alfie had grown
up terrified of saying something, doing something, that would make
him fly off the handle. And there was no telling what that thing
would be. Sometimes it was simply the way he ate his dinner or the
way he sat.

He hadn't realised until now just how much he'd been hoping
and longing to hear from his mum. For her to say that she forgave
him for taking off. He was, however, still very pleased to hear from
Betty.

He had known she would understand. For many years, they
had sat in Bishops Park under an old spreading oak tree and
imagined what life was like outside of London – outside of Fulham
really – and outside of their parents' control. Their father's demons.
They'd imagined getting their own place together somewhere, him

starting his own carpentry business and Betty setting up her own store selling the latest fashions. They'd dreamed about being able to go out with people they fancied. Other days they imagined getting a farm and keeping lots of animals and being self-sufficient. Milk from the cows, eggs from the hens. Vegetables from a plot behind the farmhouse, which Alfie would lovingly sow and nourish and watch grow.

The reality he had now, while different to what he had imagined with Betty, was still living up to his highest expectations. Some days he felt drunk with the freedom, and that was before they got out the bottle of Old Fitz.

He would write Betty back this weekend, perhaps over a cup of coffee at Esme's. He smiled as he thought about Grace and the prospect of seeing her again. He hadn't stopped thinking about her. The sheen of her hair. The perfect red pout of her lips. The way her hips swayed when she walked. He'd started building futures for them together. The children they would have, the little house here in Exeter. Small, but perfectly formed. They would name their first girl Esme, in honour of where they had met. Grace would obviously stop working once they were married and would just have time to get the house in order before Esme came along. Followed one – no two – years later by Walter. And two years after that by Joyce.

He wondered if she'd been thinking about him too. The daring and adventurous traveller. A much better impression than a wandering vagabond thankfully.

Yes, he could spare a few pennies for a coffee to sit in Esme's and write his letter. Not only would it be more comfortable, but maybe telling Grace he was writing to his sister would make her think better of him. After all, Grace must be somebody's sister too. Unless she was an only child. Or perhaps she'd had a sibling who had died and him bringing up his sister would only upset her. Or maybe she'd just think that he was nice for writing to his sister. Or maybe she wouldn't think anything at all.

He sighed and mentally threw his hands in the air. Perhaps he just needed to stop worrying for a change.

*

The Crown and Goat was unusually quiet when they arrived on Friday night. "Where is everyone?" Joe asked George as he slapped down money for three pints of bitter.

George shrugged. "Who knows, me boy, who knows? Might pick up later."

"Maybe they're sick of your singing!" shouted Barry across the bar with a cackle.

"You should be lucky to be graced with my angelic singing," Joe shot back with a grin. "Speaking of missing people, where is your lovely wife these days, Barry? I haven't seen June for a while."

"Pah!" exclaimed Barry with disgust. "Who knows where that crazy woman is. Off getting drunk somewhere else, I bet." He motioned emphatically to George. "You take note of that George – no loyalty from the old cow, none at all. Not like yours truly."

George rolled his eyes and nodded. "Right-o, Barry."

"Hah!" cried Terry. "You're only loyal to this place because it's cheap and George gives you credit."

"Well, I'm certainly not here for the fucking company, am I?!"

Jack, about to take a mouthful of beer, snorted into his pint and came up spluttering with foam in his beard. Barry and Terry laughed loudly at him, laughing louder as Jack's already pink face started to turn red. "Bugger off the lot of you."

"Oh, come on Jack, lighten up. Just think, you could be stuck with June for your wife and then things would be really bad!"

"I despair for you, Barry, I really do. June is a lovely lady who you have resolutely ground down and made miserable. No wonder she drinks so much, living with you!"

"Do you want her?" Barry cackled. "You're welcome to her!"

As Alfie slid onto a seat at the table he turned to Matthew and Joe. "I didn't know Barry was married."

"Yep, June as you've just heard. She's all right. A bit of a drinker, but then so is Barry so they're made for each other that way. One day they're deeply in love and the next they hate each other. None of us can ever keep up."

"What about the other two? Are they married?"

Matthew glanced at the three of them on their stools. "Terry used to be married, but his wife died years and years ago. Some sort of illness. Jack's never been married as far as I know. I think I heard something about his first love breaking his heart when he was a younger man and him never getting over it..."

"That's sad," said Alfie, instantly thinking of Grace. If she broke his heart would he get over it? Or would he end up at the end of the bar on a stool with Joe and Matthew, the pub the only place to call home?

"So," said Joe with a cheeky grin, "what's the deal with the waitress you've got the glad eye for? Grace isn't it? Matthew made me promise to go easy on you but blow me I'm curious and I want to know what you plan to do to win the fair lady's heart."

Alfie blushed. "Ummm...I'm not really sure if I'm honest."

"You need to have a plan, man! You can't just bumble along, you especially. You don't want to make a pig's ear of it." He raised his hands. "Don't take that the wrong way, but you do tend to trip over your own tongue."

"I thought I might go in again tomorrow and have a bit more of a chat."

"That's all very grand, but you will eventually need to ask her out – you do know that, right? Or do you plan on spending the rest of your life drinking coffee for the chance to snatch a few words with her?"

Matthew raised his hand. "Go easy, Joe. She's his maid to woo how he'd like."

"Right, right. Just trying to help."

"I just need to do it in my own time," Alfie said, finding himself almost apologising.

"Of course you do," said Matthew, "and there's nothing wrong with that."

"Just don't take too long about it," said Joe, unable to help himself. "A grand girl like that won't hang around for long. In fact, I'm surprised she's not taken already."

Alfie sat stunned. He'd never even considered that she might be married or seeing someone. In his own head they were already married with three beautiful children.

Joe caught the look on his face. "You do know she's available, don't you, Alfie?" Alfie gulped and felt his face flush, and he knew he'd started to turn red. "Blazes, Alfie! Well, you better find that out toot sweet. You don't want to be stepping on another man's toes – especially if that man will beat you to a pulp."

Almost breaking out in a cold sweat at the mere thought of it, Alfie nodded and drained the rest of his pint. "Now that's more like it!" exclaimed Joe. "Matthew my boy, I believe it's your round."

The next day he resolved to come up with a plan to woo Grace. Not wanting to talk about it anymore with Joe or Matthew, he waited in his room until they'd left to go to football before going down for his breakfast.

He took Betty's letter with him and re-read it over his coffee and eggs. He would write her back today, of course. And he would go to the café and write it and he would speak to Grace again and do his best to be charming. Or at least not trip over his own tongue.

He'd counted what he had saved for going out with Grace and had been a little disheartened. It wasn't a lot, but he thought that maybe they could go see a film if he kept saving for a couple more weeks. Or maybe had a week off from the pub. Or even a week off from buying a bottle of Old Fitz – how was it possible they were going through so much every week? It cost him the bulk of the wages he had left after he paid Hilda.

He'd thought more about the possibility that Grace might already be seeing someone else and he'd decided to ignore it. He was too afraid to know the answer, even if he could get up the courage to ask the question, and this way he could go on living the life he'd built for them.

He gave himself a thorough scrubbing in his room and tried in vain to slick down his unruly strawberry blonde hair. He realised it was beginning to get unacceptably long and thought he should get it cut before he went in to Esme's. He'd been lucky that Grace didn't think him some sort of vagabond; he didn't want to give her cause to start thinking she'd been wrong.

Of course, haircuts cost money and despite only being paid yesterday, after the damage to his wallet following last night's jaunt to the pub and what he had set aside for another bottle of Old Fitz and a few other expenditures, he knew he didn't have much left at all – probably just enough for the coffee. Still, he thought, as the haircut was really for Grace that he could borrow some of her going-out money for it.

An hour later, newly shorn and sporting a very respectable haircut, Alfie entered Esme's café and took the same table as last time. What he'd now come to think of as 'his table'. Grace came over a few minutes after he'd sat down.

"Well, hello there – Alfie, isn't it?" She smiled at him, confirming his name a little uncertainly. "What can I get you today?"

He was devastated she hadn't remembered his order and seemed unsure of his name. He'd done nothing but think about her and she couldn't even remember his coffee order. He swallowed and tried to hide it as best he could. "Hello, Grace. A black coffee would be great, thanks."

"Of course." She flashed another smile at him before making a beeline for the coffee pot.

He slumped in his chair as he watched her go. He knew she must serve a lot of people and that it had been a little while since he'd last been in, but surely after what had passed between them last time she would remember him? Surely she too had been thinking about their wedding and the type of dress she would wear, how she would wear her hair just so. Perhaps get some perfume on the black market for the occasion. Or borrow some off Aunt Gladys or whoever.

Alfie sighed and reached into his pocket and pulled out Betty's letter and the slightly crumpled paper and pencil he'd brought from home. He was attempting to smooth the pages out when Grace was back with his coffee.

"That paper has seen better days," she laughed, putting his coffee down.

Alfie sat up straighter. She may have been a little forgetful on his coffee order, but she did want to talk to him.

"It has. I'm writing a letter back home to my sister, so thankfully she'll forgive a few creases. I'm not sure my mum would have."

"Well, aren't you a nice brother," she exclaimed. "How old is your sister?"

"She's sixteen. She wants to know all about Exeter and what it's like and just generally what life is like outside London."

"Sounds like it's going to be a long letter!"

"I'm not so sure about that. I'm better at writing than at talking, but that's still not saying much."

"Well, I think you do just fine at talking Alfie, so I'm sure your letters are proper." Her eyes twinkled and Alfie thought his heart would explode with all the emotions that one sentence had managed to create. "I'll let you get on with it in peace. And I have more customers to serve. But you let me know if you need anything else." She sashayed off, swinging her hips in that seductive way she had and Alfie just sat there and watched her go, speechless and stupefied. He had been determined to play it cool today but that one compliment had floored him completely.

He sat and stared at the blank pages on the table for a few minutes, trying to collect his thoughts as they ricocheted around his head. No one had ever told him that he was good at any form of social interaction before.

He took a big gulp of his coffee and picked up his pencil. Come on, Cooper, concentrate and write your letter. If she comes back and finds you staring at a blank page she'll think you're an idiot.

Dear Betty,

Thank you so much for your letter. I had started to worry when I hadn't heard from anyone and it seems my fears about our father have unfortunately been justified. I'm sad he's decided to take that stance, particularly for your sake and for our mother's. I was a little heartened to hear you think that she might be slowly coming to accept my leaving. I'd like to think that she can forgive me someday.

Life here is pretty wonderful if I'm honest. I am known as Alfie now. It felt right to have a new name for a new life. I have a local pub where the people know me and it feels great to finally be able to act, and be treated like, an adult. And to be without fear. I feel like I can breathe for the first time in my life. It's like I've had a band around my chest all my life, and now it's disappeared and I can finally breathe. Some days I just stop and stare at the sky and think about how funny it is that I can be standing under the same sky as I was only a few months ago but that it can look so different. The grass is greener, the air is sweeter. It's everything we imagined and more.

I have a lot of fun with Joe and Matthew, and we spend the evenings in the front room at the boarding house discussing politics and sport and music – whatever we feel like! I also went and got my hair cut today and didn't have to worry about what Mum would think of it – can you imagine!

I know you wish you could be here too, and I'm sorry I couldn't bring you with me. But in a few years maybe you could come and join me? You could open that store you always talked about and by then I'll be on my feet well enough to start my own business. I've already been training up a young lad at work which I'm really enjoying, so I could train up some more on proper apprenticeships. In the meantime, perhaps you might eventually persuade our parents that you could be allowed to come and visit? I'm sure I could ask Hilda about a suitable place for you to stay while you were here.

I hope everything is going well at home and that everyone is well. Please give Doris my congratulations if she'll take them. I'm sure our parents are very pleased. They always liked David, even if we both thought he was excruciatingly boring.

I'm sending this letter via Mrs Barnes at the shop as you told me, so hopefully you receive it all right.

Please write back soon and update me on how all the family are doing. And please give my love to everyone.

Your brother,
Alfie

Walking past Esme's on his way home the following week he stopped to look in for Grace. She was in there, talking to two men at one of the tables. Alfie felt a pang of jealousy, especially when she threw her head back and laughed at something they'd said. She was his! That laugh was for him! Did she not know that?

He arrived home in a dark mood and was heading straight for his room when he heard a noise from the front room and stopped to stick his head in. He found Hilda sitting on the floor in tears, a dustpan and brush in her hand.

"Hilda, what's the matter?" he asked. He went over to her and crouched down. "Are you okay? What's happened?"

She gestured to what he could now see were shards of porcelain on the floor. "I broke Una!" she wailed, embarking on a fresh round of sobbing. He took a closer look at the shards and spotted a spiral horn peeking out from under the green armchair.

"Oh Hilda, I'm so sorry," he said somewhat awkwardly. He'd never been good with emotional women. Or women. Or emotions. His hand hovered above her shoulder, unsure whether he should pat her on the back, put his hand on her shoulder in a conciliatory way or attempt to give her a hug. He was so caught up in which one to do that he did none of them, instead lamely holding his hand ineffectually in mid-air.

She sniffed and tried to rein herself back in. "I'm sorry," she said, pulling a handkerchief from her sleeve and blowing her nose. "It's just that Una meant the world to me."

Alfie looked at the shards, hoping to be able to offer to at least stick the pieces back together but he knew as he looked that it was futile.

"I was dusting," Hilda continued, "and having a nice little

sing-a-long and dance with Winston," she gestured to the framed photo of Winston Churchill above the fireplace, "and I'm afraid I – well I'm not quite sure how it happened really – I think when I spun around my hand caught her and she flew off and smashed against the fireplace." Her eyes welled afresh and Alfie saw her bottom lip tremble as she tried not to cry.

He gently took the dustpan and brush from her and started to sweep up the offending fragments. He still had no idea what to say so he remained silent. Experience had taught him this was the best way.

"I don't even know where Eric got her to buy another one, just that it was North Devon somewhere."

Alfie moved around her to finish scooping up the shards. "It was Eric that started the whole thing. The collecting of the animals. He came home one day with the squirrel, saying he'd seen it and it had reminded him of me on account of it being squat and having red hair." She smiled. "I christened him Simon straight away and he had pride of place on my dresser. Then for my birthday that year I got Tom the tiger. Eric never was one to go for the obvious – I didn't get the cat and the dog until he'd exhausted all the exotic ones he could find. Una was the last one he bought me before he died." Her eyes welled again.

"Has he been gone long?" asked Alfie, aware he'd not said anything for quite some time.

"Four long years. It was after Eric died that I started taking boarders in to make ends meet. It's been a lovely bonus that it's also provided me with the odd spot of company." She gave him a small but sweet smile.

Alfie immediately felt ashamed for not making more of an effort to talk to Hilda, instead of treating her like a housemaid who did his cooking and cleaning. He imagined if it was his mum in this situation and felt his face burn. He resolved then to treat Hilda better in future and speak to her about things outside of boiled eggs and laundry.

"Of course, if we'd had children things might have been different. But the good lord didn't see fit to bless us with any, which

I'm sure he had his reasons for. Still, it might have helped to ease some of the loneliness if he had." She wiped her eyes and gave him a big smile. "Anyway, enough of that. I'm sure you've got better things to be doing and I best be getting on with dinner or you boys won't have anything to eat." She took the dustpan and brush from him and patted his hand. "Thanks for listening, me dear."

When he got back to his room he immediately fetched his paper and pencil and scrawled out a few quick lines to Betty.

Betty,

Please tell our mum I love her and that I hope she can forgive me one day. I will try and be a better son and maybe one day she will be proud of me.

Alfie.

Chapter 11

Fred was silent as Alfie finished, and he wondered if the boy had fallen asleep on him. He knew he'd rambled on for quite some time this morning, but he hoped he hadn't bored the lad to death.

"My mum is pretty good too," Fred said suddenly.

"I'm glad. Make sure you look after her. They're the best of us, our mums." He started to get a little choked up thinking of his own mum and hastily stood, as quickly as his aged frame would allow. "I best get back now Fred, before they start to look for me. Take care of your mum and I'll see you next week."

He spent the walk back lost in memories, unaware of his surroundings. Life had been so very different then, in so many ways. A lot more innocent. Lost in thought, he didn't see the car until he'd almost stepped out in front of it. He jumped back, startled. Not only for the near miss, but because he could have sworn it was Julia in the car. Perhaps she'd started to feel better and had decided to come into work. He hoped so. He didn't like any of the other nurses.

After putting his things away he went to the dining room to find the least questionable chair for lunch. He looked around for Julia but couldn't see her.

"Is Julia here?" he asked one of the nurses.

She gave him a pitying look. "She's sick today, remember Alfie?

We had that conversation earlier this morning?" The condescension dripped from her voice. He gave her an irritated look and tried to pull the nearest chair out and sit down with simultaneously as much indignation and dignity as he could muster.

Was it really her in the car then? He tried to think back to when he'd seen her in the car park last week and what sort of car she'd had. He remembered a blue car and something with animal print but he couldn't be sure that was her car. If it was Julia, what was she doing driving around when she was meant to be sick? He admitted he didn't know Julia very well, but she didn't strike him as the sort to take spurious sick days. Even more infuriatingly, he wouldn't even be able to ask her when she got back as it would mean having to own up to being AWOL. And he didn't want to trust to her not asking a second time.

"Are you even listening to me?" Mavis' peevish voice penetrated his thoughts. He blinked and looked around him, realising that he was somehow sitting next to Mavis and that she'd apparently been talking to him.

"Can't say that I am, Mavis," he replied cheerfully, before turning his attention to the plate of mush that was put before him. Culinary delights indeed.

He had to wait until Tuesday to see if Julia would be back in, Sunday and Monday being her regular days off. It was the nurse with the hairy lip that came in to help him bathe early in the morning, so it wasn't until he got in to the dining room for breakfast that he saw that she was indeed back at work.

She looked awful, with dark circles under her eyes. And even to Alfie's untrained eye her hair looked like it was providing shelter for a bird or two. He tried to catch her eye, but she was steadfastly refusing to make eye contact with anyone, resident or nurse. But he guessed this did prove she really had been ill and he must have been seeing things on Saturday.

He hoped that wasn't the start of some new symptom of old age, imagining things. He had enough other symptoms to worry about, what with the failing eyesight and hearing and joints that could predict rain from a hundred miles away. He guessed he should be grateful he still had his own teeth.

Julia deliberately kept her head down on her return to work. She didn't feel like talking to anyone given the events of the past few days and she certainly didn't want to encourage questions. She had started out ill, struck down for almost a week with the flu. Actual flu, not just a bad cold like so many people called it these days with throwaway abandon.

She remembered an old colleague had told her about the fifty-pound flu test. If there was a fifty-pound note at the bottom of your garden and you had the energy to get it then you didn't have the flu. She was certain that had there been a wad of fifty-pound notes at the bottom of her garden she wouldn't have had the energy.

It was times like that she missed having a partner. Someone to look after her. Send her a text to ask if she needed anything picked up from the chemist on the way home. Bring her water and paracetamol in bed so she didn't have to go rummaging around in the medicine basket in the bathroom.

But she'd made the decision many years ago that a fear or dislike of being alone was not the right reason to be in a relationship. It was just a hard principle to cling on to when you were feverish and the paracetamol was what felt like a light year away.

And then, like some sort of weird thought-induced Beetlejuice, Siobhan had turned up on her doorstep on Saturday morning. Julia had stared in shock initially. She'd been over the worst of her flu fever by then, but it still took her several moments to convince herself that she wasn't hallucinating. She'd stood there in the doorway, her mouth open, looking utterly bedraggled, while Siobhan stood with a half guilty, half hopeful smile. She still looked the same as ever. Tall, and dressed in that casually well-put-together way that made it look effortless, even though a lot of planning had gone into the outfit and the hair. Although Julia noticed she had cut her thick dark hair into a short bob.

"What…what are you doing here?" Julia had eventually stammered. "How did you find me?"

"You look awful, Julia. Are you well? Can I come in and do anything for you?"

"You can come in as I need to sit down. But you can't do anything for me, no. You did enough already four years ago."

Siobhan winced, but came inside nonetheless, closing the door behind her. The echo it made in the hall made Julia think of a tomb closing. She strode off into the front room as best she could in her state, not waiting to see if Siobhan was following her.

Julia climbed back under the blanket on the couch, taking up all of it and forcing Siobhan to sit on the uncomfortable armchair that Julia hated, but had bought because it was cheap and matched the red colour scheme of the room.

"Well?" she pre-empted before Siobhan could say anything. "What do you want?"

Siobhan looked at her hands. "I want you back," she said softly, simply.

Julia rocked back, shocked. And angry. "You want me back? After everything you did?"

"I was wrong and I'm sorry," Siobhan was pleading with her now. "I just…I got freaked out by the whole baby thing, I guess."

"I never pressured you into kids!"

"I know you didn't, I know. And I honestly did think that I was ready. But the more we talked about it and the more real it got with the adoption, the more scared I got. And I dealt with it badly, I know that."

"That's a fucking understatement! You dealt with it badly!?" Julia could feel her temperature start to rise again. "You cheated on me with a random girl you picked up in a bar and then walked away and left me!"

"I'm not proud of it," Siobhan said softly. "And if I could take it all back I would. And god help me, I wish I could." She came and sat on the floor by Julia. Siobhan took one of her hands but Julia wrenched it away. "JuJu, I'm sorry."

"Don't call me that. Don't you dare call me that."

Siobhan hung her head. "You were the best thing that ever happened to me and I was too stupid to know it. And all I want now, the only thing I want, is that life with you I gave up that day when I walked away. I want us. And I want our child, however we get there."

Julia stood up, throwing off the blanket. She was too worked up to sit still, despite still being weak from her illness. "I honestly can't believe that you have the…the sheer fucking audacity to come here after all these years and say this. Do you have any idea how long it took me to put my life back together? And I don't just mean emotionally. We had a lease on that flat that I had to see out, even though I couldn't afford to pay the rent on my own. The furniture we'd bought on credit together that I had to pay back. It took me a year to get out of the debt that I racked up after you walked out. On me. On all your responsibilities. And you, where were you? Nowhere to be seen or heard! I was working double shifts to make ends meet. And let's not forget that ridiculously expensive flat was your idea – because you just had to live in Kensington. I was happy living somewhere else, somewhere affordable, but no. You had to be seen to be fashionable."

Julia stopped, out of breath and needing to sit down again but not wanting to go back to the sofa while Siobhan was still sitting on the floor. She sat on the armchair instead. She noticed that Siobhan had started crying. "Don't you cry. You're not allowed to cry. You made this whole fucking mess. You don't get to cry. And I'm not crying any more, not for you."

Julia knew she was being harsh but didn't care. After Siobhan had walked out, she'd never seen or heard from her again, and that meant there were a lot of things she'd never got to say. That she needed to say. "Who the hell just walks away without a word anyway? After all the years we had together? And where have you been for the past four years anyway?" She looked at Siobhan, a new idea forming. "Or is that what this is all about? Wherever you've been – or should I say whoever you've been with – hasn't worked out and so now it's back to good old Julia. Because she'll look after you, sucker that she is. She looks after everyone." Julia's laugh was like glass.

"That's not it, I swear it. The past four years have made me realise how empty my life is without you. And how much you made me a better person. How much I miss you."

"Well I'd like to say I'm sorry for you, but I'm not. You made your bed – or should I say cheated in ours – and now you have to lie in it. I've moved on." Julia swallowed the overwhelming impulse to ask if Siobhan still saw the girl she'd cheated on her with. But she really had moved on, and knowing wouldn't change that.

"You're not exactly blameless in all this yourself, you know," said Siobhan quietly.

"Excuse me?! How the fuck is you cheating on me and then leaving me my fault?"

"You were always emotionally unavailable. You never let me get close."

Julia opened her mouth to respond but couldn't think of what to say. It wasn't the first time the accusation had been levelled at her. Past girlfriends, short-lived though they'd been, had said the same. They'd always break up with her citing her emotional distance. Past boyfriends before she'd finally accepted she was a lesbian. Her relationship with Siobhan had been the longest by some way.

"That still doesn't give you an excuse to do what you did!"

"I know it doesn't. But all I'm saying is that our relationship had problems. It wasn't all perfect and then one day I blew it up by doing what I did."

Julia stood up. "I can't listen to any more of this. I'm still sick and this isn't helping. You need to leave now. Please don't come back."

"Fine, I'll go. But if you do want to find me, Nathan knows where I am." She gazed at Julia intensely. Longingly. "I really do miss you, JuJu. And I still love you." And with that she left and walked out. For the second time.

Julia threw herself on the couch and hugged the blanket to herself but got up after a few moments. She couldn't sit still. And she couldn't stay in this house. She needed to get out, clear her head. She grabbed the car keys and decided to go for a drive.

*

Alfie woke to a bright and breakable morning. He was on edge without knowing why and without any reason.

Trevor was still subdued, barely talking to the nurses as they gave him a sponge bath, let alone shamelessly flirting with them as he normally did, but Alfie still couldn't find it in himself to care enough to ask what was wrong.

He collected his book and went to wait in the day room for Julia to come and herd them all on to the mini bus. He hoped she was feeling better.

He saw the usual crowd waiting, as always, and sighed internally. Just once he'd like to be surprised with who was going to the library. Actually, scratch that. He'd like to be surprised about anything. Life, people, Monday's dinner.

He knew he was in a funk but couldn't seem to shake himself out of it. But then maybe he didn't want to either. What was the point in being old and crotchety if you couldn't revel in the crotchety bit every once in a while? God knew the old bit was no fun.

The minutes ticked by until everyone was starting to grumble and pointedly look at the clock above the door, like doing so would make Julia arrive any quicker. "I'm sorry, everyone!" Julia said as she dashed in, cutting off several half-formed curmudgeons. "Shall we get going? We're only a few minutes behind schedule. I'm sure Brian can make that up on the drive – safely of course."

Alfie observed her while she talked. Her voice was brittle and too bright. And the dark circles he'd observed yesterday weren't any smaller. He hoped she wasn't back at work before she should be. But then he suspected the sickness benefits at Pinewood probably weren't industry-leading.

The journey to the library passed without incident or event. Big surprise there, he thought peevishly. He clumped off the bus and headed straight for the computers, hoping that Anne had written and her letter would help shake him out of this mood he was in.

*

Dear Alfie,

I did give my lesson on England and it did go well! I've decided to use it to kick-off a series of international lessons. Next is China, so I need to study up on that some now too. Have you ever been to China? I can't imagine how different from the US it must be. I hope one day Ethan will travel and see the world. It's a shame that I never got to, and now won't get to for quite some time, but I wouldn't swap Ethan for anything.

For now, I'll content us both with trips into New York City and the annual pilgrimage to see my parents in Florida. Why is it that when people get to a certain age they all decide to move to Florida? I guess you must have your own equivalent in England?

I can't imagine having to bathe just once a week either! Didn't you all smell bad? I bet it must have been real fun back then. Did you ever see Elvis?

I'm sorry to hear your old roommate died, especially if he was such a good roommate. Did he die a very long time ago? What does Trevor do that annoys you so much? Does he snore? Or worse, does he steal from you? I used to share a room at college with a girl that stole from me. I confronted her once and it was horrible.

What did you do before you moved into Pinewood? Did you live near Slatterley or somewhere else? I guess your state pension is like our social security hey? Except I hope for your sake that you get more than we do! Still, I guess we should be thankful that we get anything...

Ethan had a dress up day at kindergarten this week and

he dressed up as Captain America. He knows his dad was in the army and he said he wanted to be a superhero like his dad. I almost cried all over him. I've attached a photo for you so you can see him – he was so gorgeous! If you don't know how to look at the photo, click on the paperclip at the top of my email (letter) and then click on "Ethan.jpg" when it pops up. It should open automatically. I apologise if you know all of this already, but based on how my grandad is I thought it might be best to explain it to you! Better to ask for forgiveness than permission right? I'm not sure that entirely fits here, but you get my drift (I hope!).

I better get going and get some sleep. There's an early staff meeting tomorrow and I'm not a morning person!

Catch you next week!

Anne

Alfie looked for the paperclip, eventually finding a spiral he thought might be masquerading as one. He followed Anne's instructions faithfully – bless her for telling him what he had to do! – and was rewarded with a photo filling his screen of an adorable blonde boy in a costume that was a little too big, which he could only assume was Captain America.

Alfie smiled at the photo, any lingering traces of his peevish mood melting away at the sight of the wide-eyed boy in front of him, clearly pleased as punch with how he looked in his costume.

He looked for how to close the photo without losing everything else – unfortunately Anne's foresight hadn't extended that far – and finally blundered his way to success. He opened a new letter and started typing at his usual glacial pace.

Dear Anne,

Thank you for your latest letter. And thank you for your instructions on how to look at Ethan's photo, they were very welcome. He's a handsome little boy and obviously so proud with his costume. I confess I don't know who Captain America is, but I'm sure he looks just the part.

I'm glad your class on England went well and that it has spurred you on to teach further countries. I haven't been to China. In fact, I've never been outside of the UK. So I guess we are well matched there. Although America is much bigger than the UK. Your comment about Florida made me smile and we do indeed have an equivalent here, called Eastbourne. I've never been but I'm told it's where a lot of us old people go to die. God's waiting room they call it. Although I reckon you could say the same of Pinewood too.

Speaking of dying, Arthur died four years ago now. He was ninety so I guess it was sort of time. He was a good roommate. Quiet, tidy, kept to his side of the room and never tried to tell me any dirty jokes. Not like Trevor. Trevor is loud, messy and constantly trying to tell me jokes that he's forgotten the punchline to. But he's never stolen from me. In fact, I guess it's me that's stolen from him taking his ashtray for my bird motel. I guess he's not so bad. Maybe I am too hard on him. If he wasn't so annoying it would be easier to like him.

Before Pinewood I lived on my own in a council flat in the village. It was a nice little flat – little being the operative word, but it felt like a mansion to me. And it was home and had been a place to call my own. For the first time in my life in fact. I miss it. I had a nice selection of porcelain animals that I was curating, but sadly they had to go when I moved to Pinewood as there wasn't room for them. I kept one though, a unicorn named Una.

When I moved to Slatterley I made ends meet doing odd carpentry jobs. I liked that. The freedom of moving around somewhere different every day, doing different things. My skills were a little rusty, but they came back to me. Then I got too old and had to stop. And then one day I had a fall and it was decided I couldn't live on my own anymore and they sent me to Pinewood. And the rest, they say, is history. It was sad as that little flat had been home for almost thirty years.

My hour is almost up so I must go. I look forward to your return letter. Along with my trips to the park on Saturday morning, reading your letter is the highlight of my week.

Regards,
Alfie

Trevor was staring rather sadly at the TV as Julia walked past, nowhere near as agitated as he normally was while watching Detective Poirot.

"Everything okay, Trevor?" she asked, going to sit next to him. "You've been a bit glum for the past couple of weeks now."

"Eh?" Trevor looked up, a little disoriented. He'd clearly been deep in thought. "Oh hi, love. Yes, I'm all right, I guess."

Julia waited for him to continue, but he lapsed back into silence. She was about to leave him to it when he started again.

"It's just… I'd always thought that the reason James never came to visit was because his job kept him too busy – he's a very important finance director at a swanky law firm you know." Julia nodded. She did know. Trevor boasted to any of the nurses who listened about how successful his son James was. *Imagine!* Trevor would always say, *the son of a house painter being such a big shot.*

"Beth always said that he wanted to come, but he just couldn't make it," Trevor continued. "But then that day we had cake for Audrey's birthday – how many weeks ago was that now? Two? Three?

Three. No, two. Was it? I've lost track." Trevor was getting agitated.

"You're right, two weeks ago," Julia said quickly.

He nodded, calming down and bringing his thoughts back on track. "Right, well then two weeks ago, Beth said that James had lost his job months ago. She hadn't meant to tell me, you know, but she let it slip." Trevor paused, whether to let this revelation sink in for her, or to let it sink in again for himself, Julia wasn't quite sure.

"So for months now James could have come but hasn't. Months! She's been lying to me!" He was getting so worked up that he brought on a wheezing coughing fit, leaving him red-faced and breathless.

"Do you need your oxygen?" Julia asked, poised to run and get the tank. He shook his head, regaining his breath as the cough subsided.

"And what does it say about me, eh? That my son doesn't even want to come and see me? I know I wasn't always the perfect father, but then who is?" Julia nodded, thinking of her own father and his unspoken refusal to accept her for who she was.

"Sure, I lost my temper a few times," Trevor continued. "Probably wasn't around as much as I could have been, but is that so bad? Okay, maybe I drank too much a few times but that's hardly a capital offence is it? And I didn't beat him. Sure, he got the strap a few times, but that's what everyone did back then." He stopped, sagging a little.

"Oh Trevor, I'm so sorry," she said, at a loss for what else to say. She'd always thought it was awful that James never came to visit, even when he'd had his job. But to continue to not come and see his father, even after losing his job, just seemed cruel.

The silence stretched out, Trevor seemingly out of steam about it all until he asked, in a small voice, "Why doesn't he want to see me?"

Her heart broke. What could she say to that?

"Maybe I shouldn't blame him," Trevor went on. "Does anyone want to spend their Saturday mornings coming to an old people's home that smells of piss and vinegar? If I had a choice I'd be somewhere else too."

She was about to say something when Trevor continued, now in full flow.

"And the conversations are always so awkward. Beth trying to act like I've got something to say that's worth a damn – have I won at bingo that week? What was the Friday night dinner special? But you can tell she doesn't care. Hell, I don't care." He laughed a grating, brittle laugh that sounded like it was being scraped along the floor.

Julia thought about when she'd seen Trevor with his daughter on Saturday mornings. The stilted conversations laced with that special brand of condescension children reserve for their parents when they get old.

She hated seeing Trevor like this. "Hey, this isn't the Trevor I know," she chided him gently. "I'm sure Beth does want to come and see you. And it certainly does not smell of piss in here – you know Meredith would never stand for that." She smiled at him, but he didn't smile back.

He shook his head sadly, his straggly beard seeming to droop into his chest. "Maybe Alfie has it right after all. Maybe family is just too dammed hard."

Saturday dawned grey and miserable. It was that annoying drizzle that got you soaked even though it wasn't properly raining. Alfie wished it would just chuck it down for an hour or two and get it over with. He considered not going to the park but then at breakfast, as he dutifully swallowed his medication and the multivitamins they insisted on giving to all residents to make up for the lack of nutrition in what came out of the kitchen, the clouds broke a little and the drizzle finally seemed to let up. The bench would be sopping wet though so he'd need to take a plastic bag from the kitchen to sit on so he didn't get his trousers wet. He wasn't wetting himself yet and he didn't want it to look like he'd started.

He took some napkins from the diner-style dispenser on the table, carefully wrapping the bread for the ducks. The napkins were even cheaper and thinner than normal. Money must really be tight.

Carefully clutching his bread, he waited for most people to clear from breakfast before stealing into the kitchen to find a plastic bag. He found one inside the pantry and stuffed it in his trouser pocket. He was just turning to go when the nurse with the hairy lip walked in.

"Alfie, what are you doing in here?" she asked surprised. "You're not meant to be back here. Go on now, back to the dining room," she ushered him out and he breathed a sigh of relief she hadn't waited for an answer about what he was doing in there. He was no good at thinking on his feet.

He made it out of the building without further incident and enjoyed the short walk down to the park. He breathed in the smell of recent rain on leaves and grass, a smell that transported him back to the countryside and a different time. A different life.

Fred wasn't there yet, which pleased Alfie as it gave him time for his Rosalind game. He'd been saving one up all week. *For Rosalind, who was allergic to wood.* He chuckled to himself. He was particularly pleased with that one. He thought for a moment about a second one and lighted on. *For Rosalind, who could recite pi to the 125th digit in twelve languages.*

He pulled the plastic bag out and carefully laid it out on the seat. The back of his jacket would get wet – there was nothing he could do about that, but at least he could take it off when he got back without needing to change.

Fred arrived with a sigh and a grunt, and Alfie despaired of the lad ever being able to properly master the English language.

"Good week?" he asked, not expecting much of an answer. He wasn't disappointed.

Fred shrugged. "I guess."

Alfie sighed. At least the lad was a good listener. He took out the bread and passed a slice over to Fred before unfolding the napkin on his lap and starting to break up his own slice into equal-sized pieces as he spoke.

Chapter 12

"And I say fucking chocolate!" The roar reached them as they pushed open the door to the Crown and Goat and stopped them in their tracks. They looked to find Jack the Beaver standing at the bar, his face red and his barrel chest heaving, his stool lying on the floor.

"Oh, away with you, Jack," said Terry dismissively, waving his hand. "You're mad as a barbed wire badger. Chocolate in shepherd's pie? Whoever heard of such a thing?" He deliberately turned his back on Jack, which seemed to wind him up even more.

Alfie hadn't thought it possible, but Jack turned an even deeper shade of red. "And I'm telling you," he slammed his pint glass on the bar, "that it works. It's fucking marvellous in fact."

Barry was clearly doing his best to remain out of this one, studiously examining his glass. Terry turned back to Jack. "Sit back down you old fool. And collect your stool." He noticed the three of them standing in the doorway and motioned towards them. "You'll get the young-uns thinking that it's all right to behave like that. You've got a temper like a Torpoint chicken."

Jack grumbled under his breath but picked up his stool nonetheless and sat back down heavily, still muttering under his breath. "It's proper, I tell you."

"Okay, fine. Enlighten me. How does one put chocolate in shepherd's pie?"

"Well, it's dark chocolate, isn't it? None of this milk stuff. And you grate a bit of it in right at the end. I'm telling you, it does something. It really works."

Terry shook his head. "Waste of good chocolate if you ask me."

"I'll do a batch for you to try and you'll see," said Jack emphatically.

Relieved the mood had lightened, the three of them approached the bar, although Alfie noted that George the bartender hadn't batted an eyelid.

"Don't mind them," said George, automatically beginning to pull their pints. "Jack's been threatening to bring his chocolate shepherd's pie in for as long as I can remember, haven't you, Jack? We're all still waiting for a taste of this culinary marvel."

"I bloody well will bring it in this time, just you wait."

Several pints and a few glasses of Old Fitz later, the three of them were comfortably ensconced in their corner when Joe turned to him and said, "Now, Alfie. Tell us. What's the latest with your lovely waitress?"

Alfie had spent the past few weeks since his last meeting with Grace planning and imagining their first outing, often while watching her from his spot across the street outside Esme's, and was ready with an answer. "I've decided that I'm going to ask her out tomorrow." He allowed himself a small smile.

"Well, well!" Joe whooped, banging on the table and drawing disapproving looks as well as a call to keep it down. "Surely this calls for a drink! Matthew, some more Old Fitz!"

Once Matthew returned with the Old Fitz, Joe turned to Alfie. "So then, tell us what you have planned."

With the courage that only alcohol could give him, Alfie told them both about the money he'd been saving and how he now had enough to take Grace out to the pictures.

They toasted Alfie's intentions several times before George

called time and turfed them all out. In too good a mood to go straight home, they decided to walk home the long way.

They stumbled down the streets, bouncing off each other like pinballs in an arcade game. As they got further into the centre of town they started to encounter others also making their way home after closing time. Alfie suddenly pulled up short, causing Joe to walk into him. "Blazes, Alfie, don't just stop like that," he said, rubbing his nose.

"What is it?" asked Matthew, coming back after realising the other two had stopped. He looked to where Alfie was staring at a couple standing on the corner. They were standing very close to each other, their bodies almost touching and she was looking up at him. He said something and she laughed, a pretty tinkle that they could hear from where they stood. The man reached out and grabbed her hands, pulling her even closer towards him for a kiss.

Matthew looked at Joe, who shrugged.

"Grace?" Alfie whispered before, emboldened by alcohol, he charged off towards the couple.

Joe and Matthew looked at each other. "Grace?" they said together.

"Best go after him then!" said Joe, and they both started running, catching up with Alfie as he arrived at the corner. The couple turned to the three of them, startled and taken aback by the sudden and somewhat aggressive arrival of three men breathing hard and smelling of beer.

"Grace, how could you?" Alfie demanded, his heart thudding in his chest.

"How could I what? Who—? Are you drunk?"

"I thought we had something special. And here you are out with him!" Alfie spat the last word and flung his arms wildly towards the man with her.

"Hey now," said Grace's companion stepping towards him, "Take it easy. Grace, do you know him?"

"Not really. He's come in to the café a couple of times."

Alfie stumbled back, stunned. How could she say such things?

That she didn't know him? They had three children! "Is that all you've got to say about me? About us? I've been saving up and saving up to take you out to the pictures and here you are out with him! And as for you," he swung around to the man in question, losing his balance and almost toppling over in the process, "you stay out of this. This is between me and Grace."

"Pictures? What pictures?" asked Grace. "You're not making sense and you're clearly upset and very drunk. Maybe you should go home." She looked to Joe and Matthew for support.

"We were going to have kids you and me," said Alfie desperately, stumbling to keep himself upright. "Esme, Walter and Joyce. And Betty was going to come and have her clothes shop and we were all going to eat gammon and pineapple."

Grace's companion drew himself up to full height and leaned in to Alfie. "I think it's time you went home and stopped bothering the maid." He cracked his knuckles.

"I really do think it's time you went home. And please don't come in to the café again." She grabbed the man's arm. "Let's go, Malcolm."

Alfie watched her go in despair before slumping to sit in a heap on the kerb. Joe and Matthew looked at each other helplessly and very uncomfortably as Alfie started to sob.

"Come on, Alfie," said Joe at last, "don't worry about her. She's obviously a tart, giving you ideas while she's carrying on with someone else. You're better off without her."

Alfie lurched to his feet. "Don't you say that! Don't you dare say that! She's perfect!" He clumsily tried to take a swing at Joe but only succeeded in unbalancing himself and falling over.

"Feck this," said Joe. "I'm going home."

Matthew looked sadly at Alfie, torn between staying and going. "Sorry Alfie, I really am. Perhaps it won't be so bad come the morning."

"Leave me alone!" Alfie cried, struggling back to his feet before stumbling off down the road.

"Come on, Matthew, let's go. He obviously needs some space.

Not that I know quite why he's so upset. He's spoken to her what? Half a dozen times if that? And they've never even gone out together. He never did tell us if she was seeing someone – that could have been her bloody fiancé for all we know!"

Matthew sighed and followed Joe back in the direction they'd come, their high spirits well and truly gone.

Alfie drunkenly stumbled down the street, his footsteps as erratic as his thoughts. He took no notice of what he passed, lost in his own misery. How had it all gone so wrong? Admittedly, he was inexperienced in these things but he'd been sure she'd been giving him signals. She'd smiled at him, said he spoke well. She'd called him adventurous, for crying out loud! And he'd loved her. He'd spent evenings lying in bed planning their life together and the children they'd have. She would look as beautiful with a swollen belly as she did now and they would have beautiful children who took after their mother rather than him. He was going to buy her yellow ribbons for her hair to match the daisies that he'd plant for her outside the kitchen window. But now it turned out that all along she was seeing him – Malcolm. He mentally spat the name out. How could she do it to him? Did she not love him the way that he loved her? Maybe she didn't like yellow ribbons. He wondered if Malcolm would buy her yellow ribbons. Plant daisies for her under the kitchen window. He hoped the daisies all died.

For the first time he cast his gaze outwards to look at his surroundings and realised he'd unconsciously walked to Esme's. It was closed up and dark, just like her heart. His heart, meanwhile, was bleeding. For her, for his love, and for the golden future that they wouldn't have. His hopes and dreams now ash and dust. There would be no taking her to the pictures. No holding hands. No yellow daisies.

He kicked the door of the café angrily. How dare she? How dare she take away his dreams? They were good dreams. Decent dreams. And she's spurned them for someone called Malcolm and a kiss on a corner. He kicked the door again and again, letting the anger consume him. He beat his fists against the door, imagining it to be his own unhappiness.

Eventually, anger spent, his feet sore and aching and his hands bloodied, he collapsed in the doorway and curled up in a ball feeling sorry for himself. His heart hurt so much he thought it might actually be breaking in two. He lay his cheek on his knees and willed the pain to go away.

He woke some hours later, stiff, cold and miserable. He picked himself up and blearily made his way back to Hilda's.

The following morning when he finally woke he felt even more wretched. He was just as miserable as last night but now he was sober and hungover and his feet and hands throbbed for some inexplicable reason. He lay in bed and tried to forget everything. To make the pain go away.

Despite his best efforts to not think about the night before, bits kept flashing back. Grace leaning up to kiss a man who wasn't him. The way she looked at him when he'd confronted her, her big brown eyes full of reproach. The way the night had shattered, piercing him, wounding him.

And – oh – he'd taken a swing at Joe. He groaned and hid his face under the blanket. He couldn't believe he'd done that. He'd never in his life tried to hit anyone. He would have to issue a very swift and sincere apology. And possibly to Matthew too. He couldn't remember trying to punch Matthew, but there were quite a few black spots in the evening and he couldn't remember everything. It was all very hazy after he'd seen Grace and he couldn't for the life of him remember what he'd done to his right foot and his hands, which were bruised and crusted in dried blood. Perhaps he'd tripped and fallen into a hedge?

He looked at the scrap of yellow ribbon pinned to his cupboard that he'd found when he was walking home one day, tangled up in the undergrowth. He'd stopped and fished it out, thinking the colour would look lovely in Grace's chestnut-coloured hair. It was this that had got him thinking about the daisies and he'd kept it pinned to his cupboard ever since, gazing at it as he lay in bed dreaming his dreams of their future together.

He rolled over and stared at the ceiling. That was all over now. His future, his dreams, were over. She would never speak to him again, regardless of that other chap. He sighed and looked at his watch, still on his wrist. Ten o'clock. Joe and Matthew would both be gone to football, which would give him time to figure out how he was going to apologise for his awful behaviour last night.

Thankfully he wasn't hungry as he'd missed breakfast and he certainly wasn't going to Esme's for something to eat. He turned on his side to face the wall and pulled his knees up against his chest. Maybe he would just stay here for a while and pretend the world didn't exist.

Several hours later he had to admit that it was time to get out of bed. He splashed water on his face and was pulling a shirt out of the cupboard when he spotted the envelope he had hidden away inside. It was full of the money he'd been saving to take Grace out to the pictures. In the end he even had enough to buy some flowers and a bag of boiled sweets as well. He grabbed the envelope and stuffed it in to his pocket. He could think of a much better use for the money now.

He snuck down the stairs and quietly lifted his jacket from the hook in the hall, not minded to talk to Hilda either. It was a broken kind of day, mirroring how he felt. He set off for the off-licence. He didn't want to go to the one attached to the Crown and Goat in case he saw anyone he knew – he couldn't bear to sit through one of Terry and Jack's conversations. So instead he went to the Duke of York, which was a few streets further away.

In good time he was on his way with a bottle of Old Fitz in hand. He would save some to give to Joe and Matthew tonight by way of apology, but not all of it. Some of it was earmarked for making sure he was numb for the rest of the day. He thought about going back to Hilda's but then thought better of it. He needed to be outside today, even if it was on the cold side. Perhaps the cold would finish the job of numbing him.

In the end he couldn't really settle on anywhere and ended up roaming the deserted back country lanes around Exeter periodically swigging from his bottle of Old Fitz. Even in the warm haze that settled over him, he had to admit that this wasn't one of his finer moments.

He started talking to Grace in his head, eventually without realising, talking out loud. "Oh Grace, why did you forsake me? I had it all planned out for you and me. Our life, our family. How our children would never want for affection and would always know we loved them."

He blinked back tears, whether for his lost future or for his own wretched past he wasn't sure. He took a long swig from the bottle. "Walter was going to play football and I'd go and watch him play in the Exeter junior league in the park while you and Esme and Joyce cooked lunch and darned our socks. It was going to be perfect." It had been so real that he could hear the shrill of the referee's whistle, could taste the corned beef. The smell of the house a comforting blend of boiled meat and soap as he and Walter returned, conquering heroes. The touch of Grace's hand as she reached up to kiss him.

He stumbled and the world vanished, disappearing like smoke. That was all over now. It was just him. Alone. Well maybe that was just fine. He'd been on his own his whole life anyway, even if he had been surrounded by people. Well, he'd just keep on going that way. He didn't need Grace. He'd make his own future without her. Without anyone. He'd never liked daisies anyway.

He took another swig from the bottle and realised he'd drunk significantly more than he'd intended. There wouldn't be much left for an apology to Joe and Matthew now. He also realised that the light was almost gone and it was starting to rain. He looked at his watch and saw it was getting on for five. He'd been out wandering and drinking and talking to himself for hours now. Probably best get back to Hilda's for dinner and face the music with Joe and Matthew.

He stole in as quietly as he could given his drunken unsteadiness, hanging his wet jacket in the hall and taking a deep breath before sticking his head around into the front room. They were both there, sat on their respective chairs with a bottle of Old Fitz on the small table between them. They looked up and as he entered and there was an awkward silence.

"So listen—"

"Alfie—"

"Well—"

Joe inclined his head towards Alfie to indicate he should go first. "So I just wanted to apologise for last night. It wasn't right lashing out at you both. I was drunk and upset." He laughed bitterly. "I still am drunk and upset, but that's no excuse." He held up the now largely empty bottle of Old Fitz he'd bought earlier that day. "I bought this as an olive branch, but I appear to have drunk most of it. But here," he stumbled over towards them, "take what's left. I don't think I need any more tonight." He collapsed into his red floral armchair and sighed deeply, running his hand over his face.

Matthew leaned over and clapped him on the shoulder. "Don't worry about it. We've all been there."

"Easy for you to say," grumbled Joe. "He didn't try and hit you."

Well that answered that question. He took his hand from his face. "I am really sorry Joe…"

Joe waved his hand. "It's okay, truly. As Matthew says we've all been there. Although I may not forgive you for drinking most of this bottle without us. Frankly, that is bordering on truly unforgiveable. Lucky for you I'm a forgiving man. Matthew! A glass for our comrade and let's drink to friends and the destruction of women."

The three of them clinked glasses and Alfie felt a sense of relief they had both been so understanding. Perhaps he wasn't ready to do away with everyone just yet after all.

They shortly went through for dinner and Hilda gave him a knowing and disapproving look as she swished in with plates piled with mashed potatoes and Spam fritters. There were a few slices of carrot sitting mournfully on the side.

"Alfie, there was some post for you today," she said as she bustled around the table depositing the plates. "Let me go and fetch it."

Alfie, faced with the sight and smell of food, suddenly remembered that he'd not eaten all day and barely heard her as he tucked in with gusto, quickly putting the odd carrot or two out of its misery along with huge swathes of the mashed potato. So he was a little startled when Hilda came back in and handed him what was obviously a letter from Betty.

He looked at it for quite some time before deliberately putting it aside unopened. He would read that tomorrow. Sober. For tonight, he intended to get more drunk than he had in his life so far, which was, admittedly, a short history to judge against.

With that thought he grabbed the bottle of Old Fitz and poured the last of it out between the three of them. "What say you both to an evening at the Crown and Goat? I could do with some distraction." He realised he was slurring his words and didn't care.

"What a grand idea!"

"Yes, all right. Why not?"

Chapter 13

Fred looked at him somewhat incredulously. "All of that over a girl? And one you barely even knew?"

Alfie nodded, staring out over the lake. That night he'd seen Grace had been the turning point that determined the rest of his life. He was too old for if onlys, but he did sometimes wonder, even after all these years, how things might have turned out so very differently. Better. How he might have been a better person. That night set off a series of events and decisions – he knew ultimately that it came down to his own bad decisions – that ended up with him leading the life he was, rather than one he might have had. One that had been tantalisingly in his hands for a time. Before he'd crushed it. "I know. Seems silly doesn't it?"

"I'll say!"

"But you have to remember I'd barely spoken to any girls who weren't my sisters. I'd lived a very sheltered life in London, even by the standards in those days. I'd never been out with a girl. I'd never even kissed a girl. There was a peck on the lips with Jocelyn Everton behind the bike shed at school one day, but that had been my entire experience with girls before meeting Grace. I just got caught up in it all. And in my head we were already married and had three children." Alfie realised he was over-explaining, knowing what he would have to reveal next time.

Fred looked unconvinced. "Still seems like an overreaction."

"I'm sure it does, lad. Looking back, it does to me too." He sighed. He'd thought about, talked about, Grace for enough today. With difficulty, he hauled himself up and tipped his hat. "Until next week."

Halfway back the drizzle set in again, and by the time Alfie got to Pinewood he was decidedly damp. He successfully slipped in unnoticed and was trying to shake the rain off his jacket when Trevor came in.

Alfie looked him over surreptitiously, thinking he looked a little sallow. And the usual Trevor spark clearly wasn't lit. He kicked himself mentally before asking, against all better judgement, "Trevor, is everything okay?"

"What?" asked Trevor distractedly. "Oh hello, Alfie. Yes, I'm fine really."

Alfie gave a small mental cheer and began to head to the day room – it was the only room that would have heating on to dry him out before lunch – when Trevor continued. "It's just... Well, it's James."

Alfie sighed. Loudly. "Trevor, you know he's never going to come and visit. I know you keep insisting he's just busy with that job you're always boasting about, but maybe you'll be happier if you just accept that he's not going to come."

"Funny you should say that actually. Turns out he hasn't had a job for months but still hasn't come to see his old man." He gave a sharp bark of a laugh, all pointy edges with no humour. "Turns out you were right after all, Alfie. He just doesn't want to see me."

"Oh shit, Trevor. I'm sorry."

Trevor stared at the blanket on the bed for a few moments while Alfie flailed around for something to say. Trevor saved him by continuing. "I just don't understand, Alfie. And I think that's the hardest thing. Is he just a selfish shit after all, like you've been telling me all these years? Did Sylvia and I really raise such an awful and ungrateful son?"

Having never had any children himself, Alfie felt desperately underqualified for this conversation and struggled to find something useful to say. "I guess sometimes kids are just shits?" he said a little helplessly. "I know I wasn't as good a son to my mum as I should have been."

"Maybe you've got it right after all," continued Trevor, and Alfie wasn't sure if he'd heard what Alfie had said or not. "You don't have any visitors and you don't seem bothered about it. Maybe I should follow your lead and let off poor Beth as well. I'm sure she only comes because she has to, not because she actually wants to see me." He brightened a little. "I could come with you wherever you go every Saturday during visiting hours."

Alfie staggered under the weight of sheer horror and panic those few words had managed to generate. "Now, now, Trevor, let's not be hasty. Just because James is an ungrateful arse, doesn't mean that you should write off Beth. I'm sure she doesn't keep coming just out of a sense of duty. Besides, who would bring you your Scotch and cigarettes?" Alfie threw the last comment in desperately, hoping the idea of a sober and non-nicotineised existence at Pinewood would convince Trevor to continue Beth's visits. And leave the sanctity of Alfie's Saturday mornings alone.

Trevor sighed and seemed to shrivel into himself. "Maybe you're right. I just always get the feeling she'd rather be somewhere else, talking to someone else. Anyone else. It was so much easier when we were younger, eh? Living an actual life rather than what's just called life inside here. When things actually happened to you. But what do I have to talk about now? Instant mashed potato for dinner and Mavis talking endlessly about something or other. Oh and let's not forget this week's episode of *Pointless*." He laughed bitterly. "I'm just not relevant anymore."

Alfie took in Trevor like he was seeing him for the first time. The earrings, the dirty jokes. Were they just a desperate attempt by Trevor to try and stay relevant? He sat down next to him on the bed. "I don't think any of us are, are we?" He gave a short, sharp laugh. "I'm pretty sure I haven't been relevant for most of my life. But at our age we're not meant to be relevant anymore are we? Whatever that means. Surely by our age we can just be ourselves." Alfie laughed again, a proper laugh this time. "In my case, I'm a grumpy bastard who doesn't like anyone and would be quite happy if everyone would just bugger off."

Trevor gave him a sidelong look. "I think grumpy would be an understatement most days wouldn't it, Alfie." He grinned, and the straggly beard irritated Alfie all over again.

He stood up. "Yes well, it's a good job you're used to it." He snatched his book and stalked out.

Sometimes he lost trace of the days. Sometimes the anchor of Saturday and Wednesday were enough to guide him through the unending beigeness and banality that was life at Pinewood. Other weeks he lost the thread, and it was only by checking the front page of the *Daily Mail* that he maintained a grip. Even then, sometimes he had to go back to the front page more than once.

This was one of those weeks. Since Saturday he'd felt increasingly like he was floating through a fleeting unreality, his normal clarity maddeningly slipping away every time he tried to grasp it.

On Wednesday, he felt like he'd woken up in somebody else's dream. The colours too bright, the noises out of sync. And he was so off-kilter with things that he was on his way to the park when he walked through the day room and saw everyone waiting patiently to be collected for the library.

He hurried back to his room before anyone could notice his canvas bag over his shoulder and his hat in his hand. He disposed of the bag and hat and grabbed the book sitting on his bedside table. He glanced at the cover. *Black Creek Crossing*. He couldn't remember if he'd finished it or not. He read the blurb on the back. *The dark history and dire secrets of a peaceful small town are summoned from the shadows of the past.* Yes, yes, he remembered now. He had finished it. He remembered thinking that perhaps Mr Saul had had Slatterley in mind when he wrote it. Well, without the supernatural bit of course.

He hastened back to the day room, anxious now to get to the library and check for Anne's next letter. Now that he knew what day it was.

Dear Alfie,

I'm glad you were able to open Ethan's photo and see him in his costume. (FYI, Captain America is a comic book hero who is a soldier with superpowers – hence the connection with his dad). I had a hard time getting him out of the costume let me tell you! I may have to get another one as he keeps insisting that he wants to wear it and I'm going to have to launder it eventually! Either that or I'll have to try and get him equally excited about Batman or someone so I can alternate between the two. I take it you know who Batman is? :-)

Trevor sounds like a real character too, although if he's loud and messy I appreciate that you might not want to share a room with him. I'm sorry you had to give up your apartment and having your own space. But is it nice having company at least? I bet it must have got awfully lonely sometimes living on your own, even with all those porcelain animals. It's a shame you could only take one with you. What did you do with them all when you moved? Did you have someone you could pass them on to? I inherited my grandma's antique perfume bottle collection when she had to move into the nursing home. I bought a nice art deco corner cabinet and I have them all in there. Every time I go into the dining room I see them and they remind me of her.

You'll probably love the cabinet – it was handmade so they told me in the antique shop. It's certainly sturdy – they were built to last back then hey?! You say you used to be a carpenter? Did you make furniture too? Or were you not that sort of carpenter? A friend of mine is an electrician, but every time I need some electrical work done he always tells me that he's not that type of electrician! (Although really I think he's just trying to get out of doing any work). I guess there are different types of carpenter too?

Anyway, I'd better stop blabbering on and do some of that aforementioned laundry – oh the glamorous life I lead!

See you next week!

Anne
P.S. – what is a bird motel?

Alfie went back to the beginning of Anne's letter and tried to decipher what the strange punctuation was at the end of her remark about Batman. Of course he knew who Batman was! But he didn't know what the colon, hyphen and one bracket was meant to signify after that. Perhaps she'd accidentally leaned on the keyboard.

Dear Anne,

As ever, it was lovely to receive your letter. And thank you for telling me who Captain America is. I don't believe he made it to the UK in my day, or if he did he passed me by. Although rest assured I do most certainly know who Batman is. I was a little perplexed by your strange use of punctuation after that though. Is it a mistake or is it meant to mean something?

In answer to your question about my porcelain animals, I didn't have anyone to give them to, but they found a nice home at the RSPCA charity shop on Slatterley high street. It seemed fitting somehow. All except Una the unicorn, I kept her. I'm glad your grandmother had a loving home for her perfume bottles. I've not heard of anyone collecting those before. Is it common in America? I don't know what an antique perfume bottle looks like, I must admit.

Your cabinet sounds lovely too. I was actually a cabinet-maker, but funnily enough not that sort of cabinetmaker. I built house interiors – kitchens and the like. I also trained unofficially as a construction carpenter. So between the two trades I built houses, inside and out. Well, at least before I joined the funfair. After the war there were a lot of houses that needed rebuilding, so it was good solid work for a young man. And then after the funfair it was just those odd jobs around Slatterley. So no, in answer to your other question I never made any furniture. And you're right, they don't make them like that anymore. All the furniture at Pinewood is either from IKEA or from a fire sale. I particularly hate the dining room chairs. They look like they came from a cheesy cruise ship. Although as I've never been on a cruise I am basing that purely on my television viewing.

As for the bird motel, it's just a silly name I've given to Trevor's ashtray that I've filled with seeds and an old ice cream container filled with water that sit outside my window at Pinewood. It's not much, but I have some regular house sparrow visitors that seem to like it well enough and I enjoy watching them from my room. I like birds. The freedom they have to just go wherever they want to. They were the only wildlife I saw all those years I was in prison.

Alfie stopped typing, a little stunned at what his fingers has poked out on the keyboard without his brain being fully conscious of it. Was he ready to talk about that yet? And he'd have to talk about it. He couldn't put that in there and expect Anne not to come back with questions. His finger hovered over the delete button. No. No, he wasn't ready just yet.

The freedom they have to just go wherever they want to. Although I'm not so mad about pigeons.

Anyway, enough about birds. Until next week.

Warm regards,
Alfie

He slowly stood up, hating the old man noises that escaped from him involuntarily. When he was younger he'd always hated the sounds old people made, thinking they made them deliberately to remind everyone around them that they were old. How they were laughing at him now.

Picking up the John Saul novel he made his way to the front desk to see Emma and hand it back in. "Why, hello Alfie," Emma greeted him with a big smile. "How are we today?" Alfie never understood why Emma used the royal we when speaking to people. She wasn't the Queen for goodness sake. But then he wasn't sure why the Queen used the royal we either.

"Morning, Emma. I'm all right. Just need to exchange this one please."

Emma took the book he handed her and scanned it in. "Enjoying the John Saul then I take it?"

He nodded, growing a little weary of the small talk already. He was about to move off when she said, "Oh, and Alfie, you know that *Persuasion* is due for renewal this week?" He stopped. He hadn't remembered. In his muddle this morning he hadn't even thought about it.

"Ah...so I..."

Emma smiled at him indulgently and, Alfie couldn't help feeling, a little condescendingly, but maybe he was just being particularly prickly in his embarrassment. "It's okay, Alfie. Just make sure you bring it next week. I won't charge you the late fee."

"Thanks, Emma. I'll bring it back next week for certain."

*

Friday. Porridge and prunes for breakfast and then the singing activity session that he steadfastly avoided by reading the *Daily Mail* in the lounge, or in his room by the window if he could smuggle it out. They didn't like you to take the newspapers out of the communal areas, but as he always brought it back Alfie couldn't see what the uproar was about.

Today, the nurse with the hairy lip had been there to prevent him taking the paper, glaring at him over her purple glasses. In defiance, he'd planted himself in Mavis' floral armchair in the lounge rather than in the battered brown corduroy armchair in the corner that he normally sat in. He'd always found it funny that the meals were a free-for-all with where people sat but armchairs in the TV lounge were staunchly territorial and vigorously defended. Well, as vigorously as a bunch of geriatrics could get anyway.

He settled down with the paper and tried to drown out the caterwauling drifting down the corridor from the day room with the cryptic crossword.

Julia loved Fridays. Fridays were sing-a-long days and so many of the residents came along and got involved. Alfie never came obviously, but that was par for the course. They really came alive, and you could tell the old songs were transporting them back to younger, happier times. Joan in particular loved the singing. She would always arrive early to secure one of the seats at the front. Not that it mattered where they sat really, not when they were just sat singing to the tunes played on the organ by Helen's nephew, but Joan liked to be at the front all the same.

Julia watched them all come in and settle in for the singing session. Joan at the front and Ethel in her usual spot by the wall, magazine open in her lap. Ethel spent every singing session reading her magazine, never looking up at anyone. But she sang every word to every song. The rest of the singing regulars were also there, Ben, Mavis, Muriel, Audrey and Phyllis.

They all sat down and waited patiently for her to hand out the songbooks. Even though all the songs were old songs from their youth, they still sometimes forgot the words and liked to have the books there.

"Ooh, thank you, Julia," Joan said with glee as she took the book from her. "You know, I look forward to this time more than any other time of the week apart from visiting hours on a Saturday morning. When we sing I can forget about the pain in my back, just for a little while." She closed her eyes and hugged the songbook, humming to herself.

Julia was about to move on when Joan continued, "They remind me of when life was like an adventure waiting to happen. Riding the bread cart, delivering bread to the neighbourhood. Going dancing in the village hall with the soldiers back on leave. You should have seen the green dress I used to wear, the way it moved like water around me as I danced."

Julia smiled. She'd heard these stories many times before, but she never tired of listening to Joan tell them. "And don't forget London," Julia said a little cheekily.

"Oh yes, London! I arrived in London fresh from Kingsley, that tiny village I'd grown up in, with nothing more than a suitcase, a small sum of money and a whole lot of hope and optimism."

Scott, Pinewood's volunteer organist, nodded to Julia that he was ready to start. She patted Joan's hand and moved to stand next to the organ. "Okay now, Pinewooders," Julia called out. "Are we ready to have a singing good time?" She got some nods and even a few 'yeses' called out. There was an enthusiastic, "Ooh yes, I'm very ready," from Joan. "All right then, Scott, take it away!"

The opening strands of Frankie Laine's 'I Believe' left the organ and the unsynchronised and muddled singing began. "I believe for every drop of rain that falls, a flower grows…" Some murmured, some mumbled and some of them, like Joan, belted it out as best they could. It could only be called noise rather than singing, but they were all smiling, even Ethel.

Then Ben stood up and started conducting an invisible orchestra, much to everyone's annoyance.

"Sit down!" called Mavis irritably. "You bothersome old fool." Phyllis and Audrey echoed the sentiment, but still Ben carried on conducting, his eyes closed and a blissful smile on his face.

Julia couldn't help but smile. Ben stood up and began conducting every week. And every week the women would shout at him to sit down. And every week he'd ignore them and keep conducting his unseen orchestra.

Finally Saturday arrived again. Alfie was anxious to get to the park to see if Fred was coming this week or not. It was only the beginning of the revelations about his behaviour and its consequences, and Alfie worried the boy would stop coming to listen to him. He could – and would – still go to the park every Saturday, even if Fred wasn't there. After all, he'd been going to the park on Saturday morning long before Fred came along. But it wouldn't be the same, much as he hated to admit it, even to himself.

He creaked his way down to the park, more apprehensive than he could remember feeling in a long time. It was a grey and grim kind of day, and Alfie hoped it wasn't an omen.

He made his way through the park, lost in thought. He stopped at his bench and looked at the plaque. His heart wasn't quite in it but he would give it a go anyway. *For Rosalind, who was always sneezing. For Rosalind, who was named after an orchid.*

He sat down and took out his bread, placing it on his lap. He began to tear the bread into evenly sized small pieces, certain that Fred wouldn't come today. He was ready to start feeding the ducks that had started to gather around his feet when Fred appeared, as abruptly as he always did.

"Fred!" he exclaimed with the closest thing to joy he'd shown for decades. "You came."

Fred shrugged. "Yeah, why wouldn't I? Nothing better to do."

"I just… I wasn't sure, that was all." He handed a piece of bread to Fred, who settled himself into the bench and began to tear the slice up. Alfie glanced at him and settled himself in as well. "Right, then. Where was I up to?"

"You were drunk," said Fred bluntly.

Alfie winced. "Ah yes. And we were all heading to the Crown and Goat."

Chapter 14

The following morning – or was it afternoon? – Alfie woke with the fiercest hangover of his life. His stomach muscles ached, which he realised must have been from throwing up at some stage as he spotted vomit splattered on the bottom of the trousers that he was still wearing. He was lying on top of the bed still fully dressed. He couldn't remember throwing up but the evidence – and the smell of stale sick – would seem to indicate pretty resolutely that he had. He looked blearily at the watch still on his wrist. Eleven o'clock. It was still morning, just.

He looked around his room, trying to bring some sense to his addled thoughts, and spotted a letter addressed to him on his dresser. A vague memory fought its way to the surface. Hilda must have brought the letter up to his room after they'd left to go to the pub last night. He tried to force himself to remember other events from the night before but could only recall snatches. Mashed potato. Drinking with Joe and Matthew in the front room. A beagle. Surely the beagle was part of a dream?

He gave up on being able to put together any sort of coherent memory and rolled over in an ill-advised attempt to get up to retrieve the letter. But even the action of rolling over had him worried he was going to throw up again and he stopped and waited until the wave of nausea had passed before he attempted to move again.

Lying there, he tried not to think of Grace but it was no good. All he could picture was the curve of her neck, her shiny brown hair and her smiling lips, bright red from cosmetics. "Oh Grace," he whispered, "why did you have to leave me? We could have had such a life together." A few tears escaped and rolled down in to his hair and he lay there for a while, revelling in the depths of his self-pity.

Eventually his overwhelming thirst forced him into a second attempt to get out of bed, and with many feeble groans, gasping curses and sweat he managed to heave himself out of bed and gulp down some water. He splashed and scrubbed his face and immediately began to feel a little better. He took off his soiled trousers and disposed of them in the farthest corner by the door, mentally preparing an apology for Hilda.

He took Betty's letter and went and sat on the bed, his knees pulled up to his chest and the blanket wrapped around him like a cape.

Dear Alfie (how strange it is to use that name for you!),

I was heartened to hear further about your new life and that you appear to be doing so well. Matthew and Joe sound like interesting gentlemen. Imagine talking politics after dinner! As you know very well, the most interesting the dinner conversation gets in the Cooper household is how big the cow was that Dad had to butcher.

I was somewhat startled to hear you now have a local pub, but I must admit I think that is purely because it is such a departure from anything our parents would allow or approve of. What is it like? Is it as noisome as they have always suggested those establishments are? Or is it a romantic haven where intellectuals debate international events?

Alfie thought of Joe the Beaver, Beetroot Terry and Barry the Burglar and had to laugh, as much as it pained his stomach and made him feel like he was going to be sick again. Their conversations were as far from intellectual debate as he suspected it was possible to get.

I was also envious to hear of your new haircut. How I wish I could do the same. The styles and fashions are all changing now but of course I am not allowed to do anything so dangerous as cut my hair in a fashionable manner. I'm sure our mother is convinced that the beginning of the end of the world will come about from a fashionable haircut. I laugh as I write this but I don't think I'm ever so far from the truth.

I would love to come and visit you if I can, truly. But given the way our parents still feel towards you I do fear it may be some time before I can even broach the subject, let alone hope to get a favourable response. I had thought that Mum was softening somewhat towards you and your, what Dad is calling, betrayal of this family. But I fear he has undone any headway that Mrs Cooke may have achieved on that front.

Alfie slumped upon reading this. He'd been so hopeful from Betty's last letter that his mum would come around and they would be reconciled. His dad had always been a hard man and Alfie had long ago stopped caring if his dad would ever forgive him. But his mum was a different story. She too had always been hard in her way. But she had also been loving and caring, pulling out the bee sting from his painfully swollen foot when he was seven, extracting countless splinters from his hands. Reading him to sleep at night when he was young. He'd made her read *The Story of Babar* to him so many times that he was sure she could still recite it by heart. He forced himself to keep reading.

I will obviously keep working on her from my side, and Mrs Cooke and I may yet prevail. I do hope so as she is ever so miserable, despite trying to hide it.

And now my dear brother I must sign off and get this posted to you. It is difficult to write to you as our parents cannot see me writing it and they still maintain such an oversight of all my time. Even more so since you have left. Please do write back and keep me abreast of your news and your new life.

Your sister,
Betty

PS. I have just received an obviously hastily written note from yourself about our mother. Whatever is going on? Is everything okay?

Alfie sat not moving for some time after finishing Betty's letter. He was devastated that the likelihood of his mum forgiving him seemed to be moving further away. He'd not realised until now just how much he'd been counting on that happening. The gulf he'd created between them was an ache inside him.

Like prodding a bruise, he kept thinking of happy moments they'd shared; sitting together in the front room on a Sunday after church doing the crossword in *The Daily Telegraph*. Her beaming at him with pride as he fixed a broken kitchen cabinet in their kitchen. Teaching him how to tie his tie.

The thought that that bruise might never be healed left him distraught and reaching for a bottle of Old Fitz that wasn't there to numb the pain.

He looked at his wristwatch: noon. The Crown and Goat would be opening soon and he was sure George would give him a little more credit. That was one memory he did have of last night, if very little else, although he couldn't recall just how much he owed.

The pub was quiet, although having never been on a Sunday Alfie didn't know if it was quiet for a Sunday or just in comparison to a Friday night. It seemed to be just the usual locals in; namely, Terry, Jack and Barry.

And it wasn't George behind the bar. Instead, it was a plump older woman whom Alfie had never seen before. "What can I get you, me handsome?" she asked.

"Ah…um…" he stumbled, not really sure what to do now George wasn't there. He felt awkward asking someone else for credit, especially as that person was a stranger and he was sober. He stood there prevaricating and at a loss, desperately wanting a drink to take the edge both off his hangover and off Betty's letter, but too embarrassed to ask someone he didn't know.

"Oh for god's sake, give him a drink on tick, Rose," called Barry. "George opened up a tab for him last night." Alfie flushed, embarrassed all over again that he'd been so embarrassed someone else had had to speak for him.

"A pint and an Old Fitz please," he said rather gruffly, trying to make up for it.

"Right you are," Rose said, moving to the pumps. "So I've not seen you before. You new here?"

"Newish," he mumbled.

"He's from London," called Jack with a grin.

"Oooh, well, la-di-da," Rose said, with a smile to take the sting out. "How are you finding dreary old Exeter?"

"Fine thanks," he said rather shortly, just wanting to take his drink and go and sit in the corner and pretend the rest of the world didn't exist.

"How's the head this morning?" asked Barry with a knowing laugh. "You were a bit worse for wear last night, I dare say."

"I dare say he was a bit worse for wear this morning too!" Jack crowed.

Alfie gave them a tight smile and raised his pint glass. "Nothing this won't sort out, don't worry, gents."

Managing to cut the rest of the pleasantries short, Alfie slumped at the table he sat at with Joe and Matthew, staring glumly into his pint glass. A short time later the door opened and a man entered with a beagle. A beagle! It hadn't been a dream!

The man gave him a small nod as he entered and went to the bar, the dog keeping close to his side. "Afternoon, Charles," came the chorus from the end of the bar.

"Gentlemen."

"Charles, you didn't get to meet Alfie properly last night given the state of him." Beetroot Terry gestured towards where Alfie was collapsed in the corner.

"Alfie, this is Charles and his dog Frank."

Alfie raised his pint in Charles' direction. "Nice to meet you, sir. You have a lovely dog."

"Yes, you said something to the same effect last night," Charles said rather sardonically.

Alfie flushed and mumbled an apology as he desperately tried to recall what Charles was talking about. He couldn't even remember Charles, just a brief flash of the dog.

"It's all right, son," Charles said, "It's happened to the best of us." He picked up his beer and led Frank to a table by one of the grimy windows.

Alfie couldn't help looking at them. There was an equilibrium about the two of them that Alfie envied, like Charles had owned Frank forever. He'd never had that. Not with a person or with an animal, his parents resolutely refusing to allow pets. Too messy, they'd said. Too unpredictable. Too expensive. Too needy. Never mind that Alfie had desperately wanted some sort of pet, any pet. A companion who would love him unconditionally. He'd begged and begged his parents when he'd been younger, to no avail. As he'd got older he'd realised his parents would never concede and he'd given up on the idea. Given up hope.

"How long have you had him?" Alfie called across the pub, unable to help himself.

Jack the Beaver swivelled on his stool before Charles could respond, "If you want to talk to good old Charles here, then be decent about it and go over. Don't yell at him across the pub. We have manners here."

"Apologies," he mumbled, lifting his now empty pint glass in an apologetic salute. He grabbed his glass of Old Fitz and pulled up a stool with Charles, being careful of Frank under the table.

"Let's start that again, shall we?" said Charles. "Frank here

153

I've had for eight years. I rescued him off the streets for which he remains eternally grateful, don't you, Frank?" Charles reached under the table and gave Frank a good scratch.

"Off the streets?" said Alfie with surprise.

Charles nodded. "I found him shortly after I moved here. We've grown into Exeter together you might say."

Alfie nodded, thinking of his own growing into Exeter, and the growing pains that were coming with it. He realised he'd finished his Old Fitz and motioned to ask Charles if he'd like another drink. Charles shook his head, gesturing to his still-full pint. "I've only just started mine."

Alfie couldn't tell if Charles was having a dig at how quickly he drank or not, and then decided he didn't care anyway and stood and went to the bar.

"So Charles," he said when he returned, "what do you do for a living?"

"I work for the County Steam Laundry."

"Washing clothes?" Alfie asked incredulously.

'No, of course not. Driving the delivery van."

"Oh." Alfie nodded. He was trying to think of something else to say when he felt something nudge his leg. He looked down and saw Frank's big brown eyes looking back at him. They were kind eyes. Soulful. The type of eyes that would have given him comfort growing up in a household that was all too often without comfort and full of anger and reproach instead.

"I can understand why you rescued him," said Alfie, choking off a wave of emotion that was threatening to overcome him. He gave Frank a scratch behind the ears before downing his pint in one and quickly standing to go to the bar before Charles could see the hint of a tear in his eye.

An hour later he was rolling drunk again and back at his usual table, Charles having excused himself three pints and an Old Fitz ago. He blearily looked at his watch: Four o'clock. God, was it only four? He had hoped to drink the day away in here before having a feed at Hilda's and dropping himself into bed to sleep and forget everything. But Rose was getting increasingly wary about giving him any further credit and he thought the pub shut soon anyway. He'd go for a walk.

He stumbled outside, blinded by the sunlight after so long inside. He turned up his collar and breathed in the crisp fresh air. He automatically turned to walk back to Hilda's before stopping. Another way today. He turned right instead and headed for the centre of town. He'd been walking for a while when he realised his feet were taking him to Esme's. He stopped. He didn't think he could take seeing that place again. He felt like he was teetering on a knife-edge already.

He spotted a small alley off to his left and decided to take that instead. Halfway down he startled a cat that was daintily picking through some rubbish. The cat retreated a distance before stopping to watch him warily. A cat. He would have loved a cat. But no, his parents had to have their way. Even when he'd got a job and was earning money he still wasn't allowed a pet. Was still treated like a child being told what he could and couldn't have, could and couldn't do. Could anyone blame him for leaving them? His dad was angry at him? Well, he was angry at his dad! If his dad had been a more reasonable man, a kinder man, a less violent man, then maybe he wouldn't have had to leave and break his mother's heart. His mum. His poor mum. It broke his own heart to think that she was so upset. And it was all his father's fault.

He kicked the rubbish bin in anger, causing the cat to flee. No one had ever stood up to him, that was his dad's problem. God knew that Alfie had never had the courage. And maybe that had been the problem. Maybe that look of disdain he'd always imagined he saw in his dad's face really was there. Perhaps his father did despise him for being weak and it had all been a test that he'd failed by not being strong enough. Not standing up for himself. Well, he could put that right.

"I hate you!!" he yelled to his father, punching the wall. His hand, still recovering from whatever he'd done to it on Friday night, exploded in pain and he yelped. He kicked the wall a few times for good measure before drunkenly stumbling on, cradling his throbbing hand.

Hilda was in the front room tidying up when he got back and she immediately took in his inebriated state and his now swollen hand. "Will you look at the state of you!" she exclaimed disapprovingly. "And what have you done to your hand?"

"It's nothing," he mumbled, ashamed that she should see him in this state.

"Well, it certainly doesn't look like nothing. But I'll leave you be if that's what you want. Dinner is in half an hour if you decide you want to consume something other than alcohol. You've missed your bath." She brushed past him, leaving a tangible trail of disappointment in her wake.

He stood for a few minutes in the front room, at a loss for what to do. He had a vague sense he'd not eaten today and that he should indeed eat something. But at the same time he wasn't in the mood for company. And he especially didn't want any more of Hilda's recriminations. He'd go to his room and splash some water on his face and have a lie down for fifteen minutes and then see how he felt. Maybe he'd feel a bit more sociable then.

When he opened his eyes it was dark. Really dark. He got up and turned on the light to look at his watch – eleven pm. He'd slept for more than five hours. And he was ravenous. He sighed and got undressed before slipping under the covers. He closed his eyes and tried to forget about his empty stomach. Two boiled eggs were hardly likely to cut it tomorrow morning, but he supposed it was his own fault.

When he next opened his eyes, dawn light was weakly coming through the window he'd neglected to draw the curtains on. He stared around groggily for a few moments trying to get his bearings on where he was and what day it was. Shit. Monday. It was Monday. He desperately scrabbled for his watch on the bedside table before realising he was still wearing it. Wide-eyed he wrenched his wrist to his face to bring the watch into focus. Five forty-four. Shit. Shit shit shit shit shit.

He leapt out of bed and frantically cast about for his clothes in the half-light, before his brain started functioning enough to tell him to turn the light on. Five forty-eight saw him out the front door and racing down the road to make it to the corner in time for his lift with Derek.

He arrived panting and light-headed at five fifty-eight. Bob was already there. Alfie doubled over, gasping for breath and desperately trying not to vomit all over his shoes while Bob looked on in something approaching amusement.

"Sleep in, did we, boy?" he asked with a grin.

As Alfie caught his breath and stood up properly, Bob dropped the grin as he got a good look at him. "Christ Alfie, you look a mess! And you smell a right state – when was the last time you had a bath?! Surely it wasn't this week from the smell of you. Did you even have one last week?"

Alfie waved a hand vaguely in answer and attempted to smooth down his hair and his clothes. He was rescued from any further questions by Derek's arrival. He quickly hopped in, nodding briefly to Adam and Harold before sinking low on his seat and keeping his head down. It was going to be a long day. And he'd been in such a hurry to get out the door that he hadn't even got to have his boiled eggs.

Chapter 15

Alfie sat in the corner and watched them all. Getting on. Talking. Laughing even. He couldn't remember the last time he'd laughed. Really laughed. He envied them. He pretended he didn't care with his curmudgeonly demeanour and to an extent it was true.

He'd always been awkward around people, never knowing what to say, how to behave. Which meant he'd always felt like an outsider. Except with Betty. And Evie for that brief, glorious time. Yet even at his most social, he'd never felt completely at ease, comfortable in his own skin. And after a lifetime of feeling separated from the rest of the world by some sort of invisible divide that even he couldn't quite put his finger on, he thought that he might have been immune to it by now.

But every now and again when he watched people interacting so naturally, so easily, he was envious. Followed closely, if he was honest with himself, by an even bigger sense of loneliness. He didn't want to need people or company and it irked him. This inconvenient need to belong.

Even Trevor with his worthless shit of a son had friends within the home, a daughter who visited more weeks than not. He had no one. And he knew it was his own fault – for so many reasons – but it didn't make it any easier to ignore.

It was better since he'd started corresponding with Anne, and he had surprised himself with how much he not only looked forward to reading her letters, but also replying. He'd never been one to enjoy talking about himself, but lately it felt like things needed to be talked about. Needed to be said. Perhaps his brain – his soul? – could sense he was old and wanted some catharsis before he kicked the bucket. God knew he wasn't about to confess to a priest anytime soon or get the last rites.

He'd never understood the concept of the last rites. He didn't understand how someone could do all sorts of bad and horrible things, say sorry on their deathbed and then get into heaven. He certainly wasn't going to heaven after what he'd done, even if he had believed in it. And God, if he did exist, knew how sorry Alfie was. How soul-achingly sorry.

He'd never had a knack for making friends. Always saying the wrong thing or not knowing what to say. The closest he'd come was his time in Exeter and the few years he spent in the funfair, which even now after all these years he looked back on as some sort of golden age.

He knew they all looked on him with pity. The miserable old man with no family, no friends. And he knew they all whispered about him when he wasn't in the room. Why didn't he have any friends or family? He never received any letters, had no visitors. No Christmas cards at Christmas, no birthday cards to mark the years.

Perhaps that was why he and Fred got along so well as he sensed the same aloofness in Fred. The same inability to connect. Two strangers connected by their disconnectedness.

Julia observed Alfie in the corner and was filled with a deep sadness. He wasn't so bad once you got to know him a bit – which admittedly took a long time – and it was awful to see him sitting there on his own. An island of loneliness and solitude in a heaving sea of socialness and gaiety. He was pretending to read, but Julia knew he hadn't turned a page in a good few minutes and was just watching everyone.

Pinewood never did anything over the top for Easter, but they still dished out cheap Easter eggs to the residents and engaged them all in some egg painting. She and Helen had pushed a few of the tables from the dining room against the big bingo table in the day room and currently everyone except Alfie was sat having a great old time painting eggs in all sorts of colours, with varying degrees of artistry. Ben was showing a great aptitude for it, rather skilfully painting delicate yellow chicks on the eggs.

She couldn't tell if Alfie wanted to join in but just wasn't sure how to go about it, if he was just observing, or if he was simply sat there hating all of it and wishing they'd all go away so he could concentrate on his book. She suspected he'd been playing the cantankerous old man for so long that even he didn't know anymore.

She switched her attention back to the table, smiling as she saw Trevor pretend to swipe paint all over Joan's egg, much to Joan's outrage before she realised what'd he'd done – or not done. The two of them were so sweet together and she was pleased they'd found each other. With family and friend visits restricted to Saturdays she thought the week in between must feel pretty long and lonely without someone to share it with.

This thinking took her back to Alfie again. She'd still not got to the bottom of where he went every Saturday, but she'd decided to let him keep his little secret. It was probably better for her that she didn't know anyway so she could genuinely plead ignorance if she was ever questioned. She knew from a care worker point of view she should be telling him not to leave the premises and should be forcing him to stay for his own safety and well-being, but she just couldn't bring herself to do it.

She saw something of herself in Alfie. Not the grumpy exterior, but the not belonging. She'd never really felt like she belonged anywhere. Born and raised initially in England, she moved to a small town in Queensland, Australia with her parents when she was eleven. As it was a small school in a small town it wasn't exactly international, and she was always 'the English girl', 'the Pom'. Something other than them. She'd tried to diffuse it by throwing herself into adopting all the Australian habits and customs. But she could never really lose the accent, and kids can be cruel. As a teenager, going through the usual teen existential crisis, she realised she would never be accepted as one of them and decided to embrace her Englishness instead and be decidedly and deliberately English. If they were going to see her as English then that's what she would be.

It got better when she moved to Brisbane to go to university. But by then she'd spent her formative years feeling like she didn't belong anywhere and it had kind of stuck. It hadn't helped that now she'd moved back to England she was regarded as 'the Aussie' and she was the 'other' here too.

Her flatmate at university, Naomi, had studied English and had done a unit on post-colonialism. One night over a bottle of wine in the flat, Naomi told Julia what she'd been learning and it had struck a chord with Julia and stayed with her ever since.

Naomi had told her about 'the man between two worlds' theory, which was based on the indigenous inhabitants of the lands that the British, amongst others, had colonised. The indigenous people were 'educated' by the British 'for their own good'. The British encouraged them to give up their native garb and dress in the Western way. To speak their language, adopt their habits and culture. Most resisted, but some, perhaps to make a living in a world increasingly appropriated by an invading culture, turned to the white man lifestyle. Most acted as translators, guides, trackers, manservants. And while those that did this were able to make a living and support their family, they were ostracised by their own people. Forever now seen as a traitor to their race. But on the other side, they were never accepted by the white settlers, condemned to be seen as no better than a native attempting to imitate better habits. And thus, a 'man between two worlds' was born, consigned to a limbo world where he wasn't accepted by either side.

It had resonated for Julia and spoken to her soul. That was exactly how she had felt ever since she was eleven, and to find it so well explained, and by academics, made her feel vindicated.

Mavis' increasingly strident voice brought her back to the present. "Joan, you don't know. You don't *know*. I know. And I'm telling you, it's all a load of codswallop. Nobody with any real sense believes it."

Julia never got to find out exactly what Joan did or didn't know, as at that moment Trevor knocked over the glass of water they were using to rinse the paint from their brushes. All over Mavis and her eggs.

"Oh shit!" exclaimed Mavis, startling everyone, including herself from the look on her face. Mavis never swore.

"Oh dear," said Trevor rather mutedly and with a decided lack of contriteness. "I'm ever so sorry, Mavis. How clumsy of me."

As Julia went over to help clean up she couldn't help but see both Trevor and Joan doing a very poor attempt at smothering their laughter. She saw an outraged Mavis open her mouth and cut her off. "Come on, Mavis. Let's get you cleaned up and changed. I'm sure Trevor didn't mean it." She shot Trevor a pointed look.

"No, of course not. Sorry Mavis."

Julia managed to get Mavis out of the room before the peals of laughter rang out, bouncing down the hallway.

He woke and lay in bed in the dark, staring into the void around him. He knew there was a water stain on the ceiling above him and he tried to trace the shape of it in his head. Even though he was awake he would have to lie there until one of the nurses came. Despite being reasonably mobile during the day, he couldn't manoeuvre himself from lying to sitting without some sort of help. He should have been able to just press the button on the rail to get the bed to sit up, like a hospital bed. But the controls were broken – something he'd been promised for the past few months would get fixed.

The nurse would help him to sit up and then give him a sponge bath and help him dress. It was only a sponge bath today, being a Wednesday. At least he was fairly sure it was Wednesday today. Real showers were reserved for Tuesdays and Saturdays.

At first it had been humiliating. But gradually he'd come to realise that he was no different to anyone else in Pinewood, who were all attended to in the same fashion. The fact he didn't know any of the nurses' names helped keep it purely professional too, and he came to realise that the nurses simply saw it as items one through three on their morning checklist. At least it was when they dealt with him. They always chattered away with Trevor at an excessively unnecessary rate and volume considering how early it was. Thankfully they did him first and he could sit in his chair in the window and try and block them out with his book.

It was raining as the minibus pulled up outside the library, and so it took an interminably long time to get everyone off the bus. By the time Alfie finally got inside the library he was agitated. He'd lost a full twelve minutes of his hour. He didn't even bother checking if the hour would be extended by twelve minutes to compensate. He'd asked before. He was so out of sorts he didn't spot that both the computers were taken until he was already past Emma's desk and halfway there. Bugger.

He turned to the desk and was preparing to ask Emma how long they'd been on there and when he could expect to have his turn when he stopped. It wasn't Emma. It was someone else. Now in the six years he'd been resident at Pinewood and coming to the library this had obviously happened before. But on top of the late arrival and the full computers it threw him.

He reluctantly approached the desk. "Hi!" the girl exclaimed rather too brightly from her seat behind the desk. "What can I help you with today?" Alfie noticed she was incredibly short, and seemed to peer up at him from a long way down through round tortoiseshell glasses. She spotted *Persuasion* in his hand. "Are you returning that one or would you like to borrow it? If you're returning it you can pop it in that little chute just there and we'll take care of it for you."

"Well, you see… I am returning it, but I'd also like to take it out again."

"Why, of course! Not quite finished it yet hey? That's no problem at all. Do you have your library card?"

Alfie flushed. He never brought his card, as Emma knew him.

163

It's not like he took a wallet around with him these days. "Well, you see, Emma knows me so I never normally need it. I have my borrower number memorised if that helps."

"Well, I'm not really meant to lend books without the card, but seeing as you came in on the Pinewood bus it's not like I don't know where you live!" she laughed. A grating laugh like two balloons being rubbed together. It made the hairs on Alfie's arms stand on end. She seemed to be waiting for some sort of response, but he just stood and waited.

"Okay, well, right then. If you give me the book and your borrower number I'll get it renewed for you." He handed *Persuasion* over so she could scan in the barcode stuck to the inside cover. "Borrower number?"

He dutifully reeled off the twelve digits. Amazing how he could remember that but not what he'd had for lunch. "Right, okay then, Mr Cooper. Let me just go in and renew this for you… I just need to find the right screen…these computers are a bit old and clunky now so sometimes it takes a while. Still, I guess we should be glad we have anything at all. Really we should be glad that the library is even here given the government seems determined to close them all." She talked incessantly, Alfie thought. It was like every single thought that ran through her head came out of her mouth. She reminded him of one of those wind-up toys that just kept going and going.

"Right so – oh!" She finally paused for a brief second. "Well, this is rather odd. Your record shows that you've renewed this book…" He could hear her counting under her breath as she stared at the screen. "My goodness, I've lost count. But it looks like you've had it on permanent loan for what must be years. That can't be right."

"Um…er… Well, you see…"

She stared at him, agape. "It is right?"

"Yes, well…"

"Well, that is most irregular. And, might I say, against library policy." Alfie's heart started to thump and he felt himself break out in a mild sweat. He had to renew the book. He had to. He always had a copy of *Persuasion*. It had never occurred to him that his constant borrowing of the book might be against some sort of policy. His mind was racing through what he could say to convince this chattering complication to let him take the book when Julia appeared, as if by magic.

"Is there a problem here?" she asked.

"Not a problem as such," the wind-up toy answered. "More of an irregularity. It seems Mr Cooper here has had this book on the equivalent of permanent loan for years. That is most definitely against library policy."

"Yes, well, Pinewood has an agreement with Emma in this matter. Perhaps you'd like to call her to check?"

"She's at a doctor's appointment."

"Well, perhaps you'll see your way clear to reissuing the book to Mr Cooper today, and you can check in with Emma once she's back for future reference for next time?" Julia smiled sweetly at the toy. "Pinewood can vouch for him, I assure you."

"Well... All right then. But I will be checking with Emma when she's back later today and raising this. It's most irregular."

"Of course. We're most grateful to you, aren't we, Alfie." She nudged him.

"Ah, oh, yes! Yes, most grateful. Thank you, lass." He almost snatched the book from her, shot Julia a look full of gratitude and almost ran to the now vacant computers. Well, in what amounted to a run for his eighty-six-year-old body. Really it was a vaguely faster shuffle.

He sat in front of the computer and just stared at the screen for a few minutes, trying to still his racing heart.

Hi Alfie,

What a week it's been here! You'll be glad you're over there rather than in the Davenport household. Ethan came down with a stomach bug, which meant I had to take a couple of days off work to look after him. Poor little thing, he was so sick. Don't worry, I won't go into detail! He's okay now though thankfully. I just hope he doesn't come down with anything else between now and the end of the school year as I don't have many sick days left!

How's your week been over in England? What's the weather like there in spring? It was a pretty cold start to spring here in New Jersey, although it's finally warming up as we get closer to summer and things are starting to flower now.

My class on China went really well too, I think I forgot to tell you. I took in fortune cookies for everyone, which they loved. And I told them about the Great Wall of China. Which is pretty topical these days with the President promising to build his own! I didn't think that they'd make the connection but Diana, who's a precocious little thing, piped up about the 'great wall' that her daddy said the President was going to build and how it would keep us safe. Republicans hey? Anyway, enough about politics! My own daddy always told me that you don't discuss politics or religion.

How are things at Pinewood Alfie? I hope Trevor isn't being too annoying for you. I like the sound of Una the Unicorn too! I don't think I've ever come across a porcelain unicorn before. Where on earth did you find that? Well, I say where on earth but then I'm guessing England as you haven't travelled! Unless you got it on eBay? You never know these days! I mean, you're online writing with me! Your comment about the furniture there did make me laugh too. All the furniture at the school looks like it's come from a bargain basement so I know what you mean! So what did you do between the carnival and moving to Slatterley? Or did you work in the carnival for all that time?

Speaking of travelling, I've been saving like crazy and I've decided that I'm going to take Ethan to Florida for his birthday to go to Disney World! I mean, going to Florida isn't exactly new for him given we go there every year to see my parents, but I've never taken him to Disney World. I think he's old enough now that he'll enjoy it properly and remember it.

Speaking of the little devil I can hear him up and about so best go see what he's up to as he should be in bed!

Until next week!

Anne

Alfie sat back and digested the letter. It was a long one this week and a little all over the place. He was also feeling quite smug about the fact that he knew what eBay was, even if he'd never used it.

Dear Anne,

Thanks for your letter. I was sorry to hear that Ethan was sick. It's never nice to be sick, but especially so when you're young I think. Or old. It's not very nice when you're old and sick either. If you don't actually die you think that you might.

Was that too dark? Too flippant? Phyllis' old roommate had kicked the bucket only the past winter when she came down with the flu. He worried Anne might think him morbid so he deleted the last bit.

Or old. It's not very nice when you're old and sick either. I am glad to hear he's feeling better now though. When is his birthday? I imagine he will be very excited about the trip to Disney World. Are you going to tell him or are you going to surprise him?

There's not much else to report from Pinewood I'm sorry

to say. Or Slatterley for that matter. Although at least our politicians aren't as crazy as yours, just can't seem to make their mind up about anything and are constantly squabbling over this whole Brexit nonsense. The world does seem to be a much more uncertain and crazy place these days. It was never like this back in the fifties. But I'll stop now, before I start harping on about the 'good old days'.

As for Una, I found her in a jumble of an antique shop in a little village in East Anglia, I forget where exactly. I always meant to send her to a friend, to replace one that was broken but I never got the chance. So she just stayed with me.

Spring here has been a mixed bag of weather, but then that's standard. It's not been a particularly cold one though, just wet. The daffodils and tulips are all out down the park and the trees have all mostly grown back now. I like it when the daffodils are out. I didn't see them for such a long time.

He looked at *Persuasion* sitting next to the keyboard and decided it was time. He needed to tell someone. And he wasn't all that far away from the part of his story where he'd need to tell Fred. Writing it could be like a dry run for when he'd need to speak it.

In answer to your question about what I did between the funfair and moving to Slatterley, well, there's no easy way to say this, but I was in prison. For a long time in fact. I'd like to say it's behind me but it's not, not even now. No one at Pinewood knows. Nobody knows, except you now. I hope that hasn't shocked you and that you'll continue to write to me.

I hope to hear from you.

Alfie

Chapter 16

The next few weeks passed in a drink-sodden haze. He was drinking so much he was out-drinking Joe. He didn't care. He knew he was wallowing in self-pity, painting himself in it, but he didn't care about that either.

He couldn't remember the last time he'd done his fifty push ups in the morning, and he also knew his work was suffering. And while he did care about that to an extent, it wasn't enough to stop drinking. He was a little worried he was behind in his payments to Hilda as so much of his pay was going towards the drink, but again, not worried enough to stop drinking.

Joe and Matthew had tried to talk to him, to get him to stop or slow down, but he'd just angrily shrugged them off and gone to the pub without them. He didn't need them. He had all the regulars at the Crown and Goat he could talk to. Or he could just eschew conversation in favour of his own black thoughts and the company of a pint glass, which he had started to do frequently.

He continued to correspond with Betty, but his letters were shorter, the content more erratic. And the fact his mum still hadn't written to him, still hadn't forgiven him, continued to eat him up inside. And if he was honest with himself, the fact it did, that at his age he was still so reliant on his mother's good opinion for his own self-worth, only contributed to his desire for a drink to numb everything.

How had it all gone so wrong, he wondered? Everything had started so well and he'd been so happy here when he first arrived. And now here he was, less than six months in, in a pit of despair, in debt and in danger of losing the few friends he'd made.

Perhaps he should cut back on the drinking, he mused as he considered the almost empty glass in front of him. There did seem to be a correlation, he had to admit. Although everything had been fine until Grace had rejected him.

He'd not been back to Esme's café since, at least not inside. He was still walking past on his way home though, and stopping to look at Grace. Alternately hating her, loving her, missing her, mourning her. He had also taken to walking past at night when he was deeply in his cups. Some nights he would sit on the kerb outside and weep. Other nights he would try and batter the door down, waking with bruised and swollen knuckles the next morning that prevented him working properly.

He knew his mentorship of Adam was suffering, and Derek had even pulled him aside and told him to get his act together. And he had for a few days. He'd cut back on the drinking, got some more sleep. But it hadn't lasted. And he was still getting the job done anyway, so Derek couldn't complain too much. But he did feel bad that he wasn't being as good a mentor to Adam as he could be. Not bad enough to stop drinking though.

Thinking of work, he looked at his watch and realised that he should probably call it a night if he was to be in any sort of fit state for the morning. He got up to go but spotted Charles walk in with Frank. Maybe just the one more while he petted Frank.

The next morning he woke in a fog, having stayed for far too many more at the pub and then carried on back in his room, starting another newly bought bottle of Old Fitz. He just made it to the corner to be picked up, again running out of time to grab his boiled eggs.

They were currently out on the army site, and this time the army really had gone to town. He thought that they'd let off some sort of explosives this time around, and much of the upper floor and roof had to be rebuilt. He and Adam had been working on fixing the roof, and they were almost done. Today would be their last day and then they could get to work on the upper floor.

He slowly climbed the ladder, trying to keep a wave of nausea at bay. Adam was already up there, positioned on one side of the gaping hole that they would be fixing today. They already had most of the support struts in, they just needed to fix the last few and close the hole in.

Alfie eventually made it to the top of the ladder and hauled himself up to the roof. He made the mistake of looking down as he did and felt a wave of nausea again as he looked straight down to the ground floor, the section of floor on the first floor also having been ripped apart from whatever explosives they used.

They'd left the planks up on the roof from yesterday, and Adam was already wrestling one of them on to the struts as Alfie reached him. "Careful there," said Alfie, grabbing one end. Adam looked at him with what Alfie thought may have been contempt. He shrugged. He was feeling too ill to care at this stage.

They worked in silence for another hour, before a light drizzle set in making Alfie feel even more miserable as he got uncomfortably damp. He stopped to sweep the rain from his dripping hair and the abrupt motion from being bent over to standing sent a wave of dizziness through him and he fought back the urge to vomit.

He swallowed, and tasted bile in the back of his throat. "Be back in a minute," he mumbled to Adam as he made his way down the ladder as quickly as he could. He just made it to the tree line before he bent over double, retching into the bushes. He wiped his mouth and slowly unbent himself, a sheen of sweat on his waxy face despite the cool October day. He took several deep breaths and stood there for a few minutes more, making sure he didn't need to throw up again.

He was just deciding he was probably okay when he heard a crash and shouts from the house. He turned and lumbered back as quickly as his unsteady legs would carry him. He arrived breathless and dizzy, entering by the back door. He looked around and heard raised voices from the front of the house. He went through the kitchen and saw Bob and Harold huddled around something on the floor.

"What is it?" he asked as he approached, wiping specks of vomit from his mouth and fighting the black spots at the edge of his vision. He stopped when he saw. The blood drained from his face. It was Adam's body lying broken and twisted on the floor like some macabre marionette. Derek was knelt beside him, checking his pulse.

"Is he…is he…?"

Derek looked up at them all and nodded silently. Sadly.

Alfie dropped to his knees by Adam, heedless of the blood that had started to pool around his body. He had no idea what to do. He started to reach for Adam's hand but then wasn't sure if he was meant to touch him.

"I'll go and call for an ambulance," said Derek. "There's a pub not too far back that will have a telephone."

Alfie barely heard him. If he ignored the blood and the mangled body and just concentrated on Adam's face, he could almost convince himself that Adam was simply asleep. Perhaps if he stared hard enough Adam would wake up. He'd never seen a dead body before. Not really. He'd seen limbs poking out of bombed houses during the Blitz, but not this up-close reality. It was quieter than he'd imagined. He noticed even Adam's perennial pimples had lost their anger, bereft of a place to call home. Time stood still as the world dropped away. There was just Adam.

"Where's the bloody ambulance?" Bob muttered anxiously, pacing. "And why isn't Derek back? God, I hope the pub was open."

Eventually they heard the rumble of Derek's van. Alfie stood up and they all turned as he walked in. "Ambulance and police are on their way."

Silence descended, thick and airless, as they all stood around Adam, lost in their own thoughts for a time. A shaft of sunlight sliced the room, and Alfie concentrated on the dust floating in it rather than Adam's bloodied and lifeless hand, which it lit up in gold.

"How did this happen?" demanded Harold, rounding on Alfie and shattering the silence so it pierced them all like knives. "You were up there with him weren't you?"

"I…I…" Alfie took a step back, not sure what to say. "I was having a piss…"

"Pissing out last night's excesses more like. He was a good boy and he didn't deserve to go like this. He deserved better. You owed him better." Harold's face was bright red from barely contained anger and a vein in his neck was throbbing. Alfie took a step back, worried Harold was about to make a lunge for him.

"You've been a fucking disaster for weeks now and Derek, lord knows why, has gone easy on you. And now this has happened."

"Hey now," said Derek holding up his hand, "I hope you're not implying this is somehow my fault."

"Well, you're the one who's been so soft on Alfie, letting him carry on in this state." Harold looked Alfie over, sneering. "It's pathetic really. You're pathetic." Harold spat on the floor at Alfie's feet.

"Hey, hey!" Bob came in, putting a restraining hand on Harold. "Let's not do this now. Later, for sure," he added casting a look of loathing in Alfie's direction, "but not right now."

The sound of sirens stopped any further conversation. Derek went in to the kitchen to give a statement to the police, while the rest of them stood in respectful silence as the ambulance attendants took Adam's body away.

A gaping hole was left in the room, much bigger than the space Adam had occupied. It was a space none of them wanted to fill and they all remained silent until Derek returned.

"The police want statements from all of you," said Derek as he came back in. "Starting with you, Alfie."

By the time he got home that afternoon, Alfie was exhausted. Mentally, physically and certainly emotionally.

Rather than sink straight into bed he instead picked up the bottle of Old Fitz on his bedside table. He looked at it for a few moments and then opened his bedroom window and poured it all out, throwing the bottle after if for good measure. If only his own regrets could be disposed of so easily. After that he sank down on the bed and wept.

He curled up in a ball and thought of the last proper conversation that he could remember having with Adam, when Adam had spoken about his dream of starting his own building business with his cousin. Starting off small with a few jobs and then growing until they could afford to employ an apprentice or two and Adam could mentor someone, like Alfie had taught him.

The light in Adam's eye and the hope on his face as he'd talked about it wracked Alfie anew with more emotion than he could bear. Guilt and grief vied for dominance and he sobbed uncontrollably. Eventually he exhausted himself and slept.

He was lost in a huge house, a mansion. It was dark and the house was empty except for the echo of his footsteps. He walked through room after room trying to find his way out but no matter which way he went he kept coming back to the same room, over and over.

Then he noticed a small door he'd not spotted before, hidden in a corner. He went over to examine it further, bending low to get a proper look at it. He turned the handle and tentatively pushed on the door before recoiling in shock. Behind the door was a cliff edge beyond which was a nothingness, a blackness so profound Alfie couldn't discern anything, except Adam dangling from the cliff, hanging on for dear life. "Help me," pleaded Adam as he looked up at Alfie. "Save me." Alfie lunged for Adam's hand to pull him back but grasped only smoke. He looked into Adam's eyes, trying to fathom what was going on. "You've killed me," whispered Adam as he dropped away into the nothingness.

He woke with a start, panicked and gasping for air. His heart was pounding and he was covered in a cold sweat. He tried to calm himself, taking deep breaths to bring his racing heart back to normal.

He automatically reached for the bottle of Old Fitz that for the past few weeks had been his constant bedside companion. But like his attempt to grab hold of Adam, his hand encountered nothing but air.

He looked at his watch and saw he'd been asleep for no more than an hour. In fact, Joe and Matthew would shortly be home if they weren't already and Hilda would be calling them to the dining room for dinner. He splashed some water on his face and tried to pull himself together a little more before he had to face anyone. He desperately wanted a drink and was both glad and angry that he'd poured the Old Fitz out the window.

He really didn't want to have to see or speak to anyone, but he was afraid that if he stayed on his own his unspoken and newly half-formed resolve to stop drinking would waiver and he'd find himself down the pub again. So, much as he didn't want to, he went downstairs.

He could hear Joe and Matthew's voices from the front room as he came down the stairs and he stopped at the bottom for a few moments to collect his sharp, scattered thoughts. He walked cautiously in to the room, aware his recent behaviour in no way guaranteed him a warm reception. They both looked up as he entered and then looked away, disgusted. Joe shook his head. "Look at the state of you Alfie. You're a disgrace."

Alfie swallowed deeply. "I know," he said softly, almost inaudibly. The tears started again, much as he tried to fight them back, and he struggled to get the words out. "Adam…Adam… Oh god, Adam died on site today." He collapsed into the armchair, covering his face as he began to sob. "It's all my fault," he mumbled into the shocked silence.

Joe and Matthew looked at each other aghast at the news and also unsure how to deal with Alfie. A weeping man was new territory. "I'm sure it's not your fault," said Matthew eventually, shifting uncomfortably on the orange ambiguity. "I'm sure it just feels that way."

"No!" said Alfie vehemently, wrenching his hands away from

his face. "It was my fault! It's all my fault. No wonder my own mother won't talk to me anymore." He stood up abruptly and lunged for the door. "I need to be on my own," he mumbled as he stumbled out into the cold air, leaving Joe and Matthew to stare at each other in bewilderment.

Alfie blindly wandered the streets, not taking any notice of where he was going or how cold he was without his coat. The same thoughts kept going around and around in his head. His dad's disapproval. His mum's disappointment. Grace's disinterest. His own deformed sense of entitlement.

Without consciously guiding himself there, his feet had taken him back to the Crown and Goat, like a single-minded homing pigeon. Blinded by tears and desperate to numb the unrelenting pain he was feeling, he didn't allow himself to think before pushing open the door and falling into the warm and familiar embrace of oblivion.

The following morning dawned like glass, shards of sunlight penetrating the gloom in his bedroom and piercing his eyes. As consciousness and the memory of his own weakness returned, Alfie rolled over into the foetal position, screwing his eyes shut and wishing he could just disappear.

He vaguely recalled Joe and Matthew coming to find him at the pub and him angrily refusing to leave, before eventually relenting and being led away, sobbing. But he could recall little else. How truly pathetic he was. Even when he'd cost a man his life he couldn't find enough backbone to stop drinking. He felt like he was bleeding to death with shame.

Eventually he uncurled himself and looked at his watch. Nine o'clock. Derek had let him go yesterday so he had nowhere to be. And he didn't think he could go back anyway, even if Derek hadn't fired him.

Maybe it was time to move on, make a fresh start. Start all over again and make better choices. Where would he go? What would he do? He owed money to Hilda, and to George at the Crown and Goat. He couldn't just up and leave. But he also knew that he couldn't stay.

Chapter 17

Alfie stopped and stared at his hands. He'd known it wasn't going to be pretty talking about those days, but he'd forgotten just how bad he'd been. How appalling his behaviour. And he'd not even hit rock bottom yet. He thought it was pretty clear already, but he desperately wanted to make sure Fred knew how bad drinking was. How dangerous. He was about to broach it when Fred said, "You were a right git, weren't you?"

Alfie sighed, hunching even further under the memory of his younger self. "I was. And all the drinking only made everything worse. No good comes from the bottom of a bottle, lad, let me tell you."

"My parents don't drink at all. They say that alcohol is the work of the devil." Alfie looked at him surprised. He'd never thought of Fred growing up in a religious household. He waited for Fred to go on, but it seemed that was it.

"They're right too. Maybe not about the devil bit, but they're right that no good comes from it. Steer clear of it would be my advice."

Fred shrugged. "I'm not bothered." Alfie waited. Again, that seemed to be it.

He struggled up off the bench as Fred watched under hooded

eyes. The boy never offered to help him stand up. He wasn't sure whether to thank him or curse him. He definitely needed to get a cane. He'd have to talk to Julia to see how he'd go about it. He certainly had no money to buy one. He wasn't sure if it was the type of thing the NHS would cover or not. Alfie patted his now empty canvas bag to make sure he had it and tipped his hat to Fred. "Until next time."

Alfie was stuck next to Trevor at lunch. And he was in an even more talkative mood than normal. For once, Alfie didn't mind. He let Trevor's constant diatribe of whatever was going through his head wash over him, the white noise an unlikely balm for his exposed soul.

"I'm telling you, Alfie, my life would have been so much better if I'd met Joan decades ago when we were young. She's such a wonderful lady. The kids we would have had must have turned out better than the ones I bred with Sylvia.

"No, that's unfair," continued Trevor, seemingly content to blather on without any sort of input from Alfie, which suited him just fine. "Beth is a lovely daughter. It's James I'm talking about. Do you know I can't even remember the last time I saw him? I keep wondering what I did to make him so indifferent, but I think maybe he's just an arsehole." Trevor waved his fork around, bits of the pasta sauce plopping all over the place. "I mean, there's no covenant written that children have to be nice to their parents, is there?" He shoved the laden fork in his mouth and continued to talk around the food. Alfie closed his eyes against the offending sight. "It's both liberating and depressing in a way. Liberating to think it's nothing I've done, and depressing to think I've fathered and raised an arsehole."

Joan could be heard laughing from a few tables over. "God, I love that laugh," continued Trevor without breaking stride. Without seeming to chew or even swallow. "Do you know, when they left me here in Pinewood I felt like it was a death sentence. All my little pleasures in life were gone – a quick wager on the horses, a cheeky half at the local next door to the betting shop. And who wants to spend all their days with a bunch of boring old people?" He laughed his wheezing cackle.

"They put me in here because the doctors told them that with my emphysema getting worse I needed round the clock care. Make sure I took my medication correctly. Honestly, it was only the one time I got the meds wrong and ended up in hospital and you'd think it was the end of the bloody world!

"At first it was it awful in here, sharing a room with you, you grumpy sod." He laughed again as he jabbed his fork in Alfie's direction. Alfie restrained the desire to take the fork and stab him in the eye with it. Trevor's prattling had gone from soothing to grating. "Then I met Joan. Oh Alfie, how I wish we'd met when we were younger! I would have taken her out dancing. I bet she was a wonderful dancer. And she would have been just the right height for her head to nestle in under my chin for the slow dances," he winked at Alfie.

Alfie, unable to bear Trevor's onslaught any longer, stood up and left without a word.

Julia moved through the tables dispensing the plates of pasta that managed to be both dried out and soggy at the same time, lost in her own thoughts. Siobhan had called her again last night, pleading with her. What was worse was that Julia found herself wavering.

She'd been single since Siobhan had left and if she was honest with herself she was lonely. She had few friends in Slatterley, having not gelled with any of her fellow nurses at Pinewood – at least not in that 'shall we go out for a few drinks on a Friday night' sense. And Slatterley wasn't exactly huge. Or brimming with opportunities to make new friends.

She'd moved here almost three years ago. After she'd seen out the lease in Kensington she'd decided she needed a total change of scenery. Somewhere she could lick her wounds in private and start to pay off the mountain of debt she'd been left with. She supposed she could have made more of an effort to make friends here. Should have made more of an effort. In the early days she'd relied on her friends in London, less than two hours away by train. But over time she'd gone to see them less and less. And making new friends in Slatterley just seemed like more and more of an effort.

And she was still yet to meet anyone who she thought she might get along with anyway. They were all so…so… Well, if she couldn't say it in her own head, where could she say it? So small town. And it wasn't the nicest of villages either, so most of the people were of a certain type. God, she sounded like such an elitist snob, even to herself.

Emma at the library was nice. Intelligent, kind, and one of the few people who had a view on the world wider than the Midlands. But she was married with three kids, and the few times Julia had proposed catching up it had been impossible for Emma to be able to get out. Julia wasn't quite sure why the husband couldn't look after the kids for just one night – surely he couldn't be that incompetent? But she hadn't pushed it, worried it was Emma's polite way of saying she just didn't want to go out. Or at least not out with her.

So here she was. Four years on from a disastrous, calamitous breakup, and finding herself softening towards the idea of getting back together with the one who had broken her heart. Surely she couldn't. Surely she wouldn't? No. No she wouldn't. She couldn't. She would just stay single. She would stay alone if that's what it meant.

She spotted Alfie leave the room. He did it. He was alone. So it must be possible. Maybe she would take a leaf out of his book. If she kept going this way, she'd have to. She thought again of Alfie's file. No family, no next of kin. Just blank spaces where people should be.

She wondered if there ever had been any family. A wife. Loved ones. Was it just one solitary road, driving straight through the heart of loneliness? Or was it a wandering path, visiting loss and regret before ending up at a final destination of just one, alone? Suddenly she felt compelled to find out. If this was her future, then she wanted to know how she got there.

The minibus ploughed through the lashing rain on the way to East Slatterley Public Library, the mood inside subdued, like the beating rain on the roof was wearing them all down. Eroding them, like sand.

Maybe we are all just sandcastles, Alfie thought moodily. His skin was so dry that sometimes it certainly felt like he was made of sand.

Even Mavis was quiet, although Alfie noted she was sitting next to Clyde. With the noise from the rain and his already terrible hearing, even Mavis had given up trying to make him hear what she had to say.

He was worried. Worried that Anne wouldn't have written back to him after his revelation. Worried she would judge him unkindly. He had come to depend on Anne's letters and he didn't want to lose what he'd come to regard as her friendship. He shouldn't have said anything, he fretted. It was too big a thing to reveal, to anyone. What must she think of him? He tried to remember exactly what he'd written but couldn't. He'd already forgotten and remembered several times this week that he'd even said anything to her.

The bus stopped at a red light outside Wetherspoons, the smokers all huddled under the scant cover desperately puffing away. Although he'd never taken to smoking, he still thought it was a little sad they'd now banned it in pubs. His memories of the Crown and Goat in Exeter were so intrinsically linked with the smell of cigarette smoke, hanging especially thick in the air on a Friday or Saturday night. He tried to imagine walking in to clean air, his vision unobscured by plumes of smoke but just couldn't see it. And he certainly would have barely seen Joe. The way the man smoked he would have been constantly outside. Matthew had been a little better, more sensible and cautious as was his nature, but he still would have been outside almost as much. Mind you, the whole pub would have been.

"Okay everyone," called Julia, "if you just wait, Brian and I will take you over under the umbrellas." Alfie looked up, startled. While he'd been lost in thought they'd arrived at the library. It was amazing how easy it was to get lost in your thoughts when Mavis was quiet.

He walked as quickly as he could to the computers. Would she have written? What if she hadn't? Should he write to her again? Try to explain? How to explain? How do you explain that you spent time in jail? And how would he ever explain what he was in for?

He hurriedly logged on, going straight to the pen pal site and not even thinking about BBC Weather. He diligently typed in his log-in details but hesitated with the mouse poised over the log-in button. This was it. There would either be a 1 blinking at him or there wouldn't be. He hadn't properly appreciated just how much this correspondence with Anne had come to mean to him until he was about to lose it.

He took a big breath and stabbed the mouse key.

Hi Alfie,

Well, I can't pretend I wasn't shocked, that's for sure. But we do all make mistakes and I am a believer in serving your time and doing your penance and then not being judged on it. We all make mistakes right? Some small, some huge. And you're right, they do live with us for the rest of our lives.

As you've trusted me with your own secret, I will trust you with mine. I also made mistakes and have done things I'm not proud of. Shoot, I didn't think it would be quite this hard, but here goes... When I was younger I went through a wild and reckless phase and got pregnant on a one night stand. I was too young to keep it – I was only seventeen – and I knew that it wouldn't be fair to bring a baby up with the type of life that I could have given it. So I had the baby and put him up for adoption. It was an English couple in the end, funnily enough. They'd been living in the US for a long time but were moving back to England and took my boy with them.

In some ways it's been easier knowing he was so far away. It means I haven't been looking at every little boy for all these years and wondering if he was mine. I do constantly wonder what he's like though, and what sort of young man he's grown into. He'd be fifteen by now. I don't know where he's living in England, but I do find myself making up lives for him in my head. Sometimes he lives in London and is going to a posh private school, destined for Oxford or Cambridge someday. Other times he's living in a chocolate box English village, enjoying all the fresh air and wholesome living that I imagine quaint little English villages offer. But I signed the form and so I'll never know unless he chooses to find me. I don't know if that's better or worse.

Somehow all of that made Ethan extra special. So it was even more cruel when Mark was taken from us.

I'm sorry Alfie, I don't think I can write any more this week. I hope you don't think any less of me for telling you this and you're not horrified by what I've done.

Anne

He sat back, feeling like the weight of the world had been lifted from his shoulders. She didn't hate him! Nor had she pushed him for any further details, acknowledging his privacy. Instead, she had shared her own shameful secret, returning his confidence with trust and openness.

He couldn't say he wasn't a little surprised. He'd never pictured Anne as the promiscuous type. But then as he well knew, our adult selves are shaped by the mistakes of our youth.

Dear Anne

Thank you for not judging me and wishing to continue writing to me. I was worried that my revelation would shock you too much for you to want to keep up our correspondence.

And thank you also for returning the confidence. I am

certainly not horrified or think any less of you. I can't imagine how difficult that must have been for you when you were so young. I know times are different now regarding all of that compared to when I was young, but I imagine it still can't have been easy. Were your parents supportive? I hope they were. It would have been a lot for a young girl to go through. I also hope the young man in question did the honourable thing and stuck by you? Although that was never guaranteed even in my day, so I don't know why I would expect that in yours.

Sadly I never had any children of my own. I would have loved to though. Certainly as a young man I always imagined I would. Passing my tools down to my son. Teaching him the skills to be a master cabinetmaker. It's strange how unpredictable life can be sometimes. My life turned out nothing like I intended it. But then does anyone's? Perhaps for a lucky few it does.

He felt himself growing maudlin and decided on a change of tone. He would end the letter on a lighter note.

I hope Ethan is well and that your international lessons continue to be well received. Please do send any further photos of Ethan that you may have.

I look forward to your next letter.

Alfie

He made his way over to the bookshelves, his latest John Saul in hand. He was ready for another one and looking forward to browsing through the collection to find his next literary conquest.

As he crossed the library, he spotted Julia and Emma deep in conversation. Emma looked up as he passed and looked away quickly. Strange, he thought, normally whenever she caught his eye she gave him that big smile of hers. He shrugged mentally. He was the last person to have a go at someone for not being friendly.

Julia watched Alfie walking across the library and realised how bent over he looked. She made a mental note to look into getting a cane for him and turned back to Emma. "So…?"

"So I opened it up and realised it was an email to someone called Anne. And I read it. I couldn't help myself. I didn't realise until I got to the bottom that Alfie had written it. He obviously hadn't logged out properly."

"So what did it say?" asked Julia, curious more than she wanted to admit, even to herself.

Emma looked all around her, which Julia couldn't help thinking was a little over the top. "He was in jail," she whispered theatrically, clearly relishing the drama of it all.

"In jail?" Julia repeated rather stupidly, trying to take the nugget of information in. "When? Why?"

"He didn't say why. Criminals never want to admit what they did."

"He's not a criminal!" exclaimed Julia, rather too loudly in the quiet of the library.

"Shhh!" admonished Emma in her best librarian tone.

"Sorry," said Julia more quietly. "But he's not."

"Well, he's done time in jail, so I think you'll find that technically he is."

"Yes well, yes but, oh all right, technically maybe. But not really. When was he in there? Did the email say?"

"He said it was after the funfair and before he moved to Slatterley. Do you know anything about a funfair?"

Julia shook her head. "I know very little about Alfie. No one does. At least not at Pinewood. I wonder what jail it was?"

"What does that matter?"

"If it was a maximum security prison then we know he did something really bad."

"The email didn't say, but if you can figure out when he left the funfair then that will give you some idea how long he was in for. It sounded like he pretty much went from the funfair, to jail, and then came here. Do you know when he came to Slatterley?"

Julia shook her head. There was some digging to do.

She passed Joan in the day room when she got back, an unusually grumpy look on her face. "Hi there, Joan! How are we today?"

"Well, yes I'm okay, I suppose. I shouldn't really complain. Although I'd be a lot better if I had a new back and maybe some better ears."

Julia crouched down next to her. "Is your back bad again?"

"It's always bad. But I don't like to complain."

Julia hid a smile. Joan never liked to complain, but would tell you constantly about how she didn't like to complain.

"And what's this about your ears?"

"They're just not working as well as they used to. And the nurses always look at me like I'm an idiot when I have to ask them to repeat themselves. But it's not because I'm daft you know, it's because they speak so dammed quickly I can't understand a word they say. It annoys me," she said irritably. "The whole thing annoys me. Having to admit my hearing is going, the looks from the nurses when I have to ask them to repeat themselves. Growing old. It all annoys me."

Julia sat through it all, torn between amusement that Joan had forgotten she was talking to one of the nurses, and pity. How bright and alive she must have once felt, reduced to this.

"Oh dear," continued Joan, "of course I didn't mean you, Julia. You're always lovely. I'm sorry, I'm just feeling a little crabby today."

They all had their off days when they got crotchety, even the best of them like Joan. She supposed she'd be crotchety too if everything constantly ached and she was stuck in here all day. Truthfully, she was surprised they weren't all like Alfie all the time. "Honestly, Joan, it's okay. If you can't be a little crabby at your age then what's the point, hey?" she joked gently, hoping to lift Joan out of her mood. "Maybe you should have come to the library, got a change of scenery?"

"I still haven't finished the book I'm reading. I should have finished it by now, of course. But I keep having to go back and re-read so much of it every time I pick it up because I've lost all trace of what was going on since I'd last read it." She sighed, seeming to shrink a little more. "I feel like that about the days sometimes. I keep losing the thread of what's going on."

Like trying to hold on to a fistful of sand, Julia imagined sadly, thinking of the faculties, the memories, falling away, one by one.

She decided to change the subject, try and shake Joan out of her mood. "So Joan, I was wondering if Alfie had ever mentioned anything to you about his life before he came to Pinewood?"

"Oh well, I don't know. I don't think so. You know what he's like. I've only had a few conversations with him, you know." Julia nodded. She hadn't really expected anything, but thought that of everyone in Pinewood, Joan would be the most likely person that Alfie would have confided in.

"Well, thanks anyway, Joan." She stood up, unsure where to go to next in her sleuthing. For all her watching Benedict Cumberbatch play Sherlock Holmes, she clearly hadn't picked anything up.

"I mean, he mentioned something about a sister in the south somewhere – Bath, I think – but nothing apart from that. I think her name was Betty." Joan mentioned it all almost as an afterthought.

Julia froze. A sister in Bath?! Now that was a lead. If she could figure out what to do with it.

Chapter 18

In the end he decided he would sell his tools. The price they would fetch would be enough to cover his debts and leave him a little left over to get set up somewhere else. Of course, setting up somewhere else would be harder without his tools, but it was the only way forward he could see.

Derek was the only person he knew who might want to buy them, and so reluctantly he got up early the next day and walked to the corner, dreading the meeting and having to see Harold, having to see any of them. He stared at his feet the whole journey, not looking up as he plodded along. The morning felt painted on, and he a badly painted figure in it.

He still had no idea what he would say to any of them. Indeed, he was still trying to figure out what he was saying to himself about it all. All he knew was that he was so immensely sorry for everything. For letting everyone down. For letting himself down. Maybe his parents had been right after all. Maybe he wasn't ready to make it on his own.

As he walked down the final stretch he could see Bob in his peripheral vision, already on the corner. Alfie didn't raise his head until he was standing in front of Bob, delaying that moment of contact for as long as possible.

Eventually though he had to look up. And when he did he was surprised to see something approaching concern on Bob's face, rather than anger or reproach. "Alfie. How are you, boy?"

The question took Alfie aback. He'd not expected this and rather than give a superficial answer he stopped to think. Finally, he said, "You know how it is when you go into a new place and it's packed and you don't know anyone and you just stand there in the doorway, looking for something or someone that you recognise? That's what I feel like."

Bob looked at him for a few seconds, as if trying to figure him out. Eventually he nodded. "I think I do know what that's like, boy. I think I do." He checked down the road for the van, but it wasn't in sight yet. He gave Alfie a sidelong glance. "I have to admit that I didn't expect to see you again. I'm not sure the others will either, or be happy about it if I'm honest."

Alfie held up his tool bag. "I've just come to see if Derek wants to buy these off me. I need the money to square a few bits and then I'm leaving town. I need a fresh start."

Bob nodded. "Good ideas, both of them. And Derek's a fair guy. I'm sure he'll give you a fair price."

As if the mention of his name had conjured him, Derek's van turned into the street and pulled up in front of them both. It sat there, idling, like some sort of menacing mechanical beast, and Alfie felt himself shrink away from it. Bob took the initiative, walking over to Derek's window to tell him why Alfie was there when they had all expected him not to be.

Derek stepped out of the van then, coming over to where Alfie was still standing, staring at his feet again like a naughty schoolboy. "So Bob tells me you're leaving town. Probably for the best."

Alfie nodded glumly, reluctantly raising his gaze and holding up his tool bag. "I thought you might want to buy these off me? They're good tools and I wouldn't part with them except I need the money to put things right."

Derek eyed him up, staring at him intently as if trying to see through to Alfie's soul. Seeing enough to make up his mind, Derek nodded abruptly. "Right, I'll buy them off you. Not because I need them, but because I do believe you want to get yourself sorted, and for the sake of Adam's memory if I can help make that happen then I will. The boy looked up to you," – a dagger through Alfie's heart – "and I'd like to see you deserve that again." Derek looked through the bag. "I can't give you what they're worth mind, but I'll give you a fair price."

Relief flooded through Alfie. "Thank you Derek. Thank you so much."

Derek nodded. "Come by the office tonight after five and I'll sort you out." He gave Alfie a long, hard stare. "And stay off the liquor in the meantime."

Alfie nodded earnestly, taking back his tool bag. "You can count on it." He shouldered the bag and set off for Hilda's, glancing into the van as he passed it. Harold sat immobile in the passenger seat, staring fixedly ahead as Alfie walked past.

When he got back to Hilda's he went straight upstairs to pack his few belongings. He had no more than what he'd arrived with, and it felt strange to be leaving Exeter outwardly the same as when he'd arrived. So much had happened, and he'd changed so much, that it didn't feel right somehow. In that sense, he was glad he was selling his tools to Derek. At least it felt like physically something would be left behind to match the piece of himself that would forever be in Exeter.

Once he'd finished packing, he went to find Hilda. He found her in the kitchen, boiling and pickling beetroots. The resulting purple carnage in the kitchen reminded him too much of Adam's blood on the floor and he went white and almost retched.

"Alfie, dear, are you okay? Come and sit down." Hilda ushered him back into the dining room where he sank into a chair and gulped air in, trying to fight down the urge to vomit.

Once he was feeling better, he turned to Hilda. "Joe and Matthew told you about Adam?"

She nodded sadly. "I'm so sorry, Alfie."

"It was all my fault, Hilda, and now I have to go. I have to leave. From Exeter, from the drink." She went to speak, but he kept talking, afraid that if he stopped he wouldn't get it all out. "I've sorted out a way to get the money I owe you, so don't worry about that. I just wanted to say thank you. For everything. I know I've in no way been the best lodger for you. I lost my way for a while, but I'm determined to set things right and be a better man. I just can't do that here. I hope you understand and it won't leave you out of pocket, not having a third lodger."

"Oh Alfie, bless your little cotton socks. You are good at heart, I know that. And don't worry about me, the rooms are never empty for long." She looked him over with a critical eye. "But where will you go? You still look a mess if you don't mind my saying so."

He tried to smooth down his hair self-consciously, noticing the stains on his trousers for the first time. "Honestly, Hilda, I have no idea. All the adventure has kind of been taken out of things if I'm honest." She patted him on the knee.

"I'm sure you'll think of something, me dear. Just stay off the drink and I'm sure you'll do fine."

Alfie nodded disconsolately. He'd not given a lot of thought to what came after getting out of Exeter. He should have a little money now at least, once he got the money for the tools from Derek. But it wouldn't be enough to last him long. He'd need to find something quickly.

He decided to go for a walk to clear his head and distract himself. The day loomed long ahead of him until he could see Derek, and with nothing to occupy himself he worried he'd end up back in the Crown and Goat, despite his best intentions. He'd go for a walk out of town, out to the countryside. He couldn't give in to his weak will there.

He set off in the opposite direction of the pub, just to be extra careful, and soon left the town behind. Before long he realised he was on his way back to where he'd ended up that day after his fateful meeting with Grace. How long ago that all seemed now. How much had happened, and not for the better. How quickly his life had fallen apart. Each strand that made up who he was – his family, his job, his newly-made friends – falling away until he stood there, vulnerable and exposed with nothing left except an emptied-out mockery of himself.

He was deep in these thoughts when he noticed a general commotion in the field off to his left. There were lorries parked in the field, and lots of people moving around with purpose. He stopped to observe and figure out what was going on. As he moved closer, he saw painted on the side of one of the lorries in brightly coloured letters *Crompton's Travelling Funfair*. So that was it. They must be setting up, as he'd not seen anything about it. Although he had to admit to himself that even if they'd been there for weeks he wouldn't have noticed, so deep in the drink had he been.

He wandered in to the field to take a closer look at what was going on. A stocky bald man came over to him. "Can I help you, lad?"

"Oh sorry. I just thought I'd come to have a closer look. I've never been to a funfair before. Are you chaps coming or going?"

"We're coming. Opening tomorrow for three days before moving on." He wiped his hands on his trousers before holding his hand out. "Bill's the name."

"Alfie," he returned, shaking Bill's hand. Alfie looked around him, taking it all in. "So how does this all work exactly? You travel around in the lorries going from place to place?"

Bill nodded his head. "That's pretty much it. We've got coconut shys and rides and a Whip. Me, I run the Whip." Bill said this with obvious pride.

"That must be great, travelling the country, getting to see new places," Alfie said with awe and a touch of envy.

"You could probably join us if you want," said Bill. "People are always coming and going so we're normally always looking for people to do something. Do you have a trade?"

"I'm a qualified cabinetmaker and also a carpenter," said Alfie, with the closest to excitement he'd shown for weeks. "Although I don't have any tools anymore," he said, his heart sinking just as quickly as it had risen.

"I don't think that would be too much of a problem. Ray's got loads of tools. But look, best speak to Ray about it if you're interested. He runs the team of manual labourers that set everything up and pull it down again." He looked around. "See that bloke there in the blue shirt? The one over by the lorry? That's Ray. Go and see him and he'll be able to let you know if he's got anything going. I need to go and check on how the set up of the Whip is doing." He shook Alfie's hand again. "Hope to see you around, Alfie."

Alfie looked over to where Ray was now climbing into the back of one of the lorries, turning the idea over. The more he thought about it, the more it appealed. Travelling the country, meeting new people and seeing new places. And he didn't feel like he was ready to put down new roots again just yet. He would go and see what Ray had to say.

Alfie hummed to himself as, some hours later, he walked to Derek's office with his tool bag. There was a spring in his step that there'd not been for some time and Alfie was astonished to find himself approaching cheerful. He then thought about Adam and instantly felt guilty. He stopped humming.

He'd spoken to Ray who, as it turned out, was in need of someone who knew one end of a tool from the other. He started tomorrow. Tomorrow! Once again Alfie was struck by how things could change so quickly.

He stopped outside Derek's door and looked down at his tool bag for the last time. The tools had served him well and when he'd set out with them from Fulham he'd had such high hopes.

He went in to Derek's office, struck once again by how tiny the room was. "Ah, Alfie." Derek motioned to a clear space on the floor. "Drop the bag there." Alfie did as he was told and then stood awkwardly, not knowing if he should sit or not. "So I've had a think about it today," Derek continued, "and I can give you twenty pounds for the tools. I know it's not what they're worth, but it's all I can afford."

Alfie nodded gratefully. It wasn't quite as much as he'd hoped, but it would clear his debts with a little left over. And now he had the job at the funfair, complete with bed and board, he could afford to accept less.

Derek opened the drawer of his battered desk and took out the cash, handing it over to Alfie. He held the notes for a fraction longer than necessary to catch Alfie's eye. "I wish you the best of luck, boy," he said, releasing the money. "I just hope you do what you say and sort yourself out. Adam was a good boy and he didn't deserve to go like that." Alfie nodded again, swallowing a lump in his throat.

"I know, Derek, I do. And I just wanted to say thank you for the opportunity you gave me and for the work. And I'm sorry I repaid you for it all in such a terrible way. Most of all—" He started to choke a little and fought back tears. "Most of all, I'm sorry about Adam. I don't know if there was anything I could have done to save him if I was on the roof with him, but even if I couldn't, that's where I should have been." He stopped and took a few deep breaths to get himself back under control. "Have you spoken to Adam's mum?" he asked, dreading the answer.

Derek nodded sharply. "She's devastated. Her whole world has collapsed."

Alfie nodded again, sadly. He wasn't sure what other answer he had been expecting. "Well, thanks again, Derek. Really. And I am so, so sorry."

Derek nodded and waved him out, turning his attention back to the papers in front of him. Alfie slipped out of the door, closing it behind him. The gentle thud of the door in the frame felt like a coffin lid being shut on part of his heart.

His next stop was the Crown and Goat to square up his bill. He knew he had to get in and out quickly, before his resolve could break. He'd become self-aware enough in the few days since Adam's death to realise that his will was weak. Perhaps that was what his dad had seen in him and despised.

He pushed the thought from his head – thinking about his parents was not the way to avoid drinking – took a deep breath and opened the door. He stood on the threshold and scanned the bar.

Beetroot Terry, Jack the Beaver and Barry the Burglar were all on their regular stools, and Alfie spotted another regular in a darkened corner at the back. Apart from that, it was empty.

He approached the bar, trying not to let the unmistakable smell of the pub, that melding of stale beer, cigarettes and sweat, overwhelm him and undo him. He nodded to the three on their stools, hoping to be able to keep it at that. Their conversation was clearly audible as he approached and it seemed that they were back on the Turkish lira argument Alfie had heard them have some weeks before.

"I bet you twenty pounds that I'm right," Jack was saying emphatically.

Terry snorted. "Twenty? You don't have twenty pounds."

"All right then, two bob. I bet you two bob."

"If you produce a genuine 2,000 lira note – from Turkey mind, I'm not that stupid – not only will I give you two bob, but I'll eat Barry's hat,"

"Hey!" protested Barry, "I like that hat."

Alfie turned away from them to speak to George and settle the bill, which was even higher than he'd thought it probably was. He handed over a few of his precious notes, gazing longingly at the pumps as George got him his change, which seemed to be taking an age. He tried counting to ten, then twenty. He was on his way to thirty before George handed him the few shillings in change. He thanked George and quickly walked to the door.

He paused again on the threshold and turned back to look at them all. The three on their stools, red-faced and thoroughly entrenched not only in the pub but in their merry-go-round of conversations, recycled every few weeks to be rehashed and re-argued.

He realised how easily this could have been him. How easily his life could have become nothing more than the local pub and the liquor. Waiting outside the pub every morning for the doors to open so he could seek refuge in the dim, smoky haze and forget the outside world. The morose local in the corner that newcomers would ask about and be told the story of Adam's death and the girl that got away. He could see himself there, could see his own smoky outline years from now settled in to his corner table, a pint and a glass of Old Fitz before him. His youth gone, his life gone. Still listening to arguments about the existence of 2,000 lira notes and putting chocolate in shepherd's pie.

He shook his head and opened the door, flooding the dim interior with the weak afternoon sunlight. For the first time since he had run into Grace that night that felt like a lifetime ago, he thought that maybe he might be all right.

All that was left was his final night at Hilda's and saying his goodbyes to Joe and Matthew. In some ways that would be harder than anything else. Joe and Matthew had befriended him and he'd repaid that in the worst way possible. He'd not seen them since the night he'd told them about Adam. He'd heard them downstairs of course, and had even gone so far as to go halfway down the stairs for dinner. But he'd turned around and retreated to the sanctuary of his room and his own miserable company.

Tonight, he was waiting for them in the front room, sunk into the red floral armchair as deeply as he could be. As he waited he looked around the room with the purple walls and the mismatched furniture. He realised he would miss the place. He glanced over at Hilda's porcelain animal collection, wincing when he spotted the hole she'd clearly left for the dear departed Una.

He heard the front door open and close and hurriedly stood up to meet whichever one of them it was. Matthew.

"Alfie!" said Matthew, surprised. "How are you?"

Alfie shook his head. He felt like he'd been doing an awful lot of that lately. "Not great if I'm honest. But I'm getting better." Matthew entered the room properly and Alfie sunk back into the armchair, Matthew perching on the edge of his orange ambiguity.

Alfie opened his mouth to tell Matthew that he was leaving when the front door went again, and they heard the unmistakeable clump of Joe's tread in the hallway.

"Joe!" called Matthew. "Alfie's here."

Joe stuck his head around the door and harrumphed, looking Alfie up and down with a critical eye. "You look like hell," he said bluntly. Perhaps then remembering Adam's recent passing, his face softened a little and he edged a little further into the room. "You do look sober though," he continued, "which is a miracle in itself."

Alfie nodded. "I am. And I'm planning on staying that way." He looked between the two of them. "That's actually why I've been waiting for you both. I wanted to tell you that I'm leaving Exeter. To start again. Sober."

Joe moved forward. "When?"

"Tomorrow."

"Tomorrow?! Where are you going?"

"Well, here's the crazy thing. Initially nowhere. Well, I mean… I'm joining a travelling funfair, and they're in Exeter for the next few days. But after that, who knows?"

The two of them looked at him, clearly caught off balance by the news. But then Alfie guessed it wasn't everyday someone announced that they were running away with a travelling funfair. Funny. He'd not really thought of it as running away before, but he guessed that was exactly what he was doing. Running away from the mess he'd created.

"Well," said Joe, "I can't claim that it's exactly been a lot of craic, but I do wish you all the best. And I especially hope that you manage to stay sober. Some people aren't meant for drinking and you're clearly one of them."

Matthew shot Joe a mildly reproachful look. "We both wish you all the best." He glanced at the clock on the mantelpiece. "Still a while until dinner," he said, sliding off the arm of the armchair and into the seat proper. "Enough time to discuss Arsenal's loss to Liverpool on Saturday."

For the second time in his life, Alfie slipped out of the house when everyone was asleep, his bag of belongings slung over his shoulder. He clicked the front door quietly shut behind him, stopping outside the gate to turn and give Hilda's one final look.

He'd paid up what he owed Hilda the night before and said his goodbyes to everyone. That was enough. Now, it was on to the next chapter.

Chapter 19

Alfie stared at the crossword in the *Daily Mail*, trying to keep as many answers in his head as he could. He never marked the answers in the paper, just did them in his head. He couldn't bring himself to. It was all so final. So absolute. He preferred it this way, the not marking. This way it felt more private.

He caught himself staring at his hands holding the paper. So big and once so full of power. Of rage. Now it was all Alfie could do to still the tremor in them.

He remembered looking at old people when he'd been young. How full of pity he'd been for them all. The blatant irrelevancy. He sighed. How little he'd appreciated then how full of life some of them must still have felt, at least on some days. How much of a life they'd led.

He wondered if that was how they all saw him now. The nurses, that lad that came to play the organ on Fridays, Fred. He supposed it must be. They, too, would learn in their own time.

Thinking about Fred made him think of Anne's revelation in her letter. Her boy would be about his age. He understood Anne's point in her letter that in some ways it was better that her son was in the UK so she didn't look at every boy his age and wonder. Alfie only knew one boy that age in the UK and already it had started to make him wonder.

He concentrated back on the crossword. *Does it come softly from the coop? (3).* He smiled. Almost his own clue. He thought about it for a few moments and mentally penned in coo in 2 down.

Some days were easier than others, and not just because it was an easier crossword. Some days he looked at the clues and they were an indecipherable labyrinth, with no discernible way through from clue to answer. Like he was twelve years old and staring at a cryptic crossword for the first time with his mum as she sat and patiently tried to teach him the rules. *Remember, any words like broken or assemble mean it will be an anagram,* she'd told him. He smiled to himself as he remembered her then having tell him what an anagram was.

He was particularly good at those. For some reason, he could just see the new word floating out of the old one. It was why he could always get the nine-letter word in Joan's puzzle so quickly whenever he sneakily looked over her shoulder.

His thoughts were interrupted by Julia's increasingly loud voice as she spoke to Phyllis. Her hearing, never good to begin with, seemed to be getting worse. "He's dead, Phyllis." Alfie glanced at the TV and saw that Roger Moore had died. They were showing old interview clips with him in tribute.

"Oh," Phyllis nodded. "But why would he want to kiss a little potato?" she asked, clearly confused.

It was now Julia's turn to look confused. "A little potato?" Suddenly she burst out laughing. "No Phyllis, he said he'd got to kiss Liz Taylor."

Even Alfie had to chuckle at that one. Phyllis' declining hearing had been a source of benign amusement for the nurses and a lot of the residents for weeks now. Last week while watching *Pointless*, she'd asked, very confused and more than a little outraged, why one of the contestants taught a sex class with her brother. Mavis had taken great delight in pointing out that she'd said she liked to do a stretch class before supper. Secretly they were all just waiting for Mavis' hearing to go so they could all take great delight in pointing it out to her.

*

Julia watched Alfie out of the corner of her eye. She couldn't help looking at him differently since Emma's revelation. As soon as she'd had time, the first thing she'd done was go online and start googling. The prison records allowed her to search by name, but without knowing the charge or the year, it had thrown up quite a list. And because the records were still closed, she couldn't see any useful detail beyond the name and charge anyway.

She'd stopped for a minute at this point and wondered if she was crossing some sort of line. It was Alfie's life and his secret after all. Should she really be digging through dirt that wasn't hers? But in the end, despite the admitted dubious morality, her curiosity got the better of her. Over a glass of wine she'd gone through the 300-odd search results and whittled them down to a list of what she thought were possibilities. She'd narrowed it down to six.

Was his record the one from 1957 for manslaughter? Or for sexual assault in 1959? Causing death by dangerous driving in 1962? Arson in 1973? Or the one from 1985 for fraud? Burglary in 1990? She looked at him as he sat with the paper. She thought maybe arson. Or possibly burglary.

And then there was his sister in Bath, Betty. As it turned out, there was a character called Betty Cooper from some TV show called *Riverdale*. So her initial searches came back full of news and gossip about the American actress who played her.

She'd then realised, agonisingly, that the chances of Betty not having married were slim indeed. And that all she had to go on was Betty from Bath.

In the end, she'd stumbled across an incredibly useful site that allowed her to search just by first name, location and age. It searched the electoral roll, shareholder records as well as the good old-fashioned phone book. Assuming Betty was on one of those, then she was one of eighteen Bettys over seventy in Bath whom Julia would be calling on her day off on Monday. Thank god Betty didn't live in London. She'd done a search in London out of curiosity: 1,128.

Julia had to admit she felt a thrill of excitement about it all. Sadly, this was the most interesting thing that had happened in her life since she'd left London. And the fact it was probably required some more thought. Was it time to move back? Perhaps it was. She couldn't deny that she felt stifled here. Stagnant. Originally when she'd moved here it had been a haven. Somewhere no one knew her or Siobhan and she could lick her wounds in peace, without the constant reminder of Siobhan and the life they'd built together.

As she'd sold off the pieces of their life one by one to help cover the rent until the end of the lease, she'd felt like she was selling off pieces of herself. Until she'd reached Pinewood with no more than what she could fit in her car and a shell of who she used to be.

Slowly she'd rebuilt. Both herself and her home. She'd been a regular at the charity shop buying things for the flat, and she was still on their Christmas card list. And as she'd filled her own space with her own things, so she'd filled herself with her own ideas and thoughts. It wasn't until Siobhan had left and she was on her own for the first time in six years that she'd realised how much of herself had been made up of Siobhan. How Siobhan's views on things had come to be her own.

There were the small things, like being able to watch trash TV if she felt like it, and being able to eat coconut. But there were also the big things. Like realising she was probably a Lib Dem supporter, not Labour. And that she did like Christmas, and didn't just think it was a deification of consumerism.

It had disturbed her when she'd first realised how much of herself had been subsumed by Siobhan. So much so that she'd started a list of everything that she thought she believed and challenged herself on it. She also continued to eat coconut at least once a week.

*

Hi Alfie!

Thank you so much for your kind words in your last letter.

202

I feel so much better having told someone. I'm sure it must have been the same for you.

And now on to lighter things – would you believe I went on a date on Saturday night?! An actual date! It's the first date I've been on since I met Ethan's dad and it felt kind of weird. On the one hand I felt guilty, like I was betraying Mark, but then on the other hand, he has been gone for three years now. I didn't tell Ethan of course. There's no need to upset him unless things are going to go somewhere, and nice as Finn was, it's not going to go anywhere. You know what it's like, you can't get into a relationship with everyone you meet!

Alfie stopped and thought about that. He'd only been in two relationships with women in his whole life – the only two women he'd ever met in a romantic sense. Although he'd technically never been in a relationship with Grace of course, so in fact it was only really one. So he guessed that he probably didn't know what it was like.

He also didn't know what was going on with the name Finn. It sounded like the name for some sort of car. One with fins of course, like they used to make back in the fifties.

He was a nice enough guy, there just wasn't a spark. And he was so caught up in going to the gym and working out, and trust me, that's not me! I'd much prefer to spend my Saturdays trawling through a bookstore or reading a book over a long, drawn-out coffee or two (if I didn't have Ethan of course – I sure as heck can't do any of that now!). Speaking of books, what are you reading at the moment? I've just finished Jodi Picoult's latest novel and it was brilliant.

I've also booked our flights to Florida for his birthday

trip to Disney World – he's going to be so excited. His birthday isn't for another month though so I need to make sure I keep it a secret until then. I'll try and remember to film the reaction for you – although I warn you now there will be a lot of screaming!

I have also decided to do my next international class on Russia. Seemed fitting somehow with everything going on. It's great, because I'm learning things about Russia too by planning the class. Like did you know that it has the most time zones in the world? I thought we had a lot here in the US! How many does England have? I guess just one, being so small?

Anyway, I best be off now and do some more research on Russia. Hope your Wednesday in England is going okay!

Anne

Dear Anne,

I'm glad to hear that your trip to Disney World is on course. Please do send me a video if you can, along with instructions for what to do with it of course, as I'd love to see his reaction.

I was sorry to hear your date with Finn didn't turn out as you'd hoped. I can't comment on dating too much, having only ever dated one woman and that was my wife. I imagine what a date looks like now is quite different to what it looked like back then. Do they still involve going to the pictures?

Your class on Russia sounds like it's going to be interesting.

I did not know that about the time zones. You're right that England only has one time zone. Although the UK as a whole has two, with Northern Ireland. Slatterley feels like it's stopped in time, but I'm not sure that counts as another time zone.

I realise as I sit staring at the screen that there's not a whole lot more to report this week. I am reading *House of Reckoning* by John Saul, which I have almost finished. Trevor is keeping me awake with his coughing all through the night. I'm sure it's got worse this past week. I think he's even cut down on his cheeky cigarettes, so it must be bad.

As I re-read that last paragraph I am boring even myself so I will sign off.

Until next week,

Alfie

Chapter 20

Time flew by for Alfie at the funfair. Right through 1954 with West Brom's FA Cup win and Roger Bannister's incredible four-minute mile. And a surreal solar eclipse that stopped everyone as they stared up at the sky through smoked glass or overexposed film as the skies turned dark, the temperature dropped and the few birds hanging around the fair flew back to their nests. Before Alfie knew it, it was 1955 and Winston Churchill had resigned. He wondered how Hilda had taken the news.

Alfie loved being in Crompton's Travelling Funfair. The peals of delight from whoever won the cake on the cake-walk, the screams of fear from ladies in carriages on the Whip. The smell of popcorn wafting on the breeze and bright colours and lights as far as the eye could see. And most of all, somewhere different every fourth day, or sometimes every seventh or eighth if they were in a bigger town.

There was a rhythm to life at the fair. After arriving at a new town the men would set up the mess hall tent. More marquee than tent, it served as kitchen and dining room for all the fair hands. The women would then put up the folding tables and chairs and cook dinner for everyone while the men went and pitched all the tents that they slept in, the women sleeping in the cabs of the lorries. Those men who had annoyed Ray would be tasked with digging the latrines and pitching the toilet tents. Those who had annoyed Ray even more would be given the task of striking down those same tents and filling in the latrines upon departure.

Shy, hesitant and still scarred from his experiences in Exeter, like a neglected animal rescued from the streets Alfie at first only made short forays into the world outside his own head. But gradually he relearned how to interact with people, steering well clear of the drink and keeping his head down, throwing himself into the work.

Of course, it wasn't all work. And the travelling around England also did much to soothe the raw and exposed parts of Alfie's soul. With each town left behind, with each mile he put between himself and Exeter, Alfie felt himself stand straighter, think clearer. It wasn't that he forgot about Adam and what had happened. He would not, could not, forget that as long as he lived. But as the days and months passed, it was like a weight had been lifted from his chest and he felt like he could breathe again.

So much so that one glorious and crisp spring morning he caught himself standing outside the tent he slept in, his face to the early morning sun breathing the air as deeply as he could. His eyes closed as he smiled to himself. The air even smelled sweeter. Tasted sweeter.

"Well, good morning there, handsome. You look as mighty pleased with such a beautiful morning as I do." Startled, Alfie opened his eyes to find a petite blonde looking up at him with a wide grin on her face and a sparkle in her blue eyes. Even without the accent, she looked like what Alfie had always imagined an American to look like. She had on a checked blouse tucked into a pair of tight-fitting jeans, all of which served to show off her tiny frame.

"Ah…umm…" Alfie stumbled over his tongue, suddenly thrown totally out of his depth. "Can I help you with something miss? The fair doesn't open until tonight – if you come back after five o'clock we'll be all set up."

She laughed, and the sound was like jewels tinkling as they fell. "Oh, aren't you sweet." Alfie couldn't tell if it was a statement or a question. "Honey, I'm part of the carnival. I'm here to run the coconut shy."

Alfie had heard that Bertha, the woman who had run the coconut shy for years had finally decided to move on. But he had sort of been expecting her to be replaced by a like-for-like counterpart; fat, a touch smelly and with a wart on her chin. The woman standing before him was the complete opposite to that. Granted, he was standing upwind so he couldn't tell if she was smelly or not, but Alfie suspected not.

As he continued to stand there with his mouth open, she took pity on him. "I'm Evelyn Davis," she said, holding her hand out. He looked down at her hand, unsure what to do with it. Did she expect him to shake it or kiss it? In the end he did a poor attempt at both, earning himself more jewel-tinkly laughter.

"I'm Alfie," he eventually managed to stumble out. "Alfie Cooper. I help put all the stalls and rides up and then take them all down again."

"Well, Alfie, it's real nice to meet you. Can you tell me where I can find Ray? He told me to report first thing this morning and I don't want to be late."

Alfie pointed her in the direction of Ray's tent. "Thanks, Alfie," she said with another one of her wide smiles. "I'm sure I'll see you around."

As Alfie watched her walk away, there seemed to be a void left where she'd been standing. Alfie had never met someone so small who filled so much space. She was the total opposite of himself, who despite his size always tried to be as small as possible.

"Hey Coops!" boomed a voice behind him, startling him for a second time that morning. He turned to see Andrew, one of his fellow fair workers. A red-haired Scotsman with a big red beard and more freckles than days he'd been alive, at fifty-three it was fair to say Andrew was covered in them. "Don't forget the card game tonight. I'm only five games away from you owing me one hundred pounds."

Alfie grinned. "I'll be there. I've been practising though, you know, so it might take you seven games to get there."

A few months ago, feeling ready to be around groups of company again, Alfie had joined in the regular show poker game that a few of the labourers had going. They didn't play for real money of course; Alfie would never allow himself to get in debt again after Exeter. But they did keep a tally. Betting was in denominations of one pound – ridiculously high stakes, but it made them all feel like high rollers, even if it was just on paper.

Alfie as it turned out, was either an atrocious player or just had the worst luck in history. He still wasn't quite sure. He'd played 120 games now since he started and had lost ninety-five of them. He knew how to play, but somehow the cards – or the final outcome – never seemed to reflect that. The other blokes who played – Andrew, John and Stephen – all thought it was hilarious, and Alfie's card luck had become a running joke. Alfie didn't mind. It felt good to have that camaraderie again.

John and Stephen approached and Alfie could hear John saying, "I just don't think she was looking at you, that's all. That's not to say you don't have a chance. I just don't think she was looking at you."

In their early thirties, John and Stephen had been friends since school. And when Stephen's wife had run off and left him a few years back in a scandal that shocked the whole town, the two friends had decided to jump ship and join Crompton's Travelling Funfair. It seemed most people in the fair were running from something. Perhaps that's why Alfie had found some sort of peace here. Stephen was the taller of the two, with an open and cheerful face and always ready for a laugh, even if sometimes nobody else quite knew what he was laughing at. John was shorter and darker, with olive skin and black curly hair and was altogether more quiet and thoughtful.

Named Mr Switzerland amongst the workers after Switzerland's neutrality in both wars, John could always see both sides of any argument. Unswervingly fair and just, he had become the unofficial arbiter of any disagreements between the crew. Secretly Alfie had started regarding John as a moral compass to guide his own actions by, still too scared to trust his own judgement.

"You're so pedantic, Johnno," laughed Stephen. "It doesn't matter if she was looking at me or not. What matters is that I have a chance." He winked at Alfie and Alfie blushed. After his disastrous non-courtship of Grace he was even more tongue-tied with anything concerning women now – a fact the other men had been quick to pick up on and tease him about, albeit good-naturedly. Not John though. John never teased him.

Andrew rolled his eyes at Stephen. "You always think you have a chance."

"What can I say? I'm an eternal optimist."

Andrew sighed, seemingly always a little exasperated with Stephen. "Optimism – or pure fantasy – aside, we've got a lot to get through today. Let's sort out who's doing what and crack on."

Alfie was assigned to John for the day and they were to set up the Whip and Swirl rides as well as several of the game stalls. Alfie liked all three of the men in the team, but he especially liked working with John. John got on and did the job and didn't expect a lot of banter or conversation.

This had been a particular blessing when Alfie had first joined the funfair. Still reeling from Adam's death, Alfie had retreated into himself at first, having dealings with his fellow workers only as much as was needed. He had been grateful for John's companionable silences then, and he still enjoyed them now as they let him lose himself in his work. The rhythmic rise and fall of the hammer, the cathartic pounding of nails into wood.

The day passed quickly, most of it caught up in assembling the rides. It wasn't until the early afternoon that they got to setting up the stalls. Most of the stalls were open-fronted tents, but a lot of them required carpentry work as well. Everyone helped to pitch the tents, although the women stuck to the lighter duties.

Alfie was crouched on the grass sorting through tent pegs when he saw a shadow fall in front of him. He turned to see the American woman from the morning, whose name, embarrassingly, had managed to entirely escape him.

He stood up, wiping his hands down his trousers. "Hello," he managed, frantically racking his brain for her name. "Ah…umm…"

"What can I do, Alfie?" she said, making him feel both relieved that she'd taken control of the conversation, and guilty that she'd remembered his name. "Ray gave me a few things to do, but I've finished those and I don't want to be the only one standing around with nothing to do."

He gestured to the pegs on the ground. "You can sort through these if you like. They've all got a bit muddled and they need to be grouped according to size."

She smiled that dazzlingly wide smile at him. "Why, sure thing, Alfie. I'd be glad to."

"Great, thanks…Evelyn!" Her name came back to him in a bolt of revelation, resulting in him almost shouting her name. She gave him a puzzled look before settling on the grass to sort through the pegs.

Alfie walked away to get on with his other duties, mentally slapping himself as he did so and wondering if he would always be incapable of talking to women.

That night at cards, Evelyn inevitably came up in conversation. "Did you guys see the new coconut shy girl that's started?" Stephen blew out his breath, somehow managing to do so in a suggestive manner. "Now there's a different kettle of coconuts from Bertha!" They all chuckled. Bertha had been lovely, but she'd not exactly been easy on the eye.

"She's a wee slip of a lass," said Andrew. "I do wonder if she'll be able to keep up. The fair isn't for everyone."

"She's American though," said Alfie, as if that answered Andrew's question. In Alfie's mind, American women flew planes and drove racing cars and did all manner of things that English women didn't.

The three of them turned to Alfie. "And how, pray tell, do you know that she's American?" asked Stephen. "Has our young Alfie been speaking to this blonde, nymph-like goddess and neglected to tell his colleagues? Nay, his very best mates? I am wounded sir, wounded!"

"Oh shush," said Andrew. "You do go on." He turned to Alfie. "But we would all like to know."

Alfie shrugged, embarrassed to be in the spotlight and wishing he'd kept his mouth shut. "There's not much to tell really." He outlined his two encounters with Evelyn.

Stephen sat back with a whoosh of air. "Evelyn," he rolled the name around on his tongue. "Evelyn. How do I love thee? Let me count the ways!"

John and Andrew both rolled their eyes. "This better not turn into another Rosemary," said Andrew. "None of us can take that again."

Alfie raised an enquiring eyebrow.

"Rosemary used to run the hoop-la game for about six months a few years back," explained John.

"And Stephen pined for her the whole bloody six months," interjected Andrew. "All we heard was Rosemary this and Rosemary that. Thankfully the lass had the good sense to steer well clear of him, despite his mooning."

"Don't listen to them, Alfie," Stephen leaned across conspiratorially. "I know that she loved me in her heart. She just chose not to show it." He laughed, leaving Alfie unsure if Stephen actually believed anything he was saying or not.

"Oh, for god's sake, can we just get on and play some cards?" Andrew exclaimed. He nodded in Alfie's direction. "I've got a hundred quid to win."

The following day, a hypothetical four pounds poorer, Alfie rather inevitably ran into Evelyn again. He and the other labourers relieved the game and ride operators on their lunch breaks so that the fair was always fully operational, and Alfie found himself assigned to the coconut shy.

"Why, hi there, handsome," Evelyn greeted him when he arrived. "I was hoping to see you again."

Alfie blushed. "I'm here to cover you," he said shyly.

"Cover me with what? Sugar?" She laughed her tinkly laugh again. Alfie felt his face flame, his face and ears radiating so much heat he was surprised his hair didn't catch fire. Granted, his experience with English women – or any women for that matter – was incredibly limited, but he was fairly certain English women didn't speak like this and he wasn't sure what to make of it. "Oh relax, Alfie, I'm just teasing. I didn't mean to embarrass you." She put on a serious face. "I promise I won't tease you anymore."

Alfie nodded rather awkwardly. "I'm not sure if Ray explained, but you've got thirty minutes for your break. After that I need to go and cover for someone else."

"Sure thing, Alfie." She trailed a fingernail up his arm as she walked past him. "I'll be back in a jiffy."

He watched her saunter off, her attractively rounded hips swinging suggestively, and closed his eyes, mentally counting backwards from ten to try and distract himself.

"How much for a toss?" asked a voice by his right shoulder.

Alfie jumped. "I beg your pardon?" He turned around to see a young woman with a small boy in tow.

She gestured to the piles of coconuts at the back of the tent. "How much per throw?"

"Oh…umm, it's a penny." He shook his head and focused on the job at hand, deciding he would avoid Evelyn as much he could from now on. There was no way he was ready to get involved with a woman again, especially one like that.

But despite his best intentions, life, the universe, whatever you wanted to call it, conspired to continue to throw them together. It seemed wherever he looked or wherever he was, Evelyn was there. As promised, she had stopped teasing him, although he still did his best to limit conversations.

It then all came to a head one wet and stormy night. Alfie was loading some tools into the lorry, in preparation for an early exit to the next town the following morning. It had suddenly grown dark, thick and threatening clouds obscuring what moonlight there was. He was well behind schedule and he should have finished up already.

As he picked up the final box to load into the back of the lorry there was a bright flash, followed by a sound that felt like the sky was being ripped in two. It was so loud, and so near, that Alfie dropped the box he was holding, catching the edge of his right foot. He howled in pain, hopping around on his left leg as the rain started to pour.

Evelyn came running from the front of the lorry. "Alfie, are you okay?" She took in his hopping and yelps of pain and quickly took charge. "Here," she said, going over to him and grabbing his right arm, "lean on me and let's get you into the cab and out of the rain. Then we can take a look at how bad it is."

In too much pain to protest, Alfie hobbled with her to the front of the lorry. It was awkward given their substantial height difference, and Alfie wasn't sure how much it actually helped in the end, but it was sweet of Evelyn nonetheless. He slowly and somewhat awkwardly hauled himself up into the passenger seat in the cab and closed the door against the rain. Moments later Evelyn joined him in the cab, water dripping from her hair, which was now plastered to her head. Alfie thought she looked lovely.

He turned on the interior light and eased his shoe off to inspect the damage, Evelyn peering over to take a look. A big bruise was already starting to form. "I don't think anything is broken," he said, moving his toes.

"Well, that's a relief. Granted, I've only known Ray for a short while, but he doesn't strike me as the understanding type."

"He's all right. His bark is worse than his bite."

There was an awkward silence as they both stared out of their respective windows. "Looks like a wild storm coming in," Alfie said finally.

"Uh-huh. Mind you, this ain't nothing on what we get sometimes back in the States. One winter in New York we had a huge snowstorm that near crippled the entire city for a week." She laughed and Alfie could feel the silver tinsel dancing around him. "I remember seeing folks out in the snow with tennis rackets tied to their shoes…" She caught Alfie's puzzled look. "Instead of snow shoes. That was the winter before I came to merry old England."

"When was that?"

"Nineteen fifty-two I arrived in Cornwall. On the maiden voyage of the *United States*," she said proudly. Alfie nodded, but it obviously wasn't the reaction she was after. "The record-breaking voyage," she pressed, still waiting for recognition. Alfie looked at her blankly. She sighed. "The *SS United States*. Her maiden voyage was from New York Harbour to Cornwall in July of 1952. We broke the world record for the fastest time – three days, ten hours and forty minutes." She was so proud Alfie was beginning to wonder if she was part of the crew. He decided to ask.

That silver tinsel again. "Oh lord, no! I was just a passenger. But how many people get to say that they were part of breaking a world record?"

Alfie had to concede that it wasn't very many.

"And what about you Alfie? Tell me about yourself. It looks like we're stuck in the cab of this truck for a while until there's a break in the rain."

Alfie wasn't quite sure where to start. He hated talking about himself and he'd done well since joining the fair to avoid too many questions about his past. It was still something he didn't want to talk about. He decided to focus on his life before Exeter.

"I'm from London. I left to get out and see some of the world."

"That's why I left New York! I figure there's a whole world out there to explore! And where better to start than England?"

Alfie shrugged. "I suppose. I've never been anywhere else so I wouldn't know. But I've always thought America would be fun to see."

She nodded. "America is great. But we don't have the history you have here. Or Austen." She got a dreamy, far-away look. "I love Austen."

"Jane Austen?"

"Mm-hmm. My teacher at school was from England and had all the books and she lent them to me. *Pride and Prejudice*, *Mansfield Park*. I love all of them. But *Persuasion* is my favourite." She sighed and fell back against the seat. "Captain Wentworth is a dream."

Having never read any Austen, Alfie was somewhat at a loss for what to say. Thankfully, Evelyn was proving so much of a chatterbox that he didn't really have to say much at all. He quite liked that.

"I know everyone is always wild about Mr Darcy, but I guess I like to buck the trend. That's probably why I ran away."

Alfie looked at her sharply. "You ran away?"

"From my parents. They just didn't understand that I wanted to travel and see the world. They wanted me to settle down and get married and play the dutiful housewife and that was just never going to be me." She stopped. "You probably think I'm some sort of loose woman, setting off on my own to the other side of the world, and only nineteen, but I promise I'm not."

He shook his head emphatically. "No, not at all. In fact, I ran away from my parents too."

"You did?"

"I just had to get away from them. They were suffocating me." He swallowed. The conversation was veering dangerously close to Exeter and Adam.

"I thought we were kindred spirits!" she exclaimed, reaching over and squeezing his forearm. A small hand-shaped fire left behind.

He had felt so comfortable sitting here talking with Evelyn that for a time he'd forgotten his habitual awkwardness. But her touch, and the reminder of Exeter, brought him crashing back to his usual levels of discomfort and he found himself looking out the window to see if the rain had eased off enough for him to escape.

She sensed his desire to go. "Please don't leave, Alfie. I've so enjoyed talking with you just now. Besides, you should probably rest your foot a little more just to be safe."

He stared at the glovebox in front of him, torn between wanting to go and wanting to stay. "You don't even have to talk much," she continued. "I know you're not really a talker." She gave a small laugh. "Besides, I know I talk enough for two people. The danger of being an only child I guess. No one to talk to growing up means I haven't stopped talking since I became an adult."

"No brothers or sisters?" Alfie asked, surprised. He wasn't sure he knew anyone who was an only child. He knew people who were the only siblings left following the war, but everyone he'd grown up with had been one of at least two siblings, more often one of three or four, sometimes five. He'd even had one schoolmate, William, who had been one of nine.

"No, it was just me." She laughed again, and this time it wasn't silver tinsel, but brass. "I was enough of an inconvenience to my mother on my own. I think the thought of the impact two children would have on her social life was enough to sufficiently turn her off any more." She paused before shaking her head and turning her wide smile on him. "But that's me. What about you? Do you have any brothers or sisters?"

"Two sisters. Doris who is two years older than me and very disapproving of pretty much everything and everyone. And Betty. Betty is four years younger than me and the total opposite of both me and Doris."

"What do you mean?"

Alfie shrugged. "She's the best of us. She's so generous and accepting and warm-hearted, which is the total opposite of Doris. And she's so confident in herself and comfortable around people. Which, as you've probably noticed, is the opposite of me," he laughed self-consciously.

"I think you do a lot better than you think."

"Betty and I were going to leave London and set up somewhere together. I was going to start my own carpentry business and she was going to have a dress shop." He looked away. "The naïve dreams of youth, I guess."

"But why does it have to be just a dream? You can still have that can't you?"

"I used to think so but I don't know anymore. Life got all a bit turned upside down and I'm still trying to figure out which way is up."

"Shoot, I don't think I've ever known which way is up. Don't let that stop you, Alfie Cooper."

There was another silence, but this time a comfortable and companionable one as they both pondered life and the future. Eventually Evelyn broke the silence. "Well, I think the rain has let up about as much as it's going to. Let's get some food before it all gets eaten." She turned to him and gave him another one of her big wild smiles. "Thanks for waiting out the rain with me, Alfie."

"My pleasure, Evelyn," he said, and surprised himself by actually meaning it.

"Evie," she said. "Call me Evie."

In the weeks following that night he found himself constantly thinking about Evelyn. Evie. That laugh. That smile. The way her eyes twinkled when she tilted her head back to look up at him. He found himself making excuses to see her. To be near her. A few times he was lucky enough to be the one responsible for covering her lunch break, and so he got a few precious moments at the start and end of that break to talk to her.

This was already so much more than what he'd had with Grace – or more to the point, not had with Grace – he could see that now. But he was careful not to let himself get carried away. There were no cottages in the sky with yellow daisies. He simply found himself enjoying Evie's company. He relaxed into it, and discovered that once he relaxed he stopped agonising so much about what to say. He still didn't say overly much – he'd never been a big talker – but when he did speak it was easier, more natural.

The fair finished up in St Helens and moved on to Warrington. It wasn't far and so they got there early enough to set the stalls and rides up in time for the fair to open that night.

Alfie, Andrew, John and Stephen all regrouped to assign tasks, and Alfie found himself volunteering to set up the coconut shy tent. Andrew gave him a knowing look when he did so but said nothing. John gave a small smile but also said nothing. Stephen, on the other hand, wasn't going to give up his chances lying down. "Hang on there, cowboy. We all want to set up the stall with the pretty American. I'll flip you for it."

Alfie groaned. He had awful luck with coins – and cards – and everyone knew it. Flip a coin a hundred times and ninety-five times he'd call it wrong. He'd played a hypothetical game with Stephen one night where Stephen had flipped a shilling and asked Alfie to choose heads or tails. If he guessed right, he kept the coin. If he guessed wrong, he had to give Stephen a shilling. Naturally, Alfie had called it wrong and had dutifully handed over the stake. Stephen had then challenged him to a pretend game of double or nothing, whereby the stakes were doubled each correct, or incorrect, guess Alfie made. Within a few minutes Alfie owed Stephen somewhere in the region of one million pretend pounds.

Not wanting to appear overly eager to set up Evelyn's stall and invite scrutiny as to why, Alfie acquiesced to the coin showdown. Alfie had tried everything over the years to beat his own luck with these things. Going with his first instinct, doing the opposite of his first instinct. Using external cues to help make his call. None of it worked. He feared in a previous life he'd angered whichever ancient god was responsible for gambling.

"What's your call?" asked Stephen, sending a shiny new penny high into the air.

Alfie screwed up his eyes and sent a quick mental plea to the heavens. "Heads."

"Well, bugger me!" said Stephen. "You finally got one!"

"What? Really?"

"Aye," said Andrew, "looks like your luck may finally be in, lad. Use it well." He winked at Alfie and then addressed the group. "Right, let's get cracking then, shall we?"

Having won the right to set up Evie's tent, Alfie found himself overcome with shyness and went to set up the tent without finding her first. He was halfway through pitching the tent when she arrived carrying a bag of coconuts to set up as prizes.

"Well, hey there, Alfie. I didn't realise you were setting this up already – I was expecting you to holler. It was only because Andrew told me that I knew you'd started."

"Sorry," Alfie mumbled, not quite sure what to say. There was no rule to say that he was meant to tell her that he'd started pitching the tent. After all, she couldn't do anything until it was up. But he had to agree it was odd he'd not told her he was going to start. He couldn't even explain to himself why he hadn't. Fortunately Evie seemed happy to let it go.

She shrugged. "Well, that's okay. It gave me time to finish my crossword." She started to unpack the coconuts next to the tent.

"You do crosswords?" he asked, crouching down to hammer in a tent peg.

"Oh sure. I love the one in *The Times*. The cryptic one that is. I do it every week. I don't usually get all of them though. Some of them are really hard!"

"Well, if you ever fancied some help with them, I'd be happy to oblige. I used to do the cryptics on the weekend with my mum when I was younger." Alfie kept his eyes resolutely glued to the tent peg he was positioning in the ground.

"Why, thank you, Alfie Cooper. I'll be sure to take you up on that very kind offer." He heard her laugh softly behind him. "And maybe when I do you'll be able to look at me."

He blushed and started to mumble something when she put her hand gently on his shoulder. "It's okay, Alfie. Baby steps are fine with me."

He felt awkward crouched down while she was standing and stood up abruptly, almost knocking Evie over in the process. She grabbed his arm to steady herself and his skin burst into glorious flames. "Way to knock a girl off her feet!" she laughed.

"Oh, I'm so sorry!" he exclaimed, flustered.

"It's okay, Alfie. Really." She looked up through her fluttering eyelashes. "You can knock me down anytime."

He didn't know what to say to that. He was pretty sure Evie was flirting with him, but it was such an unfamiliar experience he couldn't be sure. Or be sure how he was meant to respond. For she did seem to be waiting for some sort of response. Caught though, in a perpetual spin of uncertainty on all fronts, in the end he said nothing.

Eventually she stepped back and picked up the bag she'd brought the coconuts in. "Well, I guess I better keep working. I don't want Ray to fire me. Bye, Alfie. Come do a crossword with me sometime, won't you?"

*

Later that night Alfie sought out John for some advice. He'd turned the encounter with Evie over and over in his head. And not just that one but all of them. Playing them and replaying them over and over again. He liked her. He really did. But he was so scared after everything with Grace that he felt paralysed with doubt. And fear. He couldn't risk it again. He just couldn't. And he liked his life here at the fair. He didn't want to risk messing it all up.

Having got nowhere all day within his own head, Alfie had decided John's very even shoulders and level head might be able to bring some order to the chaos of his thoughts.

As they didn't have to strike down or set up the next morning, this evening was the designated card night. Obviously not wanting to have the conversation in front of the others, Alfie went to find John before dinner. He found him sat on a toolbox in a patch of fading sunlight polishing his shoes.

"Mind if I join you?"

"By all means," John waved his hand, shoe stuck on the end. "Pull up some grass." Alfie flopped on the ground next to John, somewhat awkwardly arranging his long limbs.

John continued to methodically polish his shoe, and Alfie found the rhythmic sound of the brush over the leather a little hypnotic. An easy silence settled over them, and Alfie thought that he could quite happily sit there forever in the fading light. It reminded him of afternoons spent in Bishops Park with Betty. They would lie under the oak tree in the far south-west corner and stare up at the sky, building their imagined future together. Betty's store, his carpentry business. The cottage with the daffodils. He mentally recoiled, that future now forever tainted. It shattered the tranquillity he'd been feeling and gave him the push he needed to begin the conversation with John. And it was a conversation that he needed to start. He knew John well enough by now to know that John would happily sit in silence if he felt he didn't have anything to say.

Knowing he needed to broach the subject and knowing how to go about it, though, were two totally different matters. With his hands furiously pulling up bits of grass, he gave it a go. "So…ahh… John. I wanted to… I wanted to get your take on something."

John nodded, head still bent over his now military-standard polished right shoe. "Go on."

"I…I…ah…" Alfie fumbled for the right words, the pile of exhumed grass growing around him.

"This wouldn't be about Miss Davies, would it?" asked John mildly, his brush not breaking rhythm.

Alfie flushed. "Is it that obvious?"

John gave a small shrug and put his right shoe carefully down next to him, picking up its mate and starting to rub in the polish in small circular motions. "Probably not to most unless they're in direct proximity."

Alfie felt himself relax, relieved his feelings for Evie weren't the gossip of the fair. "You like her," said John, looking up from his shoe. When Alfie nodded, John turned his attention back to his shoe before continuing. "But you don't know how to make that jump between liking her and telling her that you like her." Alfie nodded again. John was making this a lot easier for him than he'd anticipated. "Am I right in thinking that you don't have a lot of experience with women, Alfie?"

Alfie gave a tight smile. "No good experiences anyhow."

"Ah. Well, I won't pry. That's your own business." Alfie silently blessed John for his discretion. "But my advice would be to just be yourself. I know that's not exactly ground breaking, but it's the only path to follow if you want the relationship to succeed. If you're not true to yourself then how can you possibly expect her to be?"

Polish applied, he set down the cloth and picked up the small brush again. But rather than applying the brush, he paused. "When I met my wife I was terrified too. She was beautiful and smart and she could have had her pick. It took me a long time to work up the courage to ask her out. Too long." John paused and swallowed before continuing. "After she died, I just kept thinking that if only I'd worked up the courage sooner we would have had all that time together." John fixed him with a solemn stare. "If the war taught me anything, Alfie, it's that life is short. Don't waste your life wondering."

"But what if I mess it up? I messed up the last one terribly – so very terribly, John, you have no idea. It was the darkest time of my life and I'm terrified that if it doesn't go well it will mess up everything again. And I like it here."

"Courage, lad. You just need to pluck up the courage and ask her out. We've got the first night off at the next stop as we'll get there too late to set anything up. Take her out for a drink." John paused and looked askance at Alfie. "Although I'm minded you don't drink, do you? I've never seen you indulge in any liquor."

Alfie gave a small shake of his head. "I won't touch the stuff anymore."

John nodded. "A sensible decision if you ask me. A couple of fingers of whisky at Christmas is about all I drink myself. I've never liked the taste of most of it anyhow." Left shoe now also polished to the same immaculate standard as its mate, John began to carefully pack the bits back into a battered box. "But I reckon that's probably enough talking about it." He stood and nodded in the direction of the tent where the ladies were setting up the tables for dinner. "Harness your courage, Alfie. Don't overthink it and just ask her. Oh, and don't forget to breathe." John gave him an encouraging nod and walked back towards the lorries.

Easy for you to say, Alfie thought, as he watched John walk away. He sat for a few moments longer, revelling in some time alone to think. He'd never taken a woman out before. The thought was terrifying. At least paying for it wouldn't be a problem. Although the wages on the funfair were small, not needing to pay for bed or board – and not spending a fortune on Old Fitz or down the pub – meant he'd been able to save most of what he'd been paid.

Closing his eyes and muttering a small prayer to a god he didn't believe in, he did as John instructed and screwed up his courage. He would do it. Tonight. He would ask Evie out tonight and trust himself to deal with whatever came next.

*

223

He felt as nervous as he imagined schoolgirls must feel at their first school dance. Or possibly schoolboys too. He'd never been allowed to go to his school dance so he didn't know. He had an army of butterflies in his stomach and there was a faint sheen of perspiration on his brow he couldn't get rid of, no matter how often he dabbed it dry. He'd splashed some water around out of a bucket and had put on his least smelly shirt. And he'd done his best to bring his unruly hair into line. Now, it was all up to him not to put his foot in it and be able to master the skills needed to ask a girl out. He wasn't hopeful.

As he approached the mess tent, he saw her inside talking to Lydia, the lady who ran the pop-gun tent. Despite being so petite, to Alfie Evie stood out from the crowd. Her blonde hair gleamed and he wanted so desperately to run his hands through it. He bet it smelled like strawberries.

Thinking of strawberries reminded him of family trips out to the country to go strawberry picking. He and Betty would run out into the field and pick the berries all higgledy-piggledy, much to Doris' extreme distaste. Doris never did anything other than methodically. He felt a strong pang of regret that things had had to turn out the way they had with his family. He still got the odd letter from Betty, but he'd not seen or heard from the rest of his family since he'd left London. He was sad that leading his own life, claiming his own freedom, had had to come at the cost of his relationship with his family, but so be it. They were the ones who had dictated those terms, not he.

He shook his head to clear himself of the sad turn his thoughts had taken and refocused on Evie. She was wearing a fetching blue dress that showed off her tiny waist, and Alfie couldn't help but think she looked like Cinderella. He'd heard some of the other men say Evie wasn't as pretty as she thought she was. That her nose was too big, her eyes too close together. But Alfie couldn't understand what they were talking about. She was beautiful.

He paused outside the tent and tried to gather the shreds of his courage, taking a few deep breaths to try and convince his heart to stay inside his chest. Without giving himself time to question what he was doing, he strode in and went straight over to Evie, who was on her way to deposit some dirty plates in the washing up bucket.

"Oh! Alfie, you startled me! You're lucky you got here in time, I think most of the food is gone." She stopped and stared at him. "Alfie, what is it? Is something wrong?"

Now or never. It was now or never. Now. Or Never. Now. Now, Alfie. Now, Alfie!

"Evie, will you go out with me?" he blurted out. He could feel his face burning, positive that everyone in the tent was staring at him and laughing.

"Oh! Oh Alfie…I…"

He nodded curtly. "You don't want to. It's fine, I understand." Fighting back tears, he turned quickly on his heel and strode out of the tent as quickly as he'd marched in. Stupid. How stupid he'd been. He should have known better. Should have just kept his mouth shut.

"Alfie!" He heard Evie call out behind him. "Alfie wait!" He turned around and saw her running after him. "Alfie," she puffed as she caught up with him, "I would like to go out with you. I would like that very much. You just caught me by surprise, that's all. The look you had on your face, I thought something was wrong." She stopped talking and reached for him, her tiny hand lost in his huge one. "But I would love to go out with you, Alfie Cooper. I've been waiting weeks and weeks for you to ask, haven't I?"

He couldn't believe his ears and a huge grin broke out on his face. "Really? You really want to?"

She nodded, her blue eyes looking up into his. "Really."

As he looked down at her, he noticed she only had one shoe on. "What happened to your shoe?"

She gestured behind her, back towards the tent. "It fell off when I started running after you."

Alfie burst out laughing, an involuntary and much needed release of so many conflicting emotions, while Evie looked at him confused at how her shoe falling off could be so funny. His own Cinderella indeed.

Chapter 21

"You were a real smooth operator, weren't you?" snorted Fred, laughing.

Alfie glared at him. "And how many girls have you asked out in your life?" he snapped.

Fred physically recoiled, holding up his hands to ward off Alfie's displeasure. "Okay, okay, I'm sorry. Jeez, you're touchy."

Alfie cursed himself for letting Fred get under his skin. It wasn't the boy's fault. He didn't know. "No, I'm sorry. Evelyn just meant a lot to me."

Fred shrugged to show his indifference. "So how was your date anyway?"

Alfie smiled as he remembered the evening. He'd been filled with such a sense of anticipation beforehand that he'd barely been able to eat. In fact, he'd been lucky that he'd not been fired, his head was in the clouds so much that week. "I took her to the pictures. *20,000 Leagues Under the Sea* was playing. We shared a bag of sweets." He chuckled. "The film was Stephen's idea. Take her to something scary so she'd get frightened and want my protection."

Fred looked at him sceptically. "Do people actually do that?"

"Well, I did. It worked too. In the scene where—" He stopped and looked at Fred. "You've got no idea what I'm talking about, do you? Well, never mind. Suffice to say that in a scary part of the film she did grab my arm. And she never let go the rest of the film."

The park had disappeared and he was back in the picture theatre, Evie's hands wrapped tight around his left arm as Ned discovered the human skulls and Nemo's boat was pursued by the cannibals. He closed his eyes and he could taste the sweets. Smell the roses in Evie's hair as she rested her head on his shoulder. It had smelled like roses, not strawberries.

A child's shriek of pain as she fell off her bike broke his spell, the tatters of his memory falling to the ground. He sighed. If only. If only things had turned out differently. He'd been working up to talking about Evie and it was just as hard, just as painful, as he'd imagined it would be.

Fred was staring at him, probably wondering if he'd finally lost his marbles. "I'm all right, lad. But it is time for me to go. The delights of Pinewood's pea and ham soup await."

As he got himself up off the bench he felt heavy. Heavier than before he'd sat down. So many memories weighing him down. He'd thought telling the boy would make him feel lighter, but Alfie couldn't remember ever feeling this heavy.

Eyes downcast, Alfie shuffled his way back to Pinewood, leaving a breadcrumb trail of regret.

Julia watched Trevor as he left the day room, an almost visible ball of disappointment being kicked along by his slippered feet. There had been no James again today and Julia knew Trevor got his hopes up every week only to have them dashed. She supposed in this place you had to hold tight to even the tiniest thing to look forward to.

She saw Trevor pause as a coughing fit overcame him. His coughing had been getting worse this past week, and she made a mental note to get the doctor in to look at him. Suddenly he put his hand out to grab a chair before collapsing in to it.

She ran over to him. "Trevor, are you all right?" She could hear him struggling to breathe and his eyes had a panicked look. The air sounded like it was being strangled out of him. "Helen, call an ambulance!" she yelled across the room as she grabbed Trevor's hand. "It's going to be fine, Trevor. I'll get your oxygen and that will get you through until the ambulance gets here. You'll be okay." He gave her hand the smallest of squeezes as his eyes started to glaze over. She ran.

Alfie watched Joan tug at the blanket on her legs as she sat and clearly worried about Trevor, her tablet and nine-letter word puzzle ignored and evidently forgotten. The nurses had been giving him updates on Trevor and he thought it wasn't sounding particularly hopeful. But perhaps that was just his own natural pessimism. Or wishful thinking.

He thought he should probably go and speak to her. Try and reassure her, or at least comfort her in her hour of need. But then every time he was about to go to her someone else beat him to it. Another resident or one of the nurses. People were falling over themselves to try and comfort her, lovely woman as she was.

The nurse who read the Lee Child books walked past and stopped. "Joan, are you okay?" Joan gave a small, tight smile and nodded her head almost imperceptibly. The nurse looked at her more closely, her head cocked to one side. "All your lipstick has come off. I'll go and grab it for you and you can put some more on. Can't have you going around with naked lips!" She smiled at Joan and went off in search of lipstick.

Alfie watched Joan sigh and reach for her tablet, noticing a tremor in her hands as she did so. For her sake he hoped Trevor came back, even if it did mean having to live with the sod for a few more years.

She had been number twelve. By then Julia had been a little on autopilot with her opening gambit. Did you used to be called Betty Cooper? Do you have a brother called Alfie? After some initial confusion, she'd realised excitedly that she did indeed have the right Betty.

But her excitement had quickly turned to dust when Betty

brushed her off. Yes, she had a brother. No, she didn't want to talk about him. But thank you for calling.

Julia had sat staring at the phone. In none of the scenarios she'd played out in her head had this happened. She'd imagined tears – of joy at the chance to be reconnected, of anger as Betty recounted why they were estranged. She'd imagined excited, elderly exclamations and gushing praises of thanks for bringing her back to her brother. But in all scenarios, even the one with angry tears, the conversation had ended with Betty thanking Julia and promising to be up to visit that coming Saturday to see her brother. She had not imagined the polite thank you and the quiet click as Betty hung up.

She felt deflated. The mystery and the chase of Alfie and his story had utterly captivated her. She knew she'd become a little obsessed by it all – after all, what did it matter to her if he was in jail, why he was in jail? What did it matter to her if he did have family but just never saw them? What difference to her if he had no friends or connections?

But it did matter to her and she knew why. It was because she was worried she was going to end up like him. She was essentially estranged from her own parents, even taking into account the difficulty in remaining close when you lived on opposite sides of the world. She was single, with no prospect of that changing anytime soon and she had few, if any, genuine friends. She had worked every Christmas Day since she started at Pinewood, as she had no one to share it with. She felt like she was sleep-walking through her life, disconnected from everyone around her. And in that disconnection she felt herself slowly dying. Emotionally, not physically – she wasn't that dramatic. But dying emotionally nonetheless. Withering away without the nourishment of genuine human interaction. Someone she was connected to. In short, she saw herself heading for exactly where Alfie was now and she was desperate to stop it.

She'd thought for a while that getting back with Siobhan might be the answer, but even in her darkest, most malnourished hours, she'd known in her heart of hearts that it wasn't right. What was the motivational quote she always saw people posting on Facebook after a breakup? It always had clouds or a sunrise in the background. Something about better to be alone for the right reasons that with someone for the wrong ones. True, but cold comfort on yet another lonely and empty Saturday night.

She'd been worried Siobhan was going to be devastated when she told her firmly no, after she'd clearly been softening to the idea. But in true Siobhan fashion, she'd shrugged it off and said she'd decided to go travelling anyway. Far from making Julia feel relieved that she'd clearly made the right decision, it just made her sad. Or, if she was honest, even more sad.

And even though she was aware of how much she was throwing herself in to uncovering Alfie's story, she hadn't realised how emotionally invested she was until she'd heard that soft click as Betty hung up. She'd sat staring at the black screen of her mobile, not quite sure what to do next. That was it. It was over. There was nowhere to go from here. She couldn't access the prison records, not without inhabiting some sort of spy thriller movie and knowing someone who was willing to break the law and hack into them. So that was it. Her one and only proper lead was dead in the water. It was over. She was done.

The envelope was blinking at him, showing him the red '1' which meant Anne had written to him. He tried to remember what had been in her last letter. What had been in his last letter? But he was struggling to remember. He'd found that more and more lately, this trouble recalling things. It seemed the more he remembered his past, his old life, the harder it got to remember what was going on in his current one.

He wondered if it was the same for the others. He knew it was common for old people to get lost in memories of their yesteryears. The closer you got to the end of your life the more vividly you remembered the beginning. He'd certainly overheard Joan talking about dancing with the soldiers in her youth. Phyllis would talk at length about her childhood sweetheart Bob and the small hardware shop he'd owned. And they were just the ones he'd accidentally remembered. But he wondered if their here and now was becoming hazier too as they lost themselves in those memories, or if it was just him. Sometimes he felt like he was losing his grip on the present. Like trying to grasp a bar of wet soap.

He realised he was still staring at the blinking envelope and that his mind had been wandering again. He knew he didn't have time to go back and read past letters to remember what had been said – not now he'd wasted so much time sitting there like an old fool lost in his thoughts – so he'd just have to hope that Anne's latest letter jogged his memory.

Hi Alfie,

So tell me all about your wife! How did you meet her? Were you married long? What was she like? I can't believe it took you so long to tell me you were married! I say were as I couldn't help but notice you used the past tense. So actually apologies if this is something you don't want to talk about. And if that's the case then just ignore everything I've written so far!

He'd told her about Evie? Alfie sat for a few minutes, trying to gather his scattered thoughts. No, he thought he'd just mentioned being married. Not the rest. He'd remember if he'd told her about the rest.

My lesson on Russia was real good. There are so many super interesting facts about the place that it was easy to get the kids involved. The fact it has the world's largest McDonald's sure did help! Apparently the world's largest one used to be in London temporarily when you had the Olympics, but you took it down. I don't think it ever would have gotten dismantled here – I think there would have been riots!

In other news, Finn called asking if I'd like to go out again. I don't know why but I said yes. And I know I said that there wasn't a spark and that it wasn't going to go anywhere, but it was so nice to get out. To dress up for once and do my hair nice. I thought one more date couldn't hurt... And everyone deserves a second chance right?

My brother is also getting married! Did I tell you I had a brother in Michigan? I think maybe I didn't so maybe that makes us even for you not telling me you were married! He's engaged to a real nice girl called Aimee. She's a nurse and he's a police officer so between the two of them they're like the ideal crisis couple! I know it's hard for them sometimes though, both doing shifts. I think sometimes they're like ships in the night, only speaking to each other via notes they leave on the fridge. Which must be weird – almost like being single within a relationship. Still, they seem to be making it work somehow!

Anyway, I better get on and make Ethan's lunch for tomorrow. And *The Bachelor* is starting soon and I don't want to miss the start!

Take care Alfie and I hope Trevor isn't keeping you awake too much.

Anne

Dear Anne,

You asked for me to tell you some more about my wife, so here goes. She was American, like you, and we met on the funfair. She ran the coconut shy. She was a tiny little thing and had hair that shone like gold and a laugh that

used to tinkle like silver. Her name was Evie. Well, actually
her name was Evelyn, but to me she was Evie.

Alfie stopped typing, his eyes closed as he remembered that laugh,
that smile that was so big and so bright that it lit up the world. Lit
up his world.

You asked about Trevor and if he was still keeping me
awake and the answer is no. The poor old bugger
collapsed on Saturday and has been in hospital ever since.
Pneumonia on top of his emphysema. He's in a pretty bad
way from what the nurses at Pinewood tell me. I can't
think he'll last long. Joan is distraught at the thought not
only of him being so ill, but also of him being all alone in
the hospital. I'm sure his daughter would have gone to see
him, but I doubt his shit of a son

Alfie stopped. He shouldn't swear with Anne. Not even when it
came to James.

But I doubt his son will show up. I hope he does visit
before the end, for Trevor's sake.

That is good news about your brother. And I don't believe
you had told me you had a brother, so that does indeed
make us even. They sound like a very upstanding couple
and I do wish them all the best.

I also did not know that about McDonald's, but then I've
only ever eaten in one a handful of times. I seem to recall
everything tasting like salty cardboard. But I know they're
very popular so people obviously like them. Does Ethan
like McDonald's? Or perhaps he prefers one of the others
ones? There does seem to be many more fast food chains
in America than there is here.

I hope your second date with Finn goes better than the first and I'm sure you'll look lovely. Please do let me know how it goes.

Warm regards,

Alfie

Chapter 22

The day after his date with Evie he walked on cloud nine all day, completely distracted. He'd been on a date! An actual date! And he hadn't tripped over his own feet, either metaphorically or literally.

After the pictures they had gone for ice cream and discovered they both disliked strawberry flavour. They had shared a scoop of chocolate instead, Evie insisting that she couldn't possibly manage a whole scoop on her own.

The conversation had flowed as easily as the fizzy drink, or soda as Evie called it.

"So how are you finding working at Crompton's," he'd asked her between slurps of Coca-Cola.

"It's certainly an adventure! My parents would be horrified if they knew I was travelling around with a carnival and sleeping in the cab of a truck every night. But that just makes it all the better." She'd smiled a sneaky smile, reminding Alfie of a naughty child. He laughed, delighting in her mischievousness. He also loved how she called it a carnival.

Her smile had clouded over a little then. "I just wish I got along with the other gals a bit better. Apart from Lydia I'm not that friendly with any of them and it can get a bit lonesome sometimes."

"Lydia is nice," he said, thinking of the slightly pasty woman from Lancashire who ran the pop-gun tent and was always ready with a grin and a bawdy laugh.

"She is. The rest of them not so much though. I did try, Alfie, honest I did. But they're just all so stuck up and so…so English!" She stopped and put her hand over her mouth. "Oh, Alfie, I'm sorry, I didn't mean…"

Alfie felt himself fall headfirst over a cliff for her in that moment, she looked so cute. "It's okay, some of them are a bit stuck up," he agreed conspiratorially.

"And old," Evie added, giggling.

"And ugly." Alfie burst out laughing then, unable to contain his mirth. They had laughed until they'd cried, drawing looks from several other patrons in the café.

Alfie smiled again to himself now, remembering it. He promised himself that if things worked out with Evie he would be her friend as well as her… He didn't dare finish that sentence even in his own head without blushing. But he would fill that void for her.

Later, back at the funfair in front of her lorry, he'd scuffed his feet and floundered as to how to end the evening. Should he kiss her? Did she want him to kiss her? Should he kiss her on the cheek or on the lips? Or on the back of her hand? Did people even do that anymore? In the end Evie had taken it out of his hands, wrapping her hands around his neck to draw his face down and kiss him on the lips. He thought his head would explode.

"Thank you for a lovely evening, Alfie," she'd smiled at him before jumping into the cab.

His lips had felt like they were on fire and he'd walked in a total daze back to his tent before lying down and barely sleeping all night as he replayed the whole night – but particularly the kiss – over and over in his head.

The following morning – this morning   Andrew had assigned him Evie's lunch cover with a knowing wink. Now, as he approached the coconut shy, his heart was in his throat. Even though the evening had clearly ended well, he was still nervous about seeing her.

He realised he should have bought her some flowers. That was what gentlemen did when they went out with girls, wasn't it? Turn up on the doorstep with flowers and chocolates? Admittedly, the cab of a truck wasn't the most traditional of doorsteps, but still, it was an oversight he was now kicking himself for.

He nervously sidled up to the coconut shy, hovering until she'd handed a coconut to the couple inside and noticed him.

Her face lit up when she saw him. "Alfie! There you are!" Encouraged, he finally entered the tent. "I was hoping they'd send you today."

"You were?"

"Well, of course, silly! Why wouldn't I? We had such a lovely time last night." Her brow furrowed in an impossibly cute way. "Well, at least I thought we did. Didn't we?"

"Oh yes!" he burst out. "We did. Well, at least I did. And I thought you did but I didn't know and I didn't want to assume because the last time I assumed anything it was just awful and I hoped you did, but I didn't know." Alfie stopped, realising he was babbling and that Evie was laughing at him.

"Oh Alfie. You really are so incredibly sweet." She grabbed his arm. Almost the way she had done in the picture theatre but a little different. This time it was softer. "I'm sure we'll both have a lovely time again on our second date too, once you get around to asking me out on one."

He gulped. This was better than anything he could have hoped for. Even so, the words still came awkwardly. "Ah, so, well Evie… umm…I guess I should…ah… Would you like to go out again with me?"

She laughed that silver tinsel laugh. "Oh Alfie, you are just adorable. I would love to." She sashayed out of the tent, leaving him almost levitating with happiness in amongst the coconuts. "Oh and Alfie," she called over her shoulder, "I wouldn't say no to some flowers this time."

*

237

The next three months of his life passed by in a blissful whirl. Every night off he and Evie would go out on a date, no matter which town they happened to find themselves in. They were officially an item, and Alfie couldn't remember ever feeling this happy.

All his reservations about women, about courting, everything he'd been scared about since it had all gone so wrong in Exeter, had evaporated. Dispelled into nothing more than smoke by the sheer force of Evie and of his love for her.

And he was in love, he realised. At the same time, he also saw that what he'd felt for Grace had been nothing more than infatuation. Obsessive infatuation, granted, but infatuation nonetheless. What he felt for Evie was so much more. She brought out the best in him. And when he was with her, for the first time that he'd ever known he wasn't agonising over what he said or what he did. As they'd got to know each other he'd relaxed into himself, into them, and become a better version of himself.

Lately they'd taken to staying at the fair rather than going out, holing up in the cab of the lorry, just the two of them, talking into the night or doing one of Evie's crosswords by the light of an oil lamp. He liked those nights and he looked forward to them. They felt comfortable, and like the sort of home he'd always wished he'd had, rather than his own angular upbringing where he could never find somewhere soft to sit.

And at the end of the night, before they went their separate ways, Evie would read him a chapter of *Persuasion*. A bedtime story of sorts. He found himself enjoying the story much more than he thought he would. Although he thought some of that was down to the way Evie delivered it, attempting to do the voices of each character for the dialogue. It was especially endearing when she tried to do the male voices, her deepest pitch still hovering somewhere near an alto.

Eventually he'd suggested that he read the male parts, and so they'd squeezed in to the passenger seat together, Evie all but curled up on his lap as they read together by the warm amber light of the lamp. In the latest instalment, Louisa had hurt herself showing off to Captain Wentworth, and Alfie found himself quite eager to find out what was going to happen.

"Hey, lover boy, don't forget it's card night tonight – I'm not letting you miss another one!" Alfie turned to see Stephen approaching him from the row of tents. He'd been spending his nights off with Evie for the past three months and the boys had been getting more and more vocal about his extended absence from the card nights.

Before he could answer, Stephen was on him. "I'm not taking no for an answer, Coops," said Stephen, slapping him on the back a little too hard.

"Well, maybe just for an hour?" Alfie offered somewhat apologetically, thinking that if he did the first hour with the lads he could still get across to spend the rest of the evening with Evie.

Stephen gave an exaggerated sigh and shook his head. "Fine, if that's the best I'm going to get out of you it's better than nothing." He grinned at Alfie. "Seriously though, mate, it's good to see you so happy, even if it is at the expense of my imaginary wealth."

Alfie smiled. The last count had him down £268, mostly to Stephen. There was a time when he thought he'd run out of luck given how much he lost at cards. But he now realised that fate, the universe, god, whatever you wanted to call it, had been saving up his luck for Evie. "Thanks, Stephen."

"Now, don't forget about tonight," Stephen pointed at him, walking away from him backwards, in the direction of the parked lorries. "You may be in love, but you can't spend all your time with her – don't forget about us blokes."

"Don't trip over!" Alfie called after him, smiling.

Later he sought out Evie and explained the change of plans. She smiled at him and reached up to cup the side of his face. "Alfie my love, of course you should go and play cards with the men. Just don't stay away from me all night – I'll be waiting for you."

He beamed at her. "I really am the luckiest man in the world."

"And don't you forget it." He watched her walk away and was hit with the realisation that he was going to have to ask this tiny, amazing woman to marry him.

He spent the next three months carefully saving any spare money he had. He'd become more free and easy with his money since he and Evie had started seeing one another, but the need to buy an engagement ring had reined that back in. Although they'd been spending most of their nights off at the fair anyway, he'd put a stop to even the occasional foray out. And while at first Evie was perfectly happy to go along with that, as time went on he sensed she was getting frustrated.

Alfie chewed the inside of his cheek. He didn't want to tell her why he didn't want to go out anymore, but at the same time he didn't want Evie to break it off with him because he'd become boring and unromantic.

He was focusing just on the ring-buying part of the proposal at present. Although courting Evie had made him more confident, he was still terrified at the thought of having to get down on one knee and pop the question. Frankly, he thought any man who said he wasn't scared of doing it must be lying. Or crazy. Or both.

He decided to go into the next decent-sized town the fair stopped in and look at rings. He really had no idea how much they cost and so it may turn out that he had enough already. Or nowhere near enough. The thought of it being the latter worried him even further, and he gnawed away furiously at the already tender inside of his cheek.

He heard his mother's voice in his head telling him to stop that and that it made his face look awful. That one day the wind would change and he'd be stuck looking like that forever.

He sighed and his shoulders dropped a little. He missed his family. All of them, even Doris. But he especially missed Betty. He'd sent a few letters home when he first joined the fair, but it was so difficult to get to a post office to mail the letter off, and near on impossible for Betty to reply given how frequently they moved the fair on, so in the end he'd given it up.

Betty's last letter hadn't exactly told him anything to make him want to keep corresponding anyway. His father continued to refuse to even utter his name, and his mum was still conflicted about wanting to make contact, oscillating back and forth between standing firm behind her husband and wanting to reach out to her only son. The trouble was that as more time went by, the gap she had to reach across went from a crevice to a chasm to an unending void. And his mother, never firm in her convictions at the best of times unless it involved the evils of drinking, how unsafe his job was or how best to make a Bakewell tart, appeared to be simply crumbling in the face of it.

Alfie couldn't deny he was disappointed. He'd made it clear to Betty that he was ready and willing – eager – to make amends with everyone, even Doris. Even his father. But sadly he'd received nothing in return.

It was one of the things he and Evie had bonded over, their strained relationships with their families. Although at least he had Betty. Being an only child meant Evie hadn't had an ally growing up, isolated between her mother's disdain and her father's disinterest. She sought refuge in books, particularly in her beloved Jane Austen. Which in a rather weird way Alfie was eternally grateful for, since it was those books that had inspired her to leave America and come to England.

He walked to Ray's tent to look at the schedule of where they were due to go next. The next stop he'd never heard of, but after that they had a four-day stop in Salisbury. There must be a jeweller there.

Evie was talking to Lydia by the Swirl as he approached. They were huddled together and they both looked upset. "Is something wrong?" he asked, as he got close. Something was definitely up. Evie had spots of colour high on her cheeks, which only ever happened when she got overly emotional, and Lydia was dabbing her eyes with a handkerchief.

"It's nothing, Alfie," Evie tried to reassure him, waving her hand.

He wasn't convinced. "Are you sure? Is there something I can do?"

"No one can do anything!" Lydia wailed, bursting into a fresh bout of tears.

He looked helplessly at Evie. "She got some bad news from home today. Her father has lost his job."

"Oh Lydia, I'm sorry," he said rather awkwardly, not quite sure what to do.

"He's the only one my mum and three sisters have got and now I don't know what they'll do. I've been sending money home but it's not enough. He's only ever worked at the textile factory. I don't know what he'll do now." She had got her sobbing under control, but her bottom lip still wobbled alarmingly. "And then bloody Olive and Jan and the others had to wade in with their snide remarks."

Again, Alfie looked to Evie for an explanation. "It's nothing, Alfie. They were just making some mean comments to us both, that's all. You know none of them like us."

"To the both of you? What were they saying?" He felt his male protective instincts kicking in, even though he had no idea what to do with them.

"Really Alfie, it doesn't matter. Just mean-spirited remarks from mean-spirited women." He kept looking at her. She sighed. "Oh, all right then. They were making spiteful comments about the unfortunate circumstances around why Lydia ended up here." Everyone at the fair knew that story. The married man she'd got involved with back in Preston. The scandal and disgrace after they'd been found out. Her only option had been to run away from it all and she'd ended up at Crompton's. Not for the first time, Alfie realised that everyone at Crompton's was running from something. It made him think about Adam again and his own reasons for running away.

He took a deep breath before prodding Evie. "And what were they saying about you?"

"Oh, it was nothing really, Alfie. They just have a problem with my American ways I suppose." Even Alfie could read between those lines. Evie was very different to any English lady he'd ever known – forward, forthright and flirtatious. It was no surprise that women like Olive and Jan, the self-crowned matriarchs of the fair, were threatened by her.

"Well, I just think they're jealous. And stuck up." He shot Evie a grin.

"And old," she returned with a smile, starting to look more like her usual self.

"And ugly!" They both shouted together, laughing.

Finally the fair arrived in Salisbury. The intervening days had seemed interminable to Alfie, and he'd counted and recounted the money he had for the engagement ring more times than he could remember.

Evie had spoken to him about going for a walk by the river, excited to be in such a beautiful part of the country, and she'd looked hurt when he'd refused. But he only had a small window to find a jeweller and get back, and he didn't have time.

He raced into Salisbury centre with absolutely no idea of where to start looking. He walked up and down the main streets, getting more and more frantic as he lost time. Eventually, when he'd almost given up hope, he spotted a small jewellery shop. He almost ran across the street, giddy with anticipation. He got to the window and gaped at how lovely the rings were. The diamonds seemed as big as hens' eggs and sparkled just like Evie's smile did. One in particular grabbed his eye. It caught the sunlight streaming in over his shoulder so that it radiated a rainbow around the display. Then his smile dropped. It cost more than ten times what he had.

He felt tears well up. He could save for another six months and still not have the money for it. Never mind that they could be anywhere in the country by then.

Shoulders slumped, he turned from the window and walked away, staring at his feet as he kicked leaves along the footpath. He was so lost in his own black thoughts that he almost knocked himself over by walking into a lamp post. As he stopped and rubbed his throbbing shoulder he saw he was outside a pawn shop called Honest Dan's.

His eyes roamed disinterestedly over the assorted junk in the window while he rubbed his shoulder. There was a china dinner set, a television, a telephone and an assortment of smaller items strewn around. He'd always wondered about where the contents of a pawn shop came from. Who it was that had fallen on hard times. Their sorrow at parting with treasured items. The hope as they left that they would someday be back to reclaim it.

He was about to keep walking when a glimmer behind the plates caught his eye. He moved over to the window and saw a small ring at the back, sitting in the jumble of junk like an island of calm.

It was perfect. The diamond was small, but perfectly formed, just like Evie. The ring was understated, but he realised now that was much more like Evie than the garish rings he'd initially looked at. He couldn't see a price tag on it though, and before he got his hopes up too much, he went in to ask Dan about the price, hoping he was as honest as the sign proclaimed.

Ten minutes later Alfie emerged beaming, his newly acquired tiny purchase burning a not-so-tiny hole in his trouser pocket. Now all he had to do was actually ask the question and not lose the ring in the meantime. Easy.

Exactly one week later he was ready. Well, not ready. He wasn't sure if he'd ever be ready, but he was prepared. The boys had helped him out and everything was set. Inside the newly arranged semi-circle of parked lorries was a blanket spread out on the grass surrounded by candles waiting to be lit.

After dinner that night he would ask Evie if she wanted to go for a walk and he would lead her there. John and Stephen had agreed to run ahead and light the candles for him so that when he arrived with Evie the self-made glade would be lit by what he hoped would look like a sea of fireflies. Well, maybe not a sea. He hadn't been able to afford that many candles. Maybe a small lake. He'd never seen fireflies, but Evie had talked about being enchanted by them on family trips to the woods when she was younger, and he was hoping to evoke something of that feeling tonight.

He didn't have a speech prepared. He'd thought about it, but then decided he'd just worry that he couldn't remember it. And he had enough to worry about without adding to it. He'd also thought about taking Evie out somewhere and popping the question there. A nice restaurant or some such. But apart from the ring wiping out the money he had saved, he also thought having an audience would add an extra level of pressure he could do without.

He had on his best shirt for the occasion. As he walked to the mess tent, he spotted a purple iris growing by the lorries that had managed to avoid being trampled. He picked it and carefully stuck it in his jacket breast pocket to give to Evie at dinner. It would look beautiful in her hair.

He stopped outside for a moment to gather his thoughts before he entered. He took a deep breath of the cooling air and readied himself for what he hoped would be the evening that changed his life.

A torturously long hour later, all the staff fed and plates cleared away, he left the tent with Evie, the flower tucked cutely in her hair. His heart was pounding, and he was certain he was even more nervous now than he had been when he'd asked her out that first time. Despite the cool air he could feel himself sweating, and Evie glanced at him, concerned. "Are you all right, Alfie? You look flushed. I hope you're not coming down with something."

He fanned his jacket to try and cool himself down and smiled at her reassuringly. At least, he tried to smile at her reassuringly. He suspected it was more of a grimace. He took her hand and started to lead them both over to his purpose-built glade inside the circle of lorries.

"I thought we were going for a walk," Evie said. "It's such a beautiful evening, I don't want to go straight back. And we've been spending so many of our nights off in the truck."

"I just need to go and pick something up," he told her. "I promise it won't take long."

"Okay," she said reluctantly.

He threaded them through two of the lorries, parked tightly front to back and stopped, crestfallen and confused. Instead of a glade full of fireflies he faced a void. The candles weren't lit. But he'd seen John and Stephen leave ahead of them, Stephen tipping him a cheeky wink. So why hadn't they lit them? As he turned to Evie, he saw the breeze tug on the flower in her hair and realised the candles must have blown out.

His shoulders slumped. He'd had it all planned and now it was ruined. Evie, meanwhile, had peered around him and made out the blanket in the fading light. "Why, it's almost set up for a picnic but without any food!" she exclaimed. "But why would anyone want to picnic in the dark?"

"It wasn't meant to be dark," he mumbled.

"Alfie?"

"Oh Evie, I had it all sorted in my head and this wasn't how it was meant to go at all. There was meant to be fireflies and it was going to be all romantic. Well, not real fireflies, but candles, and now the breeze has blown them all out and ruined everything." Alfie realised he was yammering on as he knew he could do sometimes – funny how he veered between uncommunicativeness and jabbering – and stopped himself.

"Alfie, I don't quite understand. What's going on?"

He was just going to do it. Blown out candles and darkness be damned. Silently, he took her tiny hand in his giant paw, enveloping it several times over, and led her to the blanket. Before he could stop and question himself or get any more nervous than he already was he dropped to one knee.

"Evie, before I met you I was lost. I'd led myself down a track that had left me in a hole that I didn't know how to get out of. And then you came along, Evie, and you were like a great big ladder." Brilliant Alfie. Very eloquent. Women always liked to be told they were like ladders. He certainly wasn't going to win any awards so far. He took a deep breath and steadied himself. It was from the heart and that was all that mattered. "I can't imagine my life without you anymore, and I don't want to. You would make me the happiest man in the world if you would agree to be my wife."

As he spoke the words, he watched Evie's face go from surprise to bemusement to that great big beaming American smile of hers. Encouraged, Alfie fumbled around in his pocket for the ring.

"Now it's not the biggest or fanciest ring in the world," he apologised as he eventually managed to yank it from his pocket, ripping several threads in the process, "but it is small and beautiful, just like you." He looked up at her in the thickening gloom and proffered the ring. "Evelyn Davies, will you marry me?"

"Oh Alfie, yes of course I will!" She flew at him, knocking him back on to the rug and smothered him with kisses all over his cheeks and forehead, finishing with a gentle kiss on the tip of his nose. She stopped and stared deeply into his eyes. "Alfie Cooper, I can think of nothing I'd rather do more than marry you."

Dear Betty,

I'm sorry I haven't written for quite some time. The difficulty of corresponding when you're on the road is a poor excuse, but one I'll use nonetheless.

Are you well? I hope you're not too lonely now that Doris and myself are no longer there. Or perhaps you have a beau yourself these days?

Speaking of these things, I do have some news myself. I am engaged! To a wonderful, lovely woman called Evelyn. She's American, which I know would fill our parents with horror, but she's so delightfully refreshing. It's one of the many things I love about her. It feels strange to talk of love given our family has never been open about such things – never mind that it's not something men talk about! – but Evie has opened up a side of me that I never knew I had. And I'm so happy Betty, truly I am.

I would love to invite you to the wedding, but it's going to be such a small affair, and we don't even know where yet. We plan to continue working in Crompton's Travelling Funfair for another year or two and save as much as we can and then settle down somewhere and start a family. I can have that carpentry business we always talked about, and Evie wants to open a beauty parlour.

She says English women don't know how to make themselves look nice. Or maybe it's that English women could look nicer than they do. Something along those lines.

You will have to come and stay with us once we're all settled. I'll make sure there's pineapple.

Your brother,
Alfie

Chapter 23

"Fireflies?" Fred snorted.

"Yes, fireflies," Alfie retorted shortly. "It would have looked lovely if all the candles had stayed lit."

Fred shrugged. "Seems like a lot of effort for a girl."

Alfie resisted the urge to pat him on the arm. "You'll understand one day, truly. But suffice to say that that was the second happiest day of my life." He glanced at Fred. "The happiest being the day we got married of course." Alfie closed his eyes, picturing the day like it was yesterday. The white summer dress Evie had worn, a posy of hedgerow flowers clutched in front of her as she walked down the aisle of the small church.

They'd got married in Shrewsbury in the end. The funfair had passed through a few months after they'd got engaged and Stephen knew the church vicar there. Evie, who had had her heart set on a church wedding, had been delighted. Alfie had even bought himself a new shirt for the occasion.

Evie had never looked more beautiful than she did that day. Her blonde hair gleamed in the sunlight streaming through the church windows, and the tiny flowers she'd woven in to it had smelt intoxicating.

John, his best man, had been a godsend on the day, managing

Alfie's nerves and making sure Alfie got to the church on time. Ray had given everyone the day off in honour of the occasion, and the whole fair had come, packing into the tiny church and threatening to blow the lid off with their thunderous applause as they were wed. After the ceremony, they'd all gone back to the field where the lorries were laid up and had a wedding feast.

That night, Alfie and Evie had spent their first night as husband and wife in a hotel. Ray, in a fit of uncharacteristic generosity, had given them both the following day off too, and they had lain in bed together all morning, wrapped in each other's arms and luxuriating in being in a proper bed for the first time since they'd joined the funfair.

Alfie smiled to himself as he thought of that morning. They'd ordered coffee to be brought up to the room and they'd sat up in bed drinking coffee and doing a crossword together. He remembered there was one clue that they couldn't get, no matter how hard they tried. *Preserving jelly, so pretty* had been the clue. They'd tried all week to puzzle it out, to no avail. It was funny to think how an elusive five-letter word could be so frustrating.

Fred's voice jerked him back to the present. "So where is Evie now, then? You never talk about her."

He knew that question would come. It had been inevitable. Yet he still didn't know how to answer it.

"She died," he said quietly. Outwardly he was looking out to the lake, but his eyes could only see Evie. The shine of her hair. That big smile, too big for her face if truth be told, but that he could never help smiling back to. The silver tinsel of her laugh. Her tiny hands locked in his huge ones. How small she was. How fragile.

"I'm sorry," mumbled Fred, clearly unsure how to respond.

Alfie stood slowly. "It's okay, lad, it's not your fault. Nothing to be sorry for." He tipped his hat to Fred. "Until next time."

Alfie luxuriated in the silence as he sat by the window and watched the birds. Trevor was still in the hospital. Nobody really expected him to be coming back, but until he actually kicked the bucket they couldn't allocate Alfie a new roommate either. It was bliss.

He wasn't heartless. He did hope Trevor wasn't suffering, but he was enjoying the peaceful silence too. No wheezing, no half-forgotten jokes.

Another few house sparrows came to join their friends, and they splashed around in the water. Alfie smiled. Birds had been the only part of the natural world he'd seen while he was in jail. Birds, and the tops of a few trees some distance outside the walls. The birds had come to represent not just the world outside, but also freedom. Freedom to fly above it all, away from it all. They were still that now. When he watched them he thought about being able to fly away from this life, this body. His past and all his mistakes. His regrets.

He sighed and reached for *Persuasion*.

Alfie had slept terribly. His rest so shallow he could scoop it out with a spoon. He stared at the watermark on the ceiling. They were still promising to fix the bed, but until they did he was a prisoner most mornings while he waited for the nurses.

He heard their hushed voices in the hallway approach and then die away again as they moved on. They were late this morning and he was beginning to grow annoyed. He'd be so late for breakfast at this rate he'd end up having to sit next to Mavis.

He thought of Evie and those first few days after he'd proposed. How happy they'd both been, with constant grins you couldn't wipe off either of their faces. Everyone at the fair had been so excited for them. They were the fair's first marriage and the team had really gone to town in decorating the mess tent one night in celebration. He lay in silence, letting his sorrow lap at his ankles as the silence washed over him.

When the nurse with the hairy lip eventually came for him she was subdued. By that time Alfie was even more grumpy than normal having waited for so long.

"Nice to finally see you," he sniped. "Just because I have nothing better to do you'd think I had nothing better to do than wait for you all morning." He wasn't even sure that made sense, but he was hungry and irritable and needed to piss.

She helped him sit up and then unexpectedly sat down rather awkwardly next to him on the bed. "Eh?" said Alfie a little startled, "What's this?"

"Alfie, I have some rather unfortunate and upsetting news." His mind raced. Was library day cancelled? Had they found out about his weekly visits to the park and they were going to kick him out of Pinewood? Were they finally introducing chair yoga and forcing him to take part?

"Trevor passed away in the hospital early this morning." She patted his arm. "I'm sorry, Alfie."

He nearly laughed. In relief. In surprise. At hairy lip thinking he needed to be delivered the news with kid gloves. Although if he was honest with himself there was a part of him – a very small part, way deep down – that would miss the old bugger. Would miss his complete zest for life and the way he grabbed it with both hands and wrung every last drop out of it. Rather than the way life was wringing every last drop out of the rest of them in Pinewood. Out of himself.

He thought of Joan. Of her tugging at the blanket over and over again. She must be devastated. "Does Joan know yet?" he asked.

Hairy lip nodded sadly. "She's terribly upset as you can imagine." Alfie hoped it didn't break her but he feared it might.

Julia walked slowly through the dining room distributing the porridge, lost in her thoughts. She still couldn't quite believe Trevor was gone. Even though in her head she had known the odds were slim, in her heart she'd still expected to see him again. Or at least hadn't let herself believe that she wouldn't see him.

The general hubbub in the dining room made it clear that the news had spread through Pinewood. People dying wasn't exactly an uncommon occurrence at Pinewood, after all it was the only way anyone left. But Trevor had been popular with both residents and nurses and it was clear the news had affected everyone more than normal.

She'd broken the news to Joan this morning. She would never forget the way her face had crumpled in on itself, like all the life had just been sucked out of her. There had been no tears, no plaintive cries. Just a slow shrinking in to herself and a deadening of the eyes. Something had broken in her, Julia could see it. She just wasn't sure if time would fix it.

She'd also called the family this morning. She'd deliberately called James rather than Beth, hoping to hear some sort of grief, some sort of remorse or sadness in his voice. For Trevor's sake. There had been none. Just a matter-of-fact promise to ensure his personal items were cleared from the room as soon as possible.

She spotted Alfie walk in and sit down. He also seemed subdued and she wondered how he was taking the news. She'd tried to stop dwelling on him in the days since her failed detective work. All it did was depress her. That she'd failed. That her life was so empty that she had nothing else to fill it with. That she was on track to end up exactly like Alfie and she didn't know what to do to stop it.

She'd been so down about it all that she'd even called her parents in a desperate hope to reconnect. But the call had been the same as all the others. Awkward, stilted conversations where they danced around her 'lifestyle choice' as they insisted upon calling it. Gushing praise for how successful her brother was, with his wife and children. The emphasis always on the wife and children part.

She sighed. She was stuck and she didn't know how to get herself unstuck. Or, to be honest with herself she did know, she just wasn't sure if she had it in her.

*

Dear Alfie,

Evie sounds wonderful. And American! Whereabouts in America was she from? You should definitely tell me more

253

about her – if you want to that is. I'd certainly love to hear more about her, and not just because she's a fellow countrywoman!

And I was sorry to hear about Trevor. How is he doing now? Is he still in hospital? Pneumonia as well as emphysema must be a tough one to get through. I hope he pulls through.

So my second date with Finn went better than expected… I think maybe he was just super nervous the first time. He seemed to be a bit calmer this time and only mentioned the gym three or four times. Much as I don't like to hear about the gym (or go to it for that matter) I certainly can't argue with the fact that he has a nice body! Not that I saw it, just to be clear, it's just from what I can tell. So we're going on a third date next weekend, and if that goes well I might think about introducing him to Ethan. Finn seems keen to meet him, which is a good sign. I mean, I would never date anyone who wasn't keen to meet Ethan. It will be interesting to see how that goes. It feels weird to be thinking about it all, but I keep telling myself that I can't stay a single mom forever. And I'm sure that Mark wouldn't want me to. And if it does all work out, it would be so nice for Ethan to have a father figure.

Oh shoot. The laundry is done so I must go and hang that out. I'm not sure there's much more to report this end anyway! It's all been a bit quiet on the Western front recently. Or should that be Eastern given New Jersey is on the east coast?

Hope everything is going well your end.

Anne

Dear Anne,

I was so pleased to hear that it seems things might work out with Finn. I look forward to hearing how your third date goes, and especially how his meeting with Ethan goes if it gets to that.

I wonder if Evie and I had got to have children if they would have looked like your Ethan, with the blonde hair and blue eyes. She was a real adventurer my Evie. She was from New York, so not quite New Jersey but the same state. She came to England all on her own, on a ship. I can't recall the name now, but it set a record for the fastest passage between New York and England. She was very small and petite – did I tell you that already? – and ran the coconut shy at the funfair. We used to do crosswords together.

He closed his eyes, remembering the nights spent in the cab of the lorry doing the cryptic crossword in *The Times* together by lamplight, too scared to use the light in the cab in case they drained the battery. How they'd try and eke out the crossword to make it last the whole week until the next one. Evie's excited impatience at checking all their answers when they got the paper the following week.

As for Trevor, he died in the hospital. Strange to think I'll never hear that awful wheezing laugh of his again. He may not have been as quiet or as clean as Arthur, but he did make more of an impression, I must admit. I'm told his daughter is coming in to clean out his room and make all the necessary arrangements.

James couldn't even make it in for that and Alfie felt himself getting angry on Trevor's behalf. He wondered who would make the necessary arrangements when he died. He guessed it would have to be one of the nurses. There was probably a standard procedure for it, for when people who were all alone died. Meagre possessions given to charity? Tick. Budget pinewood coffin purchased with government stipend? Tick. He wondered if Pinewood got a discount on pinewood coffins. Maybe they should think about sponsoring a line of them. He chuckled. He knew younger people would think it morbid, but he knew that the closer you got to death the less it scared you. And depending on how much pain you were in, the more you welcomed it.

Are you planning on doing any more international lessons? I do like the facts you tell me about all the different countries. I guess you're never too old to learn after all! Perhaps you could do your next class on Italy. Evie and I always talked about travelling there but we never did.

Until next week.

Alfie

Julia looked around her house and felt nothing. She'd put down no roots in Slatterley. Never mind roots in fact, she hadn't even put down seeds. There were no picture frames filled with photos of friends, no keepsakes bought while travelling proudly out on display. She had those things, sure, but even after three years they were still in a box in the loft, waiting to see life again at the next stop.

She realised that Slatterley had always been just a pit stop for her while she recovered. Somewhere to lick her wounds before continuing with her life elsewhere. But then life had continued. Just without her noticing or taking part. That was why she'd never invested emotionally in the place. Why she'd never made proper friends. Because she knew that she'd be moving on soon and what was the point? But four years on from Siobhan leaving, she finally had to admit to herself that she hadn't moved on. Instead, the world had moved on around her.

It was time to go. To continue life and the real, proper living of it, somewhere else. Her first thought was London, but then she thought, why not somewhere else? Cambridge, Manchester, Edinburgh. Bristol. Liverpool. Her choices were endless. As she thought of moving on and starting life afresh somewhere else she felt a lightness of spirit she'd not experienced in so long that it almost took her breath away.

Yes, she would move on. Her only regrets were not getting to the bottom of Alfie and the thought that she'd be leaving poor Joan, still distraught at Trevor's passing. In fact, all of Pinewood seemed to have had the wind knocked out of it.

Intellectually it shouldn't have been a surprise to anyone, especially given Trevor's poor health. But emotionally they'd all felt it, even Alfie she thought. Trevor had been so full of life that he'd left a void behind him.

That's what I will do, she thought as she looked around her shell of a house. Her shell of a life. I won't be Alfie, I'll be Trevor. Full of life and love and leaving a trail of sparkles. Yes, she smiled, I will be Trevor. Only without the arsehole son.

Alfie walked down the footpath towards the park, lost in thought. Pinewood had been decidedly quiet the past few days since the news about Trevor. It was like someone had pressed a giant mute button.

It was strange. He hadn't liked Trevor, but now he was gone it did feel a little bit like Lex Luther had died midway through the film.

The ding of a bike bell brought him out of his reverie. A girl of about three on a small pink bike with training wheels, ribbons streaming from the handles, rode past him on the footpath, followed closely behind by what he assumed was her father on foot. "Jessica, slow down," he called out as he chased after her, shooting a smile half full of apology and half full of thanks in Alfie's direction.

Alfie thought about when his father had taught him to ride a bike. A proper bike, as his father had called it, not a baby bike. There had been no mollycoddling, no gentle cajoling to get his confidence up. Just a straightforward instruction to keep the bike upright and not to fall off. He had fallen off of course. And he remembered trying his hardest not to cry at the scraped knee and palm of his hand. His bottom lip trembling as he tried to hold it in. His father's disgust and shame.

He'd been determined that when he taught his own children to ride a bike he would do it a lot differently. With compassion and empathy. And perhaps – heaven forbid – even a sense of fun. He sighed and his shoulders drooped a little more.

The park was strangely quiet when he arrived, and he took several deep breaths of lavender to help restore his spirits. He stopped in front of the bench. He'd not really had much time to think about alternatives for Rosalind this week, what with Trevor and everything. He knew it would not be one of his finer weeks. *For Rosalind, who never learned how to parallel park. For Rosalind, who cooked a mean scrambled eggs.*

He settled himself on the bench and pulled out the bread, enjoying the peace of the park and allowing it to wash over him. His mind wandered, so when Fred appeared it seemed like he'd arrived out of nowhere.

Alfie nodded to him without speaking and handed over a piece of bread. He took a deep breath. This next part of the story wasn't going to be easy.

Chapter 24

The first six months of married life had been bliss. They had a marital tent all to themselves – an unheard-of luxury – and as they truly got to know each other they continued to fall deeper in love. Alfie's world had never been so full. Of colour, of happiness. The sky had never been so blue, the smell of grass so sweet.

Of course, like everything, after the initial period the novelty wore off and they were consumed in the day to day. And having started marriage like two pieces from a jigsaw puzzle, each of them filling holes and gaps in the other, as life went on a distance seemed to open between them. Their edges poking each other rather than fitting together.

"Would you please stop leaving your dirty socks in the middle of the tent, Alfie," Evie snapped at him one night as she picked up the offending items and threw them in the corner.

He held up his hands in surrender. "Sure. Do you think you'd be able to stop leaving your shoes right in front of the tent flap?"

He hated that they sniped about such trivial and mundane subjects. At no point in all of his imaginings of what married life with Evie would be like did arguing about his dirty socks come into it. In fact, arguing hadn't come into it at all.

Evie sighed and her shoulders slumped a little. "Must we do this again, Alfie?"

He resisted the urge to tell her that she had started it. "No, we don't," he said instead. "I'll try and not leave my socks there."

She nodded. "Thank you." He noticed she didn't offer to move her shoes.

Alfie was stood with Andrew, John and Stephen one morning as they allocated jobs when Ray strode up to them, a look of thunder on his face. "All-company meeting. By my tent. Now." He stalked off. The four of them looked at one another agape. Ray was well known for his temper, but they'd never seen him like that before.

They trailed behind him as he proceeded to round up the rest of the fair. Everyone looked as lost as they felt.

Eventually everyone was assembled outside Ray's tent and he stood in front of them on top of a crate, arms crossed across his broad chest. "Right, you lot," he yelled, "Listen up. Someone here has been stealing and I'll find out who and have them. Twenty pounds has gone missing. If you know who it was, or if it was you, then come forward now. Otherwise, I'll be talking to the lot of you and getting to the bottom of it one way or another."

He stopped and looked around. Nobody moved forward. Instead, everyone was craning their necks trying to see if anyone was moving or looked guilty. Ray nodded like he wasn't surprised. "Right then, we'll play it that way. Everyone back to your jobs, we've still got a bloody fair to run. But I expect you all to come as soon as I call for you. I will get to the bottom of this and there will be hell to pay."

He stomped off, leaving a vacuum in his wake. Everyone looked around at everybody else, secretly sizing them up. Were they the thief?

Alfie was at a complete loss. He couldn't believe anybody at the fair was capable of stealing, and the only thing that convinced him it wasn't Ray pulling some elaborate prank had been the black look on his face.

That night at cards – a practice Alfie was now fully back in the habit of, despite Evie's constant annoyed protestations – it was all they could talk about.

"So who do you think it is?" Stephen whispered conspiratorially. He looked askance at Andrew. "Is it you?"

"Oh, away with you, you fool," Andrew dismissed him with a wave of his hand.

"Am I such a fool?" Stephen decried. "You could have stolen the money."

"As could you!" Andrew retorted. "Did you steal it?"

"Certainly not!"

"Well then," said Andrew, as if that settled it.

"It is a good point though," said John in his steady manner.

"What?" the three of them all spoke together as they turned to him. John didn't speak overly much, so when he did they all listened.

"Well, any one of us has reason enough to steal the money, don't we?" he said. "Is it so unreasonable we should turn the torch on ourselves to free us from suspicion?" They all looked at each other, unconvinced.

"For instance," John continued patiently, "Andrew, you have two children to support and regularly send money back to their mother. Perhaps you needed some extra for something important? Or maybe she was demanding more money? You have been heard to say before – and I quote – that she is 'a money-grabbing bitch'."

While Andrew sat there, mouth agape, Stephen chipped in with a chortle, "Plus he's Scottish!" Andrew glared at him while Alfie sat there at a loss, unsure where John was going with this. Surely he didn't think it was Andrew?

"Now you, Stephen," John turned to him, "you also had motivation to steal the money."

"Did you get some girl pregnant?" Andrew interjected, revelling in the chance to get his own back now the spotlight was off him.

"What?!" Stephen spluttered, "No, of course not! What sort of man do you think I am?"

"A reasonable question," John said with a smile to take the sting out. Alfie couldn't tell if it was Andrew's question or Stephen's own that John was referring to. "But," he continued more seriously, "you did receive a letter a few weeks ago that clearly upset you. Whatever was in that letter may have been the catalyst to turn thief."

Suddenly Stephen sat back, the wind knocked out of him. Alfie held his breath, certain Stephen was about to confess to stealing the money. "It was from Adele," he said quietly. "She wants a divorce."

"Oh jeez, Stephen, I'm sorry mate," said Andrew, all rivalry forgotten. John simply shook his head sadly.

Alfie was stunned. He didn't know anyone who was divorced. Nobody got divorced. He looked at Stephen with pity. First, Adele had run off with another man and left him, a huge scandal, which had driven Stephen to join the fair in the first place. And now, to rub salt in the wound she wanted a divorce, which was another scandal. Oh sure, it was getting more common, but it was still shameful. Suddenly his own marital problems seemed insignificant.

"She wants it granted on the grounds of her own adultery if you can believe it," Stephen said bitterly, knocking back his whisky as if to take the edge off. "I'll give it to her, of course," he continued, and Alfie was no longer sure if Stephen was talking to them or to himself. "In some ways it will be a relief to be free of her. And I guess it makes no difference really. I couldn't have married someone else while I was still married to Adele, and now no one will want to marry me because I'm divorced. Same result." He shrugged and knocked back another whisky. "Anyway, enough about all that. Let's play some cards."

They all picked up their hands and play resumed, John's detective work forgotten. Alfie could only be grateful for the return to the game. He wasn't ready to have his own past examined so closely.

He was whistling to himself a few days later as he erected the tent for the pop-gun game when he heard a familiar voice behind him. "I'd recognise that off-key whistle anywhere."

He stopped. Betty? Could it be? But how? He turned and like a dream it really was his sister standing in front of him. "Betty! How? Why?" he stuttered, overcome with several emotions at seeing her again.

She laughed. "What, no hug for your baby sister after all this time?"

He dropped the hammer he'd been using and moved to sweep her up in a jubilant hug. "Of course! I'm just so surprised to see you! However did you get here? How did you even know I was here?"

"I'm in Norwich visiting a friend and saw the posters for Crompton's Travelling Funfair. I couldn't quite believe my luck so I came down immediately to try and find you."

"I can't quite believe it either! It's so strange to actually be seeing you! I have so much to fill you in on! And what about you? How are you?" Alfie was almost babbling in his excitement at seeing Betty again. "And I don't even have any pineapple!" he lamented, before Betty could even get a word in.

"Pineapple?" she asked, a small furrow in her brow.

"For your gammon and pineapple!"

"Oh…Oh yes. I remember I used to eat that for a time."

"Well, I'll be sure to have some next time. So go on, tell me how everyone is." He finally paused. "How's Mum?" He stopped himself asking anything further. Since Evie, he'd realised he didn't need his parents, especially if they were going to be so harsh and unforgiving. He wasn't going to tie himself in knots anymore waiting for them to love him. Evie was his family now. Just as he was hers.

"Mum is… She's—" Betty stopped, her eyes filling with tears.

"Betty, was it is? What's wrong?" There was a sinking feeling in his stomach he didn't like, despite his new-found emotional freedom.

"She's sick."

"How sick?"

"We're not really sure. So far she's refused to let a doctor see her – you know what she's like – but Dad and I are worried. If Doris were still around she'd bully Mum into it, but she's moved to York with David and Dad is strangely letting Mum have her own way. It's like all the air has gone out of him."

Competing emotions warred within Alfie. On the one hand, he was terrified that his mum was ill and his first instinct was to rush to her side. On the other hand, she had made it quite clear in the years since he'd left London that she didn't want anything more to do with him.

"So what do you want me to do about it?" he asked more harshly than he intended.

Betty looked taken aback at his tone. "I...I'm not sure. But I thought you'd want to know. You did ask!"

"So you want me to run home to look after her? Abandon the life I've built? I won't do it. I like it here."

"No one is asking you to! I just thought you'd like to know that our mum is ill and might die!"

The tears in Betty's eyes spilled over and Alfie regretted how harsh he'd been. He was angry at his parents, not her. He realised he wasn't emotionally free from his family, simply shut off. And Betty suddenly appearing with bad news had opened old wounds right back up again.

"I'm sorry," he relented, pulling her in for a hug. "I'm not angry with you."

"Alfie?" He heard Evie's voice, several rungs higher than normal at finding him in an embrace with a strange woman.

"Evie!" he exclaimed, excited to see her but also wishing he'd had more time with Betty to himself. "This is Betty! Betty, this is my wife, my Evie."

He stood there and watched his short, blonde wife shake hands with his tall, black-haired sister. So unlike in appearance and yet quite similar in themselves. Neither of them suffered being told what to do or think.

He stood by for a few minutes, just watching them before he snapped to action. "Come!" he called to Betty, "you must meet John and Stephen and Andrew. Although you're not to be on your own with Stephen," he added as an afterthought.

He saw as much as he could of Betty while she and the fair stayed in Norwich. Luckily Norwich was a bigger town so the fair had an extended stay and they had a whole glorious week together. He and Evie didn't even argue much that week. He was so happy to see

Betty that he merely nodded when Evie started to nag him, her sharp tongue blunted by his joy at spending time with his little sister again.

They didn't talk about their mum's illness again, staying on happier and safer subjects. Alfie told her all about life at the fair and selected slices of Exeter. She was particularly amused by the regulars at the Crown and Goat.

"You're teasing me," she said after he told her about Barry the Burglar. "Surely he wasn't…?"

Alfie nodded emphatically. "It's true, I swear."

"Extraordinary. Of course, I would have heard all this before if you'd continued writing to me a little more regularly," she chided gently.

Aware they were in danger of getting in to territory he didn't want to venture in to, he simply nodded, not trusting himself to say much, and changed the subject.

"So tell me about Doris and David. Do they have any children?"

"Not yet, although I presume they're trying. You know what Doris is like – she still deems personal details distasteful."

He nodded. Doris had always been as pointy as their father, but with cold indifference rather than the violent fits of rage.

"What about you and Evie?" Betty continued. "I presume you'll be settling down soon and having children."

"A boy and a girl," Alfie responded, without hesitation.

Betty laughed. "Alfie, you do know you don't get to choose what you have!"

He blushed. "Yes of course." He resisted the urge to poke his tongue out at her as he'd done when they were children. "But that's what I'd like. Boy first, then the girl. So he can look out for her like I always did for you."

She smiled. "You always did. Remember the time—" She cut herself short as Evie approached them, and Alfie felt a wave of anger and resentment towards his wife before he could stop himself. He had precious little time with Betty before they both had to move on, and Evie kept inserting herself in to it. Why couldn't she just stay away and let him have his separate worlds? He liked them separate.

It was neater. Tidier. Never mind the fact that Evie and Betty got along like a house on fire, leaving him often feeling like a third wheel in a triumvirate that included his own wife and sister!

He watched them talk and stewed in his own sullen thoughts. At least his worlds would separate again in a few days when Betty left, and his life could go back to being neat and tidy.

All too quickly, it was time to say goodbye. Betty was heading back to London early the next day and Alfie was due to leave for a small village he'd never heard of.

"I don't want to make you angry again," Betty started, and Alfie knew immediately where she was going. "But she is quite ill. Won't you at least consider coming home to see her?"

Evie looked at the two of them sharply. "Who is quite ill?"

"You didn't tell her?" Alfie stood sullenly silent. I'm surprised you didn't tell her, he thought, now that you're the best of friends.

Betty sighed exasperatedly. "Our mother. We don't know what's wrong with her as she refuses to see a doctor, but she is rather sick."

"Alfie, why didn't you tell me?"

"Because it doesn't matter!" he cried. "I'm not going back to see her and neither of you can make me!" He was conscious he sounded like a child but he was too upset and angry to care. He stopped himself short of stamping his feet and walking off.

"Alfie," said Evie gently, cautiously reaching out to stroke his arm like one would approach a snarling dog. "It's okay. We don't have to go back to see her if you don't want to." She shot a look to Betty that he couldn't quite read.

Again, he felt a wrench that they were getting along so well. He'd even overheard them promising to write to each other regularly when he'd been eavesdropping one day. Betty was his! And Evie was his! Couldn't they see that? By establishing their own relationship he lost that.

He realised that was probably the real reason he hadn't invited Betty to the wedding. He could have organised it so Betty could come. Could have planned in advance to tell her where and when it would be. But he hadn't. Evie had encouraged him to do so in fact, but he'd resisted. Always finding reasons why it was too hard and they couldn't do it. But he realised now that deep down he just didn't want them to meet. He knew they'd get along famously and he didn't want that to happen. They were his. His sister. His wife. No one else's. Couldn't they see that? And now here they were, exchanging secret glances he couldn't read and promising to exchange correspondence he wouldn't be party to.

They'd both been looking at him all this time, waiting for what would come next. He didn't know what to say to either of them, so in the end he simply walked away.

He went to find the men. He needed to get away from the women. Not just now, but generally. He spent far too much of his time – had spent far too much of his life – subsumed or consumed by women. It wasn't right. It wasn't normal. And it certainly wasn't manly.

No wonder they felt they could manipulate him. Well no more! From now on he would act like a normal man and spend his time with other men rather than clinging to women's skirts.

He found Stephen at the Swirl, fixing a broken beam but couldn't spot John or Andrew. "Fancy a hand of poker before dinner?" he asked Stephen.

Stephen stood, tossing his hammer in the air before catching it by the handle and tossing him a wink. "You know I'm always up for taking your money, Coops. I'm not sure where the other lads are. But if we can't find them we can always play with a dummy hand." Alfie shrugged. It was less about the cards and all about the escape.

Stephen clapped him on the shoulder. "Let's go to my tent, the cards are there. If we don't find the others on the way then more imaginary money for me!"

Back in the tent, Stephen tossed him the deck of cards while he rummaged in his metal footlocker, grumbling to himself. It was a beast of a thing and took up a large amount of real estate in the cramped tent but Stephen resolutely wouldn't get rid of it. If he'd managed to steal it from the army at the end of the war then he could manage to get it around England was always his response when someone suggested he use something a little more travel-friendly. Eventually he exclaimed with delight and pulled out an almost full bottle of gin. "Now for a glass," he mumbled, diving back in. "Don't forget the dummy hand," he called to Alfie over his shoulder.

"I'll have one of those," Alfie said abruptly, surprising himself. The cards sat undealt in his hands.

Stephen turned around. "Are you sure? You've not had a drink in the two years I've known you."

Alfie nodded curtly. "You pour. I'll deal."

He woke the next morning in the back of one of the lorries. What had he done? He'd thrown away two years of sobriety. And over what?

He lay there for a few moments trying to piece together the events of the night before. He had a vague recollection of Betty and Evie coming to find him and urging him to come away. He'd refused. Instead, he and Stephen had polished off the rest of the gin and played cards, Alfie getting further and further into imaginary debt. Or had it been imaginary? Had he insisted that they play for real money? With a sinking feeling he thought perhaps he had insisted on playing for very real, very non-imaginary money. He groaned. How much had he lost? Quite a lot he thought. More than he could afford.

He screwed his eyes shut and tried to make the world go away. His head was pounding, the familiar dead animal from Exeter days was back in his mouth and every little movement made the lorry spin sickeningly.

He dreaded to think what Evie thought of him. What Betty thought of him. He wondered how long he could hide out in the back of the lorry. Not long enough given he was almost certainly already missed at work.

Flashes of Exeter ran before his eyes. The disappointment on Hilda's face when he finally stumbled down the stairs reeking of stale alcohol and cigarettes. The eventual contempt from Joe and worse, the compassion from Matthew. Then it was Adam's face he saw. Lying on the floor haloed by a pool of gradually spreading blood.

He rolled over and retched, tears streaming down his face. Whether from the retching or for Adam or for his own sorry existence at that moment he wasn't sure.

Eventually he sat up. It was time to find Evie and face the music. He knew without even going outside that he'd be too late to find Betty before she left, even if he could have just abandoned his job. He'd deal with that later when he was up to writing to her. For now, he needed to find his wife and do some damage control.

He found Evie by her coconut stall, packing away the coconuts. She was stony-faced as she watched him approach and he gulped. This wouldn't be easy. Not by a long shot. He didn't know where or how to start and so he just stood there, watching her load string bags with coconuts. A hostile silence cloaked them both and turned the otherwise sunny morning dark.

Eventually she started talking for him. "What on earth was all that about, Alfie?" she demanded, whirling on him. "Storming off and disappearing? Getting drunk? You don't even drink! And let's not forget your appalling language when Betty and I came to find you." She was rattling off his sins with alacrity now she'd got started.

Alfie hung his head and let Evie's anger wash over him. He thought, hoped, that if he took it all without rebuke it might wash some of the shame away. It didn't.

"Who were you last night, Alfie? Because you weren't my husband. The man I saw last night was a vicious drunk full of anger. My husband doesn't drink and does not act like that." He caught the double meaning in her tone. "Frankly, I'm disappointed as much as anything."

He stumbled back. It was like she'd put an ice dagger through his heart. *I'm disappointed in you.* How often had he heard those words from his father? Or worse, from his mother? Thinking of his mother made him remember her illness. How had everything turned so upside down in the space of a week? A week ago he had been happy. Or at least relatively happy. Constant arguing with Evie and the growing distance between them aside. Just a week! And now look at him.

He felt tears threatening to well up and swallowed several times to try and clear the lump in his throat that threatened to choke him. He wanted to look at her but didn't dare. He continued to stare at his feet.

"Are you even going to look at me?" Evie demanded. Slowly, almost shyly, he raised his head and saw she was in tears.

"Oh Evie, I'm so sorry! Really I am. I don't know what came over me." He'd never told Evie about his dark days in Exeter. He hadn't told anyone. Not about Adam, about his drinking problem. He'd told her the beginning part when everything had been fine, leaving out Grace of course, and then simply skipped to the end when he left to join Crompton's. "The news about my mum's illness, I guess it was just such a shock." He wouldn't mention his jealousy over her and Betty getting so close. It just sounded petty. "And I am so, so sorry. It will never happen again, I promise you." He considered getting down on his knees but instead tentatively reached for her hand.

Somewhat reluctantly, diffidently, she let him take it. "Fine, Alfie Cooper, you're forgiven. But just this once. You'd better make sure it never happens again." She drew her hand free and turned her back, in a manner that told him in no uncertain terms that he was not, in fact, forgiven, but that it was the end of the conversation.

Next up he went to find Stephen to discover just how much he owed him and if it was real or imaginary money. As he walked, he mentally squeezed his eyes shut and promised himself that if it only turned out he hadn't been betting with real money last night that he would never drink again.

He found Stephen with John striking down the Whip, and marvelled how he could be up and working after last night. "Well, hey there, Coops," Stephen boomed as he approached with a knowing smile. "You look a right state. How's the head this morning?"

Alfie tried to act nonchalantly, even though his head was, in fact, swimming. "It's all right."

"I'm surprised to see you up and about, the way you were putting it away last night."

Alfie thought he caught a look of disapproval from John, but was too miserable to care. He pulled Stephen aside a little. "So Stephen…I…ah…I was wondering about the cards last night… ah… Exactly how much did I lose?"

"Sixty-two pounds!" Stephen laughed. "You were on a roll – well, a roll of sorts anyway."

Alfie staggered a little. It was so much worse than he had thought. If it was real money they'd been playing with he was finished. That was all of his savings and then some.

"And was that…was that real money we were playing with?" Alfie whispered the question, mortally afraid of the answer.

Stephen clapped him on the back with a grin. "It was. But don't worry about it old chap. I never took you seriously." For a second Alfie thought about stubbornly insisting that he pay his debts. But then Evie's face swam before him and he tried to imagine exactly how he'd break the news that he'd lost all their savings. So instead he simply shook Stephen's hand in relief and gratitude.

"Now I'd go and find Andrew before he finds you," Stephen told him. "He was livid this morning when you weren't there. I've never seen his face so red!"

Alfie gulped and nodded. More music to face. At least he could be sure that Andrew wouldn't cry.

As he set off to find Andrew he realised that the only thing left was to write a letter to Betty apologising for his behaviour. He had a hazy memory of speaking with her last night, and what he remembered he didn't like. It was the same look of shame and disappointment he'd seen on Evie's face this morning. The two most important women in his life and he'd let both of them down. Why could he not do anything right?

Later that day, after the fair had shut for the night, Ray stalked around yelling at them all to gather round. "Right, you lot, I'll make this brief. We've found out who the thief is and the police have been notified. Thank you to those who came forward with information." Alfie thought he saw a look pass between Ray and Olive. "Would the thief like to reveal themselves before I do?"

Alfie heard a woman start to sob behind him and he turned to find Lydia, red-faced and trembling. "Ray…I…" she started, trying to gulp in air as she moved forward. Evie, always nearby to Lydia, put her arm around her to help steady her, and Alfie could see a dawning look of horror on Evie's face.

"That's right, people!" Ray trumpeted triumphantly. "Lydia here is the thief."

Everyone now turned to Lydia, still sobbing and supported by Evie. "It's true," Lydia wailed. "Ray, I'm so sorry. I just didn't know what to do. I'll pay you back, I promise I will. My dad lost his job…" she trailed off as she saw Ray's face darken. Her pleas would get her nowhere.

Initially stunned to silence, a shocked murmur now began to ripple through those assembled. And then Alfie heard Olive say, "I always knew she was bad news. Her and that American." And then louder, "Harlot."

Lydia tore herself away from Evie and ran off raggedly in the direction of the lorries, the entire fair staring after her in disbelief.

The excitement stirred up around Lydia followed the fair as it moved about from place to place, crisscrossing East Anglia. It was the most explosive and fantastic happening at the fair that anybody could remember and it wasn't dying down anytime soon.

Evie, reeling from the news about Lydia and the abrupt departure of her only friend, seemed to retreat into herself. Her beaming smile, admittedly seen less and less often the more she and Alfie argued, had now disappeared completely. Alfie couldn't help feeling a little relieved – and also a little guilty – that Lydia had moved the spotlight solely off himself and his own behaviour. But if he was honest he was mainly just relieved.

He made a few attempts to talk to her, to find out if she was okay. But the ability to open up to each other seemed to be lost to them. The distance that had been growing between them was now a chasm, their jigsaw pieces so misaligned they could be from different puzzles entirely.

"I just feel so alone now," she said as she stood outside the tent, watching the fair bustle on around her.

"You're not alone," he pointed out. "You have me." He realised he should move to comfort her, and thought that once upon a time he would have done so instinctively. Now it was something he had to think about.

"Do I? Do I really, Alfie? No. Not really. Not like before." She wasn't even looking at him as she spoke, but gazing out across the field and the flurry of activity like none of it was touching her. As he searched for something to say, this time it was Evie who turned and walked away.

Chapter 25

Dear Anne,

I know you won't read this as I'm only composing this in my head, but all this talk about Evie, both with yourself and Fred, has made me need to get something off my chest. And you see, I'll need to tell Fred soon as I'm almost at that part of the story. And I'm not quite sure how to tell him. It's all been building up to this of course. But I've delayed it as long as I can and I've come to the part I've been dreading since I started.

I killed her. I killed my precious Evie. I was drunk and angry – so angry – and I killed her. Smashed her tiny head against a metal footlocker. She was so small, so fragile as it turned out. Even lifeless I could pick her up like she weighed nothing more than a doll. I didn't mean to do it. But I was so angry, and so drunk. It's all a bit of a blur, even then. I remember a lot of shouting. Me, Evie and Stephen, all shouting. And I remember holding Evie and shaking her. Throwing her aside to get at Stephen. Her tiny head crunching into that big metal box. The thin stream of blood.

It's the worst thing I ever did and I know you won't be able to get past this, because I haven't.

Chapter 26

Having had the best of intentions not to rejoin card night for a good while following what Alfie had come to think of as 'his episode', it wasn't long before he began to miss the camaraderie. And so, on the first night after they set up on the outskirts of Bury St Edmunds, Alfie somewhat apprehensively told Evie he was going.

He waited for the usual outburst but none came. Instead, she merely nodded her head. Surprised, he turned to go and then felt something hit him on the back of the head. He turned back to see Evie holding a shoe in one hand, its mate lying on the ground by his feet. Her chest was heaving, like she'd just run a race.

"That hurt," he pointed out, trying to not get angry.

"Are you really going to go to card night, Alfie?" Evie demanded, clearly having no issue with getting angry. "After everything, you're really going to go?"

"I'm sick of apologising to you, Evie! It was one night! Yes, it was a terrible lapse in judgement, but it was a lapse. You can't keep controlling me! Just because you have no friends here now that Lydia is gone is not my fault." As soon as the words were out of his mouth he regretted them.

She stared at him for a few moments, shocked, before throwing the other shoe at him. "Get out!" she screamed. "I don't want you here anyway! I don't need you. There are plenty of people who want me if you don't."

He turned and left, wondering what she meant by that last comment. She had been increasingly absent for periods in the evenings lately, but truth be told he hadn't really cared where she was, just relieved that it was somewhere else.

He found the lads in the back of one of the lorries, already set up for the night around a lamp, with John carefully shuffling the cards.

"We weren't sure if you were coming," Stephen told him, pulling out a bottle of gin and half raising an eyebrow. Alfie shook his head out of reflex, but then the intoxicating smell as Stephen pulled the cork and his own simmering anger at Evie broke all resolve. "Just one," he said to Stephen. Just one can't hurt. And it didn't hurt. It was wonderful. The heat as the glossy liquid slid down his throat, the comforting warmth in his belly. It was like being embraced by an old friend.

That night he really did have just the one. The next card night he also had one. Then it was two. Then three. And before he knew it he was stumbling back to his tent every card night reeking of alcohol as he tumbled into bed beside Evie and promptly fell asleep and started snoring.

But he continued to tell himself he had it under control. He wasn't missing work the following morning, and he didn't drink between card nights. Surely this is what normal men did? Had a few drinks with the lads once or twice a week? It was certainly what Stephen and Andrew did. It was what Joe and Matthew had done.

Evie though, predictably, wasn't happy, and she alternated between coldness, anger and contempt. Alfie wasn't sure which one he preferred, and he tried to remember back to those glory days when they'd been happy and in love and it had been the two of them against the world. But those days, that feeling, was increasingly difficult to recall, the memories disappearing like smoke every time he tried to hold one.

Lately, she'd even stopped arguing with him when he left for a card night, instead ignoring him completely as he left or not even being there at all. Again, he wondered where she went given she didn't get on with any of the women.

Tonight she was there and so he ventured to ask. "Where is it that you go when I'm at card night?"

She tossed her head back. "I don't have to answer to you, Alfie, of all people."

Of all people? What did she even mean by that? He felt his face flush as his anger rose. "I'm your husband. I think you do."

"Oh, Alfie," her voice dripped with contempt. "Don't even pretend to be one of those men."

Those men? What did that mean? Those men who could control their wives? His father had never had any problems controlling his mother. Did she want him to be more like him? Well perhaps he could be. Maybe he could be his father's son after all. Perhaps that was where all their problems lay, that he hadn't been enough like his father. Hadn't taken control of his marriage. Of Evie. He let her walk all over him and do and say things his father would never have tolerated. The way she was speaking to him now, for instance.

"Don't talk to me like that," he said in a low voice, his anger bubbling away. She didn't even bother to respond. It was like she hadn't heard him. "Don't talk to me like that," he said again, louder, angrier. Her ignoring him just proved it. How much disdain she had for him as a husband. Again, he thought of his parents. His mother always respected his father. Feared him. Well maybe Evie needed to start fearing him.

"Yes, Alfie," she sighed, pushing past him. "I heard you the first time." His hand shot out and grabbed her arm, and she yelped.

"Alfie, you're hurting me!"

He looked down at her and saw shock and anger. And also a little fear. That was all he needed. He let her go and left to be with the men.

Chapter 27

Julia stared in shock at the aged, but still tall and attractive lady in front of her, standing somewhat uncertainly amongst the forced cheerfulness of the reception area. Alfie's sister had come! After all but hanging up on her, Betty had come!

Eventually Julia collected most of her scattered thoughts. "I'm sorry, Betty, forgive my shock it's just so unexpected to have you turn up!"

"Yes, I know, dear, and I do apologise. I hope I haven't put you out?"

"No, not at all, of course not." Julia moved towards Betty and lowered her voice. "Let's go somewhere and talk."

She took Betty to what she still thought of as Alfie and Trevor's room with a pang of sadness. Alfie was wherever he went on a Saturday morning during visiting hours and Trevor's replacement hadn't moved in yet, so they had the room to themselves. She gave Betty Alfie's chair in the window and perched herself on the edge of Alfie's bed.

"I am sorry for hanging up on you dear," Betty began. Julia waved her hand to show there were no hard feelings. "It was just quite a shock. I hadn't even known if he was still alive." Betty stared out the window as she talked, her left hand unconsciously picking at a stray thread on the hem of her blouse. "Hearing that he was, though,

279

I knew I had to come, to try to mend bridges if I can." She turned to face Julia. "Nobody wants to take this sort of thing to the grave."

"How long has it been since you last saw him?"

Betty turned back to the window. "Oh… It must be sixty-five years, I would think," she said softly.

Julia's heart skipped a beat. Sixty-five years?! What on earth could come between a brother and sister to make them stop talking to each other for so long?

"The last time I spoke to him was that night at the funfair when he got drunk and stormed off." Betty's voice was far away, like she had actually gone back sixty-five years. Julia sat, rapt. "Our mother was ill and he was upset. His wife and I went to find him, to try and reason with him. But I found someone else rather than my brother. I found an angry drunk full of self-pity. I'd never seen him like that before; never seen anyone like that before."

Julia tried to picture Alfie young, drunk and angry but could conjure only a vague outline of what he must have been like. This was also the first she had ever heard about a wife. "I never knew Alfie had been married."

Betty nodded. "Yes, Evie. It was all so tragic."

A few days later Evie flung an envelope at him. "This was waiting for you in Peterborough too, just in case you did care about what your sister had to say." He glanced at the envelope on the ground, instantly spotting Betty's handwriting. "I posted your letter back in Thetford given you were clearly never going to summon the courage to post it yourself. I posted my own letter to her at the same time." He was sure there was extra spite injected into that last part.

He'd written the letter so long ago, carrying it in his jacket pocket as he – and he was annoyed both at himself for being so timid and at Evie for putting it so neatly into words – tried to summon the courage to post it. He'd been so scared about what Betty would say. But that was the old Alfie. The Alfie that let women dictate to him. The new Alfie was a man and behaved like one.

"Well, if you're not even man enough to read the reply I'll just take it, shall I?" Evie all but spat the words at him as she bent to retrieve the letter.

Enraged, and fortified by several long drinks of gin earlier from the bottle he had stashed in the back of one of the lorries, Alfie forcefully shoved her away. Her small stature no match for his strength, Evie went clear across the tent, landing on her back by the sleeping mats.

A little shocked at his own strength, he made a move towards her to help her up but she threw a book at him, the corner of its hard cover catching him right on his ear. He looked down and saw it was *Persuasion*. She didn't say anything, just sat huddled on the floor, a tiny ball of anger and resentment.

The shock having cut through his own anger, he decided to leave before things could get any more heated and out of control. He snatched up the letter and stalked off. He'd read Betty's letter over a drink.

Brother,

Thank you for your letter and for your apology. I must admit that your behaviour in Norwich shocked me. If that is what leaving home and going on adventures does for you then I think I'm quite happy at home thank you very much. I do hope it was just an anomaly, as you have said it was. Evie told me it was the first time she'd ever seen you do anything like that, so I'd like to believe it was.

Given your reaction that night I'm not sure if I should tell you or not, but our mother has taken a turn for the worse. She's now too ill to refuse a doctor, and so Doctor Bradley paid a visit. He is cautiously hopeful that she'll rally but our father is even graver than usual. Mother has asked for Doris so I have sent for her. It worries me that she evidently expects the worse. At least once Doris is here I shall have someone to share this burden with.

I must go – she is calling for me.

Betty

"I'm telling you, he swore by putting chocolate in a shepherd's pie."

Andrew shook his head, blowing hard through his nose. "Sounds like a criminal waste of chocolate, if you ask me," he said, throwing a matchstick into the centre of the table and folding his cards neatly before him.

Stephen chuckled gleefully. "I see your one and raise you two. And I agree with the guv'nor – bloody shameful waste of good chocolate. Johnno here must be mortified."

"Well, I'm not sure if mortified is the right word," said John in his mildly ponderous way as he threw his cards into the middle. "I would be interested to try it though. You never know, it might be fantastic. There's obviously a reason this chap felt so strongly about it."

"That's our Mr Switzerland for you!" shouted Stephen, the several pours of gin and the winning streak he'd had that night making him overly exuberant.

Alfie, also on several pours of gin but on a depressingly normal losing streak, threw in his cards in disgust. "I never did get to try it. Jack was always saying he'd bring some in for everyone to try – said he had a recipe that included chocolate – but he never did." He chuckled nostalgically. "Same as that 2,000 lira note he was always talking about."

"I must say, Alfie, your time in Exeter sounds very colourful. I'm surprised you've not talked about it before." Andrew paused before saying to Stephen, "I call. What have you got, big man?"

Alfie was grateful for the distraction of the game. Andrew was right. It was more than two years since he'd joined the funfair and he'd never spoken about Exeter before, not more than in passing. He picked up the gin bottle and poured himself and Stephen another measure. Perhaps he'd finally put it far enough behind him that he could talk about it now. Perhaps it was the gin.

"You're drinking a fair bit these days," said John to him quietly as the other two quibbled over who was going to show their hand first.

Alfie shrugged. "So what? It's not affecting my work."

John nodded slowly. "You're right, it's not." He paused so long that Alfie thought he'd finished speaking before he continued. "How's Evie?"

Alfie shot him a spiteful glare. He was pretty sure the whole camp had heard them arguing this morning. And again when he was leaving to come to card night. And every other time. If they didn't they must have been deaf. Alfie hadn't thought it possible, but their arguments had become even more ferocious, and more frequent.

He wondered how it had all gone so wrong so quickly. Before they'd got married ten months ago – had it really only been ten months? – everything had been fine. Evie had been the woman of his dreams and their future had been blindingly bright. Now though, that future seemed lost to him. She seemed lost to him. And downright disrespectful. He rubbed his ear, the nick that the corner of *Persuasion* had taken out still stung a little. He found himself wondering if Grace would have been so unreasonable.

"She's fine," Alfie returned shortly, defiantly knocking back the whole drink of gin in one go.

The clamour from the other two as Stephen revealed his flush broke and washed over them, effectively ending that thread of conversation. If only his problems with Evie could be washed away so neatly.

Julia rocked back on the bed. Betty's revelation about Alfie's jail sentence – and why he was in jail – had shocked her to the core. Of all the charges she'd found online, manslaughter had been the last one she would have suspected.

Betty shook her head sadly. "It was a crime of passion they said in the end. He was drunk and hadn't intended to kill her." She paused, looking out the window but clearly seeing something other than a plastic ice cream container and an ashtray full of seeds. "Thirty years he got in the end. Thirty years he was locked away."

Julia exhaled a long breath, unaware she'd been holding it. No wonder he was so cantankerous. She supposed thirty years in a maximum security prison would do that to anyone.

"We were all in a total state of shock. He was always so sweet and gentle and none of us could understand how he could have done such a thing. I kept thinking there must have been some mistake."

Julia nodded sympathetically, still reeling, and not quite sure what to say. Betty, though, didn't appear to need her to say anything. Now she'd started telling the story it was like she couldn't stop.

"I wrote to him, asking him to explain, pleading with him to tell me it wasn't true." Betty's voice was wavering, and Julia could tell that she was holding back tears. "The letter I got back just had two lines: *I did it. I'm guilty.*" Betty stopped, clearly struggling to keep herself together.

"Take as long as you need," Julia said gently. She poured Betty a plastic cup of water from the jug by Alfie's bed, which Betty took gratefully. In all her sleuthing and imagining what was in Alfie's past, not once had it been this. Not once had it been this real.

"I went to the trial, of course," Betty continued after a few moments. "My father forbade me to go, but I had to. He pleaded guilty, so it was blessedly short in the end. He didn't look at me once during the whole trial, just hung his head and stared at his hands in his lap. Except for when the judge passed sentence. Then he put his head in his hands and wept."

Betty had seemed to shrink as she told her story, ageing before Julia's eyes. "He was convicted of manslaughter only because Stephen testified that he hadn't meant to kill her. He didn't even testify in his own defence. I think he knew he deserved whatever punishment they gave him."

"This is for you," Evie said, throwing a letter at him. They were standing outside their tent, packed tightly in amongst the rest of the staff tents. The green at Slatterley was small and so they were all bunched in together, tightly encircled by the parked lorries like a menacing python. "Just in case you cared what your sister has to say. You clearly don't care about what I have to say any longer."

He stooped down to retrieve the envelope, noticing as he bent over that he was a little unsteady after the gin he'd had. He saw

Betty's looped handwriting. "How on earth?" They'd only arrived at Slatterley that afternoon and he'd not told Betty they would be here. In fact, he'd still not replied to her last letter, he thought guiltily.

"We've been corresponding quite frequently actually," Evie stated defiantly. "I told her we would be here."

"Well clearly I don't need to read this then – what does my sister have to say?"

She tossed her hair. "I don't know, there wasn't a letter for me." She paused. "It must have been delayed. I know she was going to write." She stopped and looked at him. "Well? Aren't you going to read it?"

Alfie looked at the letter. He was curious to hear what Betty had to say, but mainly just nervous it would be a reproach for not replying to her. He really wanted to read it over a drink.

She sensed his thoughts. "Oh fine, leave then if you like. I'm used to you leaving. In fact, most of the time I prefer it when you're gone. You're no Captain Wentworth, Alfie. You're Mr Elliot!"

"Well you're no Anne," he retorted. "Although maybe if you started acting more like her and less like Louisa, flirting with everyone, then you'd have some friends. I've seen you flirting with all the men – the whole bloody fair has." Their constant arguing over the past months had brought out an unkind streak he didn't know he'd had. He grabbed her upper arm roughly and dragged her in close. "Tell me, Louisa, are you sleeping with anyone else? Because the whole fair certainly seems to think that you are."

Alfie could see he was hurting her and didn't care. "Anyone else? I'm not even sleeping with you, you pathetic drunk." She tried to work her arm free, but he tightened his grip, taking a dark pleasure in seeing her wince. "And who could blame me if I was? You're a sorry excuse for a man, undone because his mummy doesn't love him enough. I pity you." She spat the last few words at him.

He snorted and let her go, flinging her arm away. "Yeah? Well at least my parents loved me growing up and weren't so horrified by me that it put them off having more children. At least my parents were sorry I left rather than being relieved." Evie recoiled, whether from the venom in his voice or what he'd said, or both, he couldn't tell. "Now fuck off and give me some peace." He muttered the last line but she still heard it.

Evie opened her mouth to reply and then stopped, before going on. "Fine. Fine I will," and stormed away. There was a finality in the way she said it which troubled him, but he was too much in need of a drink to ask. Or care.

As he walked toward the lorry that held his precious gin, he tore open the letter and stopped dead as soon as he started reading.

Brother,

Our mother is dead. She died yesterday afternoon surrounded by her family. She looked peaceful as she slipped away so I don't think she suffered. Please don't come if you were thinking of doing so. I think father would kill you.

Betty

Betty, now past the most difficult part of the story seemed to recover a little and turned to Julia as she told her the rest. "You can imagine what it was like back in Fulham in those days. People could talk of nothing else for months. Not in front of us of course, but I heard what people would whisper behind our backs. I remember praying for some other big news to happen to take people's minds off it. But 1957 was a quiet year and nothing bigger than the boy from 19 Stevenson Road killing his wife ever came along. It nearly finished my father, coming so soon after our mother's death.

"I wrote to him in jail, of course. For the first few years at any rate. Telling him about my marriage to Peter, my move to Bath. I even wrote to him about the birth of my first son, Richard, hoping news of a new life in the family might draw him out. But I never had a single response. I don't even know if he read any of them. I tried to visit him once too, once I'd married Peter. But he refused to see me."

She paused and looked around, seeming to take in Alfie's room and meagre possessions for the first time. Betty turned to her. "Can I see him now? Can I see my brother?"

Julia shrugged desperately. "We can try. He leaves Pinewood every Saturday morning during visiting hours. But I do think I know where he goes."

She stood and eyed Betty. "Are you up for a short walk?"

He felt paralysed. Dead! How could she be dead?! The woman who had always been a constant in his life was no longer a constant in his life.

He didn't know how long he stood for, numb and uncomprehending. It could have been five minutes or five hours. Slowly, the haze started to lift and he looked around. He turned back towards the tents. He could go and find Evie. Or he could retrieve the bottle of gin from the lorry. He hesitated for only a split second before turning away from the tents and heading into the belly of the python.

An hour later – or was it two or three? – he was sat in the cab of the lorry nursing an empty bottle, tears streaming down his face. He felt like he'd been here before. Wretched, drunk and mourning.

Why did she have to die? And moreover, why did she have to die before they had reconciled? He wondered if she'd died of a broken heart. Devastated that her only son had gone and left. It was his dad's fault! If only his dad hadn't poisoned her against him, he was sure they would have made up before – well, just before.

He sat up and upended the bottle to get any last little drops out of it and then flung it down angrily. A weak beam of moonlight was coming in through the cab window, highlighting the bottle. It mocked him with its emptiness. Empty. Just like he felt. An empty container of a person that he was constantly putting things in only to have them fall out. Grace, his life in Exeter. Adam. Now, more than ever, he needed to drink himself into oblivion. Being roaring drunk just wasn't enough. He glared at the bottle, focusing his building rage on it.

He snatched the bottle up and tumbled out of the cab, falling on to the grass. "Fuck you!!" he roared at the bottle. At anyone. At no one. At the world. He threw the bottle against the side of the lorry, shattering it into a thousand pieces. Shards of glass rained down on him but he just stood there, daring any of them to pierce his skin. To inflict pain. None came.

He stood for a moment and looked around him. The shards were half hidden and dark, half illuminated by the moonlight. How very like me, he thought drunkenly.

He swayed there for a few minutes more, letting the drunken haze settle on him like a comfortable blanket of numbness. Like an old friend. Drink. He still wanted a drink. Eventually a fuzzy thought percolated through his brain. Stephen would have gin. He would go and find Stephen.

He'd seen Stephen setting up his tent on the west side of the encampment earlier that evening and so stumbled his way in that direction. He ricocheted off one tent, almost collapsing it, before falling over the ropes of another and landing face first in the grass. It reminded him of the night he'd left London and he'd tripped over in front of the fox. It seemed a lifetime ago.

He picked himself up and decided to stumble around the edge instead, using the lorries as a bumper. As he made his way around he began to look for Stephen's tent. They all looked so bloody similar in the dark. Then he spotted Stephen ahead. He was holding open the flap of his tent for someone. Someone small. Someone blonde.

As they crossed Pinewood's carpark Betty asked her, "So how is Fred, I mean Alfie, generally? Is he happy?"

"Happy is a relative term," Julia replied cautiously. She paused. "I notice you call him Fred. And you were confused at first when I called you last week."

Betty nodded. "Well, I'm sure you know his full name is Alfred. But the family always called him Fred. You see, he was named after my uncle and my mother thought it would be too confusing to have two Alfreds in the family, so it got shortened to Fred. It wasn't until he left that he decided to start calling himself Alfie. I guess I'm just not used to it."

Alfie sat and stared at his hands, unable to go on. Such big hands. So clumsy. So powerful. So capable of picking up his wife and throwing her across a tent so that her head caved in. He could feel Fred's eyes on him. The silence drew out, stretching before and after them for a lifetime. His lifetime.

Eventually Fred broke the spell. "And? What happened?"

Alfie squeezed his eyes closed to shut it all out, not wanting to talk about any of it anymore. Instead, he concentrated on the feel of the bread in his hands. How malleable it was. How easy to tear apart.

He sighed and opened his eyes. This was why he'd started having these conversations with the boy in the first place wasn't it? To stop him making the same mistakes? Well, this was *the* mistake. Don't chicken out now.

They reached the small park and Julia pointed out a lone figure on a bench by the lake, under an oak tree. "I think that's him. I'll wait here and give you two some privacy."

Betty walked hesitantly down the path, glad she was approaching from behind so she had a precious extra few seconds to compose herself. To figure out what she was going to say. As she approached the bench, she could hear Alfie talking to himself. The breeze, or perhaps her failing hearing, snatched away every other word.

"Drunk…angry…metal locker…fragile…piece of lumber…" He dropped his head in his hands and she thought he was sobbing.

She raced around to the bench, as quickly as she could. "Fred? Are you okay? Alfie?"

Alfie raised his head, tears streaked down his face. "Betty?" he asked, disbelievingly, "Is that really you?" She nodded, not quite sure what to say. "Betty, I killed her. I killed my Evie." He sounded lost, like a small child separated from his mother at the supermarket.

Tears filled her own eyes and she nodded wordlessly, sitting beside him on the bench. She grabbed one of his hands.

"I was so angry, Betty, so drunk and so very angry. I saw her go into Stephen's tent – we'd been arguing again that night – and I just snapped. I saw red. I thought she was there to sleep with him. But the—" His voice cracked. "Inside the tent it all gets blurry. It doesn't even feel like me, when I look back. It's like it's someone else's memory, or like I'm in a dream."

He turned to her. "Betty, you know I didn't mean to kill her, don't you?"

Tears spilled down her face and she nodded, a lump in her throat so big she didn't trust herself to speak.

"She was my everything and I killed her. She was the best of me, the best of everyone. Her smile that could light up the world and I put it out. And my world has been in darkness ever since." He dropped his head in his hands once more, old wounds finally reopened pouring forth too much regret and sorrow to bear.

Betty's heart wrung in anguish for her brother. She put an arm around his stooped shoulders as he sobbed.

After some time she looked at the sky and saw the clouds coming in. They were grey and heavy with rain. "Come on, let's get you back to Pinewood. Visiting hours are almost over."

Enjoyed this book? Please let people know.

As an independent author, reviews are really important – and exceptionally appreciated.

If you enjoyed *The Inconvenient Need to Belong* and Alfie's story, please do write a review on Amazon or Goodreads, or wherever else you feel like leaving a review. And don't forget good old word of mouth.

Feel free to get in touch with me too with any thoughts or comments about the book. I'd love to hear from readers.

Thanks,
Paula Smedley
Danglingfromclotheslines@gmail.com

Printed in Great Britain
by Amazon